The Mosaic of Shadows

THE MOSAIC
OF SHADOWS

Tom Harper

THOMAS DUNNE BOOKS
ST. MARTIN'S MINOTAUR
NEW YORK

THOMAS DUNNE BOOKS.
An imprint of St. Martin's Press.

www.minotaurbooks.com

Library of Congress Cataloging-in-Publication Data

ISBN 0-312-33867-8
EAN 978-0312-33867-1

First published in Great Britain by Century Books

First U.S. Edition: June 2005

10 9 8 7 6 5 4 3 2 1

for Marianna

Ἄνδρα μοι ἔννεπε, μοῦσα, πολύτροπον,
ὃς μάλα πολλὰ πλάγχθη

The Byzantine Empire Around 1095

KINGDOM OF HUNGARY

CROATS

SERBS

River Danube

ADRIATIC SEA

Dyrrhacium

Thessalonica

Adrianople

Constantir

Sea o

Hellespo

NORMANS

IONIAN SEA

Athens

SICILY

AEGEAN

SEA

ME

Constantinople

Gate of Lakes

PIKRIDIOU

New Palace

Regia Gate

Adrianople Gate

GOLDEN HORN

Gate of St Theodosia

GALATA

PLATEA

BOSPHORUS

Gate of St Romanus

River Lycus

LIBOS

Column of Marcian

Forum of the Ox

VENETIAN QUARTER

GENOESE QUARTER

Palace of Isaak Komnenos

Arch of Theodosius

Milion

St Irene

Ayia Sophia

Augusteion

PARADEISION

Selymbrian Gate

Forum of Arcadius

Column of Constantine

Monastery of St Andrew

SIGMA

Harbour of Theodosius

Great Palace

Kathisma

Hippodrome

SEA OF MARMARA

Golden Gate

0   ½   1 mile

0   500   1000   1500 metres

N

ME

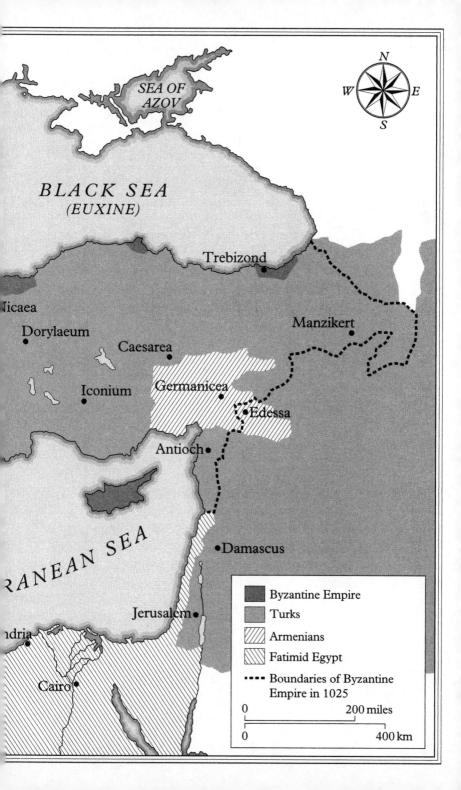

For a thousand years after the fall of the West, the empire of Byzantium, centred on the great city of Constantinople, perpetuated the living, unbroken legacy of the Roman empire. It reached the peak of its latter-day power in 1025 under the Emperor Basil II, but a dozen weak and corrupt successors squandered his accomplishments until the very existence of the empire was under threat. In these circumstances, a dynamic, young leader named Alexios Komnenos rose to the imperial throne from a cabal of the powerful military families, and through hard-fought campaigns and cunning diplomacy managed to reassert the strength and glory of Byzantium. But he was not unopposed: Turks, Normans, Bulgarians, Germans and Venetians constantly pressed at his borders, while contenders from within his own and rival families schemed recklessly to usurp his throne. With the Turks in particular advancing ever further into the hinterland of Asia Minor, Alexios was forced to beg the estranged Pope in Rome to provide soldiers to buttress the faltering Byzantine armies. Much to his surprise, and subsequent alarm, he got them: the Pope preached the first crusade, and tens of thousands of western knights mobilised to descend on Byzantium.

The language of Byzantium was Greek, but through all its history its citizens referred to themselves as Romans. Any peoples beyond the empire's borders were considered barbarians.

Why have our two consuls and praetors come out today
wearing their embroidered, their scarlet togas?
Why have they put on bracelets with so many amethysts,
and rings sparkling with magnificent emeralds?
Why are they carrying elegant canes
beautifully worked in silver and gold?

Because the barbarians are coming today
and things like that dazzle the barbarians.

C P Cavafy
tr. Keeley and Sherrard

α

It was evening when the axe-wielding barbarians arrived at my door. The sun was sinking behind the western ramparts, casting the sky and all below it in copper. In the windless air the canopies and awnings of the queen of cities were still as the myriad towers and domes above them, yet by only inclining an ear you would have met the gentle, sustained notes of the chants which swelled out from the hundred surrounding churches. All day the tide of humanity had run high in the streets, the denizens of Byzantium gathering to mark the feast of Saint Nikolas and to watch the Emperor process through their midst; now that tide was slowly ebbing, slipping back into the arcades and tenements from whence it had come. I sat on my roof and watched them go, sipping a welcome cup of wine after the week of fasting.

Zoe, the younger of my daughters, announced the barbarians. From the corner of my eye I saw her face emerge from the opening at the top of the ladder, concern and puzzlement creasing the smooth skin below her piled ringlets.

'There are men to see you,' she said breathlessly, still standing on the ladder. She paused, reconsidered. 'Giants. Titans. Three of them, with enormous axes – and one like Prometheus, with a beard of fire.'

My daughter has always been given to poetry, though I notice it more often now.

'Will they fit through the door?' I asked. 'Or should I mount my winged steed and fly up to look them in the eye?'

Zoe pondered this. 'They can come through the door,' she allowed. 'And through that opening you're standing in?'

'Perhaps. But they might break the ladder,' she added. 'Then you'd be stranded up here.'

'Then they can buy me a new one.'

Zoe's pouting face vanished, and a riotous noise erupted from the room below. Perhaps she did not exaggerate, for I could hear an almighty stamping, the tread of men who wield their feet like hammers and would flatten even the seven hills given half a day's march. The ladder trembled, and I could imagine the rungs bending like fresh boughs under the burden of that weight. I waited for the wrench of splintered wood and tumbled watchmen, but my ladder – solid, Bithynian oak – held fast, bore them up out of the darkness and into the fresh, evening air on my roof.

There were three of them, as Zoe had said, and as she had said they were giants. All wore long coats of mail hanging to their knees, girded with broad leather belts and hung with heavy, iron maces. On their shoulders they carried great twin-headed axes, which not even the perilous ascent of the ladder had unseated. Even without the insignia of their legion, a blue square of fur-trimmed cloth fastened below their necks, they were unmistakable. Varangians, elite guardsmen of the palace and protectors of the Emperor. Though I rose slowly to greet them, the wine in the cup I held was suddenly much agitated.

'You are Demetrios Askiates, the revealer of mysteries?'

The nearest of the three giants spoke. Like his companions, he was fair-skinned, though our sun had ravaged his complexion everywhere save by the rim of his collar, where it was still the shade of milk. His hair was the colour of fire, such as nature never bestowed upon our people; a mane hanging over his ox-like shoulders. He was, in short, a perfect specimen of that race which inhabits the frozen island of Thule – Britannia, as our ancestors called it when they held sway there – though he was long since departed, I thought, judging by the confident edge to his Greek.

I nodded an answer to his question, feeling the absurdity of my self-styled epithet before this brutal, unadorned power. The Varangian, I thought, would not unveil a mystery: he would crush it to powder with his mace, or slice through it with a stroke of his axe like Alexander at Gordion. What, I wondered nervously, would he do with me?

'You are called to the palace,' he said. Where his left hand played along the haft of his axe, I noticed a string of notches in the dark wood, unbroken almost from butt to blade. Were those the number of his victims?

I nodded a second time, and then – in my confusion – involuntarily twice more. 'Why?'

'That,' said the Varangian heavily, 'will be revealed when you're there.' Under the thick beard, I thought I saw his mouth twitch.

There was still light in the sky as we came outside, but already the shopkeepers' tables were drawn indoors, and the crowds of the day reduced to a scattering of hurried figures. Few would care to be caught abroad after dark, when the Watch came out. And fewer still would want to be found near the phalanx of guardsmen – a dozen more – who were, to my shock, drawn up in the street outside my house. That would do little for my reputation among doubtful neighbours, I thought ruefully. No wonder there were no children playing games in the road, no fruit-sellers and sweet-merchants hawking their wares.

It was some half hour's walk to the palace, but with a company of armed Norsemen at my back, and their red-headed captain silent before me, it felt ten times longer. Mingled glances of pity and suspicion fixed upon me from the passers-by: *he did not wear chains*, they observed, *but nor did he dress as one who warranted such a retinue*. Everywhere we walked the day was fading, with only lingering scents to tell what had passed: the stench of tanners and dyers, the warm homeliness of the bakers, the blood of the butchers and – as we at last reached the head of the avenue – the thick sweetness of the perfume-sellers.

The marbled arcades of the Augusteion were ahead of us now, with the palace gate beyond it and the vast dome of the great church on our left. The questions which clawed at my mind had reached a ringing intensity, yet were suddenly thrown into still greater confusion as the captain turned abruptly to his right, away from the palace and down a long street whose wall, I could see, was formed by the vast rim of the hippodrome. A greaved forearm against my shoulder steered me helplessly down into the darkness after him.

'The palace is that way,' I called, extending my already harried strides.

'The palace,' retorted the captain over his shoulder, 'has many gates, and not all of them serve for everyone. The fishmongers, for example – they keep to their own gate. To keep out the stink,' he added pointedly.

The walls now above us were pocked with arches and embellished with all manner of pagan and holy statues, extending far out of sight in every direction. We came under them and passed through an iron gate, a lesser entrance left curiously unlocked. For a moment we were in darkness, giddied by the echoing slap of our feet on the stone; then the purple sky opened above us and I felt warm sand trickling through the straps of my sandals. We were in the arena, on the racetrack still chewed and furrowed from the day's activity. It was empty, but the silence of a hundred thousand absent spectators only served to press the vastness upon me further, while before us a host of shafts and columns bristled from the central spine like a sheaf of spears.

'Come,' said the captain, his words muted in the oppressive expanse. He led me across the track, our feet crunching in the yielding sand, and up a narrow staircase cut through the spine. Now we were directly below the thrusting monuments, as if between the fingers of a giant hand, and for a single ludicrous second I imagined the hand closing around us in a stone fist. It was a ridiculous vision, but I could not keep from shivering.

My escorts, stout though they were, showed no more inclination than I to delay there. More steps brought us back down onto the arena floor, now on the far side of the stadium; we walked some way along the track, across to the opposite wall, and up another flight of stairs between the ranks of empty benches. These stairs led onto a terrace; the terrace, in turn onto more stairs which doubled back on themselves so often I felt dizzied. The sky was all but invisible now, only a shade removed from complete darkness, and already one horn of the crescent moon was pricking up behind the walls, but the soldiers' pace was unflagging. It was with much tripping and stumbling that I mounted the last few steps to emerge, breathless and disoriented, onto a broad balcony high above the race track.

'Welcome to the Kathisma,' said the Varangian captain, and though my lungs faltered from the climb I somehow found the air for a heart-felt gasp. True, I had been told I was going to the palace, but I had expected a side-door and a clerk's desk in one of the public court-yards; not this, not the Kathisma. This was the imperial loge itself, the dais where the Emperor paraded his untouchable majesty to the world – his world – and received its acclamation. I myself had seen him here a hundred times, though only from great distances.

One of the guards drew flame from an alcove and touched it to the lamps which hung from the ceiling. Fire sparked in the glass, and was in an instant echoed back a thousand-fold: off the golden chains which held the lamps; off the golden mosaics set between every archway; and off the golden throne which stood, empty, in the middle

4

of the room. Suddenly I was surrounded by a great host: the flickering silhouettes of a hundred kings and heroes leaped out of their gilded background, while from above the great charioteers of old seemed to be driving their horses hard down upon me, as if coming for Elijah.

'You are Demetrios, the unveiler of mysteries? The illuminator of shadows? The master of the apocalypse?'

The voice which called me was mellow, like honey, but at its first words I cowered like a kitten, for it seemed it came from the walls themselves. There was neither menace nor malice in its tone, but it was with a trembling heart that I turned my gaze upon its source – and for a moment feared that indeed the wall had come alive, for I saw instantly a figure moving forward out of the golden shadows. Only as he came into the light could I see the substance of him: the sumptuous robes stitched with the gems and insignia of high office, the round head, the beardless face as smooth as a girl's. His eyes were very bright, glistening in the lamplight like the oil in his dark hair as he stared intently upon me.

'I am Demetrios,' I stammered at last.

'I am Krysaphios,' he replied elegantly. 'Chamberlain to his serene majesty the Emperor Alexios.'

I nodded slowly, saying nothing. The ritual with which I usually greet my clients would have seemed pathetic in this august place, and there was something in the eunuch's eye which proclaimed that he already had the measure of me.

'You unravel the riddles which perplex other men, I am told,' he said. 'You reveal what was hidden, and give light to the truth.'

'The Lord has blessed some of my efforts.' I answered with more humility than I might normally have felt in those efforts.

'You found the Eparch's daughter, when her family had already arranged her funeral,' prompted the eunuch. 'That was well done. I have need of such talents.'

He had been holding his hands clasped behind his back; now he extended a fat palm towards me. The skin was fleshy and soft, but there was no softness in what it held, in what he offered me. At last I began to see why he might have brought me here, why my unorthodox skills might be necessary to him. There was much of which I remained wholly ignorant, I knew, but if the matter involved the palace, and commanded so urgent a secrecy, then it must touch on the highest possible authorities. And possibly, I thought absently, the richest possible fees.

The item which Krysaphios held was about as long as the span of a man's hand, as thick as his finger, and formed from a wooden shaft with an iron tip, which had first been hammered into a crude block and then filed into a fearsomely sharp triangular point. This point, and a good half of the protruding shaft, were encrusted with a wine-coloured stain that should, sadly, have been far less familiar to me than in fact it was. The frayed remnants of what might have been feathers were set around the blunt end.

'An arrow?' I guessed, holding it cautiously between my fingers. Despite its size it was unexpectedly heavy. 'But it seems too short for such a purpose – it would have fallen off the bow well before it was tensed.' I thought furiously, aware of the eunuch watching me. 'From a siege engine, a ballista, you could fire it, perhaps, but that would be like harnessing a plough to a dog.' I became aware that I was specu-lating too much aloud, and too much from ignorance, neither good professional practice. 'However – it is a weapon, I deduce, or at least a tool which has been used as such.' The dried blood told me that much – and more. 'Recently, I should say.'

Krysaphios sighed, and for the first time I saw lines of tension beneath his marble skin.

'It was shot,' he said, 'like an arrow but with immense power – how we do not know – at a guardsman today. Such was its force that it passed through his armour and deep into his ribs. He died almost immediately.'

'Extraordinary.' For a moment I grappled dumbly with his words – they seemed nonsensical. Or perhaps it was my exposition of the weapon which had been nonsense. In the interim, while I struggled, I reached for the well-worn safety of aphorism.

'What a tragedy for the soldier,' I mumbled. 'And for his desolated family. My prayers . . .'

'Your prayers can wait for the church,' snapped the eunuch. 'The soldier is an irrelevance. What is significant,' he added, pressing his plump fingers together, 'is that when he died he was standing, in a public street, as close as I am now to you, beside his master. The Emperor.'

I had been wrong again, I chided myself. The fees for this commission would not be rich – they would be truly beyond all imagining. If, of course, I could earn them.

I began tentatively. 'You want me to find out who attempted the assassination of the Emperor?' The words sounded no less ridiculous in my mouth than they had in my head, but I saw the eunuch nodding nonetheless. 'Someone has tried to kill him, and I am to catch that man?'

'Do you think yourself equal to the task?' asked Krysaphios dryly. 'Or have I called the wrong man from his drinking? The Eparch assured me I had not – though I naturally did not tell him the entire truth of your commission.'

'I can meet the challenge,' I said, with a confidence that I would regret the next morning. 'But at what cost?'

'Your fee, Askiates? I believe we can meet it.' The eunuch wore the graceless smirk of one who can be deliberately careless of money. 'Double, even. Two gold pieces a day should afford your time.'

'It was not the cost to *you* that concerned me,' I snapped, irritated by his easy confidence that I could be bought so easily. 'Though I could hardly do this for less than five gold pieces a day. What of the danger to *me*? I doubt this was the work of a tradesman with a grievance, a candlemaker who thought his taxes too onerous or a grocer whose balance was found crooked.'

'Are those your natural quarry?' jeered Krysaphios. The flickering gold panels behind him seemed to burn colder. 'Tradesmen who steal a coin or two when their customers are too dull to notice? If you wish to keep their company, Askiates, I can have the Varangians return you there now. Rather than winning glory and the gratitude of an Emperor.'

'The gratitude of an Emperor counts for little when he's dead. And the hatred of his enemies a great deal.'

'If you do your job properly the Emperor will not be dead. And if he does die, the hatred of his enemies will be the very least of your concerns. Have fifteen years dulled your memory so much? The fires? The looted churches? The screaming women debauched in the streets?'

I was nineteen years old when the last Emperor fell, with a young wife and a newborn daughter in my house; I had not forgotten it. Nor that the usurper of those days, whose entry to the city had supplied the pretext for the rapine frenzy that followed, was now my prospective employer, his holy majesty the Emperor Alexios. My eyes hardened at the thought, but the caution I met in Krysaphios' gaze kept me silent.

'Some things have been done which should not have been done,' he said, as if reciting his confession. 'And others which ought to have been done differently. But we have had fifteen years of peace since those dark days, and for that we should be thankful. We can build towers and walls beyond number in this city, put ten thousand men on her ramparts, but there will only ever be a single life which stands between peace and ruin. Surely that, for a man with two maiden daughters especially, is worth preserving.'

I could have struck him for drawing my daughters so casually into his web of persuasion, this half-man so haughty one moment and so devious the next, but with Varangians about me and nothing to gain by violence, I kept my fists at my side. Besides, he spoke the truth. I inclined my head in surrender, though hating myself for doing so.

Krysaphios gave a wolfish smile; evidently he relished even this trivial victory. 'In that case, Master Askiates,' he said conclusively, 'you had better make sure the Emperor stays alive. For three gold pieces a day.'

If I was to lay myself hostage to the fortunes of a doomed Emperor and an unscrupulous eunuch, I consoled myself that at least I had secured favourable terms.

β

Krysaphios had been keen for me to begin by questioning the imperial household, the men most likely to profit from the Emperor's death, but I insisted on first visiting the site of the act. Thus, next morning, a chill dawn found me outside the house of Simeon the carver, overlooking the arcades of the Mesi near the forum of Saint Constantine. Many of the ivory carvers had their shops here, with the emblem of the crossed horn and knife hanging from their arches; the house of Simeon, I guessed, was the one with the shuttered windows, the locked gate, and the two Varangians standing at the door, helmed and armed. The neighbours setting out their wares, I noticed, were careful to ignore them.

I crossed to the far side of the road and crouched low over the marble paving, scanning its grey-veined surface for signs of the murder. I had heard rain in the night as I lay sleepless in my bed, but I held out hope that blood would not wash away so easily. The stone was cold against my bare knee, and there were plenty of feet to tread heedlessly on my fingers as the morning crowds flowed around me, but I kept my eyes close to the ground until I found what I was looking for, a faded patch of pink stained into the white marble. Was this where a loyal guard had unwittingly given his life for his Emperor, I wondered, or merely the residue a hasty dyer had dripped onto the street?

'This is where he fell. I was standing behind him when he was hit.'

I looked up, to see the creased, blue eyes of a Varangian peering down on me. The axe on his shoulder gleamed like a halo beside his face, though the skin was too coarse and lined to be that of a saint. His straw-coloured hair was streaked with grey, and although he stood as tall as any of his race, he seemed old for a guardsman.

I scrambled to my feet. 'Demetrios Askiates,' I introduced myself.

'Aelric,' he answered, holding out his spear-hand in greeting. I took

9

it gingerly, and felt thick fingers clasp tightly around my wrist. 'The captain's waiting for you in the house.'

'But this is where the soldier fell?' A nod. 'Was it sudden?'

'Like lightning. All I saw was him on the ground, stuck in the side like a boar and bleeding his life out. In no more time than you'd need to blink. And straight through his armour, too,' he added in wonder. 'Like it was made of silk.'

'His right side or his left?'

The guard turned to face up the street, clearly mimicking the last steps of his dead companion, and thoughtfully lifted a hand to his right breast. 'This one,' he said slowly. 'The side where the Emperor rode.'

'So the arrow must have been fired from high up, or it would never have passed over the Emperor on his horse, and from across the street – from the carver's house.'

'Where the captain's waiting for you,' prodded the guard, the merest hint of impatience edging his voice.

'Stand here, then. I want to see what the assassin saw.' I walked slowly back across the road and up the steps between the columns, to the barred gate on the carver's door. Little light fell within, but I could see the scaly gleam of ringed armour not far back.

'Demetrios Askiates,' I called, putting my face up to the bars. The carver would have mounted them to protect his home and his goods; now, I suspected, they were become his prison.

'I know who you are, Demetrios Askiates,' said a gruff voice from inside. He stepped into the slatted light by the door, the red-headed Varangian captain of the previous night, and I saw his vast fist turning a key in the lock. The door swung inwards, opening onto a dim room filled with every manner of trinkets, reliquaries, mirrors, and caskets. Rich men and women would pay handsomely to own one of them, but in the present circumstances they put me more in mind of a tomb, a crypt, than of conspicuous luxury.

'The bone scratcher's upstairs,' said the captain. 'Lives over his workshop.' He jerked a thumb up at the ceiling. 'We've got two apprentices up there too. And his family.'

Had they been kept captive all night, I wondered, as I climbed the steep steps in the corner. I came onto the first floor, another large room covered in white shavings as fine and deep as snow. Long tables stood in the centre, still strewn with abandoned tools and half-finished artefacts, while tall windows looked out over the sloping tiles of the arcade's roof. Beyond it, I could just see the top of a helmet: Aelric the Varangian, standing where I had left him.

'The arrow wasn't fired from here,' I said, to myself as much as to the captain who had thudded up behind me.

We mounted to the next level. Here woollen curtains hung from the ceiling, dividing the room into private spaces; I brushed through them, to the front of the building where more windows – shorter, now – again looked down onto the street. We were at some height, but still there was only a narrow gap between the edge of the arcade and the dome of Aelric's helmet. I beckoned the captain to come and stand beside me.

'Were you there when he was killed?' I asked, naturally slowing my speech for the benefit of his foreign ears.

'I was.'

'And could you see – was he standing directly beside the Emperor's horse?'

'He was.'

'And do you think,' I persisted, 'that an arrow could be fired from here and pass over something the height of a horse – and maybe its rider too – yet still strike a man standing in the horse's shadow?'

The captain frowned as he stared out of the window. 'Maybe not,' he grunted. 'But then I don't know any arrow that would go through a coat of mail, whether a horse was in its path or otherwise. Ask the carver.'

'I will,' I said, more abruptly than was wise to this axe-bearing giant. 'But first I want to examine the roof.'

'The carver and his apprentices were on the steps outside when we found them,' countered the captain. 'None of them would have had time to get down from the roof so soon.'

'Then maybe they weren't responsible.' I pushed through another curtain, into a back room where there stood a table and some stools, with a ladder leading to a trap door in the ceiling. Climbing swiftly, I shot back the bolt which held it fast and emerged, shivering, onto the roof. Broken only by low balustrades, it stretched to my left and right, joining together all the houses on this side of the Mesi in one elegant line. It would have been easy, I thought, for the assassin to escape down any of their stairs. Before me I could see Constantine the Great atop his column in the forum, only a little higher than I, and behind him the domes of Ayia Sophia, the church of holy wisdom. Wisdom, I thought, that I could well use.

Turning my eyes downwards, onto the street, I could see Aelric again, still standing impassive amid the thronging traffic. Though he seemed even smaller from this height, I could yet see much more of him than from below, even when others passed beside him. And likewise he me – he waved a salute as he noticed me peering down on him.

'Yes,' I murmured to myself. This was where you could have shot an arrow at the Emperor, and hit the ribs of a guardsman beyond by mistake. I knelt by the parapet which lined the edge of the roof. There were scratches in the stone, I saw with rising excitement – and there, just at the base of the wall where moss grew in the shaded cracks . . .

'Date stones?' The Varangian captain had followed my eyes and caught what I had seen, a small scattering of date-palm seeds; now he tipped back his head and gave a great, bellowing laugh. It was not a comfortable sound.

'Congratulations, Demetrios Askiates,' he said, picking up one of the pips and tossing it in his free hand. 'You've found a murderer who shoots like Ullr the huntsman, and has a taste for dried fruits. Miraculous!'

The captain stayed with me while I interviewed the carver and his family; I doubt it put them at their ease. The carver, a thin man with fine hands, trembled and stammered his way through a simple enough story: that he had been in his shop all morning, while the apprentices worked upstairs; that they had all three of them gone out to the arcade to watch the Emperor pass; and that they had been dumbfounded to be seized by the Varangians moments later – they had not even seen the soldier die, though they had noticed a commotion on the far side of the street. The carver chewed on his nails, twisting and tearing at them as he swore that he had locked the gate behind him, that nobody could have crept in while he was outside. His wife had been upstairs, he explained, and he had had thieves before, even on holy saints' days curse them. Now, he said mournfully, he was forced to be ever vigilant. At that the Varangian captain snorted, which did nothing to soothe the carver.

The apprentices had little to add, though it took me the better half of an hour to establish so. They sat back sullenly on their stools and said nothing that was not prompted, regarding me for the most part with the inscrutable gaze of adolescence. Yes, they had been hard at work in the workshop before their master called them down to watch the procession – he was a fair man, they said, though demanding in his craft. He might have locked the door – they did not know, but he often did: he had a terror of thieves.

'Was the door locked when you came in?' I asked the captain, after I had dismissed the boys.

'I wasn't the first in. Aelric was.'

'Can you ask him?'

The captain's face, never reserved at the best of times, said plainly that he thought this a worthless task for an officer of the Emperor's bodyguard, and I fancied he made even more noise than usual stamping down the stairs. I let it pass as the carver's wife came into the room. She was younger than her husband, with a darker complexion and a fuller figure, though she dressed modestly and wore a scarf low over her face, casting her eyes in shadow. Her children were with her – two girls, very young, and a boy of about ten, none of whom would look at me. Behind them, I saw the dividing curtain twitch, and the carver's two dusty feet protruding below the hem. Was he simply a jealous husband, I wondered, or were there secrets he did not want told?

I opened with an innocent enough question. 'Are these all your children?'

'Three of them,' she said, so quietly that I strained to hear. 'I have a son, apprenticed to another carver, a friend of my husband's, and two married daughters.'

'And you and your children were watching the parade from the window yesterday?'

She nodded silently.

'Did you hear anyone else in the house at the time – someone mounting the stairs perhaps?'

She shook her head, then saw fit to add almost in a whisper, 'No-one is allowed up here but the family. My husband is very strict on it.'

Between the ever-vigilant carver, the locked gate, and the family on the uppermost floor, Odysseus himself would have struggled to creep through this house.

'And did you see – or hear – something that could have been an arrow loosed from near here?' I pressed.

'The procession caused much noise, much cheering and shouting.' She frowned. 'But perhaps there was a crack from above, just before the soldier fell across the road. As the Emperor was passing our window.'

'A crack from above,' I repeated. 'Were you up on the roof at all yesterday morning? Hanging laundry or taking some air or . . .' I paused, hearing the distant sound of boots on the stairs. 'Eating fruit?'

Another shake of the head. 'We do not go onto the roof.' It was as though Moses had commanded it thus on the stone tablets. 'Urchins and vagabonds play there. Some of the other shopkeepers and crafts-men allow them up when they should not. We keep the roof-door bolted.'

The noise on the stairs reached a crescendo, and the Varangian captain came striding into the room, almost tearing the curtain from its hooks as he did so.

'The gate was locked,' he said abruptly; then, turning to face the cowering children and their mother: 'Do you like dates?'

'Whoever fired the arrow must have come up through one of the other buildings and along the roof,' I told the captain. We were in the workshop, and I kicked up great clouds of bone shavings striding around the room in thought, while the Varangian leaned on the table and played with a small chisel that was like a toy in his hands.

'And will you spend your day asking every shopkeeper on the street whether he saw a fearsome assassin wander up his stairs, with a myth-ical weapon and a bunch of dates?'

I thought on this. 'No,' I decided. For three gold coins a day, I reasoned, such errands should be beneath me: Krysaphios would not want his treasure squandered. 'You can do it.'

The captain's red face flushed darker, and with a sudden movement he drove the chisel hard into the table. The fine point snapped at the impact. 'Take care, Master Askiates,' he bellowed, hurling the broken tool into a corner. 'The Varangians serve to protect the Emperor's life and to destroy his enemies. I have fought at his side in a dozen desperate battles, where the blood ran like rivers in the wilderness and the carrion-birds feasted for weeks. I will not be found begging gossip off merchants.'

Sunlight shone through the windows, and myriad fragments of dust and ivory swirled in the light as the Varangian and I stared at each other in silence. He glared at me with fury, one hand on the mace at his belt, while I levelled my eyes and tensed my shoulders. And in the brittle hush between us, there came the slight sound of an unguarded sneeze.

We both spun to the stairs from where it had come. There, just beyond a shaft of light and dust, was one of the carver's young daughters, sitting on the bottom step and chewing a length of her dark hair. She wiped her nose on the sleeve of her dress, and twisted her hands in her skirt as she looked shyly across at me.

'I was on the roof yesterday,' she said quietly. 'Mamma doesn't let me, but I was.'

At these simple words I almost jumped across the room, but I controlled myself enough to walk slowly over to her, a broad smile fixed intently on my face. I knelt down in front of her so that our heads were almost level, stroked her arm, and pushed some of the hair out of her face.

'You were on the roof yesterday,' I repeated. 'What's your name?'

'Miriam,' she said, looking down at her hands.

'And what did you see on the roof yesterday, Miriam?' Although I had assumed an easy, carefree tone, my face must have shown that every sinew in my body was tensed with expectation.

And doomed to frustration; she shook her head, and giggled softly to herself. 'My friends,' she said. 'We play.'

'Your friends,' I echoed. 'Other children? How about a man, a man carrying a big bow and arrow, like a soldier. Like him, perhaps,' I added, gesturing to the Varangian behind me.

But again she shook her head, more vigorously this time. 'Not like him. We played. Then Mamma found me and was cross. She hit me. I got a bruise.' She began to lift her skirts to show me, but I hastily tugged them down over her legs: there were certain things I did not need evidenced.

'And was this long before you watched the big procession?'

She considered this seriously for a moment. 'No. She hit me and then we looked at the purple man on the horse.'

She seemed as though she might say more, but at that moment we heard her name being called from above, her mother sounding far less demure than when she'd spoken with me. Miriam hopped up off her seat, opened her eyes very wide and put a finger to her lips, then turned and ran up the stairs. Her bare feet made no sound on the smooth stone.

'Well,' said the captain, folding his arms over his barrel of a chest. 'He shoots like lightning, he eats dates – and he's invisible. How do you unveil an invisible man, Askiates?'

'I'm leaving,' I said shortly, ignoring his taunts. 'There are men I must see.'

'Not invisible men, then?' Clearly he found this infinitely amusing.

'Not invisible men.'

'Aelric and Sweyn will go with you. The eunuch commands that you be guarded at all times.'

'That's impossible.' I wondered how much Krysaphios wanted me guarded, and how much watched. 'The men I am seeing are not those who would speak freely in front of palace guards.' Nor indeed welcome their company at all.

I expected the captain to protest, to offer the argument that those who would avoid the guards were those who ought most encounter them, but he did not; instead he merely shrugged his shoulders.

'As you choose,' he grunted. 'But if you want to give the eunuch his report, you will be back at the palace by nightfall. Otherwise the Watch will have you – and have you flogged for breaking the curfew.'

The thought did not appear to trouble him.

γ
───

I crossed the road, turned onto a side-street and plunged down the hill, heading for the merchant quarters and the Golden Horn. The path was steep and winding, frequently breaking into short flights of stairs where the slope was too treacherous, and I was grateful that the ashen skies had not yet delivered up their rain or I would have been upended many a time. The walls around me were sheer and tall, broken seldom by doors and never by windows: they were the fortified court-yards of Venetian traders, who kept their wares, like their lives, locked away from sight. Occasionally a slave or a servant slipped through one of the stout bronze gates, but more often the street was deserted.

Gradually, though, my surroundings became less imposing, the build-ings first unassuming, then modest, and finally humble. Shops appeared, crowding the alley with wares and smoke and the shouts of their owners, boasts of quality and promises of bargains unimaginable. Now I had to push my way through, resisting every manner of blandish-ment and enticement, while the upper storeys of the buildings reached closer and closer together, until I could imagine myself in the high basilica of an enormous church. So, at last, I came to the house of the fletcher.

'Demetrios!' As I stooped under his lintel, he put down the fistful of feathers he held and rose, limping out from behind his table to embrace me like a brother.

'Lukas.' I clapped my arms around his back, then retreated a step to let him take the weight off his twisted leg. 'How does the trade go?'

Lukas laughed, pulling a bottle and two cracked mugs from under his table and splashing out generous measures of wine. 'Well enough to give you a drink. As long as Turks and Normans keep their women mothering sons, there'll be targets enough for my arrows.' He leaned forward. 'And there are rumours, Demetrios – rumours of a new war, of a great barbarian army coming to drive the Turks back to Persia.'

'I've heard those rumours too,' I acknowledged. 'But I've heard them every month since you and I fought by the Lake of Forty Martyrs, and all I've ever seen come were adventurers who turned on us as soon as they had our gold, or visionary peasants.'

Lukas shrugged, and poured more wine. 'Barbarians or no, I'll still have a living. My masters at the palace have never reduced their order in a dozen years.'

We talked on for some minutes, swapping memories old and new, some shared but mostly separate, until – in a silence – I pulled Krysaphios' mysterious missile from the folds of my cloak.

'What do you make of this?' I passed it to Lukas. 'Could you make me a bow that could fire it, and with enough venom to pierce a steel hauberk?'

Lukas took the arrow in his hands and examined it closely, squinting in the dull light. 'A bowyer could build you a bow that would fire it,' he said, carefully. 'If you wanted a toy, a plaything for your daughter. Perhaps she needs to fend off importunate suitors?' He raised his eyebrows. 'But this arrow would make a dangerous toy – someone could injure themselves on it.' He stroked a finger over the encrusted blood. 'Indeed, it seems someone has.'

'Someone has,' I agreed.

'Someone, perhaps, who was wearing a steel hauberk?' Lukas watched me shrewdly.

'Perhaps.'

Lukas handed back the arrow. 'No. If you fired that from a bow, you would be lucky to see it stick in a tree. There's no weapon I know that could make it so lethal.'

I put the arrow back in my cloak, glad at least that the Varangian captain was not there to scorn this latest failure.

Lukas asked me to stay, but the day was drawing on and I did not want the first day of Krysaphios' gold to have yielded nothing. For three hours I tramped the streets of the Platea, hunting out every mercenary and informer I could remember in all the holes they frequented. None could conceive of such a weapon as I sought, though all expressed interest in owning one should I find it. Some tried to guess my true purpose; others blustered, and swore they could cut down a man, hauberk or no, for a fair price. One was mad, and tried – without conviction, thankfully – to stab me. At length, sitting on my own in a grim little tavern chewing some pork, I decided that if the collective memory of the brigands and hired swordsmen I'd seen could not solve this riddle, the answer must lie further afield, beyond the realm of our Byzantine knowledge.

I was right: it did. But not so very far beyond our realm. It resided, I discovered, in a small tavern behind the quay of the Hebrews, in the person of a very short, very round man, with oily skin and a miserable vocabulary.

It was pure chance that I found him. I had gone to the tavern to find a soldier named Xerxes, a Saracen I had half-known in worse times. If the weapon came from the east, I hoped he might know it. He did not, but before I could make excuses he had brought me to his table and forced me to join him in the rough wine he was drinking. It tasted like stewed pine-bark, and I held the cup well in front of my mouth to hide my grimace as he introduced the companion he drank with, a fat Genoese named Cabo who shook my hand vigorously and blew spittle in my face.

'Demetrios used to sell his sword-arm,' explained Xerxes, resurrecting a past I preferred to forget. 'Now he sells his brain. I don't know which earns him less.'

'Never as much as it's worth,' I assured him, though three gold pieces were already coming to seem overgenerous.

'Cabo's much cleverer,' Xerxes told me. 'He was in the business too. Now he's a respectable merchant.'

'What do you trade?' I asked. I hardly cared, but talking kept me from having to drink.

Cabo gave a knowing leer from under thick eyebrows. 'Silks. Gems. Gold. Weapons. Whatever men will buy.'

'Cabo doesn't like the imperial monopolies,' added Xerxes with a wink. 'He thinks they're an abomination before your God. He's like an evangelist.'

'Weapons,' I murmured, ignoring Xerxes. 'I'm seeking a weapon.'

Cabo's head lifted a fraction; his eyelids drew closer.

'Are you?' said Xerxes. 'Returning to your old ways?'

'A sword for ten gold pieces.' Cabo spoke slowly, and I guessed he would have just enough Greek to haggle for the goods and officials he needed. Drink and women too, perhaps.

'That's more than a legal profit,' I observed. 'And I already have a sword. I need a bow.'

'A bow for five gold pieces. Scythian. Very strong.'

'The bow I need must be very strong. Stronger than any bow yet made, yet short enough to fire an arrow no longer than man's arm. Strong enough to fire through steel.'

'And to sink a trireme with one stroke, and to fly as far as the moon,' said Xerxes. 'Cabo is a businessman, Demetrios, not a conjurer. You've sold your brain once too often – there's nothing left.'

'I can sell you such a weapon.' Cabo wiped the perspiration from his bald skull, and rested his fingers on the table, perhaps noticing that the cup had started to tremble in my hand. 'For seven pounds of gold.'

'Seven pounds of gold? You could buy an army with that?' Xerxes thought it a jest and waved for more wine, but I was deaf to his interruption.

'Do you have the weapon now?' I asked.

Cabo shook his head. 'Maybe in six months. Maybe in eight.'

'And what would such a weapon be like?' I did not try to hide my overweening interest; I hoped it would convince him my intentions were serious.

Cabo, for his part, did not hide his suspicion, but he had a merchant's instincts and could not resist. 'It is called *tzangra*, a crossed bow. Like a ballista, but a man can hold it himself. It will break open armour for you, if that is what you need.'

'And by what miracle of invention does it do that?' My blood and my breath both beat faster.

Cabo creased his forehead as he deciphered my question, then grinned and tapped the side of his head. 'By magic.'

'Genoese magic?' I had never heard of such a weapon among our people.

Cabo nodded.

'And do all men have them in Genoa?'

A shake of the head. 'Very expensive. Difficult to make. But possible to get, if you want. If you pay. Five pounds of gold now. Two more when I have it.'

I left his offer unanswered for a moment, feigning consideration while the sweat began to bead again on Cabo's scalp. At last: 'I shall think on it.'

'Why? Did you leave your five pounds of gold at home?' Xerxes was petulant; perhaps he worried that I truly might have such riches at my command.

'I gambled it on a horse at the hippodrome,' I told him. 'I need to collect my winnings.'

As I rose to leave, a final thought struck me.

'Tell me, Xerxes,' I said, dropping a copper coin onto the table for my part of the wine. 'It's been too many years since I retired. Where do the foreign mercenaries ply their trade now?'

'In Paradise,' said Xerxes sullenly. 'On the road to the Selymbrian gate.'

'Who's the best?'

Xerxes shrugged. 'None of them. You know what they do. Every week there's a new cock on the dunghill. Go there and ask: someone will find you. Or cut your throat.'

At that Cabo laughed, spraying wine all across the table.

Dusk was falling without a sunset as I entered the street. I was weary – it had been an age indeed since I had covered so much ground in a day, and unearthed so many long forgotten acquaintances, but the relief of having found even a single link in the chain helped my tired legs mount the hill, past the walls of Ayia Sophia and into the broad arcades of the Augusteion. A dozen ancient rulers gazed down on me from their perches: some benevolent, some wise, some forbidding, each as he would have history know him, but I ignored them all. I passed the great gate on my right, and made for a small doorway in the far corner of the square where two Varangians stood, crested plumes on their helms and axes. One of them, I saw, was Aelric, the guard who had stood on the patch of blood for me that morning.

He raised his axe in greeting. 'Come for the eunuch? They said you might.' He looked up at the fading sky. 'And never too soon.'

'I'm here to see Krysaphios. He will want to know my progress.'

'More than ours, I hope.' Aelric gave a mock frown. 'I never climbed so many steps as I did today. Sigurd had us up every house on the street asking if they'd allowed an assassin past.'

'Sigurd?'

'The captain. He said you ordered it.'

'Did he? Did you find anything of interest?'

Aelric shook his grizzled head. 'Only a girl suckling her child, who didn't pull her dress up in time when we came in. Nothing to interest the eunuch.'

'Speaking of whom . . .'

Leaving his companion on guard, Aelric led me through the door into a narrow arcade lining an orchard. The fruit trees were barren now, their branches spiny and white, but birds still called from them. We passed an enormous hall on our left, its vast doors fastened shut, and came through into a second atrium, where we skirted along another, broader corridor. We turned again, and soon I was lost in a labyrinth of halls and passages, columns and porticoes; of fountains, gardens, statues and courtyards. The very air itself was bewildering, sweet as honey and scented with incense and roses; warm as a summer's day, though outside we were in the depth of winter. The trickling of streams, the murmur of conversation and the chime of hushed instruments filled my ears; golden light spilled from the doorways we passed, framing the images of this separate world like icons. Every room was thronged with people: senators dressed in the robes of the first order; generals in their armour; scribes and secretaries under mountains of parchment. I saw noblewomen laughing in discrete circles, and petitioners with the drawn look of those who have waited long hours in vain. It was like a vision of Paradise, and through all of it I moved silently, unseen and unheeded.

At length Aelric brought me to a stone courtyard. It seemed older than the parts we had been through: here the mosaics were cracked and the walls were bare, save for the carved heads of imperial ancestors in their shallow niches. The sounds of the palace were dulled, and the perfumes in the air now had to contend with the stink of the city. The arcades were empty, excepting a lonely figure sitting on a marble bench, who rose gracefully to his feet as I approached. Aelric, I suddenly realised, had vanished.

'The Varangian captain thinks you are a fool, who dissipates his time in conversation with tradesmen.' Krysaphios stepped languidly towards me. A lamp burned from its bracket in a pillar beside him. 'And then provokes his employer by abandoning the escort I ordered.'

'If the Varangian captain knew the least thing about finding a murderer,' I said slowly, 'then I might have cause to care what he thought.'

'He says you had his men banging on doors asking futile questions all afternoon,' Krysaphios pressed. 'The imperial bodyguard. I wonder, Askiates, if you have sufficient imagination for your task.'

'Imagination enough to find a weapon that no-one else knew.' Briefly I described the *tzangra* of which the Genoese Cabo had spoken. 'And I *imagine* that this foreign weapon had foreign hands on the string.'

'A mercenary?' Krysaphios thought on this. 'Possibly. You yourself would know of such things, would you not?' He watched the guarded anger sweep my face. 'I know your story, Demetrios Askiates. I may not know the least thing about finding a murderer, but I am accomplished in the art of pinning a man to his past. Even a past he would rather forget – or hide.'

I said nothing.

'However it may be.' Krysaphios opened his palms to show me he did not care. 'The hands on the bowstring may have been foreign, but the spirit that willed them there, I am certain, is of far closer origins.' He reached into an alcove, where a roll of parchment lay scrolled up next to a statue. 'I have had my clerks prepare a list of all who might profit from an empty throne.'

I took it.

'A long list.' Headed, I noticed with a shiver, by the Sebastokrator himself, the Emperor's elder brother and the penultimate power in the empire. Perhaps Krysaphios and Sigurd were right – perhaps I should keep to the company of the merchants and shopkeepers I knew.

'A long list,' Krysaphios agreed. 'A list that could incite riot and rebellion if it were seen by those whose names appear. Look on it closely, and commend it to your memory.'

I held the paper close to the light and studied it with a furious intensity. Many of the names were familiar to me, though others were wholly anonymous. All the while Krysaphios stood silent, watching me, until at last I handed the list back.

'Repeat it,' he commanded.

'I can remember well enough, without reciting it like a schoolboy.'

'Repeat it,' he insisted, his eyes flashing. 'I have paid you for your mind, Askiates, and I will know what is in it.'

23

'You have paid me for the results I will bring you. And what am I supposed to ask of these people? "Are you responsible for the attempted murder of the Emperor? Do you own a fantastical Genoese invention called a *tzangra*?" Besides, what nobleman would even deign to speak with me?'

'You will be given the necessary introductions. As for what you should say, I would not dream to instruct you. You, after all, know all that can be known about finding murderers. Come and tell me tomorrow. Now if you will not recite my list, go. One of the guards will see you home.'

He balled up the paper in his hands and dropped it into the bowl of the lamp. It burst into flames and blazed in the glass, then quickly crumbled to ash.

δ
___

In the halls of the palace I had thought myself in heaven; the next morning, I was in Paradise. Or at least the place which bore its name: it did not merit the comparison. Once, I'm told, there had been fields here sloping up the long hill, green with wheat and fat with pasture, but those were long gone. The crops had been ground into dust, the grazing beasts slaughtered, and the extremities of the bloated city had spread inexorably over them. It was not a slum, but more a wilderness of shacks and broken shelters, where those who had used all their resources of strength and money to reach the city could collapse within its walls. Many never left, and with the watchtowers of the garrison so close at hand, it was inevitable that certain trades, those which always thrive among the poor and desperate, would flourish.

Such was its reputation, but it seemed unremarkable enough as I picked my way over the ruts and broken stones of the Selymbrian road. Children played in the roadside; wizened women hobbled along with great mounds of cloth on their backs, and every few paces there would be a gaunt, sun-scorched man sitting in front of a tray of nuts or dates or dried figs. One of these I approached, squatting down to look him in the eye.

'I seek a man for a dangerous task,' I said, using the age-old formula of the profession.

The man squinted at me, while a beetle crawled over his leg and onto the tray of figs. He seemed to be concentrating, grappling with a silent dilemma; then suddenly a fistful of fruit was thrust before my face.

I shook my head impatiently. 'No, thank you. I seek a man . . .'

I ceased talking as a second handful of figs appeared beside the first. The man was scowling now, shaking his arms in frustration.

A belated thought struck me. 'Do you speak Greek?'

The continued silence was answer enough. I raised my hands in apology, pushed the fruit away from me, and rose to leave. Ten paces away I felt a sharp stinging as a pebble struck me on the back of my leg, but I let it pass.

I walked slowly on down the road. Three or four times I tried to raise a passing traveller or hawker in conversation, but I was beyond the frontiers of civilisation: none spoke anything but barbarian tongues. I would have to return with a translator, I thought; I knew a few who frequented the harbours and sold their services to merchants. Though that would leave little of the day for visiting Krysaphios' dignitaries, and he would likely hear of it if I did not.

A tugging on the hem of my cloak returned me to the moment, and instinctively I clapped a hand on my purse to ensure it was safe. It was, and I earned a reproachful gaze from the ragged eyes of the child who had appeared beside me.

'Do you understand me?' I asked, more in bemusement than hope.

To my surprise, he nodded.

'You do?' Another nod, and the flash of white teeth. 'Do you know where I can find a man? A dangerous man?' I mimed a couple of sword strokes through the air.

The boy considered this, then nodded a third time. 'Elymas,' he said, his voice chirping like a young chick's. 'You see Elymas.'

'Elymas?'

'Yes. You see Elymas.'

I had kept a wary distance from him, but now I allowed him to grab my hand and tug me away, off the road and down a thin alley between rough rows of dwellings. I tensed, my eyes darting in all directions in anticipation of an ambush, a robbery. I had too many of Krysaphios' gold coins with me for comfort, and I was unarmed save for the dagger in my boot. But the urchin before me, in his tattered tunic and bare feet, skipped on heedless, leading me deeper and deeper into the labyrinth of ramshackle homes. Now I began to feel the weight of the area's reputation, began to feel the hostile eyes examining me from behind the splintered planks and frayed sheets which served for doors and windows. The groups of men we passed at the roadside would stop their conversation and stare insolently, while women sat with their legs lying open and offered indecent suggestions. My only solace was that none of it showed the least effect on the boy.

He brought me to place where an old woman sat by a damp fire, stirring a black pot and muttering gibberish to herself. Next to this was a makeshift tent, a wide bolt of purple cloth draped over two sticks which formed a doorway. The fabric looked remarkably like that used for decorating the streets during imperial processions, though I did not say so.

'Elymas,' said the boy, and ran off.

I watched him vanish behind a pile of rubble, which might have been somebody's house, and felt an overwhelming urge to follow. But I had come this far: I would take the final step, however ill-advised and reckless. Ignoring the crone by the fire, now giggling like a demon, I crouched down nearly to my knees and crawled into the tent.

The cloth must have been of a fine weave indeed, for within its folds all was darkness, though smoke from the neighbouring fire had somehow managed to choke the black air. I coughed; my eyes watered, and I snatched my hand to the knife at my ankle as I heard a movement beyond.

'Elymas?' I challenged.

There was a wheezing from the back of the tent, and the fluid sounds of a man clearing his throat.

'Elymas,' a voice answered at last. It spoke hesitantly, uncertainly, and did not sound Roman.

'Do you understand Greek?' My feet were flat on the ground, still poised to spring, but I had lowered the knife.

Elymas did not answer. My hopes sank. Then, in the silence, a dog barked twice, so near to me that my sword arm flew up in a blocking arc. The movement unbalanced me, and I toppled back clumsily onto the sandy floor.

'Do not be afraid,' said Elymas, his voice devoid of all comfort. 'Sophia answers all questions.'

'Sophia?' Not the hag by the fire outside, I hoped.

The dog, from somewhere close to Elymas, barked twice more. My eyes were slowly growing used to the gloom in the tent, and I could now make out the dim shape of a hunched old man, his white beard like a ghost in the darkness, sitting cross-legged before me. One hand rested on a black shadow next to him, which might – but for the barking – have been taken for a cushion.

'Sophia,' repeated my host, and again the dog barked twice.

A ludicrous notion entered my thoughts. 'Sophia is your dog?'

Two quick barks were the apparent, improbable confirmation of this truth.

'And Sophia will answer my questions?' I wondered if perhaps there was more than wood on the fire whose smoke had filled my lungs. 'And, naturally, she speaks Greek.'

This time there was only a single bark.

'What does that mean? She does not speak Greek?'

Two barks.

I looked around for the door flap, which had unaccountably fallen shut. What would Krysaphios say if he knew I wasted my time and his gold conversing with performing animals?

I saw Elymas pat his bitch affectionately on the flank. 'Not speak,' he said brokenly. 'Understand.'

I stared at him venomously. 'She understands Greek?'

Two barks protested she did.

'Tell me then, Sophia,' I began, wondering how far I was willing to take this charade. 'Can I find a mercenary for hire near here?'

Sophia looked at me disparagingly, then put her head between her feet and huffed through her nose.

'What?' I demanded, caught between impatience and the spell of this unlikely dream.

Elymas was wracked by a silent fit, rocking back and forth on his haunches. When it had subsided, he stuck a bone-thin finger into the sand before him and inscribed a circle, with a smaller circle, two eyes and a mouth within it.

Long experience of charlatans, as much as the clarity of his picture, gave me the answer. 'You want money for speaking to your dog?'

A pained expression crossed his face; he shook his head vigorously, and pointed to the bitch.

'Your dog wants money for me to speak to her?'

Sophia raised her jaw a fraction, just enough for a couple of weary barks. Internally abusing myself as an idiot, I drew an obol from my purse and tossed it into the sand in front of the dog.

She eyed it haughtily, then turned to lick her backside.

With the utmost reluctance, I added a second obol. Still she paid me no heed. A third obol followed, and then – swearing there would not be another – a silver keration.

Sophia turned back to me and gave two contented barks.

'Now,' I said heavily. 'Can I find a mercenary near here?'

Two barks, though even a dog might have known that. I would demand far more for my coin.

'Where can I find them?'

I earned scornful looks from dog and master. 'Can I find them on the Selymbrian road?'

One bark.

'Near the road?'

Two barks.

I paused, unable to think of any landmark which would help direct this line of questioning. 'Are there many men who can help me?'

One bark.

'Only one man?'

Two barks.

'Is he a barbarian? A Frank?'

One bark.

'A Roman? Like me?'

Two barks.

'And this man will find me a mercenary?'

Two barks.

'Does he have a name?'

Two barks.

Again I halted, as I came against the immutable fact that without a name or a location, this dog could tell me nothing. Nothing, in fact, that I did not already know or guess – and that, of course, was the nature of its trick. I had been a fool to convince myself that it could be otherwise, to succumb to the smoke and darkness and gnomic utterances of this false magician. I shuffled backwards, shooting the bitch a final, evil glare.

And in that second where we met each other's gaze, I swear I saw the dog lift her head, open her mouth, and say quite distinctly: 'Vassos.'

My jaw sagged in astonishment. 'Vassos?'

Two dainty barks.

'A man named Vassos?' I repeated, edging forward. 'The man I seek is named Vassos.'

And with two final barks, the dog turned her back on me and began chasing her tail.

I stumbled into daylight reeling from the strange encounter, my mind locked in a tussle of doubt and wonder. The woman with the pot had vanished, her fire now little more than embers; I breathed in deep lungfuls of cool air and hoped it would blow through my head also. During my uncommon career I had sought information from every rank of life, from city officials to notorious criminals, and often I had implored God for revelation; never, though, had I spoken with a dumb animal. What could I do but see how her story was resolved?

It soon emerged that she had done me a great service – more than many human informants have rendered me. Although I spoke no Frankish, nor Bulgarian nor Serbic nor any other of the immigrant languages of this place, the name 'Vassos' was like a charm: no sooner did I speak it to those I passed than comprehension lit up their faces and they gestured animatedly in one direction or another. I was led gradually westwards, through endless alleys of broken hovels towards the walls, until at length a gypsy loitering by a well pointed directly over my shoulder and said definitively: 'Vassos.'

I turned to see a house, itself remarkable enough in those surroundings. It seemed far older and better constructed than anything else around it: it might once have been a farmhouse, when these were virgin fields, but it was decayed and charmless now. Whoever owned it, though, had money enough to put a stout oak door on the hinges, and iron bars across the crimson-curtained windows.

I rapped on the door, wondering what business I disturbed inside. There was no answer.

'Vassos,' said the gypsy across the street, watching me and laughing.

I hammered the door a second time. Still it did not move, but in the corner of my eye I noticed one of the curtains tremble. I ran to it, just in time to see a woman's head vanish behind it.

'Vassos!' I called, trying to pull back the curtain through the bars. 'Vassos?'

'No,' said a voice within. 'No Vassos. No Vassos.'

'Where is he?' I let the curtain go and stepped back from the window. There was a silence, but my retreat was rewarded when strong arms drew open the curtain to reveal a heavily painted face glaring out at me. Her dress was a fragmented patchwork of different cloths, none bearing the least relation to the other, and tied like a girdle under her breasts so that they thrust forward toward me. There were red calluses around her mouth, and a scratch on one cheek. Her eyes were hard as glass.

'No Vassos,' she repeated emphatically. 'Vassos work. Work.'

'Tomorrow?'

She lifted her shoulders, deepening the cleft between her breasts yet further. 'Tomorrow? Tomorrow.'

'I will come tomorrow.'

Whether she understood me or not, the conversation was finished; the curtain shut and the house fell silent.

I spent the afternoon sitting in the courtyard of a minor noble, watching his fountain and playing with his cat. Every hour his steward would emerge to assure me I would be received imminently, but that lie soon tired. I preferred the honesty of the slum dwellers. I had chosen to start at the bottom of Krysaphios' list, hoping that there I might merit at least a dubious welcome, but that proved a false hope, and as it was a fasting day I could not even prevail on the steward for a drink. At last, with the shadows lengthening, I left for the palace. Krysaphios was undisguisedly unimpressed with my day's work; so too, when I arrived home, were my daughters.

'You're always home after dark now, Father,' Helena accused me. 'And late for supper.'

'"The dutiful daughter greets her father with the food of her hands,"' I quoted, smiling.

'The dutiful *wife*,' corrected Helena sharply. 'The daughter might well be in bed when her father chooses to appear.'

I settled into my chair, and took a spoonful of the stew she had prepared. 'I'm sorry,' I said humbly. 'The stew is delicious.' It was – she had her mother's gift with food. 'But my paymasters at the palace keep me working hard, and they pay me enough that one day I will not have to work so hard. Then we can have supper on time.'

'Is the palace beautiful, Papa?' asked Zoe, slurping her food like a soldier. 'Is it filled with fountains and light?'

'It is. Fountains and light and gold and laughter,' I said, and described as best I could the few corners I had seen. It needed little embellishment to make Zoe's eyes go wide with wonder.

'I thought the kingdom of God was for the poor.' Helena had been staring down at her plate while I spoke, saying nothing, but now she lifted her head contemptuously. 'I thought the Lord God would pull down the mighty from their thrones, and scatter the proud in the evil of their hearts. How can you work for such a tyrant, who glories in the trappings of sin?'

'I can work for him because his life is as valuable as any other man's.' We had argued this the previous night. 'And because in my lifetime he is the only ruler who has not brought us to the brink of ruin. He may feast in golden halls and drink from scented cups, but he keeps the borders secure and his armies far from the city. To my mind, that is enough.'

Though I believed what I said, I could understand the contempt in Helena's eyes, for I could hear my words sounding as hollow to her as they would have to me at that age. I remembered the monks who raised me preaching poverty and humility as they grew fat on the orchards I tended, and the way I burned at the injustice of it. Was I now grown into just another apologist for the orthodox?

Clearly Helena thought so; she rose from the table with a crashing of plates and chairs, and marched stiffly out of the room.

Zoe watched her go. 'She wants a husband,' she said, with the blithe indifference of a twelve-year-old. 'That's why she's angry.'

'I know,' I said wearily. 'And I will do something soon.' I speared a piece of vegetable onto my knife. 'But she should guard her tongue concerning the Emperor. He has many ears, many spies.'

And I, I thought as I lay in bed that night, was one of them.

ε
_____

It was close to midday by the time I found Vassos' house again; I
had spent the morning making some arrangements, then discovered
that his neighbours were less obliging with their directions when the
supplicant came accompanied by four monstrously armed soldiers. With
that in mind, I approached the sturdy door alone.

This time there was no need to knock. The lone gypsy who had
been outside before was now augmented by a triad of youths with
bruised, insolent faces; they loitered below the windows and stared at
me through lazy eyes.

'I'm here to see Vassos,' I said, as pleasantly as I could.

'Vassos busy.' It was the boy nearest me who spoke. He must have
been in a dozen knife-fights at least, judging by the scars, but it was
the pimples which truly disfigured him. He wore a green tunic clasped
with a leather belt, and as he spoke one hand drifted ominously behind
his back.

'Vassos is not too busy to see *me*.' A gold nomisma appeared between
my fingers, almost as if by accident, but when the youth leaned forward
to stare closer it vanished. I opened my empty palm to him with a
disingenuous shrug.

'Vassos will see me,' I repeated.

'Vassos see you.'

The boy stretched out an arm and banged three times on the door;
it swung inwards silently. With a mock bow and a sneer, he signalled
me to enter.

As I came into the dim room I saw that the boy had not been
making idle excuses for Vassos: he had indeed been busy, and seemed
only just to have concluded the business, for he was wrapping a cloth
about his bloated waist and wiping sweat from his black-haired chest.
Next to him a woman was pulling a dress up over her breasts, showing

33

not the least concern for modesty. On the couch behind them a second girl lay stretched out on her belly, shamelessly naked and glowing with a sheen of perspiration. For a moment I allowed myself to admire her openly, thinking to persuade Vassos of my complicity; besides, it was years since I had felt that pleasure, and I had the God-given desires of any man. Then I noticed the red lines scratched down the curve of her back, the slender width of her hips and the smooth skin on the flesh below her shoulder: she could not be much older – if at all – than Helena, I realised. Sickened, I looked away.

'Not to your taste, eh?' Vassos misread my look. 'Don't worry, I have more. What do you prefer? Peasant girls from the provinces who fuck like mules? Dusky Arabians from the court of the Sultan, versed in the seven hundred ways of pleasuring a man. Golden-haired virgins from Macedonia? If you're feeling patriotic, I even have a Norman wench, on whom you can revenge the treachery of their race. Though it will cost you extra if I cannot use her again.'

I stared at this ogre standing half-naked before me. Long, thick hair fell over his brutish shoulders, framing a face whose flattened nose and heavy cheekbones seemed more suited to a bull than a man. He wore a thick, golden chain around his neck, and rolled it between fat fingers as he spoke. It was with great restraint that I did not hit him immediately.

'I'm not after girls,' I said shortly. 'I seek . . .'

'Boys?' Vassos' fat lips contorted into a leer. 'I can do boys for you, my friend, if you enjoy Corinthian pleasures. Sometimes indeed I savour it myself – I must understand the tastes of my clients, you know. But it will take a little time – the boys are kept elsewhere.'

The girl who had been dressing herself when I entered had left the room, but now returned carrying a cup heavily crusted with coloured stones. She gave it to Vassos who drained its contents in a single gulp, leaving only a small trail dribbling down his cloven chin. He dropped it heedlessly on the floor, impervious to the clatter, and in the pause, I spoke again.

'Not boys. I seek men – and not for carnal pleasures. For dangerous tasks. I understood you could provide them.' It now seemed a faint hope: a lesson for trusting so much to the words of a charlatan and his dog.

But Vassos had gone very still. 'Men for dangerous tasks,' he mused. 'More dangerous than turning their arses over to you?'

34

'Men's work, not whores'.'

'I can sell you men for any task.' Vassos delivered each word with slow consideration. 'Any task which pleases me. But I do not know that I like your task.'

'Others may have paid you for similar,' I suggested.

'The business I do with others is my own affair. The business I do with you . . .' He thought on this. 'I choose not to do with you. You know the watchwords and you speak of danger, but I think *you* are the danger, my friend. Please leave my house.'

'I need to know if a man hired some men of you, perhaps in the last week or month. I will pay handsomely for the knowledge.' Again I allowed the gold coin to appear and disappear in my hand.

Vassos simply laughed, an ugly laugh that stirred the girl on the bed to look up, wide-eyed. 'You can buy my whores, and treat them as you pay for them, but you cannot buy *me* with your magician's gold. My reputation,' he explained solemnly, 'is everything. Now go.'

'Tell me who you've hired mercenaries to,' I persisted. 'Tell me and . . .'

My plea was interrupted by a piercing whistle, as Vassos stuck two fingers between his yellow teeth and blew hard through them. 'You will leave my house,' he said, smirking. 'Vassos' hospitality is legendary, but it is not to be abused. I will have my boys see you out.'

Still I did not move. I heard the sound of running footsteps, then shouts of alarm and the noises of a scuffle. A puzzled look passed over Vassos' face, but before he could act the door came crashing open and two giant bodies burst in. They moved like lions in the arena, bounding beyond me in a single stride and hurling Vassos into the stone wall behind. The back of an axe drove mercilessly into the fat of his stomach and he howled in agony; the skirt he wore slipped from his haunches and fell to the floor, exposing his shrivelled loins. Then he found the shaft of another axe pressed hard against his neck, almost crushing his throat in, and the wailing stopped.

A third figure stepped in through the shattered door. He was little more than a shadow against the daylight, but already the vast trunk and menacing arms were familiar to me: Sigurd, the Varangian captain. He leaned his axe against a chair and unstrapped the mace from his belt, hefting it in his broad hands as he approached the pimp cowering by the wall. The girl who had brought Vassos' cup screamed at the sight of him, and fled behind a curtain into the next room, while the girl on the bed sat up dazed, heedless of her nakedness.

Sigurd looked at her, at the bony ribs and breasts scarcely plumper than a boy's. He picked up the cloth that Vassos had worn and threw it over to her.

'Cover yourself,' he told her shortly. I doubt she understood him, for I guessed it would have been Vassos' custom to use foreigners and immigrants for his vile purposes, but she clutched it to her chest and wrapped her bare arms over it. That seemed to satisfy Sigurd.

'Now,' he said angrily, turning to Vassos. 'You have an ugly face, but I can make it uglier if I try. Who hired the men who tried to kill the Emperor?'

I winced; it was not the tack I would have taken. But I did not have a fearsome mace in my hands, and two of my lieutenants pinning Vassos to the wall. I kept silent and watched.

'I never hired men to kill the Emperor,' gasped Vassos, his voice now curiously high-pitched. 'I love the Emperor. I . . .'

Sigurd cut him short with an open-handed slap across his left cheek. The Varangian wore many rings, and his hand came away smeared with blood.

'You do not love the Emperor,' he told Vassos. 'I love the Emperor. You would have killed him for a fistful of silver.'

Vassos glared at him with undisguised hatred, and tried to spit in his face. But the axe-haft was too tight against his throat, and he succeeded only in leaving a gob of spittle and blood hanging from his chin.

Sigurd eyed him with contempt. 'You should never do that,' he warned dangerously. 'If your slime had reached me, I might have seen to it that nothing ever came out of your mouth again.' He held out his mace with a rigid arm, and pushed its spiked ball so close to Vassos' lips that he was forced to suckle it like a baby.

The girl on the bed stirred. 'There was a monk.'

So unexpected was her contribution that Sigurd jerked the mace away, tearing the corner of Vassos' mouth. The girl was shivering – from fear, I guessed, for she had pulled a blanket over her and was no longer shameful to look at – but her voice carried the ring of certainty.

'A monk?' said Sigurd. 'What of him? A Roman monk?'

The girl shrugged, the blanket sliding from her shoulder. 'A monk.

I was here. Vassos let him use me for free because he paid so much money.' Her voice was desolate. 'He took me like a boy. Like an animal.'

Sigurd took this news in silence, and – to judge from the tinge in his cheeks – embarrassment at hearing her degradations. In the ensuing silence, I spoke gently.

'What is your name?'

'Ephrosene.' She seemed surprised to be asked.

'Where are you from, Ephrosene?'

'From Dacia.'

'How long have you been in the city?'

She shrugged again, but this time caught the sliding blanket. 'Six months? Eight?'

'And you say there was a monk. How long ago?'

'Three weeks. Maybe four. He came several times. After the first time I tried to hide when he came, but sometimes he came unwarned. Sometimes Vassos dragged me out for him.'

'And did he come just for you?'

A tear ran down her face; I crossed to the bed and sat beside her, putting an arm around her thin waist.

'It's all right, Ephrosene,' I told her. 'You're safe from him now. From the monk, from Vassos, from everyone. Look at Sigurd,' I added, pointing to the Varangian, whose mace never wavered before the pimp's mouth. 'If he protects you, who can harm you?'

The girl wiped her cheek, and smoothed her hair back off her face.

'The monk came for soldiers. I was his entertainment. He wanted four men to travel with him – and a child.' She bit her lip, while the three Varangians and I looked on, disgusted; we could all of us imagine why he would have wanted the child.

'Did he explain his purpose with the soldiers?'

She shook her head. '"A dangerous task," was all he said. He paid much gold. Vassos was pleased. He bought me a silver ring.' She shuddered.

'And when was the last time you saw him?'

She thought for a moment. 'The monk, two weeks ago, I think. He came to meet the Bulgars, to take them away with him.'

'And did you know these Bulgars?'

'No.'

'You had never seen them before?'

37

'No.'

Her tears had stopped now; I pulled my arm from around her and made to stand up. But Ephrosene had not finished.

'I saw one of them afterwards, though. Vassos called him in. He had another task for him.'

I froze. 'Recently?' I did not hide the urgency in my voice. 'Did you see this Bulgar recently?'

To the surprise of every man in that room, the girl actually laughed. 'Of course,' she said simply. 'He was here this morning. I saw him as he left. Just before you came.'

There was an instant of dumbstruck silence in the room; then, before I could move, Sigurd had whipped the mace out of Vassos' mouth and put his face very close to the pimp's head; so close that his beard must have tickled Vassos' neck.

'What did you tell the Bulgar to do, you shit?' he demanded. His voice rasped on Vassos' ear like a lathe. 'Where can we find him?' He looked down at Vassos' sagging belly, and further down below his waist, caressing the flesh like a lover with the end of his mace. 'Where?'

Vassos seemed to have lost much of his will to speak, but once Sigurd had grudgingly allowed him to don a tunic he was willing to lead us to a place where we might find the Bulgar. As we emerged from the house I saw Aelric, standing watch over the three youths who were – with several more gashes and bruises to their bodies – lying bound in the street. Sigurd ignored them, and sent Aelric with Ephrosene to find a convent where the nuns could tend her; the rest of us accompanied Vassos ever deeper into the tangled alleys of the slum quarter. The three Varangians marched as one, crunching out their tread in perfectly measured time and keeping the prisoner always between them; I hurried along behind.

'Are you armed, Askiates?' asked Sigurd, looking back. 'You do not want to reach God's kingdom too soon. There are some mysteries you may not want revealed to you yet.'

'I have my knife,' I answered, breathing hard.

'You need a man's weapon in these parts.' Slowing his stride, Sigurd took the mace from where it swung at his belt and passed it back to me. I took it in both hands, almost overbalancing with the weight of it.

'Can you use that?'

'I can use it.' Or at least, I could have once in my past. Those days were long ago, though, and it had been many years since I swung such a weapon in anger. Now my arms ached simply to carry it.

'We need to capture this Bulgar alive,' I reminded Sigurd. 'We must discover what he knows.'

'If he knows anything. There are ten thousand mercenaries in this city, and the word of a weeping whore is a poor guarantee that this Bulgar is the one we want.'

'Indeed.' But a monk who hired foreign mercenaries from a man like Vassos was unlikely to purpose any good with them: that alone made him worth finding. And as Vassos swore – despite Sigurd's encouragement – that he knew nothing of the monk's whereabouts, the Bulgar might be our only link with him.

The buildings around us were now grown larger. Before, we had been in a shanty town of houses that never were, but here was a place where old houses had fallen from respectability into disrepair and ruin. The streets were narrower, and the lowering ramparts hid the pale December sun from our sight. I could see faces all around us, peering out from behind broken windows and rubbled walls, but the street remained empty. Perhaps the sound of the Varangians' boots had driven the populace indoors, but I doubted they would fear us when they saw how few we were. Sigurd looked back at me, and I saw my own thoughts mirrored in his worried eyes: this long, narrow road was like a mountain pass, the perfect situation for an ambush. And in Vassos we followed a treacherous guide.

We walked on, and I had begun to convince myself that I was imagining dangers where there were none, when a desperate scream tore through the silence of the alley. In an instant I was in a crouch, my hands raised with Sigurd's mace; ahead of me the three Varangians had their axes poised to strike. I stared into the dark doorways and alcoves around me but saw nothing; no arrows raining down from above, and no attackers charging against us. I remembered Sigurd's jest two days ago about the invisible assassin, and suddenly it was not so funny: perhaps after all we did face an enemy from beyond this world.

The scream came again, echoing in our ears, and I knew that – whatever else might await us – this was someone very much of our world. It had come from further along the road, and without pausing to think I broke into a run. The mace was light in my hands now, borne along by the surge of danger and excitement in my veins, and I was past my companions before they had even begun to move.

The houses ended abruptly, and the road emerged into what might once have been a pretty square. A round fountain was at its centre, seemingly dried up long ago, for weeds and mosses grew around it and the basin was riven with cracks. But it was not abandoned: a man stood on its rim, dressed in a leather tunic and standing almost as tall as Sigurd. He had his back to me, and was looking down into the fountain where another figure lay. A bloodied sword dangled from his hand.

I shouted a challenge and hurtled towards him. He spun around, surprise giving way to a snarl of defiance on his round face, and raised his sword to meet me. He was faster than I'd expected, but I was committed to my attack: as I came near I dropped my right arm back and swung it hard over my shoulder, aiming to smash my mace into his knee and fell him. But I was too slow; it was ten years and more since I had plied my trade on the battlefield, and the occasional brawl had kept neither my speed nor my strength at a pitch for defeating a mercenary. He parried my swing, crushing his sword down onto the handle of my mace and driving it clear of his body. He missed my hand by inches, but the blow served his purpose. My arm was jarred numb by the stinging impact of his blade, and the mace fell from my fingers.

Now I was exposed, too close to my opponent to retreat and without defence. Anticipating a second blow from his sword I looked up, but again he outwitted me: pain exploded through my jaw as he kneed me hard on the chin. I reeled back a step and fell flat on my back, feeling the ache in my spine and tasting blood in my mouth.

My enemy leapt down from his perch on the fountain and stepped towards me, his sword humming in the air as he took two expert swipes to steady his arm. I scrabbled desperately for the dagger at my ankle, but he saw what I did and stamped his foot down on my hand. Two fingers cracked, and I screamed, even as I saw him lift his sword over my neck for the killing stroke.

But he never struck. A new sound bellowed out in the square around us, a savage cry howled forth with a terrible anger. It was the cry Quinctilius Varus must have heard as he saw his legions hacked apart in the German forests, the cry that met the Caesar Julius as he sailed up the great rivers of Britannia, the cry of an unconquerable warrior revelling in his barbarity. A giant axe-blade sliced through the air above me and swept the waiting sword from my enemy's grip. It clattered harmless to the ground a few feet away, and the hands which had held it were still clasped empty above me as the second blow struck, knocking the mercenary backwards so that now it was he who lay winded on the ground. Strong arms held him down, while a red-faced Sigurd stood over him and held an axe to his throat.

'Move, and you lose your head,' he said, breathing hard.

I looked around, dazed. 'Is this the Bulgar? Is this the man Vassos brought us to find?' I shook my head, trying to clear some of the pain. 'Where is Vassos?'

Sigurd glanced around the square, and swore so angrily that I thought he might decapitate the captive in sheer frustration. Vassos was gone, presumably slipped away in the struggle.

'This is the Bulgar,' said Sigurd. 'Or at least, so the pimp told us. That was when we started running. None too soon,' he added, with a reproving glance in my direction.

I was heartfelt in my agreement. 'Not a moment too soon. You saved my life.'

'Saved you from yourself,' muttered Sigurd. 'Carrying a mace doesn't make you a Varangian, Demetrios. You were a fool to charge in.'

A groan from within the fountain reminded me what had prompted my impulse; I crossed to where the Bulgar had stood on its lip and peered down. The figure I had seen was still there, and I doubt he had moved an inch since I joined the battle, for his bare limbs and white tunic were covered in blood, and there were deep gashes in his leg. He lay with his knees pulled into his chest and his arms clasped about his head, making not the least sound.

'I saved someone in my turn, at least.' I stepped into the fountain and knelt beside him, lifting one shoulder as tenderly as I could to glimpse his face. He whimpered as I prised his hand from his eyes, but as it came away I almost lost my grip so great was my shock. This creature, this man whom the Bulgar warrior had been dismembering when I attacked, was not a man at all, but a mere boy whose hollow cheeks still bore the downy hairs of the first beard. He was solidly built for his years, but those must have been fewer even than the girl Ephrosene's.

'A child,' I murmured, astounded. 'The Bulgar was trying to kill a child.'

'Maybe he tried to pick his pocket,' said Sigurd. 'There's a purse on the ground over here.' He stooped to pick up the leather bag and hooked it onto his belt. 'Not that the whoreson will be needing it now. Maybe the boy fucked his sister. Who cares.'

I was about to argue the point, but Sigurd had already forgotten the boy in the fountain and stepped back to regard his captive.

'Get him to his feet,' he ordered. 'And bind his arms behind his back. I'm going to march you all the way to the palace with my axe at your neck,' he told the Bulgar. 'If you so much as stumble your head will lose the company of its shoulders.'

'What about the boy?' I asked. 'He needs help – he'll bleed to death otherwise.'

'What about the boy?' Sigurd shrugged. 'I've already detached one of my men trying to redeem a petty whore, and had that pimp Vassos escape from me. I'll see this Bulgar at the palace in chains whether he's the man who tried to kill the Emperor or a pilgrim who got lost on his way to the shrine. I won't lose him by using my men as stretcher-bearers for a pickpocket who chose his target poorly. And you,' he added, stabbing a finger into my chest, 'should clean that blood off your face and come with us, if you want the eunuch to think he spends his gold wisely.'

'I'll come to the palace in my own time,' I said fiercely, taking a step backwards. 'And that will be when I've found this boy a clean bed and a doctor. On my own, if I have to.'

'On your own, then. If you go south down that street, you should meet the Mesi.' Sigurd picked his mace out of the dust, scowling to see the gash in its handle, and returned it to his belt before prodding the prisoner forward. With his lieutenants flanking the captive, he marched away, and I was alone in the square.

My head was wracked with pain, and my right arm still numb, but I somehow managed to lift the boy into my arms and carry him out of the basin where he lay. My steps were awkward and faltering; I feared that at any moment I would topple forward and do the child yet worse injury, but with frequent recourse to the support of the surrounding walls I made some headway out of the square and down the hill. Now I could see a sliver of the main road at the end of the alley, and I hurried as best I could to reach it. Although it was a cool day and I was still in the shade of the buildings, sweat began to sting my eyes and trickle down my nose; my beard itched unbearably. My arms and back too demanded that I pause, that I sit down and rest them if only for a minute, but I suspected that once the boy was on the ground I would never raise him up again. I cursed Sigurd and his heartlessness; I cursed Vassos and his Bulgarian thug, and I cursed myself for risking my commission with the palace just to carry a dying boy a hundred paces closer to death.

In a haze of pain and fury, I reached the road. There I succumbed, and collapsed against a stone which proclaimed I was exactly three miles from the Milion.

'Are you well?'

I opened my eyes, which had drifted shut for a second. I was sitting at the edge of the Via Egnatia, my back supported by the milestone, with the boy's head resting in my arms. His face seemed peaceful – more peaceful than the rest of his ravaged body, at least – but pale, and clammy. When I touched a hand to his cheek it was fearfully cold.

'Are you well?'

I looked up to meet the insistent voice. It was a drayman, his face shaded by a broad-brimmed hat, standing before a cart loaded with clay pots. He spoke in a kindly voice which, after a moment's confusion, I answered.

'Well enough. But the boy is in a perilous state. He needs a doctor.'

The drayman nodded. 'There is a doctor at the monastery of Saint Andrew. I can carry your boy there on my cart – my journey passes it. I am going to the cemetery.'

'I'm trying my best to avoid the cemetery,' I said with feeling. 'But I would be grateful to go as far as the monastery.'

We lifted the boy carefully onto the cart, laying him over the jars of incense and unguents, and set off, travelling as quickly as we dared without aggravating his wounds on the rutted road.

'What are your perfumes for?' I asked the drayman, thinking the least I could do was reward his help with conversation.

'For the dead,' he said solemnly. 'The embalmers use them.'

We walked the rest of the way in silence, though mercifully it was a short enough journey. The drayman pulled his cart through the low arch of the monastery gate into a cloistered, whitewashed courtyard, and we laid the boy out on the flagstones. I gave the man two obols for his aid; then he left me.

A monk appeared and stared at me disapprovingly.

'We are at prayer,' he told me. 'Petitioners are heard at the tenth hour.'

'My petition may not wait that long.' Too exhausted to argue more decisively, I merely jerked my thumb to where the boy was lying. 'If the Lord will not hear my plea until then, perhaps your doctor will.'

It may have been a blasphemous suggestion, but I was past caring. The monk tutted, and hurried away.

The tinny bell in the dome of the church struck eight, and monks began streaming out of the chapel in front of me. All ignored me. I watched them pass with ever-mounting fury, until I thought I would roar out my opinion of their Christian charity to their self-regarding faces. But just then a new figure appeared, a servant girl in an unadorned green dress, with a silken cord tied around her waist. I was surprised to see her, for I would have thought the novices could do whatever chores she performed, but she seemed to have noticed me and for that I was grateful.

'You asked for a doctor?' she said, looking down on me with none of the humility or reserve expected of her sex and her station. I did not care.

'I did. Can you find me one?' I forsook the usual forms of courtesy. 'This boy is dying.'

'So I see.' She knelt beside him to put two fingers to his wrist, and laid her palm against his forehead. Her hands, I noticed, were very clean for a servant's. 'Has he lost much blood?'

'All you can see.' One entire leg was cased in crusted blood. 'And more. But fetch me a doctor – he will know what to do.'

'He will indeed.' She spoke as immodestly as her apparel, this girl, for she wore no palla to wrap her head and shoulders. Though truly, she could not be called a girl, I realised, for her uncovered face and bright eyes held a wisdom and a knowledge that only age can inscribe. Yet she wore her black hair long, tied behind her with a green ribbon like a child's. And like a child, I saw, she showed no sign of obeying me, but continued to stare with the tactless fascination of the young.

'Fetch me the doctor,' I insisted. 'Every minute brings him closer to death.'

At last my words showed some effect: the woman stood and looked towards an open doorway. But instead of hurrying away she turned, and with astonishing temerity began to upbraid me.

'Make haste,' she commanded. 'You've carried him this far, you can carry him these last few paces. The monks here are afraid to touch the dying – they think it pollutes them. Bring him inside where we can wash his wounds and get some warmth into him.'

I was almost dumb with surprise. 'Surely only the doctor will know if it's safe to move him.'

She put her hands on her waist and stared at me in exasperation. 'She will, and it is,' she said curtly. 'I am the doctor, and I say bring the boy inside so I can clean and bind his wounds before he slips beyond us.' Her dark eyes flashed with impatience. 'Now will you do as I say?'

With the colour of shame rising under the bruises on my face, I humbly obeyed. Then, when that was done, I fled to the palace.

I had never seen the dungeons of the palace before, and I would not hurry to see them again. A guard led me down a twisting stair, deep underground, to a chamber lit only by torchlight. Massive brick piers rose out of the floor and arched overhead like the ribs of a great sea-beast, while on the walls between them hung scores of cruelly shaped instruments. In the middle of the room were a roughly hewn table and benches, where a group of Varangians sat and diced. Even seated, they had to take care to keep their heads from cracking on the black lamps above them.

Sigurd threw a handful of coins onto the table and looked up. 'You're here,' he grunted. 'Finished playing the Samaritan, have you?'

'The boy's with a doctor,' I answered coolly. 'Where's the Bulgar?'

Sigurd tossed his head towards a low archway behind him. 'In there. Strung up by his arms. We haven't touched him yet.'

'You shouldn't have waited for me. His knowledge may be urgent.'

Sigurd's face stiffened. 'I thought the eunuch paid you by the day. Anyway, we didn't wait for you – we waited for the interpreter. Unless, of course, *you* speak the Bulgars' language?'

I shrugged my surrender, though Sigurd had already turned back to his game. He did not invite me to join it, and after a moment of awkward pause I retreated out of the lamplight into a dim corner. There I kept silent, and tried not to hear the dismal sounds drifting into the guardroom.

You could not measure time in that mournful place, but I must have spent almost an hour watching Sigurd's humour rise and fall in balance with the number of coins in the pile before him. Then there came a sound from above, and I peered up the curling stair to see a constellation of tiny flames descending, dozens of lamps processing down like a swarm of fireflies. Slaves in silken robes held them aloft, unwavering despite the uneven ground beneath: they filed along the periphery of the vault until they were like an inner wall of shimmering silk and fire around us. At their tail came two who did not carry lamps, one in the crimson mantle of a priest; the other in a rich gown of blazing gold threads: Krysaphios.

All the Varangians were on their feet, the silver and dice swept invisibly into their pouches.

'My Lord,' said Sigurd with a bow. He wore humility clumsily, I thought.

'Captain,' answered Krysaphios. 'Where is the prisoner?'

'In the next room. Contemplating his wickedness alone. We need an interpreter.'

'Brother Gregorias has devoted his life to the Bulgar tongue.' Krysaphios indicated the priest beside him. 'He has transcribed the lives of no fewer than three hundred saints for their edification.' That, I thought, should give him the requisite vocabulary of torment. 'If your prisoner has anything to say, he will decipher it.'

'The prisoner will talk,' said Sigurd grimly. 'Once I'm done with him.'

We left the eunuch's silent retinue in the main chamber, and stooping passed through a low tunnel into the adjoining cell. I followed Sigurd, Krysaphios and the priest Gregorias in. Here the air was closer and more unpleasant; but more uncomfortable still, I suspected, was the prisoner. His arms were hung on thick hooks above him in the ceiling, so that only his toes touched the floor: he swayed a little backwards and forwards, and moaned gently. His clothes had been torn away, leaving only a narrow strip of linen around his hips, and his wrists bled where the shackles bit into them so that he seemed to me uncannily like Christ in torment on his cross. I shivered, and banished that blasphemous thought immediately.

'Demetrios.' I saw Krysaphios staring at me. 'You are the paid expert in these matters – find out what the man knows.'

I was an expert in quizzing petty thieves and informers in the marketplace, not tearing out confessions in the imperial dungeons. But before my patron I could not be seen to falter. I stepped forward and immediately found that I did not know where to look, whether to the priest or the prisoner. My eyes darted dumbly from one to the other, and I could mask my confusion only by crossing my arms over my chest and taking deep, contemplative breaths.

47

'A monk hired you from a man named Vassos,' I began at last, addressing the wretched Bulgar. No sooner had I spoken, though, than my thought was disrupted by the quiet monotone of the priest, intoning crude foreign syllables into the captive's ear. I stammered a little, and began again.

'Three weeks ago this monk contracted you to murder the Emperor. You were to use a strange device, a barbarian weapon they call a *tzangra*, to murder him in a public street, on the feast-day of the holy Saint Nikolas.'

There was a pause while I waited for the translation to catch up with the commanding gaze I had fixed on him. The priest went silent, and four pairs of ears were poised for an answer. Only the chime of Sigurd's ringed armour broke the hush in the room.

The Bulgar lifted his face, and looked at us all contemptuously. He spoke one word, and none of us needed the priest to explain its meaning. 'No.'

I sighed theatrically. 'Ask him if he follows our faith,' I told the priest.

The Bulgar ignored the question, but after some urging from the interpreter he acknowledged that he did.

'Tell him, then, that he has sinned,' I continued. 'But tell him that Christ preaches forgiveness to those who confess their sins. Tell him that in Vassos and the monk he has served evil masters, masters who have betrayed him. We can help him.'

'We can help him screaming to his grave,' interrupted Sigurd, but I waved him to be silent and hoped the priest would not translate his words. Nonetheless, I saw the Bulgar's eyes dart towards the Varangian as he spoke.

'As long as he stays silent, he will never escape this dungeon.' Although the prisoner's continued silence frustrated me, I was at least learning to speak over the constant murmur of the translation. 'But the monk and Vassos are free to drink and whore and contrive their plots. Why should he suffer while men of far greater evil do not?'

There was a rustling of silk as Krysaphios stirred. 'You do not seem to have his ear, Demetrios,' he observed. 'Or perhaps the finer points of your rhetoric are lost in the foreign tongue.'

I worried that none of my companions understood the time it will take to pry information from an unwilling informant, however helpless and confined he might be. Krysaphios must be accustomed to seeing his will executed immediately, not waiting for an immigrant criminal to choose to speak. I feared he would soon demand more corporal approaches.

'Tell us how you attempted to kill the Emperor,' I insisted, renewed urgency in my voice. 'Tell us what the monk wanted, why he bought you to do this terrible thing.'

The Bulgar's head had sagged while Krysaphios and I argued, but now he lifted it again. He opened his mouth and swallowed; I thought he would speak, and was about to call for water when – with a convulsive jerk of his body – he spat. There was little strength in the effort, and near as I was it still landed short of me.

I stepped backwards, and gave a tired sigh of frustration. This would take many hours, and they would feel all the longer for having Krysaphios at my shoulder.

Too long, it seemed, for one man: as the Bulgar's spittle struck the floor, I heard a growl from behind me. With a single stride Sigurd had crossed to the prisoner and kicked his feet from under him; the Bulgar swung back like a pendulum, and screamed as the manacles bit deeper into his wrists. The cloth was ripped from his waist so that he hung naked and exposed, while Sigurd pressed his face very close to the man's throbbing cheek. The axe glinted in his hands.

'My friend Demetrios appeals to your sense and reason,' he hissed angrily, not waiting for the interpreter to follow his words, 'but I appeal to something to which you might actually pay heed. You tried to kill the Emperor, you Bulgarian piece of filth. You would have lifted a usurper onto the throne. Do you know what we do to usurpers in this kingdom?' He let the axe slide like a razor over the man's face. 'We pull out their eyes and slice open their noses, so they are too deformed for any man to acclaim them Emperor.' He stepped back thoughtfully, then almost casually drove a fist into the man's taut stomach. He howled again and rattled in his chains. 'Did you tell him that, priest?'

The interpreter nodded violently, trembling under Sigurd's savage gaze.

'Then tell him also,' he continued, 'that if we really want to be sure that the usurper will never trouble us again, we don't stop with his face. Oh no.' He laughed malevolently. 'We take away his manhood,

49

make sure that he'll be forever barred from becoming Emperor, and barred from inflicting any vengeful bastards on us either.' He took his axe in both hands and looked at it thoughtfully. 'Of course you could never have sat on the throne, Bulgar, but perhaps I should practice for when I catch the man who would. Shall I do that? Shall I turn you into a eunuch? Condemn you to playing the bitch if ever you want the least pleasure again in your miserable life?'

He glanced down below the prisoner's waist, and allowed derision to enter his face; I shot a quick glance at Krysaphios, but his smooth face remained wholly opaque. 'I could make you quite valuable,' Sigurd said with a leer. 'Not like some Armenian boy whose parents have simply squeezed his balls back where they came from. I can turn you into a *carzimasian*, as pure as a girl with not a shred of your flesh remaining. You'd fetch a higher price then than you ever did as a mercenary.'

He affected to tire of his monologue and fell silent. Even the priest, who had translated every word, seemed to be shivering: I think Krysaphios was the only one of us who did not cower at Sigurd's threats. Certainly the Bulgar was paying attention, his eyes fixed in terror on the evil curve of Sigurd's axe which jerked and twitched bewitchingly as he spoke. The axe which was now raised as high in the air as the dungeon would allow, hovering over Sigurd's shoulder like a vengeful angel waiting to strike.

'No,' I protested, but my mouth was dry and the words barely scraped forth. And too late: the axe swung down in a flashing arc and struck thick sparks from the stone floor; the prisoner screamed like an animal and thrashed about in his chains. Fresh blood ran down his wrists and the priest yelped in horror. But no blood fountained from the Bulgar's groin, and no gruesome lump of flesh was lying limp on the floor. The axe must have passed inches before his body.

Sigurd lifted his blade from the stone and eyed it curiously. 'I missed,' he said, surprised. 'Shall I try again?'

He had to kick the priest to translate this, but even before he had spoken a torrent of words began to spew out of our prisoner. The shock of his near emasculation had shaken something loose within him: he sobbed and ranted as though a demon possessed him, and I was glad of the chains which restrained him. Only after much soothing talk, and after Sigurd had retreated well into a corner, did he slow his speech enough that the translator could make sense of it.

His name, he said, was Kaloyan. Yes, he had worked for the pimp Vassos, mostly collecting debts and beating girls who no longer wished to work for him, sometimes protecting them from men who became angry or refused to pay. Occasionally he would do something else, something more dangerous, for Vassos was a man with ambitions and he enjoyed the thought of having a private army. Mostly, though, they were a ragged bunch of former soldiers and strongmen, who drank and brawled with each other when not called upon to fight professionally. Until, that was, the monk arrived.

'Describe him,' I said tersely, my fingers clutching the hem of my tunic in anticipation.

'He cannot,' answered the translator after a brief exchange. 'He says the monk always wore a hood, always, even in the forest.'

'In the forest?' I realised I was disrupting the story. 'Never mind. What did the monk want?'

'The monk wanted five men. The pimp provided them, Kaloyan was one. He took them to a house in the forest, where for two weeks he trained one of them in the use of a strange weapon, a barbarian weapon the like of which Kaloyan had never seen.'

'Was it a *tzangra*?' I asked, describing it as best I could.

'Yes,' said the interpreter. 'Just so. It could shoot through steel. Kaloyan wanted to try it, but the monk guarded it jealously and let no-one but his apprentice use it. Once one of Kaloyan's companions tried to steal it while the monk was sleeping. He did not leave the forest alive.'

'So Kaloyan was not the assassin.' I could not know whether to be elated or confused by how close I had come. 'Does he know the one who was?'

I saw the Bulgar shake his head weakly. 'He never knew him before,' the priest confirmed. 'Vassos found him somewhere in the slums.'

'Did the monk say what he purposed with the weapon? Why he went to so much trouble to train another man in its use?' My questions were coming faster now, for every word the Bulgar spoke demanded explanation, and the frustration of the long pauses while the interpreter spoke first with the prisoner and then formed his phrases was beginning to wear on me.

'The monk never told them his purpose, and he did not welcome questions. All he said was that he had a powerful enemy whom he wanted removed, and he could not do so himself.'

Another thought struck me. 'So if he trained only one of them in the use of the *tzangra*, what were Kaloyan and the others for? Did he fear for his safety?' Did the monk have other enemies of whom we knew nothing?

'Not for his own safety.' The interpreter puzzled at something the Bulgar had said. 'He was afraid that the apprentice would flee away if he had the chance.'

'Why would he do that?' Surely the monk paid well enough, if he could afford a quartet of bodyguards.

An even longer pause. 'Because of his age. He was little more than a boy, the Bulgar says, and wild, untameable.'

I heard the ringing thud of metal on stone as an axe-head fell to the ground. The interpreter flinched; the Bulgar screamed, though it was only Sigurd dropping his weapon. It was some moments before there was calm again, and all that time I strained with a burning impatience to ask my final question.

'A boy?' I said at last. 'The assassin was a boy? Has the Bulgar seen him since?'

It seemed an age while my words were echoed into the Bulgar tongue, then while the interpreter frowned in concentration at the long answer he was given. He curled a finger through his beard and eyed me nervously, sensing the importance that had settled on this last question, though in no way understanding it.

'Yes,' he said simply. 'He did see him again. He says he tried to kill him this morning.'

ζ

I was running out of the dungeon almost before the priest had spoken, out past the blank ranks of lamplit slaves, up the twisted steps, and into the mercy of the cool air in the courtyard above. There were shouts and footsteps behind me but I did not care: I had held the assassin in my arms only hours ago, had saved him from an almost certain death. I looked about at the great columns enclosing me like a giant cage, and realised I did not even know my way out of the palace.

'Where did you take him?'

I spun around to see Sigurd emerging from the stair behind me. He was breathing heavily, though still could hold his axe with a single hand.

'To a monastery.' I hesitated, suddenly thinking what he might do to the boy who had tried to kill the Emperor. Of course a murderer deserved death – but I had saved his life, and I had not shaken the soldier's superstition that you buy a man's life only with a small piece of your own.

'Which monastery?' Sigurd demanded. 'Christ! The boy might already be gone. There's no time.'

'The monastery of Saint Andrew. In the Sigma district.'

'Follow me.'

His armour jangling like shackles, he led me at a run through the corridors of the palace. The scribes and noblemen we passed stared but said nothing; no guards challenged us. Doors opened before us as if by some unseen hand, and sometimes it seemed that a room which I had seen cast in darkness as we approached was bathed in light when we arrived. Then the lamps became scarcer, the stairs steeper. There was little life in this part of the palace, and that, mostly furtive-faced slaves scurrying past with their eyes cast down. I hastened to keep close to Sigurd.

At length the columns and marble floors gave out and we came into a low tunnel. Sigurd nodded to the brick vaults above our heads.

'The hippodrome.'

We passed under it in silence, our footsteps mute on the sandy floor. There was a gate at the end and Sigurd had the key: beyond it I could hear sounds of life, of laughter and labour, and smell the warm odour of horses.

'Hipparch!' bellowed Sigurd. 'Hipparch! We need two horses, saddled and bridled.'

'Late for your mistress again?' A tall man, elegantly dressed, stepped into the square of the stable yard.

'At least I have a woman, you horse-fucker.' Sigurd clapped him on the shoulder. 'But she will have to wait.'

The hipparch raised his eyebrows. 'So urgent? I have two mounts awaiting the logothete's dispatches.'

'Then the dispatches can wait too. Send a boy to the chamberlain and tell him we've gone to the monastery of Saint Andrew, in Sigma.' A thought struck him. 'You can ride, can you, Demetrios?'

I could, although galloping a horse bred for the imperial post through the darkening streets of the megapolis was not something I was practised in. It taxed all my luck and concentration merely staying upright on the beast, and it was a mercy that with the day ending the crowds were gone, and that the emerging watchmen had the wit to retreat into the arcades as Sigurd and I thundered past.

We arrived at the monastery, Sigurd sliding off his horse and crossing swiftly to the gates. They were locked, but the butt of his axe-shaft was soon pounding out notice of our arrival loud enough to reach the ears of the dead in the distant necropolis.

A small door set within the gate cracked open a finger's breadth.

'Who's there?' Suspicion and fear had driven all trace of sleep from the speaker's mouth.

'Sigurd, captain of Varangians and guardian of Emperors. You keep a boy with you who I need to see.' Sigurd shouted the words like a challenge in the arena.

The monk, to my surprise, found sufficient moral indignation to resist.

'The monastery is closed for contemplation and prayer. You may return in the morning. No-one passes the gate during the hours of darkness.'

'I have almost lamed two of the logothete's finest horses to come here.' Sigurd was working himself into a powerful frenzy. 'I will not now sit on your doorstep.' Without warning, he lifted his boot and slammed it into the wooden door; there was a yelp of pain as it swung inwards.

We stepped through, Sigurd scraping his shoulders on the frame. Inside a monk was rubbing a bruised shoulder, and cursing us with words that no man of God should know, but we ignored him as I led the way across the courtyard to the arched doorway where I had left the boy. Forestalling Sigurd's axe, I knocked.

'One day your patience will betray you,' Sigurd fretted as we waited in the cold darkness. 'If this doctor's in there, let me call him out.'

'One day you'll knock down the wrong door,' I told him, 'and find so many enemies your axe will be blunted before you can kill all of them.'

Sigurd shrugged. 'Then I'll beat their heads in with the haft.'

'And leave another to clean their wounds.'

We both looked to the door, which had silently opened to reveal the woman doctor to whom I'd entrusted the boy. She held a candle, and wore only a long woollen shift which left her arms and feet entirely bare. There were rises in the fabric where her nipples pressed against it: the sight of them stirred something within me, but the look on her face was of pure anger.

'What do you mean by hammering down the monastery gates at this hour, and then calling me from my work? If you must profane the laws of God, you might at the least respect the business of healing.'

'We seek the boy who was brought here this morning,' said Sigurd, before I could offer an apology. 'Is he here?'

She gazed at him contemptuously, while my heart raced to hear the answer. Had we come so close, only to be denied our prize by my compassion?

She tossed her head. 'He's here. He could hardly have left. He cannot stand, let alone walk. At the moment he sleeps.'

'We must see him. Immediately.' Sigurd's voice was heavy with menace. 'We come on palace business.'

Two flames were reflected back in the doctor's dark eyes. 'The Emperor himself cannot raise a sick boy to health simply by his command. The boy is feverish and delirious. At the moment he is sleeping, and that is probably the most wholesome thing he has done in a month. Unless you are the man who sliced so deeply into his leg, you would tremble to wake him.'

'Lady, I am the man who *stopped* the Bulgar from killing him.' Sigurd's voice was loud now, and he stepped forward so that he almost touched her. She was minute before him, like Andromeda beneath the Kraken, but she did not waver.

'No,' she said. 'While the boy sleeps, you wait.'

'What if he escapes by the back door?' Sigurd was in retreat, now, but he would not surrender until he was satisfied.

'There is no back door, Captain – only two high windows through which you would struggle to fit your forearm. Good night.' And blowing out the candle, she left us in darkness. On the far side of the door I heard a bolt shoot home.

Sigurd stood very still, staring at his axe where it caught the moonlight.

'You can't chop your way in,' I warned wearily. I sat down on the step and leaned my back against the base of a column. 'And the boy won't move. What can we do but wait?'

Sigurd clearly had many ideas, but with a reluctant growl he at last laid his weapon on the stone floor and made a seat beside it.

'We don't move,' he warned me. 'And we don't sleep. Anyone who comes out of that door before dawn will find my axe through their throat.'

I did not ask what would happen to me if I failed to stay awake.

I hesitated to talk with Sigurd after that, but when half an hour had passed in silence I risked the hope that the chill air would have numbed his anger a little.

'Your zeal in defence of the Emperor is like something out of legend,' I said quietly, thinking he could ignore me if he chose. 'No wonder he prizes his Varangians so highly.'

'Only the English.' Sigurd stared moodily at his fist. 'There were others in the guard, Rus and Danes and their sort, but he expelled them because he could not trust them.'

'Why the English?' I was genuinely curious: to me one fair-headed barbarian giant seemed much like another.

Sigurd grunted. 'Because the English are the only men who will hate the Emperor's enemies as if they were his own. I will tell you. Fifteen years ago, at a battle near Dyrrachium, the Normans trapped a company of Varangians in a church. At first they offered gold, and riches, if the English would desert the Emperor and join them in battle, for they knew of our fame in war, but the Varangians refused. Then they grew angry, and threatened to slaughter them to the last man if they did not surrender, but still the English defied them. So at last they set fire to the holy sanctuary where they had sought refuge, and razed it to the ground. Not one man escaped. We would rather the Normans burn us alive than surrender to them. That is how deep the hatred goes.'

'But why? Why leave wives as widows, when they could have been safely ransomed after the battle?'

Sigurd leaned forward. 'Because the Normans killed our king and stole our country. Their bastard duke tricked and lied his way onto our throne, then laid the land waste.'

'When was this?' He spoke with such a savagery that it could have been yesterday.

'Thirty years ago. But we do not forget.'

'You would have been a child thirty years ago, no more than five or six years old. The same as me.'

A sound from the door behind us broke off our conversation. Before I could even turn my head Sigurd was on his feet and lifting his axe, poised to strike. I had a flash of panic that he would behead some innocent monk attending a call of nature, but it was not a monk, nor yet the boy escaping: it was the doctor. She had wrapped a stola around her shoulders, covering the indecency of her shift, and held two steaming clay bowls in her hands. Had it been me, I thought, I would probably have dropped them in the face of a lowering Varangian, but she simply set them down on the floor before us.

'Soup,' she said. 'I thought you might be cold. I did not want to find a pair of obstinate men with frostbite in the morning.'

Sigurd resumed his seat, and we tipped the hot food eagerly down our throats. The lady stood over us, watching, until we had wiped the bowls clean with the bread she gave us. To my surprise, she did not then retreat inside with them; instead she smoothed her skirts under her legs and seated herself on the steps between us.

'It's cold out here,' I warned, my clouded breath illustrating my words.

'Indeed,' she agreed. 'Too cold for two men to sit here all night keeping an unconscious cripple from wandering out of his bed.'

'We do not merely guard against his escape. There are men out there who would ensure he never left his bed again, if they could reach him.'

'And what do *you* want with him then?' she pressed. 'To offer him prayers to speed his recovery?'

'Justice,' said Sigurd harshly.

'Tell me, how did you come to be a doctor?' I interrupted, hurriedly pushing the conversation into less contentious grounds. 'And in a community of monks at that? I am Demetrios,' I added, aware that none of our unruly meetings had yet yielded an introduction. 'This is Sigurd.'

'I am Anna. And I am a doctor care of a wise father and a crass lover. My father taught me to read and learn the knowledge of the ancients – the texts of Galen and Aristotle. My lover, to whom I was betrothed, chose to abandon the marriage at the last minute. After that humiliation, none would marry me, so after the tears I chose this profession. I had friends who had suffered at the hands of incompetent surgeons, men who knew no more of a woman's body than of a camel's. I thought I could do better.'

She pressed her palms together, and in the moonlight I saw that despite her cloak she was shivering.

'Do you think me shameless?' she asked. 'Telling near strangers my intimate history?' She leaned forward. 'I see a dozen patients a day, and every one of them asks me my story. You grow used to it.'

'You could tell them you were inspired by the example of Saint Lucilla,' suggested Sigurd gruffly.

Anna laughed. 'Perhaps that would have been easier. As for the monks, their *typikon* commands them to provide a hospice with doctors who can minister to all the sexes. Usually there are two of us, but my colleague died last spring and they have not replaced him. So I do the work of two.'

I nodded. 'And is that better than marriage?'

Again she laughed. 'Mostly. Sometimes men propose it, but it is hard to be stirred by a man when you have searched the contents of his bowels for evil humours. The monks, of course, fear that I will pollute their thoughts, and keep their distance as much as they can.'

Probably they thought her a perfect succubus, hovering in their tormented dreams, but I did not say so.

'And what of you?' she asked. 'The strange man who brings me dying youths in the morning, and demands them back in the evening. Do you work for the Emperor, like your companion?'

'I work for myself,' I said stoutly.

'No man works for himself.' I was surprised by the force of her statement. 'Men work for greed, or for love, or for vengeance or for shame.'

'Then I must work for greed, I suppose. And for other men's revenge.' I thought on this. 'In this case, the Emperor's.'

'And how, Demetrios, did you become the angel of the Emperor's vengeance?'

I gestured to the monastic walls around us. 'I started in a place much like this, a monastery in Isauria. My parents sent me.'

'Did the life of a novice agree with you?'

'The food was plentiful, and regular. I had a taste for butter, which my parents could not provide, so I stayed.'

'But not forever?'

I shook my head. 'When I was fifteen I ran away to join the army. I wanted to kill Turks and Ishmaelites.'

'And did you?'

'No. The generals were too busy using their armies against each other, trying to put themselves on the imperial throne. The only chance I had to kill Turks was when we fought a lord who had hired them as mercenaries. I did not want to die with an arrow in my throat because our noble families had carried their feuds across the empire, so I went to work for myself. At least I could choose my causes. A merchant hired me to guard him and I failed, so to save my reputation I found his killers and killed them myself. Then I discovered others needed similar services.'

'So you were a bounty hunter?'

'Yes,' I admitted. 'Not a proud occupation, but a lucrative one. And as my name spread and my clients grew more illustrious, the burden of the work moved from exacting revenge to revealing the guilty. Clerks who stole from their masters, uncles who abducted their nieces and held them hostage, sons who killed their fathers for the inheritance.'

'And how did your wife view your profession?'

I looked up sharply. 'What of my wife?'

'What of the ring on your finger?'

She pointed to my right hand, where I still wore the thin lover's band I had first put on sixteen years ago. I had been nineteen, flushed with love and excitement and the weight of my first-earned coins in my pocket: I had insisted we go to the grandest goldsmith on the Mesi, though all my new riches afforded only the least of his jewellery. Later I found that he had swindled me even of that, that it was merely a cheap alloy coated with gold, but by then it was on my finger and I was too proud to take it off. Even now.

'My wife is dead. She died seven years ago, haemorrhaging from her womb.'

Unexpectedly, Anna reached over and took my hand in hers, stroking it softly. 'I'm sorry. I should not pry.'

'You wouldn't know where not to pry if you didn't ask,' I said struggling with the calm and discomfort I felt in her touch. There was a stab of disappointment when she let go.

'Besides,' I said. 'I'm speaking too much.' That was a rare complaint, but – like the touch of her hands – I was finding it at once unnatural and relieving. There was something about this woman's confidence that invited confession. 'Sigurd must be bored hearing me prattle about my past.'

We both looked over to him, and Anna stifled a giggle. It seemed I had indeed bored the Varangian, so much so that he lay with his head against the column, fast asleep.

I thought Anna would be cold, or tired, but she made no move to leave; we talked on through the night in hushed voices, until at length even my eyes began to drift closed. The pauses between my sentences lengthened, and once it was only a playful slap on my knee that kept me from joining Sigurd in the world of dreams. Anna stood, stretching her arms above her so that her body pressed tight against her cloak.

'I should sleep,' she said. 'There will be other patients to see tomorrow, as well as the boy. There is a spare bed in the infirmary if you want to come in out of the cold, Demetrios.'

Though there was not the least implication of lewdness in her plain words, I still blushed.

'What about Sigurd?' I asked.

Anna leaned over and put the back of her hand against his cheek. 'He's warm enough.'

'He comes from a frozen island at the edge of the world.' I wondered why I stiffened when I saw her touch his face. 'He probably grew up in castles built of ice.'

'I'll lay a few more blankets over him. He'll come inside if he wakes up cold.'

Anna left me in the infirmary, having assured me that there were no lepers or plague-ridden unfortunates beside me. Huddling under the covers I was soon lost in dreams, until the cock crowed and the monks filed into their chapel, and Sigurd came thundering through the door swearing he would be delayed no more.

η

The boy lay motionless on his bed, wearing only a plain tunic over his bandages. A damp cloth was stretched over his forehead so that he looked almost like a corpse prepared for burial, though his blue eyes opened wide with fear when he saw Sigurd and me looming over him. I was disconcerted to see that I had slept in the bed next to his all night.

Sigurd frowned at Anna, who stood at the boy's feet and showed no intention of leaving.

'We won't torture him,' he said. 'Just talk.' He rubbed the back of his neck; I guessed it was stiff from a cold night on a stone pillow. 'But there are things to say which you should not hear.'

To my relief, in all our talk the night before Anna had never pressed me for what we wanted with the boy. Now, though, she folded her arms across her chest and met Sigurd's ill-temper square on.

'You cannot talk to him,' she told him. 'Not without me.'

'I will talk to him, lady, whether you want it or no.' Fatigue and frustration did not sit well with Sigurd. 'And if I say that you will not be part of it, then either you will go outside until I call for you, or I will have my men drag you down to the imperial dungeon to learn obedience.' A dozen Varangians had come to the monastery at dawn, taking up stations at the doors and gates to the obvious alarm of the monks.

Anna hardened her grip on the bedstead. 'And which of you speaks Frankish?'

Now both of us stared at her in confusion. 'Frankish?' I echoed. 'Why should either of us speak Frankish?' I could see from Sigurd's silence that he no more knew the tongue than I.

'Because if you don't, you may as well talk to a fish. I spent all day with the boy yesterday, and all he spoke or understood was Frankish.'

'And you, of course, spoke and understood it too.' Sigurd's face boiled with fury, but Anna simply shrugged.

'Enough. So near to the gates I see many pilgrims in my work; many are Franks. A doctor who cannot get her patient to tell her their ailments is unlikely to work many cures.'

There was a hostile silence. Curse the monk, I thought, for employing this barbarian rabble of Bulgars and Franks. Whether he'd worked deliberately, or with the only men he could find, he had thrown every possible obstacle into our path.

'We'll take him to the palace,' said Sigurd at last, his voice alive with anger. 'One of the secretaries will speak Frankish. And we should keep the boy somewhere he can't escape.'

'If you move that boy, least of all into a prison, he will be dead before sunset.' Anna was unmoved by Sigurd's temper; indeed, she seemed to draw strength from it and breathe it straight back at him.

'He should die anyway.' Sigurd was now squeezing his fist around his axe-shaft, as if crushing a man's neck; I feared that soon the violence in his words would manifest itself in his hands. 'For his crime, death is the only justice.'

'We do not want the boy to die.' I spoke forcefully, glaring at Sigurd and Anna together. 'If the doctor says we cannot move him, then we will not move him.' I gestured around the room: its few windows were small enough that a bird could hardly have flown through them. 'If we have a guard on the door, and another within, the boy will be safe from harm and barred from escape. Now as we have waited a long night to speak with him, and as every minute we waste gives time and aid to the Emperor's enemies – with whom this boy is our only link – I propose we use Anna's gifts immediately.'

Sigurd's chest swelled so tight I thought he might burst free of his armour. He clashed the greaves on his forearms together, then slammed a fist onto the wooden table beside him.

'I will go to the palace and find someone who speaks Frankish,' he said, his voice brittle with bridled anger. 'Someone trustworthy. What you choose to do before I return is your own business, Askiates, but you will answer for it alone.'

'I will answer to the man who pays me,' I said. I was growing bored of Sigurd's rages, though I never imagined he did it in bluff. 'And he does not pay me for dallying.'

With a final, derisive snort Sigurd stormed out of the room, berating his men for imagined inadequacies as he passed them in the court-yard. Then all was still: through the window I heard the low tenor of the monks' liturgy.

I looked at Anna, shame clouding my face. 'I apologise for his temper. He has too much faith in fists and swords, and a consuming regard for his duty.'

She gave a thin smile. 'You're not to blame. But if you want to make best use of your time, you had better leave too.'

'What? Did you not hear what I told him? I need to speak with the boy immediately.'

'You'll learn more from the boy if you sit out there on the steps. Look at him. You and the guard have frightened him half to death – and death was already far too near for comfort.'

It was true. While we talked the boy had shrunk beneath his blanket, and now he clutched at the pillow like a mother. His eyes were clenched shut.

'Tell me what you want to ask him,' Anna insisted. 'Tell me, then leave me alone with him.'

For a moment I hesitated, searching her face for signs of treachery. Could I trust her? If word escaped that a boy had come within a hand's breadth of murdering the Emperor, and was now quartered here in the monastery, there would be uproar. None of us would be safe, myself not least. But by facing down Sigurd I had committed myself – and my trust – to Anna: she would have to know all, unless I wanted him to return triumphant. That was not something my pride would admit.

With a deep breath and a pounding heart, I told Anna everything. The assault on the Emperor; the pimp Vassos; Kaloyan the Bulgar and the strange monk who employed him; and how we had found the boy. I even told her about the *tzangra*, the barbarian weapon of mirac-ulous strength, for I was particularly eager to learn what the boy knew of it. When at last I had finished I took her advice: I walked outside, staved away the suspicious glances of Sigurd's guardsmen, and settled myself on the steps in the fresh morning air. There I waited.

Anna reappeared before Sigurd, thankfully. She smiled her greeting, but much of the playfulness had gone from her face, and she grew more serious still as she began to speak. I listened with few interruptions, prompting her only for the occasional detail. The story was dismally unexceptional, almost mundane, and I had few doubts that whatever the constraints of her language, it was in essence the truth. Only one facet of it struck me as false, and I had Anna go back and press the boy until I was satisfied with his answer. Then I rose to leave.

'Won't you wait for your friend?' Anna asked. 'He should be back soon.'

Or not. I doubted he would have the loan of any more of the hipparch's beasts after the use we had given them in the night.

'I think it would be wiser to leave. There are elements of the boy's story I must investigate.' And it would irritate Sigurd immeasurably to find me gone. 'I suppose Sigurd will tell you exactly what he demands, but on no account let him take the boy away from here.'

Anna bared her teeth. 'Let him try.'

'Good.' The boy was too valuable to be left in the care of gaolers and torturers, and wounds like his would rot into his bones in the foetid dungeon air. Nor could I shake off the mounting sense that part of my life was now invested in his.

'I will be back this evening, or maybe tomorrow.'

'I shall look forward to it.'

Strangely warmed by those parting words, I left the monastery and hastened towards the city, keeping off the main road to avoid any encounter with Sigurd. I visited the docks, the workshop of Lukas the fletcher, and a man who sold me three withered gourds; then I retired to the fields near the western walls, where I passed the afternoon straining my shoulders and frightening a watching flock of crows. Finally, weary but satisfied, I made my way back to the palace.

Aelric, the grey-haired Varangian, was at the gate; he smiled when he saw me.

'It's as well you came to my door, Demetrios. Your name has been spoken often in the palace today, and rarely with favour.'

'Sigurd?'

'Indeed.' Aelric shifted the weight of his axe a little. 'He swears you are an agent of those who would harm the Emperor. That is, when he does not curse you for a mercenary intent only on impoverishing the treasury.'

I snorted; I had heard enough gibes about money. 'And why does Sigurd fight for the Emperor? Is he a Roman, fighting to preserve his ruler and his nation? No. He fights for the same motives as all the other Patzinaks, Turks, Venetians and Norsemen in our legions: gold, and glory. Many would say they were the only things worth fighting for.'

A dark look crossed Aelric's lined face. 'Do not doubt Sigurd's devotion to Byzantium, Demetrios. He takes the gold and cherishes his glory, as every warrior should, but he loves the Emperor like a monk loves his God. If the Emperor was hemmed in by countless hosts of enemies, and all was lost, Sigurd would be the last man left standing beside him – whether there was gold to pay him or not. Of how many Turks and Patzinaks could you say that?'

I rolled my eyes. 'A believer may be blessed, but a zealot is dangerous – and his love too easily turns against itself. Anyway, I came to speak with the chamberlain, Krysaphios, not with Sigurd.'

'You have a gift for him, do you?' Aelric peered at the bundle I held under my arm. It was broad and flat, and wrapped about with sackcloth; it might have been a painted icon, though it was not.

'Something he will want to see,' I said. 'If I am not banned from the palace for wanting to keep valuable witnesses alive until they have told their tale.'

Aelric nodded. 'Krysaphios will see you.'

With a last suspicious glance at my package, he opened the gate and led me within the palace. Again we passed through myriad courtyards and burnished chambers, but it was different to my last visit: now none of it felt quite so magnificent as it had before. The splash of the fountains seemed quieter, the perfumes in the air less fragrant, the faces on those we met more tightly drawn.

I never saw Aelric speak to anyone, but Krysaphios was waiting for me. He stood where we had last met, in a colonnade lined with the marble heads of antique dynasties. His lips were thin with anger, and even before I had crossed the open square he met me with sharp words.

'The Varangian captain swears you have done great mischief, Demetrios. You were hired to discover the Emperor's would-be assassin, not hide him in the sanctuary of a monastery. If, indeed, this barbarian catamite is truly the one we seek.'

I had had enough of this sort of talk for one day. Without deigning to reply, I pulled the sacking from my bundle, lifted it to my shoulder and pressed on the lever. The eunuch's eyes widened in terror as he guessed my purpose; he prostrated himself on the floor in an undignified sprawl, as – with a humming crack – the bolt from my weapon sprang into the air. It went many paces wide of him and struck a bust, shattering the stone face into countless broken fragments.

I could hear the running footsteps of guards behind me, but I had made my point. I lowered the weapon, and spread my arms wide in innocence.

Krysaphios raised himself to his feet, his shimmering robes creased and streaked with dust, his golden hat knocked crooked. His smooth face was ridged with fury.

'Do you presume to enter this sacred place and murder me?' he shrieked. 'Shall I have you chained in the dungeons, for the torturers to tear you apart inch from inch? How dare you aim such a weapon at me, I who sleep at the feet of Emperors and guide the fate of nations? You might as well turn it on my master himself.'

'Did you shit yourself?' I had intended my antic to get his attention, but now we were both beyond the control of our feelings. 'This is the weapon which *was* turned on your master, which came within a hand's breadth of breaking open his skull like that marble head. I, Demetrios, discovered it. Just as I discovered the boy who wielded it against the Emperor four days ago. If you think a barbarian berserker would have done so well, one who would sooner slice off men's heads than hear their secrets, then employ him next time.'

I turned my back and looked to the bronze doors. A line of Varangians – not Sigurd, thank God – barred it, their axes raised before them. Suddenly I wondered if I had not made a terrible miscalculation.

'Demetrios.'

Krysaphios' call stilled me, but I kept my gaze away from him.

'Demetrios.'

The timbre of his voice was moderated now; he seemed to have mastered his anger. Reluctantly, I turned to face him.

'You cannot expect to shoot your bow at the *parakoimomenos* and see me laugh it off as a jest.' He may have subdued the violence in his voice, but it still burned in his face.

I smiled a grim smile. 'Believe me, eunuch – if I had shot my bow *at* you, you would have breath neither to laugh nor curse.' I lifted a hand to quell his retort. 'And nor would I, I know. I do not threaten you; I merely comment on the miraculous accuracy of this foreign weapon, this *tzangra*. And its awesome strength.'

Krysaphios looked to the shards of statue on the floor by his feet. 'That was the Emperor's mother,' he chided me. 'Carved from a relic of antiquity. He will be displeased.'

'He would be more displeased if it had been *his* head the arrow struck.'

I walked forward to Krysaphios and held the bow out for his inspection. It was an extraordinary weapon, much as the Genoese merchant had described it in the tavern, yet somehow more elegant and more lethal in form. Curved horns arced out like wings from the end of a shaft, which was carved at its butt to fit snug in a man's shoulder. There was a channel routed down the middle to grip the short arrow, and a levered hook behind it to hold the string taut. As I had discovered with my gourds that afternoon, it was wondrously easy to learn to aim it, but a wrench on the shoulders to nock the bowstring. No wonder the assassin had only been able to loose one shot.

'And you found this with the boy?' Krysaphios plucked at the string, but could scarcely move it. 'Sigurd did not tell me that.'

'The boy had hidden it near the harbour. He told me where it was and I retrieved it.' What he had really told me, at least at first, was that he had thrown it into the sea, but I refused to accept that he would discard so priceless a weapon. 'He calls it an arbalest.'

'And how did he come by it?' Krysaphios' tone was urgent now; he paced the tiled floor restlessly, kicking at bits of the broken statue with his toe.

'The boy spoke only Frankish; I had his story through an interpreter. There were many things she did not understand, or could not make understood, but I think I have the bones of his story. He came here as a pilgrim some time ago; with his parents, I think, though they are dead now. After their death he survived in the slums by thieving and begging as he could. Then, a month back, a man found him and offered gold to accompany him. He was led to a meeting with a monk, who took him with four Bulgar mercenaries to a villa deep in the forest. For two weeks there the monk trained him in the use of the arbalest – as you have seen, it takes to men's hands with miraculous ease. When they returned, he was told to climb atop a building on the Mesi and murder the Emperor as he passed. Yesterday he received a message that he should collect his payment by a certain fountain, but as he arrived he was attacked by a Bulgar and almost killed. There we found him.'

'Why the boy? Why use him for this task when four stout mercenaries were at hand? Surely they would have been more suited to wielding this weapon?'

I had pondered the same question through the afternoon. 'There are places a boy can go unnoticed where full-grown men would be challenged. Many children played on the roof of the carver's house – one other making his way there would have aroused no suspicion. And after the event, he would have been easier to be rid of.'

Krysaphios seemed satisfied with my theory, though he said nothing. Instead, he raised a finger on his right hand and a slave appeared from behind a column.

'Send word to the gaoler. Tell him to extract from the Bulgar prisoner everything he knows of the boy; also the location of this villa in the forest where he was trained. It may be that this foreign monk still has business there.' The slave bowed low and ran off, and Krysaphios turned back to me. 'Did the boy describe the monk?'

'He said he had dark hair, like mine, but tonsured. His nose was crooked, as if he had once brawled, but the rest of his features were square and harsh. He said they spoke the same tongue. I did not press him more, for he was still weak from his wounds. I thought there would be time for that later.'

'Less time than you think.' Krysaphios folded his arms. 'A great danger is approaching our city, Demetrios, and when it breaks over us we will need all our strength to defy it. If we do not find this monk within the fortnight, he may work a mischief that will ruin us all. The Emperor is the head atop the body of our nation, and if he is gone we are merely a carcass before carrion.'

'What danger?' Krysaphios had spoken almost as though the seven angels had sounded their trumpets, and the ten-horned beast was risen to engulf us. 'Are the Normans coming again? I have not heard the armies assembled on the Hebdomon, nor seen the Emperor ride out to war. Surely if such a terrible danger was near, he would go to meet it, not invite it upon us?'

'The nature of the threat, and how the Emperor forestalls it, are not your concern,' said Krysaphios darkly. 'You should address yourself to finding those who would kill him.'

'I have.' No eunuch was going to unsettle me with dire mutterings, and I have ever bridled at being told I am unworthy of knowing tantalising secrets. That, perhaps, is why I took up my profession. 'I have found the boy who would have played the assassin, and the weapon he used in the attempt. By doing it so promptly, I have even saved your purse a little.'

'My purse is deep enough. And do you really think you have succeeded, by finding a frightened boy and his barbarian plaything? What of the monk? Do you think this was a mere whim of his, and that having failed he will now trudge back to Frankia? He had money enough to buy four bodyguards, a villa and this marvellous weapon – did he collect that from alms-givers? And what would he profit from the death of the Emperor? Someone must have supplied him the money – someone who would gain much if the throne was empty. Someone who is unlikely to change his mind because his first attempt failed.' He snorted. 'You have not discovered anything, Demetrios: you have but picked up the first link in a long and tangled chain. Will your pride allow you to drop it so soon?'

He may have had a woman's voice and a cripple's body, but his mind and tongue were those of a serpent. And he knew men's hearts: I would not give up his commission, for I saw as well as he that it was barely started. To claim success now would be to mimic the physician who removed the leper's arm and declared him cured. But I would not concede that too easily.

'If I am to continue, I will need certain accommodations. The Varangians must obey me when they accompany me. The boy must be left in the care of the doctor at the monastery where he currently lies: our chain may be twisted, but he is the only link we hold and it is a fragile link. And you must confide in me . . .'

I broke off as a slave came running out of the shadows, the same slave whom Krysaphios had sent to the dungeon. He did not defer or hesitate, but fell to his knees immediately before the eunuch.

'Mercy, Lord,' he stammered, before even given leave to speak. 'The gaoler has opened the Bulgar's cell. He is dead.'

*　　*　　*

The Bulgar still hung by his wrists, as I had seen him the day before, but now his chin was slumped on his chest and his legs sagged under him. The front of his tunic was washed through with blood, almost as far down as his waist, and when I tipped back his head I saw why. Someone had taken a blade to his throat and opened his neck across almost its entire width. No air bubbled from the hanging flaps of skin, and my hand came away dry.

'The blood is hard,' I said. 'This was done some hours ago, maybe even last night. Has no-one been in here since then?'

'He was to go without food all day. To spur his appetite for answering questions.' Not even this horror could take the sting completely from Krysaphios' voice.

'No-one entered after your lordship left him,' said the gaoler. And the Varangians guarded him all night.

I turned to Krysaphios. 'It seems you were the last one to see him alive, then. After Sigurd and I had left for the monastery.'

'Not the last, Demetrios.' The eunuch's eyes were cold. 'Surely a man of your powers can see that unless he was a most accomplished acrobat, the Bulgar did not do this to himself. And the weapon which did this is gone. Whatever you say to the contrary, gaoler, someone has been in here.'

'Someone who wanted to ensure that the Bulgar could betray no more secrets,' I agreed. 'And someone who wanted to send us a message.'

'A message? Other than that he wanted the Bulgar's silence?' Krysaphios was impatient.

'A message that the palace is no defence, that he – whoever he is – can strike wherever he pleases. If he had wanted to do it in stealth, he could have taken the Bulgar down from his chains and left the knife beside him, to make it seem he had killed himself. Whoever did this walked in under the eyes of the guards. And wants us to know he can do so again.'

Krysaphios turned to the Varangian who stood in the doorway. 'Find your captain and have him double the Emperor's guard tonight. Then search the palace grounds – it may be that this assassin is still hiding in our midst.'

I had my doubts, but kept them silent. 'What about the boy?' I prompted. 'If our enemies feared for what the Bulgar might reveal, how much more must they worry about the boy?'

'Sigurd is keeping the watch at the monastery, and has more men than he needs for the task. You may join him if you wish.' Krysaphios moved towards the low-arched door. 'I must tend to the Emperor.'

'I will go home.' It had been two days since I had seen my daughters, and though there had been other nights when I did not return, it always troubled them. And me. 'Tomorrow I will see what further mysteries the boy can reveal.'

'If he lives. Remember, Demetrios, we do not have much time to untangle this conspiracy. Two weeks before the danger is upon us.' Krysaphios gave the dangling body a final, searching look. 'Perhaps even less.'

Still I did not know what looming evil might force this urgency. But if it could draw such a tremor into the voice of Krysaphios, the eunuch who slept beside Emperors and guided nations, then I knew that I, too, feared it.

θ

My daughters were uncommonly restrained when I returned home: Helena was in her bed and would only mumble when I looked in on her, while Zoe prepared me some cold vegetables with inconsequential chatter. At breakfast the next morning, however, I felt the full force of Helena's censure.

'You neglect your duties as a father,' she complained. 'What if a Norman marauder had come in the night and snatched me away? What if I had used your absence to elope with the blacksmith's son?'

'What of it? You didn't. And my first duty is to put bread in our bellies.' I chewed noisily on my breakfast to emphasise how seriously I took my obligations.

'If you are never here to protect me, you could at least trouble yourself to find me a man who will.'

'I'd rather have the bread.' Zoe bit into her own slice, and winked at me across the table. I tried to force a stern look, to rebuke her for antagonising her sister, but I fear I lacked conviction.

'The spice-seller's aunt came to visit yesterday, to discuss her nephew,' continued Helena imperiously. 'And the day before. I think she despairs of ever finding you.'

'She may never come again,' Zoe added. Her face was solemn. 'Then you'll be a spinster forever, Helena, condemned all your life to sit at your loom and weave. Like Penelope.'

I swallowed the crumbs in my throat. I knew that the spice-seller's family had been making enquiries after Helena, and that I should have approached his mother to bargain for her dowry, but there rarely seemed to be the time for it. 'If the spice-seller's aunt comes again and I am away, you have my permission to agree a dowry with her.'

'And what if I agree something extravagant? What if she claims her nephew to be the most expensive gold can buy, and I acquiesce?'

73

'Then,' I said, wiping my mouth, 'you will be grateful that I worked so hard I could afford it.'

There are men I know who eat separately from their womenfolk; many authorities, indeed, damn the practice of commingled meals as an invitation to strife and discord. If I heeded them I would be lonely indeed, but there are times when I wonder if I would benefit from a greater respect for tradition.

At the very least, though, it prepares me for encounters with argumentative women. Such as I found when I reached the courtyard of the monastery of Saint Andrew.

'You cannot see the boy, and you certainly cannot remove him.' Anna, the doctor, stood with her hands folded across her chest and her feet set apart. Her hair was tied back under a plain linen scarf – more modest than I had seen before – but she still wore her green dress. The silken belt rode high on her hips and plunged in a 'v' between them, drawing my eye immoderately low, and it was that which unsettled me as much as her uncompromising tone.

'Is he near death?' That did not bear contemplation.

She tossed her head. 'Do you have so little faith in my skills, Demetrios? Do you think a woman cannot – or should not – exercise the gift of healing?'

'Women hold the gift of life; I should think healing is a paltry business to master after that.'

'Your Keltic friend does not think so.' She gestured to Sigurd, who stood with three of his men by the door glaring at every monk and novice who passed. 'I have heard him talking.'

'He's a barbarian. But if you have healed the boy, I need to speak with him.' I had determined that I would seek out the villa in the forest, where the monk had trained the boy. 'Is he fit to ride a horse?'

Anna stared at me with open scorn. 'Two days ago he was almost hacked to pieces; today you want to know if he can ride a horse? If he tries hard, he can just drink a little thin soup. There is only one being who could heal him as quickly as you want – and I have the monks in the chapel begging His intervention.'

'Then at least let me talk to the boy.'

'You can talk to him when he's recovered.'

I swung round. It was not Anna who had spoken, but Sigurd; he had ambled down from his station by the door and was eyeing me with disapproval.

'Sigurd?' His intervention caught me unguarded. 'Yesterday you threatened to drag Anna to the dungeons because she would not let us see the boy. I thought you were as eager as I to finish this business.'

Sigurd conceded nothing, did not even blush. 'Thomas is too valuable to be pushed beyond himself, Demetrios. Our task is urgent – so urgent that we cannot risk losing him.'

I scowled, for I did not think he had decided on all this for himself. And I did not like the thought of Anna and he conspiring together against me. It made me feel betrayed. And, unjustifiably, jealous.

It would have been hard enough to haggle my way past Anna, for there was something in her manner which deterred all argument; against her and Sigurd I was impotent.

'I will return tomorrow,' I said. 'Perhaps you will have managed to work your cure. Maybe even as well as a man,' I added, spitefully.

I regretted those final words – and the furious anger in Anna's face that had met them – all the way to the docks. Of course I cared not an iota that she was a woman and a doctor: I had only wanted to sting her, as her alliance with Sigurd had stung me, just as Zoe used to poke Helena until she screamed when they were babies. My motives were just as childish.

With my foul mood thus firmly set, I passed my morning with merchants and factors, with stevedores, foremen and pilots, in a far-fetched attempt to discover when and how the *tzangra* had entered the city. The smells of fish and sewage which infested the wharves soured my humour still further, as did my predictable failure to turn up any new information. Whores propositioned me – perhaps, even after so many years, there was something of the soldier still in my stride – and peddlers begged a moment of my attention for their wares: perfumes just arrived from India; honey from the bees of Epirus; relics of the saints found in the desert, preserved so immaculately that they might have lived yesterday. I came perilously close to breaking the fast with a man furtively carrying a wineskin under his cloak, but I resisted. I had no need for more reasons to rebuke myself.

The clamour and hassle battered me all morning, until at last I broke. I dredged Krysaphios' list of dignitaries from the corner of my mind where I had ignored it, and considered the names it held. Another lesson of my time in the army: if you make no progress with the task appointed, do it precisely the way your superior commands. Half the time at least, he will care far more for obedience than success.

Earlier in the week, I had tried to start with the lowest rank on the list and been resoundingly shunned; this time I would go to the opposite extreme. The name rose easily from my memory, and my peevish temper found grim delight in the prospect of an afternoon wallowing in righteous frustration. Nor did I need to ask where he lived: on a day when my every question drew a negative, even I could probably find the Emperor's elder brother.

He did not live humbly, of course, but in a palace built out on terraces over the wooded hillside above the harbour. It had once belonged to a man named Botaniates, who had had the misfortune of being Emperor when the Komnenos brothers – Isaak and Alexios – decided the imperial diadem would suit one of them better. Alexios took the throne; Isaak got the house, though from the size of it you might have thought he had won both.

To my surprise, my name alone took me past the first gate, and into an atrium where dozens of hopeful supplicants played at dice on the flagstones. Many of the games looked well advanced, and I feared I would lose more than a few obols before my time arrived, but almost immediately a slave in an ochre tunic ushered me through a narrow door and into an inner courtyard, beyond the envying glances of the less favoured.

'I will tell the Sebastokrator you have come,' he said, excusing himself.

I paced around the courtyard, waiting. A two-tiered arcade ran around its edge, but I saw no-one in the galleries. The only light came from a square of grey sky high above me, distant and remote, but a little sun must have crept in at times, for a vine had managed to climb some way up the northern side. Its thick stem coiled around the marble pillars, branching and spreading across the face of the wall as if desperate to escape into the air above, while the withered leaves it had shed were left unswept on the cracked tiles below. I doubted the Sebastokrator spent much time here. It was a mournful place, silent and sombre.

Except in one corner. Most of the walls were crumbling and faded, but here there was a bright mosaic, newly laid and vivid even in the dull half-light. Still alone, I crossed the broken floor to look closer. It was a striking work, a triptych of bold colours whose subjects seemed to leap from their gilded background. The subject was unusual, too. In the first panel, a white-bearded man watched as a woman held a fair-haired baby to her breast; sheep grazed in the background, and three angels sat at a table laden with fruits. The second, central panel was a dramatic contrast: now the old man stood with his arms aloft, a firebrand in one hand and a knife in the other, poised to strike the helpless child bound before him on a wooden table. His eyes were wide with a terrible fervour as he stared out at his unseen audience, and by some trick of the artist the knife seemed to stretch forth from the picture, reaching almost into the air above me. A young boy with dark skin and tousled hair stood beside the man; despite the horror of the scene he witnessed, he seemed to be laughing.

The violence of the image was mesmerising, but I pulled my gaze away and looked on to the third panel. Now harmony was returned, and the old man's eyes were kindly again. He had wrapped his arm around the fair-haired son and was pointing him towards green hills in the distance. The sheep had returned, and the angel was blowing on a trumpet in the clouds. But it was not all innocence, I saw, for in the lower corner of the picture the tousle-headed boy was fleeing into darkness, his face cast down and a scorpion pricking at his bare heels.

'Do you like the mosaic?'

I started; for a second I thrilled with the fancy that the voice had come from the very picture itself. Then I turned, and saw that a new arrival had crept up behind me. He was shorter than I and a little older, with light hair and a thin beard. There was something martial in his thick arms and broad shoulders, but he was dressed simply in a white dalmatica. He seemed an unlikely clerk – but too forward for a slave.

'It paints a vivid picture,' I answered. So vivid, indeed, that it still addled my thoughts. 'So real it might almost draw the censure of the church. The artist must have a singular talent.' I considered it again, still unsure of whom I spoke to. 'But the subject confuses me.'

'It tells the story of Abraham and his sons.' My companion pointed to the first panel. 'Here he and Sarah rejoice at the birth of their son,

77

Isaak, prophesied by angels when all thought Sarah barren. In the second picture, Abraham is poised to sacrifice Isaak, as the Lord commanded to test him. Finally, Abraham embraces Isaak as the future of his line.'

Much of that I had guessed, but elements of the iconography confused me. 'Who is the dark-haired child who looks on in the middle image, and flees away at the last?' I asked.

'The child is Abraham's bastard son, Ishmael, born to him by the slave-woman Hagar. In the last picture he is cast out by Abraham, expelled into the wilderness.'

I shivered, for suddenly the images seemed every bit as dangerous as the wild-eyed man wielding the dagger. I did not need Krysaphios' familiarity with palace gossip to guess its meaning, still less in the very house of the Sebastokrator Isaak, whose father had overlooked him for the imperial throne in favour of his younger brother. Merely to think that he, like Abraham's rightful heir, might eventually be restored to his inheritance at the expense of his brother was almost certain treason. I wondered whether the Emperor Alexios had visited this room in his brother's palace.

But I had little time to think on allegory, for my host had stepped away to examine some detail in the picture, and as he moved his white gown rode up over his ankles to reveal a pair of mismatched boots. One was black, but the burnished leather of the other – identical in form – was unmistakably red.

Only one man in the empire wore red boots, and only a handful of others had the right to wear a single such boot in honour of their kinship with him. In an instant I was prostrate on my knees, touching my forehead to the floor and reciting the imperial incantations like a liturgy. I had seen too many pretenders and usurpers to believe that any man deserved the abasement that ritual demanded, but never had I imagined I would stand in the Sebastokrator's palace discussing the merits of his artist. I fastened my eyes on the floor, and prayed he had not taken offence.

'Get up, Demetrios Askiates.' To my untold relief, there was amusement in his voice. 'If I had wanted your oblations, I would have met you wrapped in my jewelled lorum, and with pearls dripping from my crown, so that you could not have doubted my rank. I wished to meet you as a man, not a slave.'

'You expected me, Lord?' I had never had to address such an exalted man before, and I struggled for the correct forms. I suspected his deliberate informality had its bounds.

'For the past three days. I had word from the palace that you were engaged to discover the brigands who tried to murder my dear brother, the noble Emperor. I greatly hoped to speak with you.'

'Why, Lord?'

'The bureaucrats and slaves at the palace would withhold things from me, Demetrios. That is how they keep their fingers mired in power. But some facts are too important to serve merely to buttress the pride of eunuchs – facts regarding the safety of my brother, for example. We Komneni trust in our own, for who else will protect with the ferocity of kin?'

Clearly his trust was not shared with Krysaphios, for there were six of the Emperor's siblings, and a scattering of his cousins and children on the eunuch's list.

'Kinsmen can be jealous,' I observed. Whatever the factions at the palace, I was here to test Isaak for treachery, not to confide in him. 'Absalom led an army against his father, King David. Simeon slaughtered Shechem and all his kin. And as Cain, not every man is his brother's keeper.'

Isaak spun about. 'And do not forget that Shadrach was cast into the furnace because he refused to obey his lord. I summoned you because I *am* my brother's keeper, Demetrios Askiates; I share all the burden of government with him, and I must know if he is in danger.'

'A wicked man might think you had cause to hate him.' I was walking the precipice here. 'That you nursed an injury that your father chose *him*, rather than you, his eldest son, to take the throne. Such a man might – mistakenly – approach you, hoping to enrol you in his conspiracy, to play on the bitterness he presumed.'

Isaak spread his hands wide, unconsciously emulating the towering figure of Abraham in the mosaic behind him. 'Bitterness? That was fifteen years ago, and it was agreed by all the leading families that my brother Alexios was the better candidate. I would need a deep heart indeed if I was now still able to squeeze bile from it.'

'And no-one has tried to whisper otherwise in your ear? None have hinted that if you coveted the throne, they might help you get it?'

'None until you.' Isaak pursed his lips. 'No, Demetrios, there are always flatterers trying to persuade me that my station is inadequate to my merits, but they say so only because they think it is what I would hear, because they think that if I did strike against my brother they too would gain by hanging on to the hem of my robe. I ignore them, and try to keep them from crossing my threshold.'

If that was so, then he had made a strange choice for his mosaic. But I had pressed the Sebastokrator too far already to impugn him further.

'You do not think any of these sycophants might intend genuine mischief?'

'No. None of them would chance raising his own hand against the Emperor simply for the right to sew a few more rubies onto his robe, or to win another farm in Scythia. Who would risk the ultimate crime, the ultimate punishment, unless he stood also to win the ultimate reward?' He must have seen the suspicion flare in my eyes. 'Yes, you say: I could win the ultimate reward. But I do not want it.'

'Do you know any who do?'

'The Emperor's daughter Anna, my niece, is recently come of age, and is betrothed to the heir of the man whom my brother deposed. He might feel he has a double claim to the throne, through both father and father-in-law, and he is of an age when men are often the victims of overwhelming impulse. My brother-in-law Melissenos once coveted the purple and had himself proclaimed Emperor, before recognising that he could not contend with me and my brother.' Isaak tipped back his head and laughed at the incomprehension on my face. 'Too many names for you, Demetrios, all twined and tangled together? There is not one of the great families which has not touched the purple at some time or another, and we marry each other with indecent frequency. Even if you confined your search only to those with a claim to the throne, you could fill the Hall of Nineteen Tables threefold with them. Now tell me what you have found, so that I can inform my brother. The bastard eunuch tells him nothing.'

'The bastard eunuch pays my wages,' I retorted. Then, foolishly provocative: 'If the Emperor wishes to hear what I have found, and cannot get it from his chamberlain, then he can summon me himself.'

I looked hesitantly at the Sebastokrator, wondering whether I had given too great an offence. His face was cold, certainly, but not malicious.

'You clearly understand little of the ways of the palace,' he said curtly. 'Do not think that merely because my brother is the Emperor, he can do as he pleases. He is hemmed in by a thousand petty restraints: traditions, protocols, conventions, precedents and promises. He is no more a free man than the slave who rows his barge. His power is brittle, and faces threats far more subtle than an assassin's arrow. He cannot be seen to antagonise his counsellors by usurping their authority.'

'No more can I.' The Lord God knew I had no allegiance to Krysaphios, but his world was murky enough; I dared not stray into realms of betrayal.

The Sebastokrator Isaak pursed his lips. 'You disappoint me, Demetrios Askiates. I had heard that you, uncommonly among men, were prepared to drive your own path. To know when the call of a higher authority befitted a judicious confidence. Clearly I was wrong.'

Without awaiting an answer he turned and marched out, ignoring the hurried bow I thought it wise to offer. As I brushed the dust off my knees, I wondered whether I had made my first enemy within the palace. It was a discomfiting thought.

I

The following day I again wanted to take the boy Thomas to the forest, but again Anna refused. Likewise the next day, and if there was one consolation to the delay, it was that I made steady progress through Krysaphios' list of nobles. As I had expected, I learned nothing from them, but at least my obedience muted the eunuch's criticisms when I reported to him. I contemplated travelling to the forest without the boy, trying to find the place where the monk had trained him by description alone, but the answers the boy gave my questions were so vague I doubt I could have found my own feet by them. And on the third day Anna sent word – grudging, even in the mouth of the novice who bore her message – that the boy was sufficiently healed to travel.

We left before dawn. Sigurd and his company of Varangians met me outside my house, their horses' flanks steaming in the cold air. Father Gregorias accompanied them, for it appeared the little priest spoke Frankish as well as Bulgar, and had been co-opted into accompanying us as our translator. On the empty street corners the Watch still prowled, enforcing the curfew, but they stepped back respectfully as our cavalcade cantered past, offering hurried salutes to these barbarians riding out of the dawn mist.

We stopped at the monastery. A dozen Varangians fanned out in a half-circle around its gate as Sigurd and I dismounted to fetch the boy. A handful of monks straggled across the courtyard, perhaps collecting the night soil from the cells, but otherwise no-one moved. I was tense, scanning every rooftop and architrave for unexpected movement, for I had grave misgivings about taking the boy out of his seclusion and into the public thoroughfares beyond. It would be many months before I forgot the sight of the gash across the Bulgar's throat, and whether it had been the work of the elusive monk, his agents, or some higher power, I did not think they would rest while their failed assassin lived in captivity. But I had spent three days fruitlessly antagonising merchants and nobles: if the boy could lead me to the house where he and the monk had trained, then perhaps there I would find something to guide my search. And I did not want to cause Anna undue risk.

Anna was already awake, wrapped in a heavy, woollen palla and bustling about purposefully with a small chest of medicines.

'This is the salve to rub on the wounds,' she told me, pointing to a small clay pot. 'And in this bag are clean bandages. You should replace them after each day's riding. There's some bark in there as well for him to chew on if the pain is too great. If you find fresh water in the forest, you can rinse his leg with it.'

I scowled; the early hour, a lack of food, and the tension of the moment had soured my stomach. 'I have fought in a dozen battles,' I reminded her, 'and seen men march twenty miles after them with worse wounds than the boy's. I do not need lessons in field medicine.'

She ignored my petulance. 'Sigurd knows my instructions; he can see to Thomas. And keep him well fed. He needs to regain his strength.'

'Indeed.' Although I did not wish the boy ill, the last thing I wanted was for him to be restored to full health while we travelled. If he escaped, I doubted either of us would long survive it.

All this time the boy had stood mutely in a corner. Anna had found him a monk's coarse tunic, which sat high on his tall frame, and a thick cloak; now she kissed him on the cheek, pulled up a fold of the cloak to mask his face, and pushed him gently towards me.

'You'll want to hurry,' she said, peering out of the open door. 'The sun will be risen soon.'

That thought had been uppermost in my mind too, yet I delayed a moment further in the unlikely half-hope that I too would merit a kiss. I shook my head in wry reproval. I was thinking like an adolescent, I chided myself, not like a grown man, a father and a widower.

I led the boy outside. He did not resist as I slipped rope manacles over his wrists and tied them fast, leaving enough slack between them that he could steady himself in the saddle. My horse was nervous, perhaps absorbing my mood, and I patted her neck to try and calm her fidgeting as Sigurd effortlessly hoisted the boy up so that he sat before me. I glanced about, ever wary of danger, for now shutters were beginning to be thrown back, and figures could be seen moving behind the windows. I looked at the boy in front of me and imagined him squinting down the stock of the *tzangra* from the ivory-carver's rooftop as the Emperor's retinue processed past. Was there another man, even now, taking the same sighting?

I kicked my horse over to where Sigurd conferred with Aelric.

'We'll make for the gate of Charisios,' he announced. 'It's the fastest way.'

'Too obvious,' I argued. 'They may be watching it. We should take the gate of Saint Romanos, and cross the river further upstream.'

Sigurd glared at me. He had a leather sling for his axe, I noticed, hanging from his saddle just before his knee. 'They? Who are your *they*? Do you think we face an army of darkness with spies on every corner? A lone monk and a handful of Bulgar mercenaries cannot be everywhere.'

'If we delay any longer they will find us without trying. Krysaphios agreed that in matters of practicality, my decision would prevail. We go to Saint Romanos.'

Sigurd pulled back on his reins, and rapped a fist against his bronze greave. 'This is what prevails, Demetrios: the power of a man's arm. If our enemies await us, let them come.'

'Your arm will be as feeble as your armour against the weapons these men wield, unless we meet them at a time of our choosing. Have you spent so long tramping the corridors of the palace, Sigurd, that you've forgotten the importance of reconnoitring your adversary?' I spurred my horse forward, before he could retaliate. To my relief, I heard the clatter of hooves following on behind me.

We rode as swiftly as I dared with the invalid boy on my horse, through the dirty light and waking streets of the morning, until we reached the gate of Saint Romanos. At the sight of Sigurd the guards waved us through, and soon we were out in the broad fields which stretched away from the walls. The harvest was long since gathered in, but teams of men and boys were there with their oxen, ploughing under the old year's stumps and chaff. The rising sun was wan through the grey clouds, but the unaccustomed effort of riding soon had me pulling my cloak back off my arms, and then bundling it into a saddlebag altogether. We had slowed our pace to avoid aggravating Thomas's wounds, and I could enjoy the freshness of the morning as I tried to ignore Sigurd's lowering bulk ahead of me. He had not spoken to me since we left the monastery.

The jangling of iron to my left turned my head, and I saw that Aelric had come up beside me. Despite his fading hair and his lengthening years, he sat comfortably in the saddle, humming something I did not recognise.

'You've upset the captain,' he said, breaking off his tune. 'He's a warrior – he doesn't care to be reminded that he's as much the Emperor's ornament as his *huscarl*. Parading to impress ambassadors and nobles sits uncomfortably on him when he'd rather be killing Normans.'

I glanced nervously forward, but either Sigurd could not hear or would not show it. 'I've heard he has no love for the Normans. He told me they stole your kingdom – as they stole the island of Sicily from us, and would perhaps have taken Attica if the Emperor had not defied them.'

Aelric nodded. 'Thirty years ago, they came, and even the mightiest king that ever ruled our island could not resist them. Sigurd was only a child then, but I was a man, and I took my place in the king's battle-line.'

'You fought the Normans?' Though there was yet a wiry strength in Aelric's arms, it was hard to imagine this genial grandfather hammering foes with his axe in the mountains of Thule.

'I fought their allies,' Aelric corrected me. 'The Normans conspired to invite a Norse army into the north, while they skulked in the southern sea which divides our island from their country. We fought two great battles by the rivers of the Danelaw; we lost the first but won the second. As the Norse king discovered, it's only the last battle that matters.'

I was already lost, for he seemed to make as many fine distinctions between Norsemen and Normans and the Northmen of Thule as the ancients once made between their feuding cities. But they must have been distinct in his own mind, for he continued without hesitation.

'That second battle, that was a warrior's day. I killed seventeen of them myself, yet while a single man stood they would not leave the field. Even Sigurd remembers it.'

I craned my head back in my saddle. Sigurd was riding in silence immediately behind us, an ill humour still written across his face.

'You were there?' I asked, braving his antagonism. 'But if it was thirty years ago, you must have been too small even to lift an axe.'

Sigurd lifted his chin contemptuously. 'I carried an axe at an age when you probably slept in a crib,' he informed me. Then, too proud to resist the story: 'But I was there at the battle. I was only six, but my father, who fought for our King Harold, brought me there and left me under a tree behind our line.'

'Sigurd saw more of it than most,' Aelric interrupted. 'More than us who couldn't even see our elbows for all the death about us.'

'I remember I saw the banner of their king, Harald the Land Waster, held aloft when all his army was routed.' Sigurd's rough voice was strangely wistful now. 'His bodyguard hacked and parried all who came, marooned in a sea of English warriors. When he fell they fought on, and when at last the fighting was done and our men came to retrieve his body, they first had to pull away seven corpses who had fallen protecting him. Later I discovered that they learned their war craft here, in Byzantium, serving as Varangians.'

Normans and Norsemen, and now two King Harolds: was it just that the barbarian words all sounded alike to my unfamiliar ear, or were they all named identically?

'I thought you said the Normans stole your kingdom. Yet now you say you eventually defeated them.'

'We defeated Harald and the Norsemen in the north,' said Aelric. 'But a week later William, bastard duke of the Normans, landed on our southern shore. We marched the length of the country and brought him to battle, but we were too weary and they fought with the desperation of men without retreat. They killed our king, and took his throne. As I said, the last battle is the only one that matters.'

'So you fled their victory, and came here?'

'Not immediately.' Aelric paused a moment to scratch his grey beard. 'For three years the Bastard contented himself despoiling the south, gorging his accomplices with morsels of our land and fastening his grip on power. Then he came north. Some of our lords who had pledged themselves to him rebelled, but too late: they could not withstand the army he led, and one by one they were destroyed, or surrendered. The Bastard turned the fertile country along that coast into a wasteland: bodies lay in the streets by their thousands, and some of the living grew so hungry they gnawed on the bones of the dead. There was not one village or field that he did not raze to the ground, not one ounce of food he did not tear up and burn before our eyes. Then he invited the Danes to come and ravage our shores, so that those few shoots of life which had survived the first devastation were uprooted and consumed. After that there was no life left in the north: a man could ride through the wilderness for days, and never hear a single voice but his own. That was when I came to Byzantium.'

'And I too.' Sigurd's face was pale under his bronze helmet, and his eyes twitched as if beyond his sway. 'The Normans came to our village one evening; they killed my father and entered his house. All through the night I could hear my mother and my sisters screaming, and at dawn they were dead. I could not even bury them, for the Normans turned our home into their pyre. I was taken away by my uncle, first to Caledonia, then across the sea to Denmark, and at last, by way of many roads, and rivers, to this city.'

He wiped a gauntleted hand over his cheek, then grasped his axe just below the head and pulled it from its sheath.

'You see these notches, Demetrios? These are the number of the Normans I have killed since then.' He snorted. 'Or at least, the number I have killed since the last haft snapped from all the wood I carved out of it.'

'It could still be worse,' Aelric observed. 'Look at the eunuch.'

'Which eunuch?' I asked, failing to understand his meaning.

'The chamberlain, Krysaphios.'

'What of him?' In his dress, his manners, his language, he seemed as pure a Roman as I had met. 'He did not come from Thule, did he?'

It was an innocent question, but Aelric and Sigurd laughed so loudly in response that their horses bucked and shied in alarm. 'From England,' Sigurd repeated. 'Why, Demetrios, do you see a resemblance to us?'

I thought of the eunuch with his smooth, olive skin and hairless face, next to these blistered, shaggy, blue-eyed giants. 'Not much.'

'Krysaphios had his own encounter with the Normans,' Aelric explained, subduing his merriment. 'When he was a young man, he lived in Nicomedia.'

'It was Malagina,' Sigurd interrupted.

'I heard Nicomedia, but it does not matter. It was in the reign of Michael Ducas, more than twenty years ago. One of the Emperor's Norman mercenaries named Urselius proved treacherous, as is their habit, and turned against the man who paid him. He took many of the Asian provinces before he was finally captured, and during his rising there was much looting and barbarity. The rumour I have heard is that one night some of Urselius' Norman army captured Krysaphios, then just a boy, and took him to their camp.' There was no humour in Aelric's face now. 'When they released him in the morning, he had become a eunuch.'

It was not the first time I had heard such a story, for I knew that the western barbarians found the third sex at once fascinating and repellent; that many derided us for our reliance on them, and believed our whole race to be tainted by their manlessness. It needed little imagination to think what torment a gang of mercenaries, filled with drink and such beliefs, might effect on a hapless prisoner. If that had been the ordeal Krysaphios suffered, I could only admire the will he must have had to turn it to his advantage, to attain the rank he now enjoyed.

Sigurd's voice broke into my thoughts. 'You know that the Emperor relies on the Varangians because of the hatred we bear the Normans. You may guess how he relies on the eunuch.'

Such tales of horror dampened further conversation, and we rode on in silence, save for Father Gregorias grumbling at the back of our column: that his horse was lame, that his saddle chafed, that the water in his flask was brackish. It seemed he did not number horsemanship among his accomplishments. After a time, we splashed through a ford in the shallow river and joined the main northerly road. A high-arched aqueduct rose about half a mile away on our right, mimicking the line of the road, and we followed it as the land grew wilder. The sporadic clusters of trees we passed became more frequent, then began to reach into each other, and finally merged into a forest which pressed constantly against our path, stretching away deep into the hills. The sound of running water was never far off, and sometimes we could see the moss-covered brickwork of a cistern or channel through the branches. A few hardy wood birds whistled their song, and occasionally we would meet a lone pilgrim or merchant, but otherwise the forest seemed deserted. Pines and oaks and beech trees towered over us, and it did not take long for my fears to begin preying on me. Every snapping twig or falling branch or rustling animal had me jerking awkwardly around, scanning the underbrush for the first signs of attack. As generations of careless travellers had found to their cost, it was the perfect place for an ambush, remote and hemmed in.

Sigurd must have shared my apprehension, for at lunchtime he posted four of his men as pickets on the edge of the glade where we halted. Our horses chewed contentedly on the grass, but even the sight of open sky above us did not lift my oppressed mood, and we ate our bread in haste.

'I'll be glad of Christmas,' muttered Sigurd, eyeing his meagre meal with disdain. 'The feast of the Nativity, as you call it. If man doesn't live by bread alone, a soldier certainly can't.'

'Ten days,' agreed Aelric. 'Then we'll have feasting.'

'If we're out of this forsaken wood by then.' Sigurd spat an olive stone into the bushes. 'If the boy can lead us to this house we're told of, and doesn't run off into the trees when we're not looking.'

Thomas, oblivious to our words, sucked on the dried dates I'd brought him. The dressing that Anna had wrapped around his leg seemed to be holding up under the strain of riding – I could see no new blood seeping through it – and I fancied that the clean air and fresh surroundings had brought a new vigour to his cheeks. It was the first time I had seen him not poised on the brink of death, and it struck me how he seemed now both younger and older. Younger in his limbs, which all seemed a half-inch too long for him, though clearly they were strong enough to wield the arbalest; younger also in his beardless cheeks, which in a year or two might be ruggedly hand-some, and in his fair, uncombed hair which blew wild in the wind. But there was a hurt in his blue eyes which, even in our pastoral surroundings, was never truly gone; a heaviness in the way he carried his broad shoulders. He had known pain, I guessed, and not merely the physical kind of a Bulgar's sword. Though he seemed placid enough for now.

'Well?'

I looked up from my thoughts. Sigurd had been speaking all the while, his words drifting past me, and now he was staring expectantly at Father Gregorias.

The priest turned on the boy and uttered a string of incompre-hensible syllables, to which the reply came in more abbreviated kind.

'He confirms that he will find where the house was,' said Father Gregorias sulkily. 'He will remember the way.'

'Did he unwind a ball of string behind him then, like your Theseus in his maze?' Sigurd was scornful. 'Or can he speak with the birds?'

Gregorias put the question to the boy. Without the sarcasm, I assumed.

'He says he did not survive in the slums of the megapolis by daydreaming. He watched the path closely, in the hope that he might escape.'

'Then we'd best get on. Dusk never lingers in the woods.' Sigurd hoisted himself back onto his horse. 'Even a boy with memories painted like icons might not find this house in the dark.'

We rode on another two hours, meeting ever less traffic on our lonely road. Our beasts began to tire, and even Father Gregorias eventually lost the energy to complain; so much, indeed, that twice I had to turn back to be sure his horse had not thrown him into a thicket. Light was fading from the sky, and although most of the trees were leafless, their canopy still brought on premature darkness.

A sharp elbow against my ribs interrupted my thoughts; I pulled back on the reins, alive to the possibility that Thomas intended to use the gloom to escape. But he had jostled me intentionally, and now had an arm stretched out – as much as the rope would allow – towards an oak tree. Its massive girth was swathed in ivy, and wrinkled roots had begun to tear the roadstead beneath us, but otherwise it seemed unremarkable.

I called a halt, and beckoned Father Gregorias forward.

'Ask him what he wants.'

I endured the usual frustrating pause.

'He recognises the tree. He says that the path to the house is around the next corner, on the left.'

'Is it?' Sigurd swayed in the saddle as his horse pawed at the ground. 'Does he also recognise the shape of the pine-needles?'

But his suspicion was misplaced; we rounded a curve on the murky road and there, just as Thomas had said, a path forked away. We had passed many like it that day, some little more than animal tracks, some so broad we had struggled to discern the true road. This one was wider than most, but rutted and broken by rain. Whoever owned it clearly cared little for its upkeep. Perhaps, in this wild place, he hoped to avoid the attentions of brigands.

Nonetheless, it had clearly been used recently. As we rode up it I could see small heaps of stale dung, and the traces of hooves imprinted in the mud. The forest was silent here, and more ominous for it. Sigurd,

I saw, had his axe in his hand, and several others of the Varangian company had followed his lead. I felt a chill of fear as I realised that the boy in front of me would be wholly defenceless and an obvious target, the sort I would have relished in my days as a bounty hunter. And any blow aimed at him would be as likely to strike me.

But no-one assailed us. We passed between a pair of stone columns, surmounted with carved basilisks, and the path began to rise steeply up a hill whose summit was lost in the trees. I touched Thomas on the shoulder, gesturing at the pillars, and he nodded recognition. The foliage around us thinned, and looking through it I could see the sky drawing steadily nearer the ground. For a good quarter hour I could have sworn that the brow of the ridge was just ahead of us, but every crick and twist in the path yielded nothing but a further climb.

And then, without preamble, we came between an opening in a wall and into a broad clearing, shaved off the crown of the hill like a monk's tonsure. It had the feel of a high place, but the tall trees growing close against the encircling wall blocked out any view we might have had beyond. The wall ran around the entire perimeter, save where we had entered, and within the enclosure there stood half a dozen out-buildings, including a stable block and, on the far side, a large, two-storied house. We rode towards it.

'It's quiet.' We were all glad to have clear space around us, but the lonely solitude was still unnerving. Even to Sigurd. 'Wulfric, Helm – see if anyone will fodder our horses.'

Two of the Varangians broke away and crossed to the stables. One dismounted, unsheathed his axe, and pushed through the unlocked door. Weeds grew around it, I saw – as indeed across much of the open ground.

I motioned Father Gregorias forward. 'Is this the place? The place where the monk and the Bulgars brought Thomas?'

I hardly needed the answer. The way that the boy's shoulders hunched forward as we saw the house, that his knuckles whitened around the rim of the saddle, told me everything.

'Empty, Captain.' The two Varangians were walking back from the stables. 'It's been completely swept out.'

We continued towards the house. It must have taken a Heraklean effort to erect it in this remote place, and you might have thought that whoever did so would have troubled himself to maintain it. But the closer we came, the more derelict it appeared. Ivy and creepers grew up its walls, and the glass in its windows was broken. The plaster was mottled and cracked; in some places it had peeled away completely to reveal the dull brickwork underneath. A short flight of steps led up to the arch of the main doorway, but there too the marble was chipped away, uneven.

Sigurd slid off his horse and threw the reins to one of his men.

'Was this the place where you came?' he asked the boy.

Thomas nodded.

'Were any others here?'

'Only those he came with,' translated the priest. 'The monk, and the four Bulgars. Otherwise the house was as abandoned as it is now.'

'We'll judge how empty that is when we've seen it.' Sigurd lifted his axe and thumped the butt against the wooden door. It resounded with a low rumbling, ominous in those lonely surroundings, but did not open.

Sigurd tried the handle, a brass knob shaped like a howling boar. It gave readily.

'Did you see the monk lock the door when he left?' I asked, alive to any clue that it might have been occupied since. But the boy did not remember.

'We'll see if anyone's here soon enough.' Sigurd pushed open the door, and ducked under the low, fractured lintel. 'Wulfric stay with the horses. The rest – follow me.'

We crossed the threshold, glancing nervously about as we entered a narrow hallway, which almost immediately gave out into a square peristyle. This too bore a dilapidated air: the tiled images on the floor – bare-chested warriors sticking bears and lions – were faded and uneven. Rainwater had collected in pools in the depressions, and in one corner a small shrub had forced its way up through the stone. Doorways in each wall led on to further dark rooms.

'Search it,' Sigurd ordered. 'Four men each way. Demetrios and Aelric can stay here with the boy and the priest. If anyone finds trouble, regroup here at once.'

Thomas and I seated ourselves on a marble bench, while Aelric paced around the courtyard and Father Gregorias looked worriedly at the mosaics. The slapping of the Varangians' boots faded away, and we were alone. From somewhere within, I heard the steady dripping of water.

I turned to Thomas. He rested his chin on his knuckles, and stared mournfully at the floor.

'Where did you stay?'

He looked up, listened to the priest's translation, then pointed to our left.

'Did you all stay there?'

'Yes.'

'And did the monk leave anything when you departed?'

The boy shook his head. I could have guessed, of course: a monk who tried to leave no living witnesses to his plot was unlikely to have left anything to identify him in this ruin.

'Demetrios!'

I looked up. Sigurd had appeared in the gallery above me, flanked by two of his men.

'There's nobody here. A few beds, a table, some stools – all of them rotting, by the smell of them. Nothing else.'

'Nor here.' One of Sigurd's lieutenants had appeared on the balcony opposite. 'House is as quiet as the tomb. Nice view though.'

Indeed there was. The third corridor led from the peristyle onto a wide terrace at the back of the house, projecting out over the steep hillside. We stood there in silence and gazed onto the furrowed landscape of hills and wooded valleys before us. On the western horizon was an orange smear where the sun was setting, while to the southeast I fancied we could just see the glittering domes of Constantinople. It was a magnificent vantage point, ingeniously constructed so that the trees would block any sight of it from below, while leaving the view from above unconstrained.

A cold breeze played over our faces, and we were turning to go indoors when Thomas surprised us all by speaking unprompted, and at such length that Father Gregorias was pressed to remember it all.

'He says the monk often came here,' he said. 'He would stare out at the queen of cities, and beseech God to annihilate her, as He did Sodom and Jericho.'

'He said all this in Frankish?' It seemed strange that a monk would address his God in a foreign tongue.

Gregorias conferred with Thomas. 'In the language of Old Rome, Latin. Thomas knew the words because the Franks and Normans use it in their worship.'

This was more curious still, and I shook my head in defeat. At every turn I found a dozen new questions, but never a single answer.

Sigurd looked up at the sky. 'We'll spend the night in the stables,' he announced. 'With the beasts. I don't want to find myself stranded here by some poacher turning his hand to horseflesh. And there's only one door to guard.'

A peal of thunder rippled through the valley.

'And,' he added moodily, 'the roof's intact.'

I spent another half hour exploring that mournful house, but found no answers among the crumbling fabric and mouldering furniture. The thunder was moving slowly nearer, and every time it sounded I would snap my head around, unsettled by the surroundings. I was glad at last to escape the building, to return to the company of the Varangians, who had tethered our horses in the stable and made a small fire in a ring of stones outside. On it they roasted salt fish and vegetables which we gulped down in haste: there was little of the usual banter of soldiers on a march that night.

We settled down on the hard floor, cursing whoever had swept out all the straw before abandoning it. As I closed my eyes, I heard the first drops of rain beginning to strike on the lead tiles above us.

It was still raining when I awoke, and still dark. A horse was snuffling somewhere on my right, but otherwise nothing moved. I lay there a second reminding myself where I was, allaying the natural fears of night with the knowledge that I was surrounded by a dozen of the stoutest warriors in the empire. That was comforting. I put my hand under the balled-up cloak I used as a pillow and felt the haft of my knife still there; then, almost from superstition, I reached out to touch Thomas on the shoulder.

My hand felt cold air, then cold stone. I stretched further, my heart whipping itself into a panic, but again felt only the slap of my hand on the hard floor. Where was he? I threw off my blanket and stood, picking my way between the sleeping Varangians to the doorway. Warriors they might have been, but none of them, I noticed, stirred as I stole like a thief between them.

None, at least, save Aelric: but he could not help it. He was sitting in the doorway, his back against the frame, and as I reached it to look outside I fell sprawling over him. He cursed, and staggered to his feet, his hand fastening around the axe at his side.

'It's me, Demetrios,' I hissed. Old though he was for his calling, I suspected I would not survive more than a single blow of his axe. 'The boy's missing.'

'Christ.' Aelric rubbed his eyes. 'Oh Christ.'

A clap of thunder exploded over our heads, and almost simultaneously a shaft of lightning cracked through the clouds.

'There!' I had been peering out into the rain, searching in vain desperation for any sign of the boy; by the white glare of the lightning, I thought I had seen something. 'Someone moving, over by the house.'

'And what's to say it's the boy?' demanded Aelric. 'Are you armed?'

'I have my knife.' His words struck a fresh wave of dread into me, as all my fears of brigands and bandits and the monk's adepts in this desolate place came flooding back, but there was no time. I launched myself out into the rain, flinching under the barrage of the water, and began running across the open ground to the house, with Aelric's footsteps close behind me. My feet dragged in the mud and puddles, and my clinging tunic hobbled me. Rain ran off my sodden hair into my eyes, which I had to keep squeezed close together, but another flash of lightning guided me on towards the house. The door, I saw, was open.

'Follow me in,' I shouted, looking back over my shoulder. Aelric was invisible, and any sound he made was now drowned out by the torrent of winds around us.

The gale stopped as I pushed through the door, and for a second my squelching tread seemed terribly loud in the small hallway. Then there was rain pelting my face again, and I realised I had come into the peristyle. The water rattled on the stone tiles, but I thought that somewhere in the surrounding darkness I could hear a more animate sound, as of someone scraping at something.

I stepped forward, trying to gain a sense of where the noise was strongest. My effort was thwarted, though, as thunder boomed out over me, resounding off the walls and galleries in a dizzying, deafening roll. I tried to steady myself against a pillar but found none; then, for an instant, lightning burst across the square of sky overhead. The entire courtyard was held in its cold brilliance, and by the light I saw the boy, Thomas, crouched in the far corner by the bush which grew through the mosaics.

The light vanished; I stepped towards him, but in that moment something blunt and heavy cannoned into my back between the shoulder blades. Instinct took over; the months of training I had endured in the legions flooded into my blood, and as my shoulder hit the ground I rolled away across the floor. If my assailant aimed a second blow at where I had fallen, he would meet only stone.

'Aelric?' I yelled, wondering if he had blundered into me in the dark.

There was no answer, and I sprang away again just as I heard something crash into the space where I had been. Someone else is here, I thought in disbelief. Some murderer intent on killing me. Did Thomas purpose to lead me here as a trap?

My knife was still in my hand, for instinct and discipline had tightened my grip when another man might have dropped it. I raised it before my face, straining every sense for a sign of my enemy. Someone was moving in the blackness before me, but where I could not tell. He did not seem to be so very near, but with the uproar of the weather that could yet be near enough.

And what of Thomas? He had been in front of me when I was struck from behind: where was he now? Perhaps my invisible assailant was not hunting me at all. Perhaps he had come to slaughter the child.

Another sheet of light from the sky broke off my frenzied speculation. Thunder and lightning seemed now to have joined themselves immediately overhead, and by the spark of their union the courtyard was again illuminated. And there, standing in the shadowy doorway directly opposite me, a huge figure with a weapon raised in his arms.

The light vanished and I launched myself forward, charging across those slippery tiles heedless of the rain and the chance of other, unseen enemies. As I came near I lowered my shoulder – as the *dekarch* had demonstrated on so many parade grounds – drew back my knife, and tensed my neck for the impact.

He had not moved in those few seconds; I struck him in the belly and drove my knife hard into him. He grunted and fell backwards, bringing me tumbling down over him, but it was I who shouted the louder, for his stomach seemed to be lined with steel, and my knife had bounced harmlessly off him. He was in armour, I realised with horror, while I lay there defenceless. I tried to pull away but he had wrapped an arm about me and was holding me down, scrabbling on the floor for the weapon he had dropped.

'Shit,' he swore.

My heart stopped. 'Aelric?' I gasped. 'Aelric? It's Demetrios.'

A sharp blade hovered against the hair on my neck.

'Demetrios?' he growled. 'Then why in Satan's hell did you try to rip my guts out?'

He loosened his grip, and I drew myself up. 'There was a man in here, attacking me.' I shook my sodden head. 'Was that you too?'

'What do you think?' Aelric's voice was surly – perhaps I had hurt him through the armour. 'I followed you in. I was only just here when you rammed me.'

'But I've been here . . .'

A flickering light by the entrance silenced us both; we drew apart, tensing our weapons in our arms as it drew nearer.

'Aelric? Demetrios?'

'Sigurd?'

The Varangian captain stepped into the room, his axe in one hand and a torch in the other. God alone knew how he managed to get it lit in the midst of that pelting storm. He held it under the colonnade, but its burning glow pierced the night to reveal the entire courtyard, frozen into a tableau where even the rain seemed to stand still.

Aelric and I were standing in the door to Sigurd's left, by the passage which led into the western arm of the house. Sigurd, flanked by two of his men, was at the main entrance, staring angrily at Thomas, who cowered in the corner where the lightning had last revealed him, his hands still loosely bound. Of whomever else I might have battled in the darkness, there was no sign.

'I suppose,' said Sigurd, 'that there is a reason for this.'

Aelric answered first. 'The boy managed to escape the stables. Demetrios and I chased after him, but in the storm I lost my bearings. By the lightning I saw him entering by the west door and I followed. As I came in here, he rammed me like a trireme and we both went down. Fortunately I recognised his voice before I took his head off.'

'But I didn't come in the west door,' I objected. 'I came by the main entrance, which was open. Where Sigurd is. And I was here several minutes before I attacked you. Mistakenly,' I added. 'But I grappled with someone well before that.'

'Perhaps it was the boy.' Sigurd had no patience for this; I guessed he would be furious that the boy had come so close to escaping. 'We'll get his explanation in the morning. Until then we double the guard and tether the boy in the stables.'

'What about the other man? He may still be in the house – or at least in the grounds. Supposing he is an assassin sent by the monk – or indeed the monk himself?'

Sigurd snorted. 'Even if this man exists, and if he is not some phantom of your dreams, I will not waste my night chasing over rubble and through mud to find him. If you want to stay in this house and seek him alone, then do it. I will not risk a sprained ankle or a knife in the dark.'

Nor, on reflection, would I.

ι α

Nothing more came to disturb my sleep, though it would have found little sleep to trouble. I lay awake, tensed by every creaking beam or rustle of blankets, until the air outside the door lightened, and the few birds which had not fled before the winter began their morning song. Glad of any excuse to be away from my restless bed I rose, passed the sentries on the door, and made once more for the house.

My head already ached from its broken sleep, and the stiff chill in the air did nothing to help it, but at least the rain had passed. I looked around, nervously scanning every yard of ground between me and the encircling woods. Nothing moved.

My pulse quickened as I reached the house, and even the sight of the empty courtyard did nothing to soothe it. I glanced up at the surrounding galleries, unable to shake the apprehension that someone might be watching me; I even walked all around the colonnade to be sure that no-one lurked behind a pillar. No-one did.

I turned my attention to the corner where we had found the boy in the night. His behaviour was a mystery, for if he had wanted to escape he would surely not have come in here. And he would be desperate indeed to try to run in a storm, in the midst of a forest with his legs bandaged and his arms tied before him. He would not have survived a day. So why had he risked so much coming here, when an overzealous Varangian might easily have cut him down in the dark?

I looked to the floor. The mosaic tiles were loose, cracked open by the bush which had pushed through them. I squeezed my thumb under one and tugged, watching as it came away in my hand. Mortar trickled off it in a fine powder, turning to a grey paste again on the wet floor.

I prised away half a dozen more tiles, looking particularly for those which were already loose. They would be the ones nearest the stem of the plant, I guessed, and I scratched my arms several times reaching under its branches to grasp them. Perhaps it was a futile exercise in eliminating an unlikely possibility, but this whole expedition had been just such a task: what were a few more wasted minutes?

And then I saw why the boy had risked so much to come here. A black tile – the stripe in the side of a tiger – came free, and as I poked my finger in the cavity beneath I felt the cold surface of polished metal. It was a ring, the gold barely tarnished by its underground sojourn, set with a red stone which was probably a garnet. A sinuous black crack was cleft through the gem, almost like a snake, and written around the shank in clumsy, Latin lettering was an inscription.

'The captain says breakfast is cooked, if you want any.'

I looked around to see Aelric. 'Tell Sigurd I've found something,' I ordered. 'Tell him to send the boy here with the interpreter.'

I rinsed the dirt from my hands in a puddle while I waited, and rubbed the ring on the hem of my tunic before folding it into my fist as Thomas stumbled in. His face was set firm in a hard scowl, and his bandages were caked with mud.

'Ask him what he was doing here last night,' I instructed Father Gregorias. 'Did he really think he could escape us?'

'He says he was called by nature.'

'And his modesty was such that rather than relieve himself against a wall, he walked two hundred yards through a driving storm to piss in here?' I rolled my eyes. 'Ask him if he was looking for this?'

As I spoke, I opened my hand to reveal the ring, keeping my eyes always fixed on Thomas's face. He may have learned his craft in the slums of the city, but he could not hide the surprise of recognition which flashed across his features.

'Where did you find that?' asked the priest, irrelevantly.

'Under a stone. What does the inscription say?'

The little priest took it in his hands and squinted at it. 'Saint Remigius, lead me in the way of truth,' he read.

I had never in all the feasts and liturgies heard of this Saint Remigius, but I recognised the trinket clearly enough. It was a pilgrim's ring, the sort sold by hawkers and peddlers near the shrines of the sanctified. Had the boy left it here? His parents had been pilgrims, I remembered: was it theirs?

'Ask him if it was his mother's.'

The boy's cheeks coloured, and he spoke angrily at some length. I twisted the ring in my hands while I waited, until the priest was ready to translate.

'He says it is his. The monk who brought him here wore it on a cord about his neck. One night the boy managed to cut the cord and hide it. The monk was furious and searched everywhere, but eventually he accepted that it must have worked loose and fallen somewhere in the grounds. The boy never had the chance to retrieve it from its hiding place.' The priest cleared his throat. 'According to the boy, he remembered this in the middle of the night and came to fetch it for you.'

What devotion. 'Tell him I do not believe him.'

The boy muttered a few short words, which Father Gregorias seemed challenged to translate.

'He says you . . . He insists it is the truth.'

'Am I to think he would simply have presented me with this ring in the morning?' I rolled my eyes. 'If he stole it once, he would not lightly surrender it.'

The priest was translating my words as I spoke, but they wrought no change in the boy's hardened face. I began to doubt I would achieve much by continuing this bout of contradiction and denial.

'Whatever his purposes,' I shrugged, 'you may tell him that by running away in the night he has done nothing to help his fate with us. Nor has he helped his wounds to heal by splashing them through mud.' I looked at his shabby clothing and the soiled bandages. 'I saw a spring in the gardens; we had best use it to clean him.'

We walked around the house – Aelric, the priest, Thomas and I – and down some stairs into a sunken, walled orchard. In its centre was a low plinth, from which a stone channel ran between the trees back to the cistern under the house. The channel was broken, feeding only into a boggy patch of ground, but the spring still rose, and fed enough water over the moss-grown lip of the trough that I could splash it over Thomas's leg.

I had just dried him with my cloak, and was wrapping on the fresh bandages which Anna had given me, when he spoke unexpectedly.

'What was that?' I asked, pulling the linen tight.

Gregorias translated. 'He said this was where the monk brought him to practise with the arbalest. They would spend much of the day shooting at targets against the far wall over there.'

I tied a knot, then paced down the garden to the wall which the boy had indicated. Like all this estate, weeds and lichens had made it their own, but there were many places where the stone showed through, clean and sharp, and pitted with white gouges. Many arrows must have struck here, each drawing the boy's eye closer to the true aim which would see his bolt strike home on the Emperor. It was as well he had not practised any more.

A shout from above interrupted my thoughts; I raised my head over the parapet and looked out across the broad enclosure. One of our sentries had issued a challenge to a man now riding between the gateposts on a handsome white mare. I saw Sigurd emerge from the stables and move quickly to meet him, with the rest of his company spread in a purposeful line behind. I ran to join them.

The man on the horse seemed untroubled by the cordon of Varangians, every one of them with an axe in their hands. In fact, there seemed to be an arrogant amusement on his face as he looked down from his mount.

'What are you doing here?' he asked. Although his green cloak and high boots seemed expensive, his accent was rustic.

'We heard rumours that the Emperor's enemies could be found here,' said Sigurd evenly. 'We came to find them.'

The man on the horse squinted. 'Did you find them?'

'None. Yet.'

I think Sigurd meant it as a threat, but it drew a laugh from our visitor. 'I am Kosmas, and no enemy of this or any other Emperor. I am the forester, and I manage this estate for my mistress, the owner.'

Sigurd moved his head in a broad arc, deliberately studying the ramshackle landscape. 'Does she pay you well for it?'

'Enough that I do not tolerate uninvited guests. If you have found all there is to find, which is nothing, you should go.'

I could see Sigurd boiling up to resist the man's demand, and did not want a confrontation here. 'Tell me, forester,' I broke in. 'Who is this inhospitable mistress?'

'My mistress, who is most hospitable to those she invites, is the noble lady Theodora Trichas. Wife of the Sebastokrator Isaak, and sister-in-law to the Emperor Alexios Komnenos.' He smiled. 'Hardly a family to be harbouring traitors and treachery.'

That was so optimistic as to be laughable. But we left anyway.

The long ride back was silent, and the arrival stormy. The road grew ever busier as we neared the city, and though we chose one of the lesser gates so as to arrive inconspicuously, we still found a mass of people jostling to get in. The watchmen were ill at ease, barking questions at the entrants and searching their belongings with brusque contempt; most of those around us seemed to have come in from the country, and many must have carried the greater part of their belongings on their backs. We might have been there until nightfall if Sigurd had not managed to push and kick a path through for us, and fortunately the guards recognised him. When the last of our company was within the walls, he called a halt.

'We'll take the boy to the palace and keep him in the gaol,' he declared. 'If he's well enough to escape once, he's well enough to get out of that monastery.'

'If you put him in there, he'll die in a week.'

'And that will be no loss to me.' Sigurd snapped his reins angrily. 'Let disease take him, if God wills it.'

'Disease is my least concern. Have you forgotten what happened to the Bulgar? The monk, or his agents, can enter the gaols at will it would appear.' Although few seemed to care about the Bulgar's death, it troubled me every time I thought on it. How had an assassin crept into the depths of the palace, through a locked gate and past a legion of Varangians? None of the enquiries that Krysaphios, Sigurd or I had made could answer it.

'We'll be more careful this time,' said Sigurd. 'For all it matters.'

'Do you want me to go to the chamberlain over this? He has given me the prerogative. I say the boy does not go into the gaol.'

Sigurd glowered. 'And where will you take him then, Demetrios? Into the monastery, to the care of monks and women? Will God protect him there?'

That thrust me onto the defensive. I had had all day to ponder it, but my thoughts had been ever distracted by other questions. Now I floundered for a solution, while Sigurd watched with a sneer on his lip.

I spoke the first thought I had. 'He will come to my house.'

'To your house?' Sigurd looked delighted with my folly. 'Your castle? Your tower, surrounded by water and guarded by a thousand archers? Or your tenement, where the boy could slit your family's throats and escape over the rooftops in a second?'

They were all sound objections, but I would not give him the victory of acknowledging so. 'If the boy wants to escape, he will succeed eventually. Unless we put him in the prison, in which case he will die. You will lend me two of your soldiers to watch my door. As for my family . . .' I hesitated. 'I will see they are safe.'

Sigurd stared at me in angry silence.

'The boy is no more the monk's ally than was the whore he used. Perhaps a little affection and charity will coax more information from him.' I raised my hands. 'Or, I can talk to Krysaphios.'

'Take care,' Sigurd warned. 'You might get your way with him for now, but who will you turn to when he loses patience? Take the boy; I will leave you Aelric and Sweyn – for the moment.'

He kicked his horse and cantered off, followed closely by all but a pair of his men.

'I must go too,' said Father Gregorias. He looked desperate to be parted from his mount. 'I am needed at my church.'

'You are needed with me,' I answered. 'How else am I to talk to the boy?'

'Call in the doctor. She speaks his tongue.'

And meek though he was, he left me. With two reluctant Varangians, and a boy none of us could comprehend.

I led my companions back to my house, and realised I had nowhere to stable the horses.

'We should take them back to the palace,' said Aelric. 'The hipparch will want them immediately.'

'I can go,' I offered. 'I ought to report to Krysaphios.'

Aelric shook his grizzled head. 'You can't go alone. It's getting dark, and the Watch will have you locked up for a horse thief if they see you. And I can't come with you: you don't want to leave Sweyn alone with your daughters.'

I smiled wearily. 'My daughters are with their aunt, my sister-in-law.' I would have to leave them there another night, though they would return primed with even more disdain for my disreputable profession, and for my paternal failing to find them suitable families of their own.

'Then you and I can guard the boy, and Sweyn can return our mounts.' Aelric swung himself down from the beast and strode over, lifting Thomas onto the ground. I dismounted, and handed both sets of reins to the taciturn Sweyn.

'Get back quickly,' Aelric told him. 'You don't want to rely on my old eyes all night.'

'Not if last night is any guide,' I said, as the horses vanished around the corner. I had not yet raised his failure to stop Thomas escaping the stable, for fear of provoking Sigurd to still greater wrath, but I had not forgotten. Nor forgiven it.

Aelric looked me in the eye. 'We all have lapses, Demetrios. You were kind to hide mine from the captain. But the boy is safe, and no harm was done. If I've learned one thing from my life, it's that when I escape the worst consequences of my mistakes, I should thank my God and forget it.' He clapped me on the arm. 'Now let's get the boy out of the street, before some arbalest-wielding monk gallops past and puts an arrow in him.'

We climbed the stairs to my home, keeping Thomas always between us.

'Is this the only entrance?' Aelric asked, as I unlocked my heavy door.

'There is a way out onto the roof inside.' I crossed my threshold, bending to pick up a scrap of paper which someone had pushed under the door. 'Unfortunately, it only bolts from the inside. This house wasn't built to be a prison.'

'But are we here to keep the boy in, or others out?' Aelric crossed the room and rattled the shutters. 'At least you've got bars on the windows.'

'A sensible precaution for a man with young daughters.' My skills as a bounty-hunter and a searcher had allowed me to move my home away from the more dangerous corners of the city, but not always their inhabitants.

Aelric continued prowling around the house while I unfolded the paper. 'The merchant Domenico wishes to see me at his house in Galata.'

'Do you know him?'

'I've never heard of him.' I put the paper on a table. 'Perhaps he wants to sell me an arbalest.'

'If that's so, you'd better see the eunuch first to collect your pay,' Aelric chuckled. He poked his head around one of the dividing curtains. 'Who sleeps in here?'

'My daughters.' Although they were away, I did not want Aelric or Thomas staying in that room. But I had yet to consider how I would manage that combination in my household. 'The boy and I can sleep in my room; you can sleep on the bench in here.'

'I'll get a palliasse from the barracks tomorrow.' Aelric was clearly unimpressed at the prospect of another night of hardship.

In the absence of my children, I chopped up some leeks and onions, and mixed in some Euxine sauce which a former client had sent me. Sweyn returned with bread he had had from the palace kitchens, and the four of us shared a coarse meal by the light of my candle. Then Aelric took the bench and pushed it against the bolted roof door, while Sweyn descended to the street.

'Better to guard at a distance,' he explained solemnly. 'Otherwise, if you miss them, it's too late.'

I retired to my bed chamber with the boy and lay down on the bed, gesturing that he could share it. Instead of gratitude, though, he recoiled, cowering by the wall like a cornered hare, his arms crossed tightly over his chest. He stared at me with bitter eyes, and his legs, I saw, were trembling.

'Do you take me for some sort of pederast?' I was angry and embarrassed. At the tone of my voice he cringed still further; a tear ran down his cheek.

With a sigh which might have been exasperation or pity, I rolled off the bed and stood on the far side, pointing first to him, then to it, then to myself and then to the floor.

Still he did not move.

'Very well.' If words and signs would not suffice, he would have to judge me by my actions – or stay cramped in his corner all night. Very deliberately, I laid out a blanket on the floor, reclined myself on it, and blew out the candle. Then I listened in the darkness.

It must have been a full half an hour before I finally heard the boy creep into the bed above me. And it was long after that that I at last fell asleep.

ι β

E arly the next morning I went straight to the palace, thinking Krysaphios would demand to know my progress immediately. He did not. Instead, a clerk directed me into a long arcade lined with benches, where scores of petitioners had already gathered, some so settled they seemed scarcely different from the marble statues around them, as if a gorgon had come and gazed on them. I tried to explain my importance to the clerk but he would not hear me: promising that my name would be noted, he vanished.

I leaned against a cold pillar – the benches were all occupied – and waited. The pale sun moved above the fountain behind me; clerks and secretaries, men and eunuchs, bustled about, talking in urgent voices and ignoring the supplicants who lined their way. In over an hour, I did not see one of them granted an entrance. And an entrance to what? I wondered. I doubted the Emperor Alexios, or even his chamberlain Krysaphios, awaited me on the other side of the doors at the end of the passage. They would admit to another secretary, who might direct me to yet another vestibule or atrium, where another clerk would take my name and ask me to wait. In these heavenly surroundings men moved like the stars, their path prescribed by a higher law and destined never to deviate, nor to touch another body.

I would go, I decided. The thought of the boy and the two Varangians in my house made me anxious, and the eunuch's gold made me only less tolerant of time wasted. I pushed myself away from my column, and for a moment thought that I had committed some grave offence: there was an almighty clash of cymbals from the far end of the corridor and a great commotion all about me. Men who had not twitched a muscle all morning were suddenly off their seats and on their knees, touching their foreheads to the ground and trying to mumble the words of an adoring hymn. I could hear the tramp of many footsteps, stamping out a rhythm over which rose the plangent cadences of flutes and harps. I knelt; but did not make my bow so low that I could not see who was coming.

First there was a company of Varangians, though none that I recognised. Their burnished axes were held over their shoulders, the hafts capped with the plumed feathers of great birds, and even in the wan light their armour gleamed. Behind them came the musicians, their faces pursed in concentration, and then a priest, swinging a censer before him and filling the air with its rich perfume. Finally came their master. The pointed toes of his mismatched boots moved serenely over the floor, as though he did not touch it; his head, under its pearl-crusted crown, was bowed in solemn contemplation and glowed with the radiance reflected up from his golden robes. It was far removed from when I had last seen him, in a simple, white dalmatica standing before his unsettling mosaic. The Sebastokrator Isaak. Whose wife's decrepit hunting lodge, I thought, I had visited only the day before.

As he came level with me, I saw my chance.

'May you live a thousand years, Lord,' I called. 'It is Demetrios. I must speak with you.'

Not one hair on his beard moved, and his eyes remained fixed on whatever it was that he could see that other men could not. Then he was past me, and the space was filled with his retinue, dozens of nobles following like crows after an army. He was long disappeared behind the bronze doors before the last of them had passed.

As soon as the way was clear I made to go, but again I was delayed, this time by a stout, dwarfish slave tugging on my elbow.

'Come with me,' he said, his eyes very bright. 'You are summoned.'

'Where?'

But he had slipped behind the column, and I had to make haste to find him again. He led me to a door – not the great doors that the Sebastokrator had entered, but a small door more suited to his height than mine, set into the wall a little to the side of the main gate. Nor did it lead into any jewelled hall, but into a tight, low-roofed passage whose lamps gave little protection against the erratic steps and turns which beset it. We met no-one, until suddenly the way ended abruptly in a stone wall.

'To your right,' whispered the dwarf.

I stepped to my right, and suddenly I was out of the tunnel and in a bright, airy room. Its high-domed roof was set with many windows, and painted with ancient kings, while the light from the gilded walls shone like an eternal dawn. I blinked, and looked back, but behind me there seemed only solid masonry. Of my shrunken guide, and the passage by which I had come, there was no sign.

'Demetrios.'

I looked back to the centre of the room, where two men stood ringed by marble columns. One was Krysaphios, more immaculately dressed than ever; the other . . .

For the second time that morning, I prostrated myself before the Sebastokrator. He took my homage with a smile, then gestured me to rise and approach.

'I summoned you, Demetrios, when I saw you in the hallway. I have come with tidings which concern you – and I am quick to share with those who will find use in it.' He lowered his chin and stared at me. 'Terrible news has reached me from my wife. Her forester has reported that a monk and a company of Bulgars broke into her hunting lodge in the great forest; I fear they used it to concoct the plot which almost murdered my brother. I rushed immediately to tell the chamblerlain, for my conscience cannot bear the burden that I may have given succour to my brother's enemies, however unwittingly.'

Now it was my turn to eye him sceptically. 'Did your wife's forester also relate how a dozen Varangians were at the house yesterday, and discovered all this before an inhospitable steward named Kosmas evicted us?'

The Sebastokrator did not flinch. 'I did not know that, Demetrios. This message only came this morning. I think it took many days to reach me. I would have sent a messenger to you, but I thought it wisest to tell the chamberlain first. I feared that he might see me more readily than you.'

'Indeed,' said Krysaphios. 'Sometimes I have more urgent matters to attend than belated, inconclusive gossip.' He was looking at me, but I felt he spoke to the Sebastokrator.

'More urgent matters?' Isaak made to defend me. 'What could be more urgent than the safety of the Emperor?'

'The safety of the empire, as you well know, Lord.'

'They are the same. And where is my brother?'

'He is at the walls, seeing to the defences. The masons have been labouring since dawn to put them in good repair.'

'Why?' I broke in. Did this bear on the crowds I had seen pouring in from the country the night before?

'Because we may soon be attacked,' snapped the eunuch. 'Why else? But that is not your concern, Demetrios. Your concern is that if a barbarian army does besiege our gates, there is not a homicidal monk at large who could destroy the Emperor when he is most needed. I do not think you will snare him by loitering in this room.'

He jerked his wrist, and the doors behind me opened noiselessly. Taking his meaning, I bowed low and left, passing a host of musicians and sycophants loitering in the next chamber. As I walked in they leapt to attention, and as quickly forgot me when they saw who I was.

As I was already at the palace, I sought out the archivist at the imperial library, for there was a small detail I wished to know better. He was a fastidious man, and would not let me touch his precious books and scrolls, but insisted I wait in the scriptorium among the rows of monks hunched over their desks, while his acolytes searched through piles of parchments and papers. It was a bright room, lit by enormous arched windows at either end; the only sound within was the reed pens scratching like chattering insects.

After a wait, which could have been minutes or hours, I saw one of the assistants emerge from the rampart of shelving and whisper something in the archivist's ear. The old man nodded slowly, then shuffled across the room to where I stood.

'We have found what you sought,' he whispered to me. His voice was like the rustle of dry papers. 'This Saint Remigius you ask of is not known in our church, but he has much importance to the barbarian Franks.'

Again the Franks. The boy had said that the monk prayed in their language; now it seemed he venerated their saints also. 'Why?' I asked. 'What is this Remigius' story?'

The archivist clasped his hands together so that they disappeared in his long sleeves. 'After the fall of the West, when the barbarians had made themselves masters of Roman Gaul, and paganism and heresy were rife, Remigius converted their king to the true faith. Thus the Franks were saved for Christ.'

'What else?' Though doubtless important for ecclesiastical history, I could see little reason why that should win the saint an assassin's devotion.

The archivist looked at me severely, as if my impatience were a slight on his scholarship. 'There is nothing else. He was made a bishop, and died at a venerable age. His shrine is in the Frankish town of Rheims, where the barbarians keep one of their few centres of learning. It is written that there he effects many miracles.'

I could not tell whether he considered the education of barbarians to be one such miracle, but it was obvious that he drew little pleasure dispensing from his hoard of knowledge to an ignorant supplicant like me. I gave my thanks and left, unsure whether I had gained anything of importance. It was another link which tied the monk to the barbarian west, but I sought ties with Romans, with men who stood ready to assume the imperial throne if the Emperor fell. Whichever saints the monk prayed to, and whether he worshipped in Latin or Greek, I needed to find his masters.

That morning, however, I had little idea where I might seek them. I could try to talk further with Thomas, but I was impatient and could not find the enthusiasm for it. There were still many eminent names on the list to interview, but I feared a shared language would not make them any more forthcoming than the boy. And walking the streets hoping to glimpse a monk with a crooked nose would avail even less.

I fished out the paper that I had found under my door the night before and re-read it. 'The merchant Domenico wishes to see you at his house in Galata.'

It would be a change to speak to someone who wished to see me. I turned onto the steeply sloping stairs, and made my way down to the harbour.

A boatman rowed me across the Golden Horn, wending his way between the dolmans and biremes, skiffs and dhows which choked the wide bay. I have ever wondered that they called the Horn 'golden', for though enough of it was loaded on the decks and wharves – in specie and in kind – the water itself was rank with flotsam: the splintered wood of discarded crates, dead fish fallen from the nets, and the floating effluence of the sewers. None of which, thankfully, I could dwell on, for the boatman had constant need of my eyes to look over his shoulder and guide him between the crushing hulls of the larger vessels.

'Fleet's come in,' he said, nodding to his right. 'Came up last night.'

I risked a quick glance where he indicated, and saw the huge sterns of imperial triremes moored further up the channel. The flag of the High Admiral himself flew from the largest, and all their decks were thronged with men.

'Why is that?'

'Barbarians.' The boatman sucked in his cheeks as he navigated the bow of a Levantine trader. 'They say the Normans will come again. Three days' march away, they say.'

'That seems unlikely. The Emperor would have fought them on the shores of the Adriatic before they ever got this far.'

The boatman shrugged. 'I repeat what I hear. I'll believe when I see.'

We pulled in towards the high walls ringing the colony of Galata on the far shore.

'Which gate do you want?' asked the boatman.

'I'm looking for the merchant Domenico. Does he keep his own wharf?'

'I've never heard his name. A Venetian?'

'Or a Genoese.' I scanned the pilings, and the ships moored against them, for any hint of their owner's identity.

The boatman hailed a stevedore on one of the quays, and shouted the name Domenico at him. The man frowned, then shook his head and gestured along the shore to the next landing stage.

'Most of the Genoese have their houses in the city,' the boatman told me, unhelpfully.

We had to ask at three more wharves before at last the name Domenico drew a response. A burly foreman waved us in, took the rope we threw him, and helped me up the ladder.

'Do you want me to wait?' asked the boatman, looking up from the base of the wall. He seemed anxious to leave, for the sky was darkening, and I sensed a squall might be coming from the Asian shore.

'I'll find another.'

As the boatman splashed his way back across the Horn, I took my directions from the foreman and began to mount the hill. The land near the shore was cluttered with warehouses and the narrow lanes between them, but as I rose higher they quickly gave way to generous houses projected on terraces, built to see over the commercial sprawl beneath to the hump of the city across the bay. The mansions grew in proportion with their elevation, though it seemed to me that that lofty magnificence would afford their owners only sore knees and tired lungs. And solitude, for the bustle of the docks below was far behind now.

The house of the merchant Domenico was not at the crest of the hill, but it was nearer there than the foot. One day he would live in considerable splendour, for it was a vast, imposing property, but for the moment the platoon of builders, plasterers, carpenters and masons he employed disrupted its elegance. The air in the outer courtyard was thick with dust, and rang with the noise of hammers chiselling stone. Plaster was caked onto the trunks of orange trees planted in fresh earth, and a pair of trestles had turned the nymphaeum into a sawpit.

I sought out the steward and showed him my letter, trying to make myself understood over the din. It must have meant something, for he ushered me into a broad room which, while in the throes of recon-struction, was at least temporarily empty. Originally the floor had held images of fish and sea monsters, snaking through the blue-green tiles, but half of the mosaic was now overlaid with wide slabs of marble, surrounded at its borders with narrow ribbons of pink and green and black. Beyond it, through three wide arches, I could see the domes of the city cascading down from the pinnacle of Ayia Sophia to the small churches by the sea walls; the pines and cypresses spread over the eastern slopes; the heroic columns of the Emperors spiking above the skyline, and the high bulk of the *pharos*, the beacon, towering over the city.

'Demetrios Askiates. Thank you for coming.'

I turned to meet my unknown host. His voice was warm and eager, though marred by a note of insincerity from the too-perfect way he formed his words. He was about my age, or perhaps a little older, and had a figure which suggested he did not make the ascent to his house very often. His cheeks glowed red, perhaps from the effort of carrying the immaculate silk finery he wore, but his round eyes danced with energy.

'Were you admiring my new floor? The workmen were supposed to finish it a week ago.' He chuckled. 'I can know to within two days when my ships will arrive from Pisa, for all that they must travel hundreds of miles at the mercy of winds and currents and storms. But ask a builder when he will finish, and he is as vague as an astrologer casting his horoscope.'

'I preferred the old floor better.'

'So do I, Demetrios, so do I. May I call you Demetrios? Good. But fashion dictates that the floors must be simple – clean lines of pure marble – and so I must follow her demands.' He rubbed his toe on the stone. 'Apparently it will focus the eye on the splendour of the walls – when the bastard painters have done their work, of course.'

I took a breath to speak, but he forestalled me.

'But you did not come to discuss aesthetics. You came because I, Domenico, invited you. And why? Because, my friend, I think we both trade in the same market.'

'Do we?' Experience had taught that any man who proclaimed himself my friend was usually either lying, or a hopeless optimist. 'Do I sell anything that you would load onto your ships for Pisa?'

Domenico laughed as though it was the greatest witticism. 'Not unless you dabble in fine cloths, or spices from the east, or miniature ivories. But the wind that drives my ships brings other commodities too, besides those I can sell in the forum. News, for example. Some wine?'

He pulled a clay bottle and a pair of chalices from an alcove in the wall.

'Not in the fasting season.'

'A pity. This I had from Monemvasia, in the Peloponnese. Very sweet.' He filled his goblet almost to the brim and sipped enthusiastically.

I paced over to the window and looked out, seeing the great warships of our navy moored in the bay below. 'You speak of news. What news? News that would interest me?'

'Almost certainly.' Domenico put down his glass with an ungainly bang. 'If we could agree its worth.'

Now it was my turn to laugh. I met many such men in my profession, worms and leeches who learned some trivia and tried to turn it into gold through dark hints and extravagant promises.

'No thank you,' I said. 'I have no need of quayside gossip, and certainly not the money to pay for it.'

Domenico looked affronted. 'Quayside gossip? Demetrios my friend, this is more than quayside gossip. And as for the price . . . I am told you have influence in the palace?'

Who told you that, I wondered? 'I sometimes have business at the palace. So do many men. But no more influence than a sailor on one of your boats has over your affairs.'

Domenico looked crestfallen. 'I had heard otherwise. But irrespective,' he persisted, 'you can take word into the palace, and let those in command choose how to reward it.'

'I can take word into the palace. But I would not trust too much on the generosity of my masters.'

'Not even for information regarding a plot to murder the Emperor?'

Domenico slurped at his wine and turned to gaze innocently at the panorama below, though he must have seen my eyes jerk open.

'What of a plot to murder the Emperor?'

'Demetrios, my friend, I am a new arrival in this city, come to establish a business and to earn an honest fortune for my dear father in Pisa. But the life of a merchant is hard here – many men before me have invested themselves with rank and position and privilege, and they do not surrender it easily. You see how I am exiled from the commercial quarters within the city, forced to trade in this remote, unfashionable suburb. How can I forge alliances, Demetrios, when none of those whose ear I seek will venture across the harbour to meet me?'

He took my arms in his hands. 'If my seed is to flourish here, and not wither and die, I must find powerful friends. Men who will unlock the doors which are barred to me, who will ensure that I am not the last to the market with my wares. I need influence, Demetrios.'

'You spoke of a plot to murder the Emperor.'

'If I tell you, will you see that the palace knows of the service I performed? Can I trust that the eparch will look favourably on me if I petition him?' He sounded almost desperate.

'You can trust the palace as much as they may be trusted.'

He wrung his hands together, then sighed. 'Very well, Demetrios. As a sign of my faith, I will tell you what I have to say, and leave it to your conscience to see that I am rewarded as I deserve.'

'None of us are rewarded as we deserve, certainly not in this life. But I will do what I can, if you warrant it.'

That seemed to satisfy him. 'Then know this. A man has approached

me, a monk, though he was no man of God. He offered me an invest-
ment. He told me that, like Christ, he would tear down the temple
of your empire and build it anew. He said the old order would be
swept away, that there would be opportunities for the downtrodden
and meek to claim their inheritance, that those who aided him now
would not be forgotten later – after the Emperor was dead, and his
throne occupied by another.'

Somewhere outside the window a seagull uttered its wheedling cry,
but inside all was silent. I could hardly move for the shock of what
the man had told me, the disbelief that he actually had something to
offer. As for him, his restless energy spent, he watched me closely.

'Can you describe this monk?' I asked at last.

'Sadly not. He wore a hood over his face and would not remove
it. All I saw was his chin: bony, and creased with age.'

'And did he explain how he was to accomplish this regicide?'

'He said he had agents close to the Emperor, against whom he
would be defenceless. All he needed, he said, was gold to make the
final arrangements.'

'Did you give it to him?'

Domenico looked wounded. 'Certainly not, Demetrios. I am a friend
of your people; I know that it is my own countrymen who conspire
to bar me, not yours. My loyalty is unswerving. I told him he would
have nothing of me, and that he should depart in haste if he did not
want me to turn him over to the Watch.'

'He said nothing more?'

'He departed, as I suggested.' Domenico licked his lips. 'Perhaps I
could have pressed him for closer detail, but I was afraid. I know the
Emperor has many ears – even in this corner of his realm – and I
would be mortified if it were thought I had any time for such treachery.'

I thought a moment as my pulse slowed again. Though the information was useful – and though I would probably send word to the
eparch commending the merchant to him – it took me no further. It
confirmed the monk's ambitions, certainly, but those I knew. It
suggested he might have spies in the palace, but that too I had long
suspected. Beyond that, nothing.

'And this would have been about three weeks ago?' I asked, thinking
back. Presumably before the monk found the money elsewhere, and
hired the Bulgars and journeyed into the forest.

But Domenico was shaking his head vigorously. 'Three weeks ago? Indeed not. Do you think I would hide such information for three weeks, when the very life of the Emperor might be in jeopardy? Not for three weeks, no – not even for three days.' He swallowed. 'This was the day before yesterday.'

Through the next week the city grew ever more oppressive, as if the very walls themselves squeezed in on us. Each day the crowds in the streets were thicker, and each night the colonnades along the great roads brimmed with those who could find no shelter. The churches were thrown open, and when they were filled the hippodrome became a vast, open hostel. Prices rose, and food became scarce.

Nor was the weather kind. A bitter wind came down from the north – a Rus wind, as we called it, after the wild men who followed it – and even the wealthiest of citizens covered their finery with heavy cloaks. By night the streets danced with the candle-flames of priests and nuns who worked tirelessly to keep the poor and the homeless from freezing, while the smell of wood smoke lingered on every corner. Never were the bakers more popular.

Through all this, the rumours spread. There was a barbarian army coming, some said; yes, but to offer their lives to the Emperor against the Turks and Saracens, argued others. No, the despondent insisted: they would finish the work that Bohemond the Norman had begun once before, devouring our lands and putting our cities to the sword. And why did the Emperor Alexios not go out to fight, they demanded? There was no hour when the streets did not echo with the tramp of soldiers, when a squadron of cavalry magnificently attired did not thunder past – why did he not use them? Had he betrayed us, or been petrified by a fit of panic? Why could he not show himself to reassure his people?

Many sought my opinion, for they knew I had dealings with the palace, but in truth I knew as little as they. Krysaphios had barely acknowledged my report that another assassination might be imminent, and I had not seen him since I delivered it. Nor Sigurd: Aelric told me that he worked every hour to get the walls into good defence, and had not even returned to the barracks for three days. Aelric stayed with me guarding Thomas, but otherwise I was forgotten, left to spend my days asking unwanted questions of distracted nobles. The fact of the villa in the forest belonging to the Sebastokrator's wife inevitably drew my attentions in his direction, but however many of his servants I discreetly questioned, I could find none who had ever heard of him having dealings with a foreign monk. With reluctance, at least until I could find greater proof, I had to allow that perhaps the monk had used the house unbeknownst to the Sebastokrator.

Every other day Anna came to my house, to examine Thomas's wounds and change his bandages. Her visits were a rare source of pleasure in those nervous days, and on the third occasion I invited her for dinner.

'The moralist Kekaumenos tells us that we should be wary of dining with friends, lest we be suspected of plotting treason and betrayal,' she said, smiling as she tucked away the loose ends of Thomas's dressing.

'The old misanthrope also tells me that you'll mock my servants and seduce my daughters. But I have no servants, and I will trust you with my daughters. If you will trust their cooking.'

She brushed back a loose strand of hair that had fallen from her hood. 'Very well. Tomorrow night?'

I had hoped she could come that same evening, when the Sunday break in the fast would allow me to serve her a finer meal, but I mastered my disappointment and agreed. So, on a cold Monday before the feast of the Nativity, Anna, Thomas, Aelric and my daughters and I sat down for supper together.

'You've made a virtue out of the church's proscriptions,' Anna told the girls, spooning another steaming portion of the meatless stew onto her plate. 'Some day you'll make your husbands fat.'

I rubbed a hand over my temples. It was the wrong thing to say, and Helena took her opening ruthlessly.

'Not if my father has any sway. The spice-seller's aunt wishes to make a bargain for her son, but my father will not even meet her. He would rather I tended him until he was dead and I was shrivelled, than that I should find happiness with another man.'

'You shouldn't cook so well then,' suggested Zoe. 'You should spit in the pots and serve nothing but beans.'

I noticed Aelric and Thomas watching their plates intently, both now taking smaller portions in each mouthful, as if trying to eke out their meals.

'When I have earned enough dowry to find you a man who deserves you, then I will look for him,' I tried. 'You don't want to squander yourself on some unworthy wretch who stinks of garlic.'

'You wouldn't want me to squander myself on a prince in the palace, even if his estates stretched from Arcadia to Trebizond.' Helena's face was red now. 'And how am I to know what a worthy man should be, if the only people I see are the women in the market?'

'A husband is not everything,' said Anna gently. 'I have survived without one.'

'But you chose that it would be so. You did not have a father who would rather see you married, like Persephone, in Hell, than in this life. And you had a noble calling to sustain you – I merely buy vegetables, and prepare them for this table.'

'Very successfully,' offered Aelric.

I turned to Anna, desperate to change the tone of the conversation. 'Talking of your calling, I must congratulate you on the healing you have given Thomas. It seems nearly miraculous. When I found him bleeding to death in that fountain, I thought he would barely survive the afternoon.'

Anna smiled, her skin golden in the candlelight. 'Wounds like his are straightforward, and whether he lived or died was more in God's hands than mine. I simply staunched the bleeding and cleaned away the evil humours which might have grown there. It was as important that you brought him to me so readily. And that you took him into your home afterwards. Few recover in prison air.'

I shrugged, embarrassed. 'I acted from selfish motives. I needed him for my work. But . . . I am glad to have helped him. He needed some kindness.'

'Hah.' Helena had her arms folded, and was glaring at her empty plate.

I frowned. 'You disagree? Perhaps, now that I think on it, locking him up with you for company was less of a kindness than I intended.'

'Hah. He was lucky I was here. He needed attention, and understanding. You could not care what he felt, or how he fared in his soul, so long as he stayed tethered here like a sheep. You were barely here to notice.'

'And you have succoured him like a Samaritan, I assume?'

'Like a baby?' suggested Zoe, giggling.

Helena tossed her head. 'Enough to know that he deserves far more sympathy than you would ever show him.'

I looked angrily at Aelric, uncomfortable with what she implied. 'You were supposed to be here to ensure that nothing untoward happened between my daughters and the boy. How else could I have conscienced leaving him alone in my house with them?'

The Varangian lifted his arms in innocence. 'I watched him every hour of every day, or Sweyn did. Nothing could have happened. Although,' he added, 'my task was to guard against anything that might befall him, not safeguard your children's virtue.'

Helena hissed like a cat. 'My virtue is better defended than any walls that Constantine and Theodosius and Severus together could have built. All I did was talk to the boy. Even that, it seems, displeases my father.'

'Talk?' Now I was quite incredulous. 'Have you also learned Frankish, then? Or did you hire a priest to come and translate for you?'

'If you had ever bothered to try, you would have discovered that the boy can understand Greek far better than you think. And, with some encouragement, speak it.'

For a moment I was silent, agape at this revelation and digging desperately through my memories to think what I might have said in front of the boy; searching for confidences revealed or insults unwittingly given. But Helena was not finished.

'And if you had spoken with him, and heard his story, you might genuinely feel for his plight.'

'And what story is that?'

'Do you really care to hear it?'

'Yes,' I said tersely.

Anna touched Helena's arm. 'And even if your father does not, I certainly do. He was, after all, my patient.'

Helena settled back, triumph written across her young face. 'I don't think I've ever heard anything so miserable. His parents were seduced by some charlatan back in their homeland, and as if under a spell left their fields to travel across the world. Their patriarch had preached that every Christian should fight the Ishmaelites, and this mountebank persuaded them that even unarmed, the hand of God would protect them and scatter their enemies.' She shook her head. 'I have never heard such stupidity.'

'I have. Go on.'

'They passed through our city last August, two weeks before the feast of the Dormition. Our Emperor gave them food, and ferried them to the far shore of the Bosphorus.'

'I saw them,' I interrupted. 'A rabble of peasants and slaves, mostly, with little more than ploughshares and pruning-hooks to fight with. They marched into the Turkish lands in Bithynia, and did not – so far as I know – return. Though I heard rumours that they slaughtered whole villages of our own people in their quest.'

'Thomas did not say that. But his people began to quarrel among themselves. Some went off in search of plunder, while others waited for their leaders to decide what to do. They heard that their vanguard had advanced, even that it had taken Nicaea, and they rejoiced, but then word came that the Turks had slaughtered their expeditions and were camped not ten miles away. Some of the knights rode out to meet them, but they were ambushed and driven back. The Turks followed, and routed their camp in a frenzy of murder. Thomas saw his own parents hacked apart, his sister consumed in the chaos.'

I saw Helena reach under the table and touch Thomas's hand, but I did not rebuke her.

'Thomas, and a few others of their company, retreated to an abandoned castle near the coast. Between the mountains and the sea, he said, there was not one inch of land that was not deep with the dead, but he and his companions managed to improvise a defence – using the bones of their kinsmen for masonry – and withstood the Turkish siege. At last the Emperor heard of their peril, and sent a fleet and rescued them, and brought them back to our city. Not one in ten of the original host survived.'

Some of this I had heard in rumour, and some in gossip, but nothing so terrible, so utterly desolate. And so vividly told: I doubted Helena's words all came from the boy's crude, untutored tongue. I have always noticed the poetry in my daughters.

I looked at Thomas with new compassion, wondering that he had survived such ordeals. He must, as Helena said, have understood much, for his blue eyes were moist with hemmed-in tears, and his hands were tight fists.

'When was this?' asked Anna.

'Two months ago. A month later he arrived in the city and was forgotten. He survived alone for a week on the streets, before a disreputable man found him and promised him gold to join his sordid designs. What choice did he have?'

Aelric reached across the table and touched Thomas's shoulder. 'You were brave. And lucky, though perhaps you think otherwise now. In my homeland, I saw many boys like you.'

'If that's his story, then I think you did well to get him to speak of it,' Anna told Helena. 'For all we smear them with ointments and wrap them in bandages, most wounds need light and air to heal. The wounds of the mind most especially.'

Helena looked pleased.

'But you should respect your father. You never could have helped the boy if Demetrios had not rescued Thomas as he did.'

Now I looked smug. Doubly so, in fact.

From there the meal relaxed, though several times I saw the others watching Thomas with oblique glances. Anna talked of her profession, with Zoe and Helena a keen audience, and Aelric let them prod him for gossip from the palace, the fashions the ladies wore and the tastes of the empress. They were genial company, and the candle was burned low when at last Anna rose and announced she must go.

'I'll walk you to the monastery,' offered Aelric.

'I can manage. The Watch have almost forgotten the curfew these last few nights, since the rumours of the barbarian army spread. The streets are so busy that under a full moon, midnight might be confused for noon.'

'But there's a new moon tonight, and if the Watch aren't looking there'll be more than late guests about.'

'Take Aelric,' I pressed. 'Think what satisfaction the moralists would derive if something happened to you after you ignored their precepts on coming to dinner.'

While Aelric sought out his cloak, I walked Anna down the stairs and helped her wrap her palla over her head. The night was freezing, and in the orb of the lamp I held I could see a few, tentative snowflakes drifting from the sky.

'That will make the plight of the homeless worse,' observed Anna. 'I've already seen a dozen families with chills and frostbite, forced to seek medicine when a warm fire would have saved them.'

'Perhaps it will freeze the barbarian army too, if indeed they exist. Then your patients can go back to their villages.'

Anna was tugging at her cloak. 'Can you adjust this, Demetrios? My brooch has come unclasped.'

I reached forward, my hands clumsy on the frozen metal. I had to lean close to see where I worked, but the honeyed perfume on her neck distracted my senses in dizzying fashion. So much that I could scarcely tell afterwards whether, as I fumbled in the dark, I had indeed felt the warmth of her lips brush against my icy cheek.

'There.' I fastened the clasp and stepped back, as the pounding beat of Aelric's tread heralded his arrival. 'Thank you for your company – and for risking the moralists' reproach. It's rare that I entertain friends.'

'It was a pleasure.' A snowflake landed on the tip of her nose, melted, and slid down onto her lip. She licked it away. 'And a pleasure meeting your family. Strong-willed girls – they do you credit.'

'When they don't abuse and insult me.'

Aelric emerged into the street and looked up at the sky. The snow was falling thicker, now: already a soft layer covered the road like goose down.

'I'll be back in an hour,' he said. 'I'll try not to wake you.'

He took Anna's arm, and I felt a burst of jealousy that she did not snatch it away immediately. I tried to laugh at myself – if I could barely think about finding a husband for my daughter, how could I contemplate my own desires? Helena, certainly, would never forgive me.

I said goodnight, and watched the pair of them disappear into the falling snow.

I awoke early after strange dreams. The house was achingly cold, and I huddled tight under my blankets to try and generate some warmth. Despite Helena's efforts of the night before, there was a hunger in my stomach which only made my limbs seem colder; the last two days of the fast would, as ever, be the hardest.

I raised myself on my elbows and peered over the edge of the bed, to see how Thomas fared on the floor. Anna had scolded me for leaving him there, lecturing that evil vapours lurked near the ground, but Aelric had found a straw mattress and the boy had seemed comfortable enough since then.

He was not there.

I rubbed my eyes and looked again. The blankets were thrown back, and there was a depression where he had slept, but of Thomas there was no sign.

I rose, and brushed past the curtain into the main room. Perhaps he had come to pick over the crusts of the last night's meal.

He had not. Nor was Aelric there – his mattress, though recently used, was empty.

I was growing uneasy, but not yet overly concerned. For the past few mornings Aelric had left early to fetch bread from the baker; I supposed this time he might have taken Thomas with him. I pushed open the shutters on the front window, hoping to see some sign of them in the street.

The shutters did not give easily – the icy night must have frozen their hinges – but as they at last swung open I was dazzled by the crisp light which poured in. The entire street was turned white, drenched in a sea of snow as far as my eyes could reach. Nothing save the wind had stirred it, and from my high vantage it seemed as smooth as the marble floors of the palace. And as cold.

Only a single figure broke its pristine coating, a solitary man almost directly below my window. He wore a monk's habit, but even in the chill of the morning he had pulled back his hood, so that the skin of his tonsure stared up at me. Breath steamed from his lips; he did not move, but seemed to be watching for something.

I stood for a moment as if the air had frozen my very soul. Was this *the* monk, I asked, the man who had contrived to murder the Emperor? Why should he be standing in the bleak dawn outside my house? But then, who else would be standing there? And Thomas was missing.

I shook free my amazement and ran to the girls' room.

'Helena,' I said, 'Zoe. Wake up. The man I seek . . .'

As my eyes adjusted to the gloom after the brightness of the street, my words fell away. One mystery at least had been solved.

'Thomas! What in all Hell's dominions are you doing here?'

He was sitting on the end of their bed, wrapped in a blanket and staring at me with wild, uncomprehending fear.

'Helena! Is this your mischief? Are you mad?' Outrage and urgency wrestled in my mind. 'Never mind; we will talk on this later. A dangerous man – the man I seek – is outside our house, and I cannot let him escape. If Aelric comes and I am gone, tell him to follow if he can. And you,' I said to Thomas, 'get away from my daughters' bed and cloister yourself in my room. I will deal with your wickedness presently. And yours likewise, Helena.'

Battling the confusion that raged within me, I pulled on my boots, grabbed my knife and hurtled down the stairs.

I came into the street and blinked; the monk was gone. Had I imagined him? No; I could see his footsteps in the snow, the trodden circle where he had waited, and two parallel lines where he had come and gone. I followed them with my eye and there, just at the crossroad, I saw a flash of darkness on the snow disappearing around the buildings.

With the chill air rasping in my throat, and my sleeping tunic no protection against the cold, I chased after him. Nothing stirred in the snowbound streets, and the tracks were easy to discern, if not to follow. The snow rose above my ankles, tumbling into my boots and trickling down so that my feet were numb and sodden. Even with the effort of forging a path my legs trembled with the cold, and I wished with a burning fervour that I had seized a cloak, perhaps some leggings, before leaving. But then I might have missed him, for those few minutes' delay with Thomas and Helena had given him a start which I could not close, and for the first half-mile I barely saw him save in fleeting seconds before he turned another corner.

Mercifully, he did not make for the heart of the city, where the marks of others might have obscured his trail, but seemed instead to aim for the walls. Up winding alleys and treacherous stairs I followed him, sliding and stumbling where the driven snow masked hard contours. Forgotten washing, frozen like lead tiles, hung on taut ropes above me; but no-one appeared at the windows to haul them in. It was as if the winter storm had stilled the entire city, all save me and the man I chased.

The silence thawed as I came suddenly onto the Adrianople road. A few bold travellers ventured along it, mostly on horseback, but I had seen the monk turn west and now, with the snow thinner and the way straighter, I could lengthen my strides and close my pursuit. For vital seconds I was unseen and unnoticed, but then the monk cast his eyes back over his shoulder, saw me, and began to run. I tried to increase my pace still further, but there was little purchase to be had on that road and my legs were already stiff with cold. Thankfully the way was wide and straight, so there was no losing the monk, but he remained as far beyond my reach as ever. We careered through the trickle of traffic, kicking up plumes of snow behind us, though there was nothing I could summon to gain on him. But soon we would be at the walls, and then he would be trapped. He must have realised this, for at that moment he veered suddenly right down an alleyway. I flailed my arms to keep my balance as I followed him, but too late – he had vanished. I cursed my luck, and his wiles, but did not succumb to misery, for the snow was thicker again and his tracks were fresh.

And then, it seemed, he flew away, for ahead of me the tracks stopped abruptly in the middle of the road. I came nearer and nearer, looking about for fear that he might have leapt into a doorway to ambush me, but he would have needed a giant's stride to make that leap and there was nothing. Was there another Genoese invention which would carry men into the air?

I reached the end of his trail and understood. He had vanished not into the air, but into the ground: the footmarks finished at a narrow hole, a dark circle in the spotless snow. The iron disc which had covered it lay discarded a little way away, and at its rim I could see the first rung of a ladder leading down. From the bottom, perhaps thirty feet below, the mirror-gleam of black water told me it was a cistern.

A more cautious man might have waited there for help, for men with swords and torches to flush out the monk like a hunted boar. But the blood was flowing quick under my skin, and I did not know how many other tunnels might lead out from the chamber. Barely thinking, I lowered my legs into the hole and slid down the ladder. My palms burned with heat and splinters from the coarse wood, but I did not dare descend more slowly for fear that the monk might lurk at its foot, might drive a blade through me as I came down on him. When I could see the water was near, I pressed my foot against a rung and vaulted out into the darkness. The searing chill of the water clenched around me and I howled; had the monk been there he could have felled me at a stroke, for I was frozen in the icy water. I feared I might never move my limbs again so tight was its grip. My scream echoed around the dark hall, resounding off the domed ceilings and ranks of columns whose dim edges I could see in the pool of light shining through from above. Then there was silence. And then, at once some way off and all around, a frantic splashing.

The monk, I thought, and that sound stirred enough within me to lift my legs and start pushing through the chest-high water. I did not move quickly, but it took only seconds to leave my well of light and pass into utter darkness.

Was this how Jonah felt in the belly of the whale? I struck out blindly and felt a low wave ripple away from my chest, then slap against the surrounding forest of columns. One by one my senses deserted me: first sight; then sound, as the rushing echoes overrode each other in my ears; then, as the water numbed my soul, touch. I scraped against pillars and their pedestals and barely noticed, though the rough stone tore my shrivelled skin. Once my hand brushed something cold and clammy, and I started with a shout, but it was only a fish carried deep under the city by the aqueduct. I wondered if I had any more chance of escape than he.

Too late, I realised the futility of my ambition. I would not find the monk down here. Even with a score of men and fires there would have been endless columns for him to duck behind; alone, and in the dark, it was hopeless. Now my only thought was to escape, to be out of these depths and back in the light. I spun around, feeling the water swirling about my legs, and searched desperately for that beacon of daylight where I had entered.

'Deliverance is of the Lord,' I mumbled through shivering teeth. 'Deliverance is of the Lord. Out of the depths have I called thee, Lord; hear my prayer.'

I thought I could see a smear of pale light somewhere to my left, surprisingly closer than I had expected. Had I stumbled around in a circle?

'Christ have mercy. Christ have mercy. Christ have mercy.'

I repeated my prayers with a ferocity I had not felt since my days as a novice, and with each 'Christ' I forced another step forward. Soon the saviour's name was little more than a whisper, a puff of air hissed through frozen teeth, but still it drove me on. The light was near now, cold and silent and beautiful, and I stumbled towards it with new hope. I could see the rungs of the ladder, shining like steel where the daylight met them; I could see the small circle in the roof where the world awaited. And there, far beneath it, I could see a dark figure hauling himself out of the water. His wet robe clung close about him so that he took the form of an eel or a serpent, the wet fabric gleaming like scales; the limbs which he stretched upwards seemed to be webbed into his body. I gave a faint, gurgling cry, and plunged forward, splashing and flailing to reach him before he escaped.

Even with the bewildering echo he must have heard me come, for I saw his head swivel round, and then his arms jerk up in frantic motion. I flung out a hand and felt it close around his foot; it pulled free of the rung as I fell back, but I did not let go. With a shriek and a howl the monk lost his grip, and there was nothing I could do to move as he came crashing down on me. His falling weight pressed me under and I sank, convulsing as my lungs drew in great gulps of icy water. I tried to stab him with my knife but my hand was empty: in the confusion I must have dropped it and never noticed.

And that was my last hope gone, for my enemy had found his footing now and was holding me under, waiting for the water to drown the life out of me. I did not have the strength to resist, and a few feeble kicks did nothing to dislodge him. I had been a thoughtless fool to think I could trap him in this cavern, and now I would pay the price of pride.

Calm descended. I ceased my struggle, and he must have been almost as drained as I, for he seemed content to hold me there and let nature take its course, without advancing the moment by further violence. I was suspended in the void; the waters closed in over me and the deep surrounded me; I could imagine that the fingers on my throat were nothing more than drifting weed. There are men I have spoken with, often after a battle, who claimed that in the moment of certain death they were transported to some earlier time in their lives, but I felt none of that: only a dull warmth creeping through my veins, a serenity in the knowledge that my struggle was gone, and soon I would be with angels. And Maria, my wife.

But not yet. Suddenly the hands which held me down drifted away. I was rising through the water, and could feel a stinging on the crown of my head where it was exposed to the biting air above. Then it was on my shoulders, my back. My body drifted and my foot touched ground; I pushed up, and gasped as my head broke free. No-one pressed it back. I gagged and choked, coughing gallons of liquid out of my lungs and trying to overcome the wracking pain which had exploded in my head. Somewhere, I thought, I heard someone call my name.

'Demetrios. Demetrios.'

I opened my stinging eyes. It was not Maria, still less the angels. It was – against all hope and reason – Sigurd.

He lifted me out of that cave and slung me over his shoulder, pumping ever more water out of me as his armour rose and fell against my stomach. Dazed and bedraggled, I saw the snow-bound city turned on its head. He carried me tirelessly, never stopping, up stairs and twisting passages, across great roads, down narrow lanes and through stout gates, until I was brought within a room and laid in a bed. I shut my eyes, and the soft voices over me did nothing to spur my consciousness. Instead, I fell into a profound sleep.

I might have slept forever, but it was still light when I woke. My first awareness was that I was warm. Beautifully warm, beatifically warm, warm like a saint in God's eternal gaze. A warm mattress was underneath me, warm blankets wrapped around me, and from somewhere behind the walls a bell was ringing.

I rolled over, opening my eyes further. I recognised this room, with its whitewashed walls and small windows: it was the hospital at the monastery of Saint Andrew, and by a chest a little distance away stood Anna.

She was not warm, not even remotely; she was entirely naked. She was brushing her hair, and the motion of the arm behind her head lifted her bare breasts like some antique statue. Her small nipples were puckered tight and hard, while by her hips the olive skin of her stomach rose gently as she breathed. Such was her lack of modesty that she did not even try to hide the dark shadow between her thighs.

For a moment I stared like some virgin on his wedding night; then, overcome with guilt, I belatedly pressed my blushing face into the pillow.

Anna laughed; a soft, forgiving laugh.

'Come, Demetrios,' she mocked me. 'You were married, and raised two daughters to womanhood. Surely you must have uncovered these mysteries before. Am I so shameful?'

'Shameless, I think.' My humour returned a little, and I risked looking back. I was just in time to see her arms wriggling through the sleeves of a woollen camisia, which tumbled down over her body to mask its temptations. I felt an ache of regret that I had not looked longer, but dismissed the thought at once.

'Do you always undress before strange men in the middle of the day?' I watched her pull on her green dress and fasten the silken cord around it.

'Only when they appear at my door half-frozen and close to death. I had to force some heat into you, so I lay beside you in the bed until you stopped shivering. You served in the legions – surely when you campaigned in the mountains you huddled together with your comrades at night?'

'If we did, we kept our clothes on.' I had endured much that day; it seemed almost too much to believe that I had risked mortal sin lying with Anna and not felt a moment of it.

Again I drove back my thoughts from the places they strayed. 'And how did I come to be here?'

'Sigurd brought you. He said he found you almost drowned in a cistern.'

'Is he here now?' Had he watched while Anna undressed and shared my bed?

'He had important things to do. He said he would return, and try to bring some fresh clothes.'

Only now did I realise that under the blankets, I too was wholly naked. I pulled the covers closer.

Anna tied the scarf over her head and crossed to the door. 'I must go. I have other patients to see. I will send an apprentice with some soup, and try to visit soon.'

'Will you share beds with all your wards?' I raised myself on one elbow.

The door closed without answer.

Not long afterwards, Sigurd came. His face was flushed despite the cold, but he waited while I dressed with the tunic, leggings, boots and cloak he had brought. He must have gone to my house, or sent someone there, for they were my own. Which was as well, for his tunic would have reached almost to my feet.

'That's the second time I've saved you from a battle you were foolish to enter,' he said pointedly. 'There may not be a third.'

'I know.' I was honest in my gratitude. 'But how did you find me? And what of the monk?'

'Your elder daughter found me with Aelric. I met him in the street; he had left his station to go and buy food.' I did not envy Aelric explaining that to his captain. 'We followed your tracks through the snow as far as the Adrianople road, where there were plenty of witnesses who could remember a bare-headed monk and a half-dressed madman chasing him. From there we searched the side-streets until we found you.'

'And the monk?'

'We saw him trying to drown you at the bottom of that hole, but as I came down the ladder he fled. I let him go; only a fool would follow a man into that abyss. My men are guarding the entrance. If he comes out, we'll catch him.' He looked theatrically at the sky, though the sun was veiled in cloud. 'If he's still down there, he'll already be dead.'

'We should go and see.' I stood, feeling the trembling in my legs as they took my weight. I was weak, but the food which Anna had sent gave me strength, and the hunger to see the monk who had almost killed me was all consuming.

'Will the doctor let you go?' Sigurd asked with a smile. 'She protects her patients like a tiger, you know.'

That was only half true. Some she protected like a tiger; me she waved away with a dismissive snort.

'If you choose to risk your health and your strength running around the city, trying to do the monk's work for him, then do so,' she said briskly. 'I need your bed for the more deserving anyway.'

Sigurd and I walked out of the monastery. It was late afternoon, and the road was almost solid with the humanity herded onto it. The snow, so pristine that morning, was now ground to a grey slush and mixed with grit and mud. It was well that the ground stayed frozen, or many might have sunk into an inescapable mire.

'I must go to the walls first,' said Sigurd. He had seemed cheerful at my bedside, but now his mood was grim. 'I need to check on the garrison. The monk will wait an extra half hour – whether he's under, on or in the ground.'

I did not argue, but pushed my way after him through the tide of men and beasts which flowed against us. It was straining work, and if I had not had Sigurd's commanding bulk to follow I doubt I would have progressed a step. There was an intensity in the crowd now which I had not noticed previously: a hunch to their shoulders and a desperation in their gaunt faces. Perhaps it was the burden of snow and cold added to their already straitened condition, or perhaps they knew that the city was ill able to provide for them after the many others who had preceded them.

Sigurd had anticipated an extra half an hour, but it was almost an hour later, near dusk, when we at last reached the walls. Along them the Watch had kept a corridor free for messengers and heralds to gallop through, and I was glad of the space to breathe as we came into it.

'My men are up that tower,' Sigurd told me. 'Will you wait?'

A squadron of cavalry thundered past, drowning my reply and spraying me with mud. Above me, a ballista was being winched up a tower on a scaffold, straining at the thick ropes which held it.

'I'll come up.' I did not want to end that day crushed under a horse or a falling siege weapon.

As ever, Sigurd was recognised, and we were waved up by the guard at the foot of the stairs. It was not an arduous climb, but my head ached again and my legs begged for rest. About me, I could see sentries scurrying about, shouting and calling, though I could not hear what they said.

We came onto the broad rampart and my interest rose. A hush had fallen, and the guards were still, their faces pressed against the embrasures as if watching for a miracle. Sigurd ignored them and continued up the steps to the turret, but – drawn to the spectacle – I crossed to the battlements and stared.

Out across the snow-swept fields the sun had sunk beneath the rim of the clouds, facing us like a glowing eye. The sky and land alike were caught in its crimson glare, shimmering red, but that was not what had silenced the watchmen. On the ridge across the plain, some two miles distant, an army had appeared. They rode towards us with the sun behind them, their spears like pricks of flame and their banners dark above them. They were moving forward, but as one row passed into the shadows below the ridge another came up on their heels and took its place. It was a host of thousands – tens of thousands – and the snow turned black underfoot as they marched towards our gate.

The barbarians had come.

'This changes everything.' I had waited three days for an audience with Krysaphios, and now that I had it I was giving full vent to my feelings. 'Can you believe it is merely chance that not three weeks after the Emperor was almost murdered, an army of barbarians arrives at our walls?'

Krysaphios stroked his beardless chin. 'This changes nothing,' he said calmly. 'Except to raise the penalties should you fail.'

'The man who directed the assassin was a monk who prayed according to the western rites, and used a barbarian weapon unknown to our people. Now ten thousand of his kinsmen, armed for war, are camped just across the Golden Horn. Can it be happenstance?'

'You disappoint me, Demetrios. You had a reputation for insight, for seeing the hidden truths which other men did not. Not for pouncing on chance.'

'I may see deeper than other men, but if I find a man standing over a corpse, with a knife dripping blood and a stolen purse in his hand, I do not presume that there must be a more subtle explanation and let him go.'

'This time you should.' Krysaphios clapped his hands together. 'The barbarian army had barely crossed our frontier three weeks ago. Even if the attempt on the Emperor's life had succeeded, they would have profited nothing from it. And besides, they are come to aid us, to drive the Turks and Saracens from our lands in Asia and restore them to their rightful owners. For all the mob may fear them, they are our allies, our welcome guests.' He did not try to hide the scepticism which underpinned his words. 'It is on that understanding that the Emperor tolerates them, that he gives them food for their bellies and straw for their horses.'

'Nonetheless,' I pressed, 'I would like to see these men. Even if it is a foolish fancy, you know that I prefer to be thorough.'

'As thorough as you were in the cistern?'

Krysaphios mocked me. Aelric and his companions had spent a day and a night standing watch over the cistern's entrance, but no-one had emerged. They had concluded that the monk must be dead, but I had insisted on finding a body, and had led many men down there with nets and torches to scour it. We found nothing except fish: the monk, it seemed, had dissolved into the water like powder. Or more likely, as the hydrarch suggested, crawled out through one of the pipes which fed it.

'As thorough as I was in the cistern.' I had not been deterred by the complaining doubts of the Varangians, and I would not defer to the eunuch's scorn. 'My instincts are sound, Krysaphios, if not always true. I need a pass into the barbarian camp, and perhaps an introduction to their captains.'

Krysaphios' eyes dipped in thought.

'After all,' I added, 'even if – as you presume – the man who would kill the Emperor rests within our city, it cannot have escaped his notice that a foreign army will give him great scope for mischief.'

Krysaphios looked up. 'I fear you are too easily tempted by digressions, Demetrios, and succumb to fancy.'

'My fancies have served well enough.'

'That is why I will give you the opportunity you seek. The Emperor will send an envoy to the barbarian captains tomorrow, and you may accompany him. If, of course, you can stand their stink. Report to me in the new palace by the walls when you return.'

The path out of that courtyard had grown familiar in the past weeks, and my face was now known well enough that the sentries did not challenge me. Winter had at last entered the palace; the gaiety and laughter which I remembered from my first visit were replaced with grim intent, and the gilded walls seemed dulled.

'Demetrios.'

One man at least could muster some warmth: Sigurd, striding toward me along the arcade. The hollows of his eyes were dark, all the more so against the pale skin, but his greeting was hearty enough.

'I thought you were at the walls.'

'I was. But the Franks are keeping quiet enough in their camp, and without siege engines or boats there's little they can do to trouble us.'

'Surely there should be nothing they would do to trouble us in any event. Krysaphios tells me they are here as our allies.'

Sigurd eyed me as a teacher with a peculiarly obtuse student. 'When ten thousand foreign mercenaries are camped before the city walls, you do not trust to kind words and noble intentions. Particularly if they are as duplicitous and greedy as the Franks. The Emperor will not believe they are his allies until they have defeated his enemies and returned to their own kingdoms. Until then, he will treat them like a tame leopard – with good will, and great caution. Otherwise, he may find one day that they have bitten off his hand and more besides.' He scratched his beard. 'But I cannot waste time educating your credulous ignorance, Demetrios, for I must get my company ready to call on the Franks tomorrow. We will be escorting the Emperor's ambassador, the estimable Count of Vermandois.'

'The Count of where?'

'Vermandois.'

'I know that the Emperor's lands stretch far across the world, but that does not sound like a Roman place.'

'No.' Sigurd grinned. 'It's in the kingdom of the Franks, not so far from my own country. The Count is the brother of their king, apparently.'

'And he's the man the Emperor chooses as his emissary to the barbarians?'

'He has been here some weeks as the Emperor's honoured guest. An unfortunate shipwreck deprived him of a grander entrance. His time here has convinced him to swear loyalty to the Emperor, for here at last he has found a man who respects his position with all the riches and women he deserves.'

'He's been bought.'

Sigurd fixed me with a warning stare. 'He has, Demetrios, he has. As have you.'

I had, but my price was a sorry trifle against what the Count of Vermandois – Hugh the Great, as he styled himself – must have commanded. He appeared before us the next morning an hour late, clothed in a robe whose very fibres seemed spun from pearls and emeralds. His skin was pale and smooth, like silk beneath his golden hair: doubtless he meant to look magnificent, almost angelic, but his eyes were too cold, too petulant for that. Nor did his beard flatter him, for it seemed a recent creation: a thin, uneven affair which would not have looked amiss on an adolescent.

He did not speak to us, but mounted his horse in a haughty silence at the head of our column. There must have been fifty Varangians in a double file, headed by Sigurd looking magnificent in his burnished mail and helm. The guards' customary axes were in slings by their sides, and they carried instead fine lances, tipped with pennants which rippled in the breeze. At their rear, Father Gregorias and I – dressed in a monk's mantle – were a less than fitting tail for the glorious cohort.

We kicked our horses into a trot and rode out of the palace, out through the Augusteion and down the broad Mesi. Our pomp drew crowds, convinced that this must herald an appearance by the Emperor, though when they saw that it was no Roman who led our column but in fact a barbarian, their shouts became jeers, and they turned their backs on us. No longer did they recede out of our way, and our lines became ragged, uneven, as each man drove his own path through them. I had worn my hood, for anonymity as much as warmth, but now I tipped it back so those around me could see I was of their race. It seemed to ease my way a little.

At the Gate of Lakes we halted, in the shadow of the new palace where, according to rumour, the Emperor Alexios preferred to keep his private quarters. Sigurd bellowed a challenge, and a fanfare of horns rang out from the tower as the gates swung open. It was a grand spectacle, though whom it impressed besides the Count I do not know.

We passed under the arch and out of the city, keeping close to the placid waters of the Golden Horn. It was almost two miles to the village where the barbarians were billeted, but in all that distance we saw hardly a soul. No-one worked the fields or shared our path; not so much as a single hen pecked at the roadside, and no smoke rose from within the dwellings we passed. I remembered Aelric's talk of the desolation wrought upon his country by the Normans, and shivered to think that it might happen here.

Soon, though, there were many signs of life ahead: the smoke of a hundred fires, though it was only midday, and the smells that men and horses bring wherever they settle. I could see a cordon of mounted soldiers stretched out across the landscape, spaced like the towers which crowned the city walls. As we came near, one of them challenged us.

'Who travels this road?'

'The Count Hugh the Great,' answered Sigurd. 'And his escort. Here on an embassy from the Emperor. Much good may it do us,' he added under his breath.

'You'll need patience,' observed the sentry. We were close enough now that I could see he was a Patzinak with a scarred face and narrow eyes, from another of the Emperor's mercenary legions. From the time I had spent talking with Sigurd and Aelric, I knew even the Varangians bore them a grudging respect.

'Have the Franks hired you as their guardians?' asked Sigurd. 'You should be protecting the Emperor, not these whoresons.'

'We protect them from themselves,' the Patzinak said with a tooth-less grin. 'They come in the name of the cross, they say, so we keep their souls free from the cares of the world beyond. Like the walls of a monastery.'

'Or a prison.'

'Or a prison.' The Patzinak pulled his horse aside, and waved us past. 'Strange enough, we had a scuffle with some of them last night. They said much the same.'

We rode on, into the makeshift town which had descended onto our plain like the new Jerusalem. They had been here only four days, but already the earth was ground to mud by the passage of a thou-sand feet, and the trees had been felled for kindling. Blacksmiths had constructed rudimentary forges under canvas awnings, and sparks flew through the blue smoke as they worked against the ceaseless demands of arms and horses. Peddlers of a dozen races proclaimed their strange and multifarious wares, while on every corner of this tented city women shouted offers which, in any tongue, were readily understood. Many of them, I saw, were our own people, who clearly had bribed or crept their way through the Patzinak cordon.

At length we came to what had once been the village square, now covered with a vast tent. The knights who stood grouped before it seemed larger, stronger than the haggard creatures we had seen before, and there was a stiffness in the way they held themselves. On a crude post behind them, beside the pavilion door, was draped a banner emblazoned with a blood-red cross and a slogan in barbarian characters: 'Deus le volt.'

'Thus God wills it,' whispered Father Gregorias in my ear.

'Does He?'

The Count Hugh dismounted, grimacing as his fur boot settled in the mire. Sigurd and the nearest Varangians followed.

'Halt.'

A guard by the door angled his spear across the Count's path and spoke brusquely. The Count responded with anger, though to little effect.

'He says none are allowed in his lord's chamber bearing arms,' explained Gregorias. 'The Count replies that it demeans his honour to be denied his vassals.'

Honour or no, he at last agreed that the Varangians would wait outside while he conducted his audience with the barbarians. Gregorias and I pushed forward.

'My secretaries,' said the Count curtly. 'So that none may falsely represent what is said.'

The guard eyed us as warily as he had the axe-wielding Varangians, but allowed us to pass into the gloom of the tent. It took some moments for my eyes to adapt, for the only light within came from a three-branched candlestick on a wooden chest, and the dimly glowing coals of an iron brazier. Behind the pole which supported the coned ceiling there was a splintered table, where two barbarians sat on stools arguing; otherwise, the room was empty. The Count strode into the open space in its midst, the only place where he did not have to stoop, while Gregorias and I perched ourselves on a low bench by the door.

Everything that followed they said in Frankish, but by peering at Gregorias' quick scribbling, and with the odd whispered explanation where his hand lagged their mouths too far, I managed a fair understanding of what passed.

In the time-hallowed manner of ambassadors, the Count began by announcing himself. 'I am Hugh le Maisné, second son of Henry, King of the Franks; Count of Vermandois . . .'

'We know who you are.' The interruption was as unexpected as it was abrupt, and came from the man at the right of the table, a tall man with unkempt dark hair and a skin so pale it was almost luminous. It seemed that long use had set his features in a perpetual sneer.

'And we welcome you, Count Hugh.' The other barbarian spoke

with calm diplomacy, in stark contrast to his companion. His hair was fair, though darker and longer than the Count's, and the months of travel had given him a weathered complexion which suited him well. He wore a handsome robe of russet cloth, and leaned forward earnestly over the table. 'We had hoped to find you safe arrived here.'

'Mincing like a Greek, and dressed like one of their girl-men. Have they made you their whore, Hugh, or clad you with so many gilded lies that you forgot your true countrymen?'

'Peace, brother,' the fair-haired man rebuked him. But the Count's delicate skin was crimson, and his chin quivered.

'The great Emperor Alexios grants these gifts in honour of my position,' he squealed. 'And I wear them of courtesy to him. Have a care, Baldwin no-lands: a single thread of this cloth would buy more than your miserable position could ever afford, yet it is but the least of the magnificence which the Emperor has given me.' He turned his eye to the other end of the table. 'To you though, Duke Godfrey, the Emperor will be likewise gracious. There is treasure in his palace the like of which has never been seen in Christendom, and he is eager to bestow it on men of good faith, those who follow the path of Christ.'

The dark-haired Baldwin made to speak again, but his brother stilled him and spoke first. 'I have not come here seeking favours, Count Hugh, and the true pilgrim needs little baggage on the holy road. Even where the path is most perilous, a sword and a shield and fodder for my mount will suffice me.' He gestured about. 'You see my quarters – a bare floor and a place to conduct my business. I need no praise or trinkets from the Greek king, only a safe passage for my men across the straits. If he grants that, I will be gone within the week. I do not wish to dally here.'

The Count shifted on his feet. 'The Emperor applauds your noble purpose, Duke Godfrey, for your pure heart is well renowned, even in these distant kingdoms. He will happily do all he can to advance your eternal victory over the Saracens. All he asks is your oath that whichever lands you take that once were his, you will restore to him as is his right.'

Baldwin's fist slammed down on the table, scattering the papers laid over it. 'He asks what? That we should lay down our lives so his miserable nation of Greeklings can spread their bastard offspring back into lands they were too weak to defend. We fight for God, Count, not for the glory of tyrants. Any lands we win in battle will be our own, earned with our swords and bought with our blood. If your master desires them, he can come and claim them himself. In combat.'

Duke Godfrey frowned. 'My brother speaks harshly,' he told Hugh, 'but there is truth in what he says. I came to serve Christ, not men, and I have already sworn my oath to the Emperor Henry. I cannot serve two masters.'

'Do not mention the Emperor Henry to the Emperor Alexios,' cautioned Hugh. 'It does not please him.'

'If Alexios gives me the boats to cross the straits, we need never meet. I have no need for the flattery of kings.'

'And do not call him a king. He commands the reverence due his office, unbroken since the days of the first Caesars.'

Baldwin stood suddenly. He walked around in front of the table, lifted the hem of his tunic, and sprayed a stream of piss onto the floor by Hugh's feet. The Count leapt back in horror, holding his precious skirts like a girl.

'I will show the reverence due his office,' Baldwin snarled. 'He cannot beg our aid and then treat us as villains. Tell him that he *will* let us pass, or he may find he no longer has a kingdom left to rule.'

'If you ever had any title of your own, Baldwin Duke of nowhere, you might have the least idea what it is to rule.'

'Better no land at all than to fuck it out of a Norse princess like you, Count.'

'Enough!' Duke Godfrey raised himself to his feet. He too was a tall man, though lesser than his brother. 'There should be no quarrel between us here. You have come as the king's ambassador, Count Hugh, so tell me plainly: how soon can we make the crossing of the straits?'

Hugh pushed out his chest like a songbird. 'As soon as you have sworn the oath he demands, to restore his rightful lands.'

'You know I cannot.'

'Please, Duke Godfrey, you must. Or at least come to the palace with me. My lord Alexios invites you to celebrate the feast of Saint Basil with him, to savour his hospitality. He is a reasonable and generous man; I am sure an hour in his company would convince you of the value of an alliance.'

Godfrey shook his head wearily. 'I do not think that would be helpful.'

'And who is to say that if we enter his city we will come out again?' Baldwin demanded. 'I have heard that the brother of the king of the Franks went in a free man and came out a slave, bound in golden chains and with his balls cut off. What will the king of the Greeks do with us, once we are inside his fortress? I would sooner walk unarmed into the court of the Saracen caliph, for at least he would stab at me in the chest.'

'I think what my brother means,' said Godfrey uneasily, 'is that he cannot understand why you would have us parley with this foreign king. He has already shown himself no friend to our people by his treatment of the hermit Peter and his humble army who came before. Now he tries to exact oaths and obligations from us simply to continue our journey? I trust neither him nor his offers. Tell him this: "Worship the Lord your God, and him only serve."'

'And tell him also that we are but the vanguard of a greater army, and that soon our ten thousand will be a hundred thousand. We will see if he still dares defy us when they are come.' Baldwin sat back down at the table, and began to pick grime from his fingernails.

'I will wait here until he gives me leave to pass,' said Godfrey. 'But I will not render myself a hostage in his city. You would do well to consider your own situation.'

'I will return to the Emperor,' said Hugh, furious. 'And remain his honoured guest. Think of that when the rains come, and the water rises under your humble bed of straw; when your sword and armour rust and the fever infests your limbs. Then you will regret this show of pride. But the Emperor is a merciful man: when you decide to show him the honour he is due, he will greet you like a lost son. Until then, you can rot here.'

143

I had hoped to have an hour or two to probe around that camp with Father Gregorias, to see if I could glean any sign of the monk having been there, but that was clearly impossible. Duke Godfrey might have managed a bare civility, but his brother Baldwin's crude spite was closer to the mood in the faces which surrounded us when we emerged. As we remounted, I saw that Count Hugh no longer took his place at the head of the procession, but dropped back so that he was in the midst of the Varangians. Gregorias and I had no such fortune: we were at the rear again, and had to endure a strained half hour in the fear that we might be dragged from our horses and butchered, or find an arrow between our shoulders, before at last we came through the Patzinak cordon.

At the Gate of Lakes we halted again, this time for Hugh to leave our column and pass through another gate into the first courtyard of the new palace. Remembering Krysaphios' instructions to report to him there, I followed.

Against the decadent sprawl of the old palace, expanded out over many centuries, the new palace was a compact building whose growth was purely, dizzyingly vertical. It was built on a hill, with a commanding view over the Golden Horn to the north and the line of the ramparts to the south. Much of the brickwork was as yet unplastered, but there was none of the chaos of construction that I had seen at Domenico's house.

A boy came and took our horses, while a guard led us up a steep stair to a high terrace, where two sets of bronze doors brought us into a high-vaulted room. There was neither ornament nor decoration on the walls, and the marble floors were of the simple, modern style. But the view at the end was breathtaking, a row of full-length, arched windows looking out to the dark sprawl of the barbarian camp. The room must be built atop the great walls themselves, I thought, on the outermost line of our defences. It would take a confident man to stand by those windows, and I noticed that neither of those present chose to risk it.

'Count Hugh. What success?' It was Krysaphios, interrupted in his conversation with the Sebastokrator Isaak.

'None.' Hugh crossed to a finely wrought chair, inlaid with gold, and slumped into it. 'They are impossible, my countrymen, full of false pride and toothless threats. They have no love of nobility, no respect for their betters. I cannot talk to them.'

'Threats?' Isaak looked at him keenly. 'What threats?'

'None that would trouble a man of your power. They say they want only boats to cross the straits, and then they will depart. But they will not swear the oath the Emperor demands.'

'With boats they could attack the sea walls, divert our strength.' Isaak paced the room in agitation. 'What exactly did they threaten?'

Hugh wiped an ornate sleeve across his brow. It came away smeared with grime. 'They said they were merely the vanguard of a greater army – this is as I told you it would be – and that the Emperor could not defy them when all their host was assembled. They said . . . I cannot recall what precisely. Your secretaries recorded it all, I think.'

Isaak and Krysaphios looked at me.

'Well, my spying secretary, what did you discover?' the eunuch asked.

'Little enough,' I admitted. 'They were rarely minded to give answers. There were two of them, Duke Godfrey and his brother Baldwin. Godfrey, I think, is an honest man, though stubborn: he will not be swayed from his path. Baldwin is more dangerous. He has nothing to lose and a fortune to gain, and he burns with pride and envy. I think he means to find a kingdom for himself, and from where he does not care.'

'And do you think he would go so far as to murder the Emperor to get it?' Krysaphios' voice was sharp. 'Is he in league with the monk?'

I pondered this. 'I think not. He did not seem a subtle man.'

'So a subtle man would have you believe.'

'He said also that they were here at the Emperor's invitation. Is that true?'

'Hah.' Isaak stopped his pacing and looked at me. 'Two years ago we sent emissaries to their church to request a company of mercenaries.

145

We did not ask for an army in its ten-thousands, commanded by our ancient enemies and bent on their own ends. They have used our need as a pretext, Demetrios, for it is well known they wish to overthrow our power and install themselves as masters of the east.'

'I must protest, My Lord,' said Hugh. 'I cannot speak for all my countrymen, but certainly for most. We came from noble motives, to free the Holy Land and the great city Jerusalem from the yoke of the Turk, so that all Christians would be free to follow in the steps of our Lord Jesus Christ. Do not let the ambitions of a base few obscure the virtue of the many.'

'An army bent on liberating Jerusalem avails little when the Sultan holds court in Nicaea,' Isaak observed. 'And even less camped outside the walls of Constantinople. If they truly desire to pray by the Holy Sepulchre, then they should swear the oath and be on their way, not bandy threats against the Emperor.

Hugh wrung his hands together. 'I know that, Lord Isaak. You know that had my army not perished in storm and shipwreck, I would even now be in Jerusalem. But these men are unreasonable, and they suspect the wiles of the Greeks. They will twist sinister meanings even out of your generosity, which I know well to be true Christian charity.'

'If they will not accept our gifts, then they can do without them until they find their senses,' said Krysaphios. 'Send orders to the Eparch that their grain supply is to be reduced. We will see how long they endure empty bellies and the winter rains. And prepare to have them moved across the Horn to Galata. They will be further from mischief, there, and easier to contain.'

'And what of my responsibility?' I began tentatively. 'How do you wish me to proceed?'

Krysaphios glared at me. 'As you see fit, Demetrios, as you see fit. Whether the barbarian captain would overthrow us or not, I do not doubt that he would seize upon any disruption to work as much evil as he could. So whoever wants the Emperor dead, you had best find him quickly. Now go.'

I returned home in haste, for it was less than a week after midwinter and the days were still short. I could no longer afford to flout the curfew, having lost my Varangian escort when I sent Thomas back to Anna's monastery, to learn our tongue and our customs, and to keep him away from my daughters. Helena, in particular, had not forgiven me for it, nor for the scolding she had received for her immoderate conduct that morning when I found Thomas in her room. She had persuaded me that nothing more reprehensible than talk had passed between them, and Zoe, unusually, had supported her story, but it had done little to placate me. Nor deterred me from sending the boy away.

It still rankled with Helena. 'After he was kidnapped and enslaved by that wicked monk, how could you lock him away in a monastery? He'll go mad.'

'I doubt the monks of Saint Andrew's will force a bow into his hands and make him shoot it at the Emperor. And why is there no meat in this stew? The fast ended three days ago.'

'The fast will continue until the barbarian armies go. At least, that is the rumour. Few drive their beasts to market for fear that they will be seized by a mob of Franks and Kelts, while the animals which do come are bought by the imperial commissary and taken to feed our enemies. So we go hungry.'

'"If your enemy hungers, give him bread to eat; if he thirsts, then water to drink, for you will heap up coals of fire on his head and the Lord will reward you,"' I told her. 'I met the King of the Franks' brother today.'

'Was he fat?'

'He was wearing an enormous, ill-fitting robe. It was hard to tell. Nor did he have coals on his head.'

'Did he say when they would be leaving?' asked Zoe quietly. She was at an age when the slightest change in her mood could make her seem almost a woman, or scarcely a child. Now she just looked afraid.

'The decision is not his to make. They need permission from the Emperor.'

'Then he should give it to them and let them go.' Her voice was rising, the words tumbling out, and she was twisting her hair round her finger as she had not done for many years.

I tried to speak gently. 'Why? Are you hungry, Zoe? The Emperor cannot simply let a horde of barbarians pass through his empire. He must ensure that they are kept from causing injury.'

'Well he should send them away. The streets are filled with strangers, and there's no food, and soon it will be the feast of Saint Basil and we won't be able to celebrate it properly, and all the time there are a thousand Franks at our gates armed for war. I hate it. I want the barbarians to go, and the city to be normal again.'

'So do I.' I put my arm around her shoulder and drew her in to my chest. 'Doubtless the Emperor will order it that they are gone as soon as is possible.'

He did not. Through a long, wet January the barbarians stayed camped by the head of the Golden Horn, while I searched with ever-mounting frustration for any sign of the monk, whether he even lived or not, and if so whether he was in consort with the Frankish army. I found nothing. After a fortnight I began to doubt myself, to wonder whether he had indeed perished in that freezing cistern. I would have trawled it again, but I no longer commanded any urgency in the palace: with every fruitless day which passed, my meetings with Krysaphios became less frequent, the hours I waited in crowded corridors ever longer.

January passed: the day of the Heirarch Basil, then the Epiphany, and even the feast of Gregory the Theologian, and still – so far as I could see – the barbarians would not demur. Every day brought new rumours: of other great armies at Thessalonika, Heraklea or even Selymbria; of villages raided or livestock stolen; of barbarians stealing through windows in the night. As my business still took me, occasionally, into the palace, I perhaps heard more tales than most, though the gossip in the gilded halls seemed no more reliable than that in the market. And still we went hungry, still the streets teemed with those who had sought refuge, still it seemed that the barbarians were as much our besiegers as our allies.

One evening, a few days before the onset of February, a messenger came to my house, dressed in the livery of the palace.

'I am come from my master, the Emperor,' he announced. Water dripped from the hem of his cloak onto my floor.

'Indeed?' I had expected this moment for some days now, the news that my services were no longer required. I could not say I would have done otherwise in his position.

'The barbarian captains have agreed to send ambassadors to meet with the Emperor and discuss his demands; the Emperor fears that the monk may try to slip into the palace disguised among their retinue. As you are the only Roman who has seen the man and lived to tell of it, he asks that you attend.'

It was comforting to know that the monk still lived in the thoughts of the palace at all. 'I will be there,' I said. It would not do to have the Emperor cut down before the barbarian envoys, and it would be interesting to hear what they had to say, after the defiance I had witnessed in their camp. At the very least, it promised to be a spectacle.

Cymbals clashed, and a thousand guardsmen stamped their feet as one. A lone trumpet sounded its mournful note and the choir began again, their voices rising a half-tone with each repetition. The light of countless candles glittered off the ranks of axes, the scaled armour, the gold and silver of the courtiers' robes and the emeralds, sapphires, rubies and amethysts that bedecked them, a mosaic of coloured light.

The imperial acclamation resounded through the hall.

> Behold the morning star approaches,
> The daystar comes.
> His eyes a mirror to the sun,
> Alexios, our prince,
> Doom of the Saracen.

A dozen priests stood at the front of the room, swirls of incense rising from the censers which swung in their hands. They chanted their own contrapuntal hymn, matching the rhythm to perfection so that the tunes flowed together like water. An Egyptian pounded on a pair of goatskin drums, rising to a climax at the end of each verse until, with a single breath, every man in the room bellowed out: 'Hail!'

'You'd think with all that cheering the Emperor would show some gratitude,' said Aelric, next to me.

We were in a gallery above the main hall, peering down from behind a curtained arch. Below us, on a throne mounted on a marble pedestal, the Emperor himself sat like a statue. A resplendently jewelled lorum covered his chest and shoulders, overlaying a dalmatica of shimmering purple silk: only as it caught the light could you see the subtlety of the patterns which curved through it. The constellated pearls and gems of the imperial diadem covered his head, and a pair of bronze lions lay like sentinels at his feet. To his right, on a lower dais, sat the Sebastokrator Isaak, regaled in finery which eclipsed all but his brother's, while on his left stood the eunuch Krysaphios. Beyond them a galaxy of lesser nobles and bishops vied among themselves for the opulence of their dress.

The choirs of priests fell silent, leaving only the drummer striking his staccato beat. It rose through the silence like thunder, sounding from the walls and columns; it seemed to fade from beneath us, yet the echo at the far end of the room grew ever louder, until I realised it had become a pounding on the golden door which faced me.

Krysaphios lifted a hand and the doors flew apart, thrown open by the hands of a half-dressed giant who lumbered in like some latter-day Polyphemos. He stood at least a head taller than Sigurd, and his skin gleamed with oil; he led an octet of eunuchs bearing silver biers on their shoulders. Seated atop them, seeming at once in awe and discomforted, were two barbarians. Their garments were dull and drab, with neither the artistry nor the ornament of our people; they seemed, if it were possible, to suck the radiance from the air they inhabited. Neither of them were men I recognised.

The eunuchs set them down on the floor before the Emperor, bowed low and left. They seemed unsure whether to stand or sit: one made to stand, but even as he did so the pair of bronze lions by the Emperor's feet sprang into life. Their jaws rose up and down; their manes flared, and their tails thudded against the floor. The barbarians watched open mouthed, as if afraid they would be devoured by these mechanical toys.

'Welcome to the court of the prince of peace,' Krysaphios intoned. 'He bids you offer your petition.'

With a hesitant glance at the nearer lion, which had lapsed into stillness, one of the Franks stood and gave a curt bow. The crowd stirred, and I guessed this was not the protocol, but he remained standing and uttered a short speech in his own language.

'I am Geoffrey of Esch, companion of Godfrey, Duke of Lorraine.' Perhaps it sounded magnificent in his tongue, but the monotone of the interpreter robbed it of any grandeur. 'It is by Duke Godfrey's command that I speak here, O morning star, most noble Emperor.'

'The interpreter's obviously been instructed to avoid trouble,' murmured Aelric. 'I doubt his true words were half so humble.'

He spoke in a slightly hollow, detached manner, far removed from his usual good spirits. His knuckles were white where he gripped the balustrade, and he seemed to sway slightly, as if he would fall without a handhold. Perhaps he feared for the Emperor's safety – I certainly did. A pack of barbarians had spilled into the chamber behind their leaders, standing sullenly by the doors, and I scanned them anxiously for any sign of the monk. With the smoke of candles and incense making my eyes water, and a bright light pouring through the doors, it was hard to see anything of them at all.

The barbarian spoke again, though not one thread of the Emperor's robes moved in response.

'Prince of peace, we have journeyed many miles, and through many dangers, to come to your aid, to join you in God's holy war against the Saracens and Ishmaelites who infest the holiest places of Christendom. But the road is long, and already we have delayed a month here, while in distant lands the ravages of the heathen continue unchecked. We ask you, great Emperor, to give us leave to pass from here and to give us passage across the water, the better to perform God's work.'

The interpreter fell silent, and every man in the hall strained to hear Krysaphios' answer.

'Honoured guests, come from all the nations of Christ, the serene Emperor embraces your thoughts to his heart. He gives thanks to the One God that you have come to fight at his side in the cause of right-eousness, and would not see your keen swords dulled through unuse. But before you pass from our walls, he would have you swear the oath customary among our people, to serve him truly and to restore to him that which is rightfully his, the ancient Roman lands of Asia.'

A murmur arose at the back of the room, and the envoy's face dark-ened. Even the translator's tact could not disguise the true intention of his words, for he spoke in haste and anger, with frequent jabs of his finger towards the impassive Emperor.

'Great star of the morning, we humbly beseech your indulgence. While nothing compels us more urgently than the desire to see your glory and power restored to its fullest lustre . . .' The translator faltered, his talent for equivocation clearly stretched to breaking. 'But we Franks are jealous of our oaths, and do not give them lightly. We beg more time for reflection.'

Krysaphios' lip curled. 'We know well how close you guard your allegiance. That is why we honour you as allies. But the munificent Emperor would have you remember that he is quick to show his gratitude to those who aid him.'

The eunuchs who had borne in the barbarians now reappeared, four mahogany caskets slung between them. As they neared the dais they seemed to trip, sinking to their knees and tipping forward their loads. The chests fell open and the barbarians gasped as a king's treasure spilled out across the floor. Golden chalices and plates, bowls and bracelets, necklaces set with pearls, myriad shining trinkets and enough coin among them to pay an army. Both barbarians were on their feet, stooping down to touch the riches before them with wonder on their faces. One scooped up a handful of hyperpyri and let them trickle back through his disbelieving fingers; the other held a drinking vessel, and stared at it as though he had found the cup of Christ.

'Great are the rewards for those who pledge their loyalty to our cause,' said Krysaphios.

But the barbarians showed little heed. They were talking urgently between themselves, fingering the treasures as they spoke. There seemed to be some disagreement.

'That's unsettled them,' said Aelric. 'That much gold could turn anyone's mind.'

'Buying allies can be an expensive habit. Allegiance bought with gold is like meat in the sun: it festers quickly.'

The two barbarians concluded their argument and turned back to Krysaphios. For all the wealth at their feet, neither looked happy.

'The friendship of the Greeks is a valued honour,' said the interpreter. 'But nothing gains merit by haste. We ask time for pause, to carry this offer' – he waved his hand at the scattered treasure – 'to our lord Godfrey.'

'The lord Godfrey should have sent ambassadors who could vouch for his thoughts and speak with his voice,' Krysaphios told them. 'But perhaps you wish to retire to a private chamber to consult your hearts.'

The envoys nodded dubiously. Again the eunuchs ran forward to raise their litters, but the barbarians disdained them, and were already walking back down the aisle to the door.

'Halt,' called Krysaphios, and they paused. 'None leaves the Emperor's presence.'

Without warning a tremendous noise exploded through the room, and a billowing column of smoke rose around the Emperor's dais. The barbarians trembled, grasping one another for support as if they expected a bolt of lightning to sear into their flesh.

The smoke began to clear, and I felt a surge of shock as I looked down at where the Emperor had sat. He was gone, and with him the gilded throne, the bronze lions, everything: all that remained was a smooth disc of white marble.

Aelric must have noticed my shaken pallor. 'Don't worry, Demetrios,' he said, touching my arm. 'That was no miraculous barbarian weapon. It always happens like that, to excite the foreigners.'

There was a touch of scorn in his voice, though I was too flustered to comment on it. Looking through the eddying remnants of the smoke, I could see the ambassadors hurrying out of the door glancing nervously over their shoulders. Krysaphios and Isaak, I noticed, had also disappeared.

'Well, I saw no sign of the monk in their retinue. Did you, Aelric?'

'None.'

'Though if he prefers to hire others to do his work, it could have been any of them.' It was hard to think of the monk while marvelling at how close I had been to the Emperor, at the glory which surrounded him; I was still remembering the splendour of the barbarians' entrance when the door behind me opened. A slight commotion in the room caught my attention, but it was only at the sound of the voice that I shook off my daydream.

'Why do we persist with all that theatre? The smoke stains my robes and scalds my cheek — it's a miracle that it hasn't burned my beard off. How would I look to the barbarians then, Krysaphios, with one cheek charred and shorn?'

'It serves its purpose, Lord.'

I turned around, forgetting even to sink to my knees. The man who had sat on that throne so motionless and unyielding, the prince of peace and the morning star and the heart of the empire, now paced only a few strides away. Beneath the well-groomed beard the cheeks were ruddy, like a peasant's; thick eyebrows surmounted his flashing eyes. Even under his shapeless robe you could see the breadth of his chest and shoulders, sense the rough strength in his arms. He moved with restless energy, barking his thoughts to Krysaphios and the Sebastokrator who stood respectfully by the door.

I collapsed to the floor and made the customary obeisance, rigid with apprehension. I had spent almost two months thinking of little other than his safety, of the cares and motives of his killers – but as an abstraction, a riddle: never had I considered him a living, breathing man. Now, as he strode around the small chamber, it was hard to imagine him otherwise.

'Who is this?' he demanded, breaking off the litany of his impatience with ceremonial. 'Why is he here?'

'Demetrios Askiates, Lord,' Krysaphios murmured. 'He is the only man who has seen the monk who tried to murder you on the feast of Saint Nikolas. He is here to protect you.'

'Get up, then, Demetrios Askiates.' The Emperor's eyes fixed their curiosity upon me. 'I have heard your name. But tell me, can you protect me against the inflammatory excesses which the credulous minds of barbarians require?'

'Lord . . .' I stammered.

'No matter. I knew when I accepted the throne that assassins, ingrates, invaders and usurpers would try and depose me from it: I did not think I would have to pose there like a statue while gouts of smoke roared about me. Perhaps I should haul the great founder Constantine down off his column and erect him on that throne. He would serve as well.'

'But did you see the terror in their eyes, brother?' Isaak asked merrily. 'They imagined you were some pagan god of the ancients, Zeus descended to claim their souls.'

'I fear the gold made more impact on them. What do you say, Krysaphios?'

'I fear even the lustre of gold will not warm their hearts. The deceit was plain in their faces. Their captain has sent them as a distraction, to divert us with hopes of promises to come until their strength is sufficient that we cannot resist them. Then he will come – and he will lay down his own terms.'

'The chamberlain is right.' Isaak's fingers twisted a pearl which dangled by his ear. 'If all Duke Godfrey wanted was to spear Saracens in the name of his church, then he could have taken the oath and be besieging Nicaea even now, rather than casting threats outside our walls. Delay favours his ambition.'

The Emperor leaned against a wall and stared at a hanging icon of the Theotokos. 'So – the barbarians are duplicitous. That we knew. What do you propose we do with them, brother?'

'Muster our armies and confront them.' There was no doubt in Isaak's voice. 'When they see the size of our forces, they will agree our demands immediately.'

'And if they do not?' Alexios probed. 'Our legions are not so invincible as they were in the age of our grandfather, even of our uncle. That is why the barbarians have come.'

There was a shout at the door, and all looked around as it opened to admit Sigurd. He wore a wolf pelt cloak from his shoulders, while his hauberk cast dappled crescents of light across the floor.

'Your pardon, Lord.' He genuflected. 'The ambassadors ask to take their leave. What are you doing here?' he added, puzzled. I thought he spoke to me, though his eyes were on Aelric.

'Let the barbarians wait,' said Krysaphios. 'They can leave when the Emperor dismisses them.'

'More smoke and toys,' Alexios muttered. I was having difficulty reconciling this reluctant, businesslike figure with the autocrat who controlled the fate of nations.

Isaak looked up. 'But what do they say? Have they agreed to take our oath?'

'They plead that they must consult their leader. They wish to defer their decision for a later time.'

'If they needed their captain's assent then he could have come himself.' Isaak punched the palm of his hand. 'I told you, brother, they will lead us a dance until they can strike us. Our only hope is to strike first.'

'But what if they do not surrender when we mass our army? What if I am sitting on my horse at the head of my cavalry and the barbarians refuse our demands? Then I will either look a coward, or be forced to press home the battle. A quarrel between us and the barbarians will draw laughter in the court of the Sultan, and will do nothing to restore our inheritance. And if we lose the battle – what then? Our walls will be undefended and the barbarians will take the city – we will lose everything.'

'We would not lose the battle, not against those barbarians. Throw gold on the ground and they would root at it like swine.'

'Dyrrhachium. Joannina. Ochrid. Arta. Have you forgotten those

156

battles, Isaak, merely because there are no triumphal columns or arches to remind you? I have not. The barbarians defeated us there, and whatever their defects, they fight at least as hard as we do – doubly so when there are riches to be won. They are a race of gamblers, and if they thought they could take our city they would not hesitate to risk the throw.'

By the door, Sigurd shifted a little on his feet. The gesture was not lost on the Emperor. 'But what to do now, you say? Tell them, Captain, that . . .'

I was genuinely curious to see what the Emperor would decree, but at that moment a movement by my side distracted me from his words. Aelric, who had stood by me in silence all this time, was moving forward, unbidden. He staggered a little, as though under a heavy burden, and there was a dull emptiness in his eyes. You might have thought he had drunk too much, save for the deliberation with which the axe lifted off his shoulder and settled into his hands. The weight seemed to compose him: his stride stiffened, and the muscles of his arms tensed as the blade came up beside his head.

'What . . . ?'

Almost numb with surprise, and almost a second too late, I saw the impossible truth and sprang forward. The Emperor's back was to us, though he must have sensed something was amiss for he began to turn; Krysaphios was looking away, and Isaak was speaking with Sigurd. A bow of light played across the blade as it swung past a pendant lamp, and a roar rose in Aelric's throat.

For an instant it seemed as if my heart stopped, and with it all time, but mercifully my body continued to move. I dived for Aelric's feet, flailing my arms forward to catch him. His axe was slicing through the air as I felt my fingers make contact with his brass-ringed boots; I fastened my grip around them and let my full weight meet his legs.

There were many shouts, but his was one. His knees buckled and he tumbled forward, tangling me between his shins as his axe struck the floor. What else it might have hit in its path I could not tell. Our momentum carried us sliding across the marble a few feet, until at last we came to a halt. Even then he was not defeated; he pulled free of my grasp and began to rise to his feet, his axe still in his hand.

A roar sounded from above, and I looked up. Sigurd was standing over me, a tower of rage and fury. His face was ashen, shaken, but there was not the least compunction in his eyes.

'You betrayed us,' he breathed. 'Everything.'

His axe swung down, and hot blood splashed against my cheek. At a little distance, Aelric's head rolled free across the floor.

For a moment we were still as the icons on the walls – Sigurd, Alexios, Krysaphios, Isaak and I. Blood welled from the stump of Aelric's neck, soaking through my robes, but I had not the wit to move. A bead of sweat or tears sank down Sigurd's cheek, and the rings of his armour tensed and slacked as his chest heaved beneath it.

The Sebastokrator Isaak was the first to find his voice. 'The barbarians,' he hissed. 'They must have planned this, to murder you in your own hall and seize the crown as it slipped from your head. Let us kill them now, and then fall upon their kinsmen in their camp.'

I saw Krysaphios nodding behind him, but Alexios raised a weary hand to still them. There was a gash in his sleeve where Aelric had landed his final, glancing blow. 'Do not touch the ambassadors,' he commanded, imposing authority on his shaken voice. 'Why would they attempt such a crime when they were my hostages? They must have known their lives would be forfeit if anything happened to me while they were here.' He paused. 'Unless, of course, there was another candidate ready to take the diadem and command the mob to save them.'

His sharp eyes glanced at each of us in turn, fixing – so I thought – a second longer on Isaak than any other.

'We will seek out all who have a claim to the throne and establish their whereabouts,' said Krysaphios. 'And we should deploy the guard in the streets, lest in haste someone has already started to move against you.'

'Can we rely on the guard?' asked Alexios. 'If one of my longest-serving Varangians will betray me, whom then can I trust?'

Sigurd winced; he seemed on the edge of tears. 'The Varangians will defend you to the death, Lord. But if you do not trust us, then take our arms and make us your slaves.' Dropping to his knee, he held his axe by its blood-swathed blade, and offered it to the Emperor.

'Take it, Lord.' Krysaphios kicked angrily at Aelric's headless corpse. 'If you do not know why a Varangian should have done this terrible thing, you cannot tell us why another may not try again.' 'Was he a traitor all this time, waiting for his moment to strike? If so, why now? Was it a moment of madness? Or did he indeed act for a wider cause among his legion?'

'On balance,' I observed, 'it would have been useful if Sigurd had not been so quick to dismember him.' I looked at the staring, lifeless eyes and shuddered. This was a man who had ridden at my side and eaten in my home: it was not easy to see him now. 'It would have been worth everything to know his motives.'

Sigurd, still on his knee, growled. 'You can wrestle a snake to the ground, Demetrios, but to be sure it will not bite you must behead it. My duty is to keep the Emperor from harm – yours is to find those who would harm him *before* they enter his presence. Which of us has failed today?'

'My task would be easier if you did not help the monk by destroying every link with him.'

Sigurd looked as though he might like to use his axe again, but Isaak spoke to me first. 'What of the monk? There is a greater power at work when the Emperor is almost murdered in his own palace, and you think only of spies and foot soldiers. Forget the monk, if he even exists, and instead seek out his masters.'

I was about to retort unwisely, for in all this argument it seemed my own role in bringing down the assassin was forgotten, but I was forestalled by an urgent rapping on the door, and the sound of voices in the passage beyond. We turned, and Sigurd raised his axe, though Alexios stayed unmoved.

'Who disturbs the Emperor?' Krysaphios' fear wrought anger in his voice.

'Your pardon, Lord, but it is urgent,' said a voice behind the door. 'The watchmen on the walls report smoke rising from the outlying villages. The barbarian army has begun to riot, claiming that we hold their embassy hostage and demanding their release.'

Isaak exploded. 'You see brother – already they are moving. Their haste betrays them. Let us chain the hostages and ride out to face our enemies.'

Alexios ignored him. 'Captain,' he said, beckoning Sigurd. 'I will not disband your legion. Long service has proven their value; I would be an ingrate and a fool to squander it because of a single man's treachery.' More immediately, I thought, he could ill afford to lose good troops with the barbarians so near. 'Fetch your company and escort the envoys to the gates. Explain that I will await their answer in the coming days.' He pulled his lorum straight, wiping a drop of blood from one of its gems. 'If so much as a single strand of their hair is harmed, either by your men or by the mob in the city, you will answer for it person-ally, Captain. Is that clear?'

Sigurd nodded, bowed, and backed from the room, while Isaak glowered in the corner.

'Now,' continued the Emperor. 'Find me the captain of the Patzinaks. I have forgiven the Varangians the traitor they unknowingly harboured, but I cannot keep them in the palace if even a single man is suspected. I will need men about me I can trust, for it will be another day at least before we know if the danger is passed.'

'The danger will never pass so long as the barbarians live outside our walls,' muttered Isaak.

'Unless the danger is already within.' Krysaphios turned to me. 'Demetrios, you remember the list I showed you once?'

It was almost two months since I had seen it, but I remembered enough of its eminent names to manage a convincing nod.

'Then take a company of Patzinaks and find where those men are as quickly as you can. Any who have taken sudden trips to their country estates, or who have hoards of arms cached in their cellars, or who have tried to slip through the gates in disguise, report back to me. I will be at the new palace with the Emperor.'

I nodded my obedience. 'And what of Aelric? Someone must know, or guess, the motive for his treachery. Some of his comrades? His family, perhaps?'

Krysaphios shrugged impatiently. 'Perhaps. You can ask Sigurd when he returns. Though do not seek him in the palace – by nightfall all the Varangians will be at their barracks by the Adrianople gate.'

I made my obeisance and left, stepping over Aelric's riven head as I did so. The blood had matted through his greying hair, and the jaw was slack, but the eyes remained as firm as ever, fixed where Sigurd's vengeful blade had swung.

★   ★   ★

The next few hours passed in a daze. The shock of what I had witnessed, the disaster which had almost befallen and my improbable part in averting it, occupied my soul as I marched my squadron of Patzinak mercenaries between the houses of the nobility. I quizzed their gate-keepers and stewards, searched their halls and cellars for signs of flight or rebellion, but found little. Most had been in the palace, watching the ambassadors; some were away in the country, and a few were at home attending to their private business. All of them I noted in the thin book I carried, recording their excuses and alibis with reflexive thoroughness. Krysaphios could scour it for whatever incrimination he sought, but none of the men I saw seemed seized by manifest guilt.

And hour after hour, as I asked the expected questions and heard the expected answers, I struggled with the motive of the crime. Aelric could not have hoped to gain from his treachery, for even had he felled the Emperor he would have died the next instant. Unless madness or an evil spirit had taken hold of him, someone must have driven him to attempt the murder with a threat greater than certain death. What could that be – and who? It might have been the monk, but whose ends did he serve? Was it as Isaak suggested, that the barbarian envoys had hoped to use the confusion to their advantage? That was madness, for they would have been slaughtered to a man. Or was it the barbarian captains, away in their camp, hoping that the Emperor's death would give them an excuse and an opportunity to take the city? That was almost too fanciful to credit. Or were the barbarians simply a distraction, an irrelevance in a political contest fought among our own nobles?

I found no answers, but when my task was done I took the notes to Krysaphios at the new palace. Such was my exhaustion, my shock, that I did not argue when the guard announced that the eunuch was unavailable: I called for a secretary, sealed the book with wax, and left it with him to relay to his master. Then, as it was not far, I walked along the hilltop in the shadow of the walls to the Varangian barracks.

'Is Sigurd the captain here?' I asked.

'On the ramparts,' answered the sentry.

'Can I speak with him?'

'You can,' he said dubiously, 'though you might regret it. He's in an evil mood.'

'I'll risk it.'

I crossed the parade ground and climbed the broad stair up to the wall, watching my breath cloud the bitter air. The sky was clear, a swathe of purple far above me, and the first stars were beginning to prick through. They reminded me of the Emperor's opulence, the glittering gems set in the imperial fabric, and I wondered who would have been wearing those robes tonight if I had been a second slower. The Sebastokrator Isaak? The Emperor's first son, barely eight years old? One of the eminences whose servants I had interviewed that afternoon? Or a barbarian from the west, sitting awkwardly on the throne watching the abomination of an empire?

I found Sigurd alone, leaning on the deep embrasure between two battlements and staring out at the sparks across the water where the barbarian campfires burned. He grunted when I greeted him, but did not turn to face me.

'It seems so tranquil,' I mused, pulling my cloak tight about me. 'Truly, night smoothes the fractures of the world.'

'But night dawns, and it will be a long time before the fragments of this day are forged back together.' Sigurd tipped a clay flagon to his lips, and I heard the gulping of liquid tumbling from its throat to his. 'Wine?'

'Thank you.' It was coarse stuff, but a welcome tonic against the cold.

'Though you've no cares. You saved the Emperor's life. You can expect a house and a pension for such service. I let a traitor destroy the honour of the Varangians, and come within an inch of razing the empire.'

'So who guards the Emperor now, if the Varangians are expelled from the palaces?' My fevered mind wondered whether Aelric's deed had merely been a gambit to discredit his legion, to leave the Emperor vulnerable.

'Patzinaks.' Sigurd's voice implied they might as well be lepers. 'Round-faced barbarians from the east: an ugly race, with ugly women and uglier habits.'

'Reliable?'

'As rocks. Once the Emperor defeated them in battle; now they worship him as a god, and serve him as zealots. I once saw a Patzinak stand for four days and nights in driving snow because no order came to relieve him.'

There was a silence as we swapped the wine again. I leaned against the massive parapet, and felt the cold of the stone on my cheek.

'I know your wounds are sore,' I began again, 'but there are questions which need swift answers before the trail fades. Did Aelric have any particular comrades in the guard? Or a family?'

'He was in a company of men who were all like brothers. But do not seek answers from Sweyn or Stigand or any of the others: they were as ignorant as me. Otherwise Aelric would never have crossed the palace threshold, except in chains. He had a family, though – a wife, Freya, and a son.'

'Do they live in the barracks?'

'None of the women do. The wife keeps a house in Petrion, not far from here. The son left home years ago – he probably has grandchildren by now. Remember, Aelric was already a warrior when most of us were still sucking on our mothers.'

'Did you know him then? Back in Thule?'

'England,' Sigurd corrected me automatically. 'No – our paths here were separate, and it was years later, when I was a grown man, that we met.'

'And his wife – did he meet her here, or was she also from England?'

'English. She fled with him after the Bastard conquered us.'

'I think I had best see her. Will she already have been told Aelric's fate?'

'I doubt anyone has thought of her until you, Demetrios. You may have to relate the news yourself.'

'Will you come?'

Sigurd drained the last of the wine and tossed the bottle over the parapet. I heard it shatter on the stones below.

'I cannot leave this place.' He kicked at the battlement before him. 'We are not allowed any closer to the palace than these walls.'

On balance, I decided, it would probably be better to arrive at the widow's house without her husband's murderer.

I left Sigurd in his isolation, walking the utmost boundary of the city, and made my way to the house he had described. Though I knew that the passing of time was no ally, I moved listlessly, rebuffing the attentions of the Watch and hating the fact that I would have to tell Aelric's wife of her husband's treason and death. All too soon I was at her door, thumping a cold fist against the thick oak. Every stroke sent numb shivers through my hand, but I persisted until at last I heard a suspicious voice within demanding my business.

'I have come from the palace. It concerns your husband.' My words haunted the empty street.

Three times I heard the sounds of bolts being drawn. Then the door cracked open.

'You are not of the Varangians. Have I seen you before?'

All was darkness beyond the door, but the voice bespoke someone old, a woman pinched by a weary life.

'I am a stranger,' I admitted, 'but I knew your husband. He . . .'

'You *knew* my husband?' The door edged open a fraction further. 'Why is it that you *knew* my husband? Where is he now?'

'He is dead.'

I had not meant to say it so baldly, but it was out now and I could curse my carelessness later. I heard a wail arise in the room within, the sound of someone stumbling about, and I pushed in through the door before she could slam it on me. Small fists flailed against my chest, and I raised my arms in defence, though there was little force in her bony blows. The darkness hindered me, but eventually I managed to catch hold of her wrists and hold them away, until the screams of defiance broke down into a forlorn sobbing.

As gently as I could, I steered her backwards, away from the door. She was weeping, calling her dead husband's name and many other things in a tongue I could not understand.

'Do you have a candle?' I asked as she took a choking breath. 'It would help if I could see you.'

Tentatively, I relaxed my grip a little, testing whether she still aimed to attack me. There was no sudden movement, nor any increase in her sobbing, and so I let her loose.

She moved away. For a second I feared she might be fetching a blade, might assault me in the darkness, but then I saw a shower of sparks in a corner and the flare of a wick. The candle was burned low, crusted with shrivelled knobs of wax, but it gave enough light that I could at last see Aelric's poor widow.

She was old, at least as old as he, and the deeply-shadowed furrows of her face added still more years. Her ragged hair was grey and untied, hanging in frayed bunches, and her skin shone with tears. Dressed only in a woollen shift, she fell back onto a stool and gestured me to take a bench. I reached out a hand to stroke her arm, but she recoiled in loathing and huddled herself away.

'Did Sigurd kill him?' she asked.

The question startled me, so much that I could do little but flounder for a minute before admitting: 'Yes.' And then, struggling to impose myself: 'Why should you think so?'

'My husband always feared it, that Sigurd would find his secret and murder him in a fit of rage. Every day in the last ten years, since Sigurd joined the Varangians, Aelric feared him.'

She scratched her scalp through her thin hair, and shivered as though a draught had blown over her.

'Why did Aelric fear him?' I asked. 'What secret could he have kept that would have inflamed Sigurd so? Was his purpose with the Emperor always . . . ?'

'The Emperor?' Aelric's wife – Freya, I remembered was her name – gave a bitter laugh. 'What did Aelric care for the Emperor? Or Sigurd, for that matter?'

'Sigurd loves the Emperor like a father.'

'Love?' Freya spat on the floor. 'None of you act from love – but from hate. Sigurd does not love the Emperor; he hates the Normans, and with a merciless passion. Why else would he not forgive Aelric, who brought him into the Varangians and was like an older brother to him?'

'But what had Aelric done?' I was bewildered; it was like trying to knead oil, reasoning with this woman.

She ignored me. 'He knew it was returning. So did I. Ever since Asgard appeared at our door three weeks ago it haunted him. Aelric, who served the Emperor long after most of his companions would have hung up their armour and taken a farm in the country. Will Sigurd still be standing his watch when he is as old as Aelric? Never.'

'Who was this Asgard? Another Varangian?'

'He came three weeks ago, and Aelric changed. His smile vanished, and his shoulders sagged; he would hardly eat. At first he did not speak of it, but I knew, for what else could Asgard have to talk to him about? Then Asgard called again and took him away: to meet his friends, he said. And now he is dead, the most loyal man who ever carried an axe. My husband.'

I leaned closer, trying to find some thread to guide me through the fog of her babble. 'And what was this secret of Aelric's that Asgard wanted to talk of?'

Freya straightened, defiance kindling within her. 'Why should I tell his secrets to a stranger, the crow who croaks his death?'

'Because all our safety depends on it – and yours especially. If you do not tell me others will come, and they will not be as gentle as I. Before he died, Aelric betrayed the Emperor and the Varangians, and that will not be forgiven lightly.' I had not wanted to touch on Aelric's treachery, and it had been a sound instinct, for Freya plunged her face into her hands at the sound of it.

'My husband was an honest man who served his masters faithfully,' she sobbed. 'If they were devious, or evil, or made him defy his nature, then God will judge *them*, not him. And you call yourself gentle – you, cursing his name to me while my tears are warm, before he is even laid in the ground. Get out of my house, and allow me my grief without poisoning it.'

'I cannot. I must know . . .'

'Out! Out!'

She would not be consoled, certainly not by me, and until then I would get no sense from her. I left her to her tears, and hurried back to the walls. It seemed the night had lasted an eternity, but Sigurd was still there, pacing the ramparts and scanning the dark horizon with vacant eyes. Neither of us offered a greeting.

'Do you know a man named Asgard?' I asked. 'Maybe a Varangian, or someone from the palace.'

Sigurd's scowl, if it were possible, deepened. 'I know Asgard,' he grunted. 'He was a Varangian, until a few years ago. I expelled him myself for stealing from us, thieving in the barracks.'

'Did he know Aelric?'

'They escaped England at the same time, and arrived in the city together: Asgard and Aelric, their wives, a few others. Most are dead now.'

'But not Asgard?'

Sigurd raised his hands in ignorance. 'I could not care. I heard that he kept a stall in the fur market, selling mangy pelts and skins that the Rus traders could not persuade any others to take. Maybe he's still there, maybe not. He was a worm, and we were well rid of him.'

'He did not keep in contact with any of your men?'

'They would have spurned him. Stealing from your messmates is like stealing from the church – except that we have no obligation to forgive. Why all this curiosity? Do you want a cheap shawl for your daughter?'

'He visited Aelric several times in recent weeks. Freya blamed him for a change in Aelric's mood, and I think he may have carried messages for the monk.'

Sigurd snorted. 'The monk? The monk is a phantom, Demetrios, an apparition. The sort of man you blame when there are no other excuses.' He paused, pondering this. 'Asgard, on the other hand – he's real enough. Seek him in the market.'

———

The furrier's market was a dismal place next morning. A fine rain had been falling since dawn, and however hard the vendors tried to keep their wares under awnings the pelts still grew mottled and bedraggled. Only the richer merchants escaped, those whom the guild favoured with places under the eaves of the stoa: they sat shivering at their tables, rarely rousing themselves to tout for custom. The stink of treated hide drifted down from the far end of the market, where the tanners and leather workers kept their stalls, and with the mouldering air of animal carcasses as well it was no wonder there were few buyers.

Rain trickled down the back of my neck and soaked the shoulders of my tunic, while my boots grew ever more like sponges underfoot. The faces of dead animals stared plaintively from every rack and trestle: rabbits and hares hung by their ears, long-snouted wolves piled above each other, deer whose antlers had already been sold to the ivory-carvers, and – on one stall – an enormous bear mounted on a pole.

I stopped at several stalls to ask after Asgard, and received a predictable pattern of replies. He was on the west side of the market, one man claimed; no, the north insisted his neighbour. Perhaps he had given up his stall altogether and abandoned the trade, suggested another, for the quality of his wares was second-rate and he rarely saw his customers twice. Some had seen him but could not remember where, and others knew of him but had not seen him that day. It was a common pattern of response, but on that mournful day, with rain constantly dripping in my eyes, it seemed more than usually futile.

Nor were the merchants amiable company. They say in the provinces that a shepherd comes to resemble his flock, and here the same was true. All the men I encountered were lumbering and hairy, with wide, untrusting faces and thick beards, some smeared with fat to keep them dry. Many must have been the bastard sons of Norse traders, and they fragmented their language with peculiar sounds which seemed to owe more to the tongues of beasts than men.

At last, though, I found my quarry. He did not warrant a shop in the stoa, nor even a covered stall in the square. He huddled in a corner in a rat-eaten fur cloak, his grey hair splayed flat across his skull and his blue eyes squinting almost shut against the rain. A tray bearing the skins of small vermin was laid out before him.

'How much for a stoat's pelt?' I asked, affecting to examine his merchandise.

'Fourteen obols.' The line of his eyes became rounder, watching me carefully.

'Too expensive. Do you have anything else to sell me?'

He blinked. 'Alas, nothing but what you see. The guild does not allow me any more.'

Wincing slightly at the dank feel, I lifted the dead stoat in my hand and weighed it thoughtfully. As I studied it, my right hand strayed to the pouch on my belt and pulled out a golden nomisma.

'I do not need your rats,' I told him, dangling the pelt by the scruff of its neck and discarding it. Asgard's eyes ignored it, fixed on my right hand. 'I need knowledge. Information. An observant man in a crowded market must witness many things.'

'Some things. When I am not occupied with the needs of my trade.'

I picked out another fur and swung it in my hand. 'Are these local furs?'

I could see that he did not like the meandering direction of my questions, that the doubt in his eyes was turning to suspicion, but he could not keep from reciting his sales chatter. 'Local? Indeed not. They are brought by the mighty Rus, from the wild forests of the north, down great rivers and across the Euxine sea to grace your garments. You will not find pelts of a higher quality anywhere in a thousand miles.'

Though I guessed the words were seldom used, they still sounded tired and hollow.

'You clearly know their provenance well. Are you one of these Rus?'

'No,' he admitted carefully. 'But they are my kin. I am from the kingdom of England – Britannia, as some of you call it, an island just beyond the Russian shores.'

'Where the holy Emperor, may he live a thousand years, recruits his bodyguard?'

'The same place. In fact, I served the Emperor myself, once, as one of his Varangians, carrying my axe in his service. He chose me for my honesty.'

'Truly?' I wiped a lock of hair out of my eyes. 'I am looking for a man who knows of Varangians. Or rather, a man who seeks to know more of them. A monk who travels the city bargaining with guardsmen past and present. Have you seen such a man?'

The gold coin I had been holding slipped from my fingers and landed noiselessly on a pile of fur. I did not pick it up. It agitated Asgard; he cast his eyes down, then to one side, and fidgeted with the clasp of his cloak. Always, though, his gaze leapt back to the glittering nomisma in his tray.

'Why should I know that?' he croaked. 'There are many Varangians in this city, and many who have left after a lifetime of loyal and honourable service. Who would come to a distant corner of a stinking market, a space which even the whore-born guilds do not value enough to rent for more than an obol, to ask questions of a luck-less merchant?'

'A man who placed great value on what that merchant might tell him,' I answered. 'As I do.'

Two more gold coins dropped before him.

'No,' the old man whispered. 'No. I have not seen your monk.'

'Yes you have. You led him to your old comrade Aelric, and revealed some terrible secret which compelled Aelric to betray everything he valued. Do not deny it.'

Asgard was shuffling back now, glancing about for a path to escape. I followed him, tipping over his tray and scattering his pelts over the wet stone.

I pulled out my knife. 'I will know what you have said and done, Asgard. You can take either gold for it, or steel. Do you know a Varangian captain named Sigurd?'

Asgard's thin jaw opened wider. 'Sigurd? He is a berserker, a madman. He would kill his own mother if she stepped too near the Emperor for his liking. I served under him in the guard.'

'And now, through the treachery you concocted with Aelric, you have ruined him. If you do not tell me what you have done, he will come with his axe to make you answer.'

All this time I had been advancing on Asgard as he retreated; now,

171

he found himself with his back to a broad column. I watched him squirm against it, and stood ready to strike if he tried to run.

But running was no more in Asgard's character than fighting: there was no strength in his time-ravaged limbs and he knew it.

'He will kill me,' he pleaded. 'The monk swore he would kill me if I told any other.'

'If the monk has finished with you, he will probably kill you anyway. At least I will give you a chance to live.'

'But I did no wrong. I did not betray Aelric – he did that himself. I never murdered my countrymen, or put innocent families to death, or burned homes and crops and poisoned wells so that the land would lie empty for a generation. Not I, no. Why do you point your blade at me, when it is Aelric's neck which should feel its edge?'

'Aelric's neck has felt its last blow.' My words were short, brusque – what were these horrors he ascribed to the genial Varangian? 'Do not try to save yourself by blackening the names of the dead.'

'If he is dead, then that is the least justice he was due. A man lives by his loyalties, and he had none.'

'Then your head should join his, for if you conspired with the monk then you betrayed the Emperor just as much as Aelric.'

'The Emperor?' Asgard gave a horrible, cackling laugh. 'What do I care for the Emperor? For some years he paid me to serve him, and then he did not. But Aelric did not betray some jumped-up Greek – he betrayed his own people. His real kin. The English.' Somehow, through his obvious fear, Asgard managed to contort a vicious smile.

'Aelric fought with your king against the invaders.' I remembered his confusing tales of Normans and Norsemen. 'Was that a lie?'

The fur-merchant shook his head. 'It was true enough. But what he did not tell you was that three years after the invasion, when the Bastard conqueror came north to wreck the land, Aelric's lord supported him, and Aelric with him. There were more than Normans up there – Englishmen turned on their neighbours too. Some say they were the worst, the fiercest. Aelric always held that he did it because his thane ordered him, but who is to tell the truth of that?'

'Aelric spoke of this? To the Varangians?'

Again that awful sneer. 'Not to the Varangians. If you so much as admired a Norman whore you'd be out of their ranks with your head cracked open. But he spoke of it to me, on the long nights during our flight from England. He used to wake up crying in the night remembering the things he had done, needing to confess. They were ugly stories, too, but I kept them secret. Then they threw me out of the barracks and he did not raise a word to protect me, after I'd kept him safe all those years. So when the monk came to my stall, asking if I knew any of the guards who were disloyal, or might be, it did not take much of his gold to draw out Aelric's name.'

'And then you took this monk to Aelric's house? You forced him to betray the Emperor?'

'I forced him to do nothing. I persuaded him to share a drink with me. When he came, I introduced him to the monk. The monk explained that if Aelric served him faithfully, he might die but his wife would live in comfort; otherwise, he would die in ignominy, his past treachery revealed, and his wife would have to whore herself to Normans simply to live. Once Aelric had agreed, and the monk had rewarded me for my work, I left them to their own business.'

'Where was this meeting?' So great was my anticipation that I moved closer, almost pricking Asgard with the point of my knife.

He whimpered, and wiped his nose on the sleeve of his cloak. 'At a tavern near the harbour. He arrived after us, alone. I never saw him after that.'

'So you do not know where he can be found? Did he not leave instructions in case you thought of another victim from whom he could extort disloyalty?'

Asgard shook his head so violently that I almost believed him.

'I will take you to the imperial prisons,' I told him. 'Then I will find Sigurd and repeat your story. Perhaps he will remind you of things you have forgotten.'

Asgard cowered back in terror, pressing himself so close against the column he might have been carved on it. 'Do not take me to Sigurd,' he pleaded. 'Not to Sigurd.' A leering hope entered his eyes. 'Perhaps there are other things I remember.'

'What other things?'

Asgard raised his chin in rare defiance. 'The monk did not leave instructions – but that does not mean I was fool enough not to make enquiries. Asgard always seeks new business.'

I stood very still. 'What did your enquiries reveal?'

'That a man who values knowledge will pay for it.'

'You were involved in a plot to murder the Emperor,' I reminded him, 'and your life will be forfeit unless you ransom it with something of singular value. Is your knowledge enough to buy your soul?'

Asgard looked miserably unhappy, but with a knife at his throat and Sigurd's vengeance to follow, he had little choice.

'I paid a boy to follow the monk when he left the tavern. A clever lad, and sly. He knew how to find the shadows when the monk looked around. Which he did often, apparently – a suspicious man. But the boy tracked him like a deer, back to a tenement in Libos.'

'Where in Libos? When was this?' I raised my knife so that it hovered before Asgard's eyes. It seemed to make the words come faster.

'Two weeks ago, perhaps three. I do not know if he has been there since. But that you can find out yourself. It is west from the column of Marcian, near the north bank of the Lycus. A grocer named Vichos keeps his shop on the ground floor.'

I stared into his eyes, trying to judge the truth of his words, but fear had long stripped all honesty from his face and I could not tell.

'If we find the monk, you will live.' Though not in the least comfort. 'For now, you will come with me to the palace, until I can judge the truth of your tale.'

Asgard's eyes widened, and he sank to his knees. 'No,' he implored me. 'Not to the palace. If I go there they will kill me. I have helped you all I can – have mercy on me now. Let me go – give me only an hour to escape, and that will be a fair bargain.'

'I will decide what is a fair bargain,' I told him, feeling no pity for this traitor. If he had hoped to win mercy by grovelling, he had misjudged me. 'Get up.'

But Asgard's serpent mind had a final draught of venom in it. I must have edged back a little as he rose, and those few inches were all the room he needed to spring forward, crashing into my legs and driving me away. My feet kicked and slipped on the wet stone beneath and I fell, landing heavily on my back. There was a terrible pain in my lungs and throat where the air had been forced out, and by the time I regained my feet Asgard was gone.

I cursed, though it was of little moment. I disbelieved at least half his story, and suspected there was another half as yet untold, but that could wait: doubtless the Watch would have him before nightfall, if the monk did not find him first. For now, the highest imperative was to reach the house in Libos, the house of Vichos the grocer. If the monk truly was there, then even Asgard's escape would be a small price to have paid.

I climbed back up to the palace and summoned the guard. It was strange to meet Patzinaks, with their short swords and pointed helmets, in the places where Varangians should have been, and my unfamiliarity with them meant further delay until I could explain myself to their captain. He listened to my story with ever greater concern, and rattled off orders to his subordinates as soon as I was finished.

'We will call out the Watch to find this Asgard, and take a company of men down to the house in Libos.'

I nodded my approval. 'Good. I will go with you.'

For all that we needed haste it took some time to assemble his men, while I wandered the courtyard and fretted that the monk might even now be fleeing his house, again just a few paces beyond our grasp. I tried to goad the Patzinaks to swiftness, but they treated me with indifference and ignored my pleas. Only when the captain was satisfied that all his men were correctly arrayed and equipped did we march out through the Augusteion.

The crowds in the streets were surging as thick as ever, despite the persistent rain, and a column of a hundred guardsmen in their midst brought constant friction. Feet were trampled, baskets spilled and clothing muddied as the Patzinaks rammed their path through. Sigurd had spoken of their single-minded devotion to the Emperor, but here they seemed like automata, like the lions in the palace whose apparent obedience was entirely free of will or reason. It felt strange, unsettling to be in their company; I would much rather have been with Sigurd and his men. Coarse and wild though the Varangians were, I could at least admire their passion, the unbridled currents which ruled them. There was nothing of that in the unmoving Patzinak faces which followed me.

Nor were they as physically arresting as the giants of Thule. If Sigurd was a bear, then his Patzinak counterpart was more a mule: shorter and stockier, but with a stride I suspected would never falter in a month of hard marches. His arms swung freely at his side, and his head jerked erratically as he walked. He had the face of a man who would prefer to knife his enemy in the back than meet him in a head-on duel, but in a fight, I guessed, he would have the guile and will to wear down mightier opponents. If once he was on the field of battle, I did not think he would leave it lightly.

We passed under the column of Constantine and through the arch of Theodosius, and further along the road to the small square where the Emperor Marcian had found a space for his own monument. No doubt walking in the shadows of the past should have inspired us to rival its legend, but with rain trickling in my ear and the carved figures in the sky almost invisible, it only depressed me. Even the prospect of finding the monk could not inspire me: I had seen too many broken men and women in the last hours for that. And it was hard to lift my mood on the strength of a traitor's desperate lies.

Past the column of Marcian, as Asgard had said, we turned left. It was a narrow, unpaved street, turned to mire by the rain and with streaming water gouging a new course down its centre. The buildings were of unpainted wood, dark and rotten with all the moisture they had absorbed, tottering over us like drunken giants. We progressed slowly down the road. The Patzinaks had their swords out, alert for any danger, but there was little life to be seen around us, and the only sound was the constant rattle of raindrops on the puddles and tiles. Though marching soldiers were a common enough sight on the Mesi, a hundred of them prowling through a private neighbourhood would sweep every resident, honest or otherwise, out of their path. With nothing to obstruct us, the grocer's shop was plain to see, and the faded paint on the lintel – just visible through the gloom – gave me the name: Vichos.

'So far your informant does not lie,' muttered the captain. 'But I wonder what he keeps in his shop.'

'You should array your men around it before we find out. It will do us no good if there are a hundred of us inside the house while the monk jumps from a window and makes his escape.'

The captain gestured to his sergeants to deploy the men as I had suggested, keeping a dozen close about us. The grocer's shutters and door were fastened shut, as tight as their skewed hinges would admit, but I thought I saw a shadow within moving across one of the cracks. Was he watching us? Did he realise that he had failed, that soon the Emperor's torturers would be heating their irons before his eyes? Or did he have a plan, another gambit to outwit us? Was he even there?

'My men are ready,' the captain told me. Though there was nothing the least secretive about our actions, his voice was hushed. 'Shall I send for the stone-throwers and ballistas, or do you think we can break this siege ourselves?'

I ignored his sarcasm. 'This monk commands weapons whose power you could not conceive. Tell your men to beware, for their armour may be no protection.'

The captain shrugged, and fell silent as his men moved towards the building. The sergeant at their head banged on the door but there was no answer.

'Break it,' said the captain.

Water was dribbling behind my ear and off my nose; my breaths emerged in ragged clouds, but despite all the misery of cold and damp I felt my heart beating faster, my mind awakening with the hope of success. At the door, the sergeant now had a mattock in his hands, and was swinging it hard against the fractured timbers. The wood did not groan or crack under the impact, for it was too sodden and rotten for that; instead the blow knocked one of the panels clean out of the frame. The sergeant bellowed an order and his men piled forward, driving their boots and shoulders against the flimsy barrier. It did not hold for more than a second. With swords outstretched and shields held before their faces the men charged in, disappearing into the dim room beyond. I heard shouts and the screams of women, the crash and clatter of upturned tables, then the curt staccato of commands.

I could not stay in the street. I ran across to the house, stepped heedlessly over the broken threshold and took in the carnage before me. Two soldiers were kneeling over an elderly man and his wife, pinning them to the ground amid a sea of broken pottery and scattered vegetables. Dried fish lay in pools of olive-oil, while pickled sauces were splashed across the earthen floor. In less than a minute, the soldiers had left barely a single thing in that room untouched.

'Where is the rest of your company?' I demanded.

One of the Patzinaks jerked a thumb towards the spindly ladder in the corner. I climbed it two rungs at a time, hoping it would not crack apart under me, and hauled myself through a narrow gap onto the floor above. Frayed curtains had once shielded the room from the stairs, but they were pulled down and bunched on the floor, revealing more carnage: rudimentary pieces of furniture overturned, clothes and keepsakes tipped out of trunks, and even an icon of the holy virgin ripped off the wall. But no Patzinaks.

A second ladder continued the ascent to the topmost level, from where I could hear shouts of triumph and anger. Without another thought I leapt up the ladder, vaulted into the room above, and set my eyes on our new prisoner.

Two Patzinaks were holding his arms, their fingers squeezed tight into his skin as he writhed and struggled between them. He was not dressed as a monk, but in a nondescript woollen tunic which reached almost to his ankles; there was fresh mud on his boots, and dampness on his clothes which suggested he was only recently returned here. His skin was dark and his features hard, set with black eyes which flickered desperately around the room. He was thinner than I had expected; his garments hung from his shoulders like shrouds, and there was a stoop which had not seemed so obvious when I chased him through the snowbound streets. He gave no sign of recognising me.

In a corner, the sergeant stood with his arms crossed over his chest, surveying his achievement. 'Is this the one?' he asked.

'I don't know.' Suddenly, after the energy and momentum of the chase, I felt a stab of uncertainty. Surely this was the right man – how could it not be? Feeling my limbs shivering with sudden tension, I walked slowly around the captive until I could see the back of his head.

He did not have a tonsure.

I cringed; I felt as though someone had kicked me in the groin, or punched my throat. Black bile flooded my stomach, and I stepped away from the prisoner. Yet still I clung to my belief, like a drowning sailor to his flotsam. It was weeks since I had caught the monk outside my house, more than sufficient time for his hair to grow back. Indeed, a man so attuned to his safety would hardly have done otherwise, especially once he knew I had seen him.

The Patzinak captain had arrived now. I could see his head just emerging from the hole in the floor where the ladder protruded.

'Send two of your soldiers to the monastery of Saint Andrew,' I told him, 'and have them bring back a boy named Thomas who is living there.' I brushed aside his puzzled objection. 'He is the only one who can tell if this is the man we seek.'

★   ★   ★

That next hour was an aching ordeal, my every hope hostage to Thomas's arrival. We searched the house, the top room particularly, but found nothing of import: our prisoner had a low bed, a crude table and a pair of stools, and little else. He did not speak, and I could not summon the strength to interrogate him, so we left him sitting against the wall with his hands tied before him and four Patzinaks surrounding him. Most of the guards were dispatched back to the palace, while others rummaged through the shopkeeper's rooms below. Every sound they made caused me to start, to peer down the ladder to see if Thomas had arrived, and every time I felt a fool for revealing my agitation.

Predictably, I hardly noticed when he did finally arrive; I was standing at the window looking out over a wasteland of broken tenements, and only when I heard the sentry's challenge did I turn to see him.

He was looking well. Anna must have seen to it that the monks who cared for him did not take their ascetism too rigorously, and in the weeks since I had seen him his chest and shoulders had swelled out like a warrior's. His pale hair was brushed and trimmed, and his young beard was beginning to close in over his chin. He looked uncertainly about the room, unsure perhaps as to why he had come.

Even before I could ask my question, his eyes told me the answer. I had seen him notice our prisoner, sitting bound and guarded, had seen the curiosity which the sight engendered. There had been confusion, certainly, and perhaps a little fear, for it was not so long since he had been in that position. But not, to my furious frustration, the least hint of recognition.

Κ

'This is not him.' A month in the monastery had worked miracles on Thomas's Greek, though I was in no mood to appreciate it. Thomas looked closer, his hesitant lips moving silently as he rehearsed his next words. 'But like.'

'Like? Like what? This man is like the monk?'

A look of pain furrowed Thomas's face, and I forced myself to repeat my questions more slowly.

He nodded. 'Like. Like him.'

'Like a brother, perhaps?' I turned to our cowering captive, who had heard every word. 'Is your brother a monk? Does he stay with you?'

I was tense enough to shake an answer out of him, but he merely snivelled a little and rested his head on his knees. One of the Patzinaks slapped the side of his face.

I looked to the sergeant. 'Go downstairs and ask the grocer whether this man received visitors: a monk. Apologise for the damage you have done his house; tell him that the Eparch will see he is well paid for his trouble.'

The sergeant looked doubtful, but I was the only man in that room who could vouch for the Eparch. We waited in silence while the sergeant thudded down the ladders; then we heard raised voices, the sound of the grocer's wife screaming accusations, and the crash of some clay vessel shattering.

The sergeant returned, flushed.

'There was another man who often stayed here. The grocer's wife had many rows with the tenant, who she calls Paul, over whether he should pay more rent for this guest. She was outraged that a man of God was taking advantage of them. "Why can he not stay in the monastery, with his brethren?" she asked.'

A flood of elation burst through me, but I tried to remain methodical. 'What did this Paul say in return?'

'That the man was his brother, brought to our city on a pilgrimage ordained by God. Who was he to deny him hospitality?'

'And when was the last time this monk visited?'

The sergeant smiled in triumph. 'Two days ago.'

I turned back to look at our prisoner. 'Your brother is the monk I seek, the man who would kill the Emperor.' I did not know whether to feel joy or anger that I had come so close. 'Sergeant, take him to the palace for the torturers to start their work. Leave six of your men here in case the monk returns.'

As I had hoped, I saw the prisoner Paul go pale when I mentioned the torturers. 'You will not snare my brother here,' he protested. 'He is gone.'

I watched him coolly. 'Of course you say that. We will see what you say after a month in the dungeons.'

The prisoner went silent and bit his lip; his fingers were now wrapped tight about each other, and his nails gouged white weals in his skin. 'He is escaped,' he insisted. 'I swear it. I saw him yesterday evening, in the forum of Arcadius, and he told me he would be gone by dawn. Whatever you want with him, you will not get it now.'

'Then we will get it in the dungeon.'

'But what more could I tell you there?' The prisoner threw his gaze desperately around the room, beseeching pity, though the watching Patzinaks evinced nothing but menace. 'He is gone, curse him, and he will not come back. You say he wanted to kill the Emperor, whom I pray to live a thousand years. Maybe he did. He was much changed, my brother, when he came here, and I think evil had blossomed in his heart, but what could I do? I could not bar my brother from my door: he would not let me – and he was my kin. "Do not be slow to entertain wayfarers," he told me, "for thereby some have entertained angels unawares."'

I snorted. 'He was far from an angel.'

'He did not think so.' The prisoner Paul shuffled his shoulders a little, trying to smooth out his tunic. 'How many nights did I listen to him, his sermons of how the empire needed a purifying fire to descend and burn away its withered branches.' Paul looked at me imploringly. 'He was not like this when we were young.'

After his earlier silence, the torrent of Paul's story left so many fragments I could scarce begin to think what to examine first. I settled on the beginning.

'When you were young,' I repeated. 'When was that?'

'Thirty years ago?' Paul shrugged. 'I have not counted. We grew up in the mountains of Macedonia, the sons of a farmer. Michael and I . . .'

'Michael? Your brother's name is Michael?'

Paul shook his head. 'It was then. But when I greeted him by it after he returned, he chastised me for it. "I am reborn in Christ," he said. "And I have taken the name Odo." After that he insisted I call him by this new, barbarian name.'

Once again the story was flowing away from me. 'After he returned . . . from where? When did he go?'

'He went not long after he was grown to manhood. He and our father . . . disagreed.'

'Disagreed about what?'

Paul lifted his bound hands and wiped his wrists across his forehead. 'Our father had arranged a bride for him, but Michael did not want to marry the girl. When my father insisted, Michael refused. Afterwards he left our village and came here, to the queen of cities. He said he would make a pilgrimage to the relics of Saint John the Baptist, and find absolution.'

'Did he find it?'

'Not here. He came, but he did not stay. He did not have the means to enjoy all the fruits of the city, and – though he did not say as much – I think he fell in with immoral companions. After he escaped them, his wanderings took him to the ends of the earth, to the lands of the Kelts and the Franks and the other barbarian tribes who cling to the fringes of the world. There he found his salvation.'

'In the western church?' No wonder he had taken a barbarian name, after the fashion of his new religion. 'When was that?'

'Some time in the past.' Paul looked at me hopelessly. 'I heard nothing from him in all those years after he left the village. Everything I know I have from what he told me when he returned. Some three months ago,' he added, anticipating my inevitable question. 'He sent no word that he was coming – I did not even know that he knew I was here. I had come much later, after our father died. One day I returned from my work to find Michael – Odo – sitting on a stone by the grocer's door. I scarcely recognised him, but he knew me immediately and told me he had come to stay with me. How could I refuse?'

'Did he say what he purposed here?'

'Never. And after one attempt, I did not ask again. He was always a private man, my brother, and he grew more so in his wanderings. He told me nothing, not even when he would be here. Sometimes he disappeared for days or even weeks, leaving no word, and I thought that perhaps he had gone back to his friends in the west, but then he would return unannounced and demand my hospitality again. Only yesterday did he say that he was going forever. As I told you.'

'Where was he going?'

'He did not say.'

I should not have been surprised. 'Did your brother ever mention any notable men of the city?' I asked, wondering if I could at least draw some hint as to his masters.

As so often, Paul shook his head, then looked up doubtfully. 'One evening I rebuked him for eating all my dinner. I had prepared none for him, thinking he would not return that evening. As was his habit, he responded with a bitter harangue on the pre-eminence of his work: he told me that he was employed by a great lord, and lesser men should presume nothing but to make straight his way.'

I kept my tone restrained. 'Did he say which lord?'

'Of course not. I assumed he meant the lord God. He often spoke of his calling as the Lord's avenger, the cleansing flame of the Holy Spirit.'

'Did he speak of what he would avenge?'

For the first time, I drew from Paul a feeble smile. 'Constantly. He wanted to cleanse the city of her filth, her heresies, and restore purity to her streets. To him she is Babylon, the great mother of whores and abominations, drunk on the blood of the saints. Michael swore that in the hour of her doom she will be made desolate and naked, her flesh will be devoured and burned with fire, and he will be the agent of this destruction.' His smile widened a little. 'If you read the apocalypse of the divine Saint John, you will understand.'

'I know the apocalypse.'

'During his years in Rheims, he had somehow been persuaded that this was his proper task.'

'His years *where*?'

'Rheims, I think he called it. A barbarian town. He spent some time at a school there, and later took orders in its abbey. It is where he was re-baptised as Odo. I do not know where it is.'

I did not know where it was either, but I knew I had heard of it. I thought back to a dusty library and a severe archivist lecturing me on Frankish saints.

'Did your brother ever speak of a Saint Remigius?' I asked. 'Or show you a ring inscribed with that name, mounted with a cracked garnet.' I reached into my pocket, fumbling for the ring which I had carried with me ever since that day in the forest, as if by holding his totem I might gain some grasp over the monk himself. 'This ring?'

Impervious to the excitement in my voice, Paul shrugged. 'He did have a ring, but I did not see it closely. It was red; it may be the one you hold. I glimpsed it only when he washed. He said it was a token of the barbarian town.'

'Did you ever see any others with such a ring?'

'None. As I have said, no-one visited my brother here.'

I spent another hour throwing questions at the prisoner, checking the details of his story and prodding for any clue he might reveal, wittingly or not. I asked about his own circumstances – he was unmarried, it transpired, and worked as a minor clerk for a notary, taking a fraction of his employer's earnings for the documents he prepared. He worshipped in the approved manner, fervently but without the zealous self-righteousness which the fathers condemned. He told me the name of his village and I wrote it down, for someone would have to travel there and ask about his brother. It would not be me: a journey through the Macedonian mountains in winter would not, I decided, afford the best use of my time and talents.

Outside the windows, evening was coming early to the dark day, and I was keen to be away. I had only a single question remaining, and it was more curiosity than hope. 'Tell me, Paul, was your brother a violent man?'

The words seemed to agitate the prisoner greatly. He did not answer, but jerked his head against his shoulder as if shaking water from his ear.

'Unbind me, and I will show you.'

I ordered a Patzinak to cut his bonds. Paul gave a grimace of acknowledgement as his hands were freed, and pulled up his sleeve. I drew in a breath, for all down to his wrist the entire arm was black, as if it had been burned or rotted away. Only after a few moments could I see that they were in fact a mottled patchwork of overlapping bruises.

'It does not become a man to speak ill of his brother,' said Paul heavily, 'but even in our childhood Michael was cruel. I told you he departed our village because he disagreed with my father's choice of bride. In truth, he fled before the vengeance of her father, after his rage had left the poor girl almost dead. He has learned many new things on his travels since then, but he has forgotten nothing. If he could throw down our city in a cauldron of blood, he would not hesitate.' He rubbed his loosened wrists. 'Indeed, he would revel in it.'

'So he is a Roman, corrupted by Franks into turning on his mother city, and returned to work violence and sedition.' Krysaphios licked the honey from his fingers as he considered this; he had been eating when I found him at the palace, and the urgency of my news would not deter him from his meal. 'And just across the waters of the Horn we have ten thousand armed Franks, who spurn our hospitality and provoke our ambassadors. Who arrived mere weeks after your monk. I imagine you have noticed the coincidence?'

'I have.'

'But how could they profit from killing the Emperor unless they could take the city. And what could give them to think they could do that? They have no siege engines to batter down the land walls, and no fleet to attack us from the seaward side. They depend utterly on the Emperor to provide for them. If they risked an assault and failed, we could starve or execute them at our leisure.'

'Then they must be confident. Or fools.' The contradictions bothered me too, for it was ever my task to question the anomalies which other men dismissed or did not notice, but here I could not resolve them. They were barbarians, I told myself – they did not think as we did. 'Perhaps they relied on the monk, or Aelric, to open the way for them.'

'It would need more than one treacherous Varangian to open our gates to an enemy horde.' A honeyed nut crunched between Krysaphios' teeth. 'And my spies have yet to discover any others who were complicit with Aelric.'

'Yet the Varangians remain exiled from the palace,' I observed. Every door and alcove still had a Patzinak by it.

'The Varangians are posted on the walls, away from the gatehouses, and will remain there indefinitely. We need men we can trust about us, Demetrios, and the Patzinaks are ferocious in their loyalty.'

'Until the monk manages to corrupt one of them.'

Krysaphios' smooth forehead wrinkled with mock confusion. 'But the monk is gone, you told me. His brother said so. Do you not think he has fled back to Frankia?'

'I doubt he is further than a mile beyond our walls, and probably safe in Galata with the barbarians.'

'You think he will come back? Attempt to murder the Emperor a third time?'

'I do. If his brother spoke truly, and I believe he did, then he is too much a zealot not to. Whomever he serves.'

Krysaphios fixed me with an inscrutable look. 'And so? How do you propose to act next?'

Here I was on firmer ground, for I had spent the march back to the palace pondering exactly that. 'First, we need to find a home for the monk's brother. I have brought him here, but he should not be cast into the dungeon. He has done nothing to deserve it, and a little kindness might repay itself with more news of the monk. We should leave him somewhere comfortable but secure.'

Krysaphios nodded. 'You have an extravagant kindness, Demetrios, but I will do as you suggest. You can quarter him in one of the houses we use for foreign emissaries.'

'Good. After that, we need to worm a spy into the barbarian camp. Someone who can see if the monk is hiding there, and listen for any word of a plot against the Emperor.'

'That will be harder. There are many eyes watching the barbarians: the Patzinaks, the merchants who supply their needs, even down to the drovers and carters who deliver it – all that they see is reported back to me. But to penetrate their darkest confidences . . . I cannot see how that would be done.'

'I can.' With brief words, I told him my plan. He did not like it; indeed, he rebelled against the sacrifice and chastised me for a sentimental fool. But, after a full hour's argument, I won him round.

*   *   *

Anna did not like the plan either when I told her the next morning.

'It will almost certainly fail,' she told me. 'Either he will abandon you the moment he has crossed the Horn, or he will be discovered and tortured to death. Either way, you would never forgive yourself.'

I rubbed my chin. 'I know. But I cannot think of an alternative. And if he does desert me, then he will be back among his own people and I, for one, will not feel his loss. There are many *poulia* in this game, and he is one who has no other role to play. If he succeeds it will be a great blessing; if not, we have lost nothing.'

It was a poor choice of words, and Anna hissed with anger. 'You've spent too much time in the halls of the palace, among the generals and eunuchs, if you believe that men and boys are all just counters in a game, to be discarded from the board at the throw of a die.'

'I'm sending him back where he belongs.' Her words pierced me like arrows, that she should think me so callous, but I hid my shame and persevered. 'A boy of his age should not be kept locked in a monastery far from home, to be tutored by monks. If he chooses to come back, then he will have earned his freedom and far more besides; if he does not, he is still free.'

'And if he tries to come back and is found and killed by the barbarians?' Anna's anger had not subsided. 'What will you do then, Demetrios?'

'I will pray for his soul. And for mine. I do not do this lightly, Anna, but there are no others who would be trusted in the barbarian camp who could pass for a Frank.'

'Thomas doesn't pass for a Frank – he *is* a Frank,' Anna observed tartly. 'And what of your monk? If he is in the camp, as you believe, then he will recognise Thomas and he will kill him, as he tried before.'

'Yes.' I had come to tell Anna that I would be taking Thomas away from her, but she had quickly forced from me the entire story of my plan and the reasons for it. 'There are ten thousand men lodged in Galata. With luck he will keep apart from the monk.'

'Luck.' Anna snorted, not at all like a lady. 'If you are trusting to luck, Demetrios, then you are a bigger fool even than I thought.' She pulled her fingers through her hair, and seemed to relent a little. 'Are you really so desperate to keep him away from your daughters?'

Despite all the gravity of the moment, I laughed. 'I would be grateful if you did not tell Helena. But I cannot force Thomas to do anything against his will, so I had better speak with him myself.'

Reluctantly, Anna acquiesced. She led me across the monastery courtyard to the kitchen door, where the sweet smell of baking bread mingled with smoke and the scent of onions. The aromas played on my stomach, for I had not yet eaten; they also reminded me of another cause for my visit.

'Anna,' I called, stopping her just before the door. 'Before we speak to Thomas, I had almost forgotten: I wondered whether you would come for supper with me. And the girls,' I added hastily, lest I seem too suggestive. 'Perhaps on some evening in the next fortnight, before the fast of Great Lent constrains my hospitality.'

Anna turned and eyed me with suspicion. She wore a reddish-brown dalmatica today, its inexpert dying giving the effect of woodgrain, or mottled leaves. It was tied over her hips with the silken cord she always wore, and the breeze in the courtyard blew the skirt close against her thighs.

'I accept your invitation,' she told me. 'But if you are merely trying to corrupt me into agreeing with your wicked plan, then you will fail.'

'It's neither for you to agree or otherwise. Thomas will decide.'

Thomas was in the kitchen, stirring a simmering pot of beans without enthusiasm, while a monk sat on the stairs and read at him from a dust-worn Bible. He scowled at the sight of Anna and slammed his book shut, locked the clasps and climbed the stairs out of the room.

'It happens often,' said Anna, without offence. 'Some of them do not like having a woman within their walls, and all of them fear what might happen if they were found alone with her.'

'Their misfortune.'

Thomas looked up from his cauldron as we approached. He gave a shy smile on seeing Anna, a broader smile on seeing that the monk had departed, and a nervous frown on seeing me. He let go of his ladle, and cursed fluently as it slid beneath the oozy surface of his broth. I doubted he had learned that expression from being lectured out of a Bible.

'Demetrios has come.' Anna spoke slowly. 'He wants to ask you something.'

I pushed past a row of iron pots to stand beside her. 'I have news of the monk.' I paused to see if he had understood me. From the way his eyes stilled and his cheek twitched, I guessed he had. 'We think he is in a big camp of barbar . . . of your people, outside the walls of our city.'

Thomas glanced hesitantly at Anna, who added a few words in his natural tongue.

'I want you to go there and find him.'

For a long time Thomas remained silent, while the pot beside him bubbled, and spat its liquid into the air. Some of it landed on his tunic but he did not seem to notice.

'If I go, he kills me,' he said at last.

I shook my head. 'No. You find where he lives. Then you go to the house of my friend.' My fervour hastened my words, and I had to concentrate to rein them in again. 'He will protect you, and send us your news. Then we will come with many soldiers and catch the monk, and lock him in the dungeon.'

Again Anna spoke in the barbarian language. I kept my eyes on Thomas, hoping Anna did not take advantage of my ignorance to dissuade him. Thomas replied in kind, hunching his shoulders and gesticulating with his arms; I felt a growing anger that I was barred from their arguments.

'I go.'

Coming at the end of a string of foreign sounds, I failed to realise that Thomas had reverted to Greek until he had repeated himself.

'I go.'

'You will go?'

He nodded, uncertainly.

'Good. Very good.'

'And when he returns, he will be free to go where he pleases, to return to Frankia or stay in Constantinople or settle in the empire, whichever.' Anna stared at me with steel in her eyes. 'You promise that.'

'I promise.' I would wonder how to persuade Krysaphios to honour that promise later, if the boy delivered the monk into our hands, and if he did not desert to his kinsmen.

If he lived long enough.

κ α

We stood by the Adrianople gate, shivering even in our cloaks. The rain which had relented on the previous day had returned with an implacable constancy in the night, beating on the tiles above my head so loudly that I could not use even the few hours I had for sleep. Two hours before dawn we had met at the gate – Anna, Thomas and I – the only light a beleaguered pitch torch in the shelter of the archway. Burning fragments dripped from it, hissing as they fell into the mud below. It was not a propitious beginning to what was already a slender hope.

'If they ask, tell them the truth of your story – how you came here, the fate which befell your parents, and how you escaped to live in the slums of the city. Perhaps blame your misfortune on the Romans: curse us for not having provided more aid to your army, or more succour when you returned.' I did not wait for Anna to translate my words, or worry if the boy had understood them. I had told him all this a dozen times the previous afternoon, and I spoke now more to quell my own nerves than to rehearse his duties.

'You will have to go all the way around the Horn and come back down its other side. It will not be a pleasant journey, but we cannot risk the chance of them seeing you rowed across from here. Give me your cloak.'

Unwillingly, Thomas pulled the sodden cloak from his shoulders and handed it to me. Underneath, he wore only a thin tunic which had been purposely torn on stones and dragged through mud.

'He'll die of cold before he's halfway to the silver lake,' Anna muttered. I half expected that, even now, she would try to persuade him to abandon the plan.

'He will look bedraggled, mud-splattered, and forlorn.' I let concern shade my voice with anger. 'As befits an urchin who has lived for weeks in the slums. He's already too fat.'

I turned my attention back to Thomas. 'Try and evoke pity with your story, and find a kind knight or soldier who will take you as his servant or groom. Then try and discover if the monk is in the camp, and where we can catch him. As soon as you know that, make for the house of Domenico the merchant. You remember where I showed you on the map?'

Thomas nodded, though perhaps only because I had stopped speaking.

A sentry ambled out of the guardhouse, his cloak pulled tight around his shoulders. The briefest glance at the pass I carried from Krysaphios satisfied him, and he started drawing back the bolts on the heavy door. I hoped that with the rain in his eyes he would be unable to see much of Thomas, for I did not want anyone to remember him leaving the city.

'I do not like this course,' Anna told me. There was sadness in her face. 'But Thomas has agreed it, and you think it necessary, so I cannot argue.'

The last bolt came free, and the sentry pushed the door open. It took the full weight of his shoulder to force it. In the night beyond, I could see only driving rain and darkness.

'Go, Thomas.' I gave him a little push to hasten him forward. He stooped to hug Anna, who held him tight for a moment, then turned his back on me and stepped out into the night. Long before the gate was drawn shut, he had vanished.

I returned home to my bed, but my broken night had upset my soul and it would not permit sleep. I lay there for hours, sometimes rolling onto one side or another, sometimes trying to lie very still, but even with my eyes shut the visions of my mind continued unblinking. A grim daylight and the hustled noises of the street pricked at my senses, and even when I could forget my concerns for Thomas, and keep from revisiting the memories of his departure, I found no solace.

Eventually, I surrendered and threw off the covers. A glance out of the window revealed nothing of the hour, for there would be little change between dawn and dusk that day, but it must have been near the middle of the morning.

I pushed through the curtains, ambled across to the stone basin and splashed some water on my face. It was as cold as the floor, though it did little to wake me.

'You've slept even later than Helena.' Zoe was sitting at the table stitching a tear in her camisia. 'She doesn't approve. She says a father should wake before dawn to provide for his daughters.'

'She can save her indignation – I couldn't sleep.' I found the end of a loaf of bread, spread it with honey, and chewed on it without enthusiasm.

Zoe looked up from her needlework. 'Did you leave us in the night? Helena thought she heard the door.'

I winced as a shard of crust scraped the roof of my mouth. 'I did. Sometimes the dark hours are the best time for dark secrets.'

'And dark fates,' Zoe admonished me.

I heard a door shut below, and light footsteps on the stairs. It seemed to take longer than usual, but at length the inner door swung open.

'You've risen.' Helena surveyed me reprovingly. She carried a basket of bread and vegetables under her arm, and her palla was streaked with mud. 'I thought you might have become the eighth sleeper of Ephesus.'

'And my heart rejoices to see you too.' A hammering pain was beginning behind my eyes and I did not welcome Helena's contempt, but I tried to remain calm. 'What have you brought for my lunch? Mutton?'

'There was no mutton.' Helena dropped the basket on the table with a bang. 'Only this.'

I peered at what she had brought. 'The fast doesn't start for another week and more,' I told her. 'Couldn't you have found some fish, or some gamebirds?'

'The righteous need no priest to tell them when to fast and when to feast,' said Helena stonily.

'Was he not there, then?' asked Zoe.

I looked between my daughters. 'Was who not there?'

'The butcher,' answered Helena quickly. 'No, he was not. He had sold his meat and gone home. The rest of this city must be as gluttonous as you, father – and they at least leave their beds at a decent hour.'

'Well, I want some stewed lamb. If my own daughter cannot provide for me, I will have to go to the tavern.' I pulled a heavy dalmatica over my head and tugged on my boots, then added: 'Perhaps in the afternoon we can go to see the spice-seller's aunt, and her nephew.'

I had meant it as conciliation, but at the sound of my words Helena stamped her foot, glared at me and swept into her bedroom.

I threw up my hands and looked at Zoe. 'Why should she do that?'

But Zoe was suddenly much preoccupied with her sewing. She stared at her needle and gave no answer, as inscrutable, in her own way, as her sister.

I abandoned my attempt at being the dutiful father. 'I will be in the tavern along the road,' I told Zoe. 'Eating lamb stew.'

But it seemed I was fated not to eat my meat that day: I emerged from my house to meet a quartet of Patzinaks. Three were mounted; the fourth, just moving away from his horse, was approaching my door. Another held the reins of a fifth horse.

'You are summoned to the palace,' announced the man who had dismounted. 'Immediately.'

I rubbed my temples. 'Has the monk been found? If not, I am going to eat my lunch. Tell Krysaphios he can wait.'

The Patzinak stepped closer, bristling. 'Your orders do not come from the eunuch. They are from a power you cannot defer. Come.'

I went.

There were many reasons I regretted the exile of the Varangians to the walls, and not least was their company. Coarse and erratic though they were, they had welcomed me into their conversations; the Patzinaks showed no such warmth. They rode two ahead of me and two behind, at a pace which allowed little more than an occasional grunted direction. I even found myself grateful to the horses for hastening the journey, though their jarring progress added a fresh dimension to my headache.

The Patzinaks' route was as direct as their manners: we rode straight up the Mesi, past the milion and the tetrapylon, and into the Augusteion, under the gazes of our ancient rulers. As soon as we halted the guards were off their mounts and on their feet, pushing away the candle-sellers and relic-merchants who flocked to the forecourt of Ayia Sophia. They barged a path to the great Chalke gate, thrust the horses' bridles into the hands of a waiting groom, and pushed past the petitioners and tourists who streamed into the first courtyard of the palace. In all this, I was their helpless obedient. I lost count of the turns we took, the corridors and courtyards we navigated, for with two Patzinaks at my back I had never a second to orient myself. The endless marble halls and golden mosaics made it hard to distinguish one part of the palace from another, and everything we passed seemed at once both strange and familiar. Only the ever-diminishing number of people around us suggested we were moving into more private quarters.

We stopped at a door flanked by two enormous urns, each taller than a man. The leading Patzinak turned to face me, and extended an arm towards the green courtyard beyond.

'In there.'

I paused a second, to draw a breath and to imply my independence. Then I stepped out of the long passage, and into a different world.

It was not a courtyard, as I had thought: it was a garden. But a garden the like of which I had never seen, nor ever imagined. Outside, in the city, it was a rainy day in the depths of winter, but here I seemed suddenly transported to the height of summer. The trees around me were not bare but laden with fruit and blossom, and a golden light suffused the air so brightly it seemed to shine through the very leaves themselves. The ground was soft, silent beneath my feet, as though I walked on cushions, though the grass seemed real enough. It was wet, but it must have been a dew for when I looked up through the tangled leaves and branches above I could see only profound depths of blue. And somewhere in the trees, birds were singing.

I began to feel giddy, dazed; I had taken a few steps forward into this orchard, and when I turned back there was no longer any sign of the way I had entered. Then I heard a sound behind me, a gentle rustling as of leaves or silk, though there was no wind, and I spun about again to see what marvellous creature might appear.

My fancy had almost convinced me to expect a centaur, or a griffin or a unicorn, but in fact it was a man. A man, though, whose magnificence could have graced any legend. The crown on his head gleamed like the sun, as though it alone was the fount of the mysterious light. His robe was dyed purple all the way to its hem, and woven through with gold, while the lorum which crossed his broad chest could have served as the armour of a god, so thick were the gems which crusted it.

Even before I had seen the red toes of his boots I was falling to the ground. The earth seemed to sink under me, absorbing me, and I had to reach out my arms to balance myself as I chanted the acclamation. Though the settings where I had seen him before – the great church, the golden hall and the hippodrome – were all magnificent in their own fashion, it was in that garden that I first believed that a man might indeed be a living daystar, might endure a thousand years.

'Get up, Demetrios Askiates.'

With some effort, I pushed myself away from the spongelike ground and stood, keeping my eyes downcast. There was something reassuring in his voice, something unrefined which seemed out of place in the fantasy of our surroundings.

'Do you like my garden?'

'Your . . . your garden? Indeed, Lord,' I stammered.

'I did not mean to unsettle you with it. I find it soothes me: a world apart from the world I rule.'

'Yes, Lord.'

He scratched the rough hair of his beard, and looked me in the eye. 'I have called you here to thank you, Demetrios. If not for you, I would have no need of craftsmen's tricks to believe I was in the gardens of heaven.'

I had never received the gratitude of an Emperor before, and I was unsure how to accept it. I opted for mimicry. 'Tricks, Lord?'

'Surely you do not believe that even I can bend the seasons and the weather to my will. Feel the leaves on that tree, those buds which are bursting to break into flower.'

I reached up and rubbed one of the leaves between my finger and thumb. It had the waxy sheen of a fresh oak-leaf, and I could see the dark lines of veins running through it. But to touch . . .

'It feels like silk,' I marvelled.

'Exactly so.' The Emperor Alexios swept his hand around him. 'All these trees – the grass and sky as well – all silk. Fires and mirrors make the sun, and if you were to pick yourself one of those plump apples and bite into it, you would break your teeth. Thus we maintain a world which is always on the cusp of summer, which never decays in the drear of autumn. Unlike my own realm.'

'Are there rooms for all the seasons?' I wondered aloud.

Alexios laughed, a throaty, peasant's laugh. 'Perhaps, but I have yet to find them. I lived five years in the palace before I discovered this room, and it took as long again for the workshops to restore its full splendour.' He coughed. 'But I did not summon you to talk about my garden, Demetrios. As I said, I want to thank you for guiding the traitor's axe past my neck.'

'I would have done the same for any man.'

'No doubt. But not every man could reward you as I will.'

'Your chamberlain already pays me more than I am worth to protect you. I was merely . . .'

Alexios smiled. 'It does not matter what *you* are worth: my chamberlain pays for what *I* am worth. And I pay for what I value. I have instructed the secretaries to make the necessary payments, in due course. I believe you will be satisfied.'

'Thank you, Lord. The gifts of your bounty flow from your hand like water from . . .'

The Emperor jerked his head. 'I do not need your flattery. I leave that to those who have no greater talents. If you must protest loyalty, do so with your deeds.'

'Always, Lord.'

'Krysaphios tells me you think it was the barbarians who tried to kill me. The men who are camped in Galata, consuming my harvest and refusing my envoys.'

'There are obvious reasons to think so.'

The Emperor pulled a leaf from the bough and twisted it in his hand. 'My brother, Isaak, believes we should fall on them at once and massacre them in the streets of Galata, then send the survivors back across the sea in chains. There are many in the court and the city who think likewise.'

'It would offend the laws of God,' I offered, having nothing better to suggest.

Alexios discarded his crumpled leaf. 'It would offend against the laws of reason. Those barbarians are there because I begged them to come, and if they have come in greater numbers than I hoped, and with their own purposes in their hearts, that does not reduce my need. Not if I am to rescue the lands of Asia which my predecessors squandered.'

'There are those who say that the barbarians have not come to rescue those lands, but to take them for themselves.' I could not believe that I was speaking thus with the Emperor, on matters of the most exalted importance, but against all expectation he seemed to welcome it.

'Of course the barbarians have come to take lands for themselves. Why else would they journey halfway across the world to fight for me? That is why I must keep them here until they have sworn to return what is rightfully mine. If, after that, they can carve out kingdoms of their own, beyond our ancient frontiers, then let them. I would rather have Christians bound with oaths on my border than Turks and Fatimids.'

'Do you trust the barbarians so?'

'I trust them as far as they keep their swords from me – which, it seems, is not nearly far enough. But they have their uses. When the Normans invaded, I fought them in a dozen battles and lost each one, yet still I drove them from our lands. Why? Because they will not trust each other for long: they are more prone to faction and jealousy even than the Saracens. Gold and ambition will divide them from each other, will keep them weak against us, while all that will unite them is their hatred of the Ishmaelites. They will gain gold and kingdoms; we will have our lands restored, and we will live together in uneasy dependence.'

'Will it work?'

Alexios snorted, in a way most unbefitting an Emperor. 'Perhaps. If the barbarians are not massacred by the Turks, and if they do not fall out with themselves before they even reach Nicaea, and if their priests do not discover that in fact the Lord God intends some wholly different purpose for their army. But none of it will happen if I do not squeeze those oaths from their captains.' He took my arm. 'Which is why you must ensure that nothing is allowed to destroy our alliance with them. If they succeed in murdering me, or are even known to have tried, then there will be war between our peoples and the only victors will be the Turks.'

The audience was finished. I left that enchanted garden of perpetual spring, and returned to the world I knew. Where the rain was still falling.

κ β

The rain fell for most of the following fortnight, splashing at my heels as I roamed the city. I spent many hours at the gates, watching as small parties of barbarians were admitted to admire the sights of the city and our civilisation. Most were content to gape in silence, though some felt compelled to mask their awe with belittling jokes and snide insults. Occasionally these would spark scuffles with Romans, but the Watch were always there, always ready to draw the combatants apart without violence. Clearly they too had had their orders from the Emperor. And all the while I wondered about Thomas.

The first two days after he left I had thought of little else, though I knew it would be weeks before I had news of him. His life was on my conscience, and I ached to ask those passing merchants who dealt with the Franks whether they had heard anything of him, but for the sake of his safety I could not dare. At least there was no news of his death, and as the days drew on my thoughts returned to more immediate concerns. Always, though, it was a weight on my heart, an itch worrying at my mind. Often it haunted my dreams.

There were also long days at the palace, when I wandered its corridors like a ghost, interviewing guards and functionaries, probing for any sign of trouble, and – as Krysaphios instructed me – keeping my eyes open. It seemed little enough to do for the gold he was paying me, but the strain of it told, for every hour I spent in those halls I lived in the terror that a slave would approach and announce that the Emperor was dead. I did not see him after that day in the unnatural garden, except once at a great distance: a gilded statue in the midst of an endless train of monks, guards and nobles, processing past a far door to the strains of music and incense. Otherwise, it was as if he inhabited a different world.

But I did see his brother, a week or so after my audience. A morning on the walls had left me too tired to face clerks who prided them-selves on the time they could take telling me nothing, and I was walking down some empty, forgotten arcade when I heard the sound of voices. Not the gaiety of courtiers, nor the grumbling of servants, but the hushed murmur of men who do not wish their words to be heard. It seemed to come from behind a small door recessed between two columns, open just enough to be ajar but not so much that you would guess anyone was within.

I walked towards it, but at the sound of my footsteps the voices paused. With a nervous glance at the solitude around me, I pressed my boot against the door and pushed.

'Demetrios.' The Sebastokrator's head jerked up as I fell to my knees, but I kept my eyes raised enough to see that he had been talking very closely with another man, who shrank back into the corner of the tiny room as Isaak stepped forward. He seemed flustered, but the time it took me to perform the full proskynesis allowed him to compose himself.

'Get up,' he told me. 'What are you doing in this corner of the palace?'

'I was lost,' I said humbly. 'I heard voices and thought I might find a guide to lead me out of here.'

Isaak scowled. 'Count Hugh, have you had presented to you Demetrios Askiates? He works for us to thwart our enemies.'

I bowed. It seemed that Count Hugh had forgotten the scribe who accompanied him on his embassy to the barbarians, though it would be many months before I forgot the preening Frank who had almost been pissed on in the barbarians' tent. 'An honour, Lord.'

'Count Hugh is one of the few Franks who understands the need for all Christians to unite under the banner of God and His Emperor,' Isaak explained. 'He hopes to persuade his countrymen to follow his good sense.'

'Thus far without success,' said Hugh mournfully. He fingered the agate clasp on his mantle. 'Some of them are reasonable men, yes, but too many listen to the poison which the whelp Baldwin spouts.'

Isaak looked at me carefully. 'But these great cares are not for Demetrios. If you seek the way out, take the north door from this passage and continue until you find the chapel of Saint Theodore. You will find your way from there.'

I bowed. 'Thank you, gracious Lord.'

He attempted an insincere smile. 'A Caesar's duty is to aid his subjects. And perhaps I will see you next week – at the games?'

I did see him at the games, though I doubt if he saw me. He was seated on a golden throne beside his brother on the balcony of the Kathisma, while I shared a bench high on the southern side with a group of fat Armenians, who cared for nothing but gambling and honeyed figs. Worse, they supported the Greens.

'Why would anyone support the Greens?' I asked of my neighbour, a thin man who chewed his fingers incessantly. 'You might as well declare yourself in favour of the sun.'

The man looked at me with terror, and returned to his fingers.

'Demetrios!'

I glanced up warily, for one meets many men in the Hippodrome and not all are to be welcomed. This one I was happy enough to see, though I barely recognised him without his axe and armour. He wore a brown woollen tunic with a studded leather belt, and high boots which had little difficulty poking a space between me and my timid neighbour.

'Shouldn't you be at the walls?' I asked.

'The walls have stood safe for seven centuries, and broken every army which came at them. They may survive an afternoon without me.' Sigurd shuffled along the bench a little, taking advantage of the newly vacated space. 'I thought I could take a few hours to see the Greens win.'

I groaned. 'Not the Greens. Why would you want to see them win?'

Sigurd looked puzzled. 'Because they do win. Who would not support the strongest team? Don't tell me that you support the Blues?'

'The Whites.'

Sigurd guffawed, happier than I had seen him in weeks. 'The Whites? You can't support the Whites – no-one does. Have they ever won once in your entire lifetime?'

'Not yet. Their day will come.'

'But they don't even race to win. Their only purpose is to act as spoilers for the Blues, to knock the Greens off the track and let the Blues past. They're not competitors. You might as well see me supporting the Reds.'

If you supported the Whites, as I did, these were not new arguments. 'Perhaps there is nothing I would rather see than the Green chariot upturned on the spina. The first and only time that my father brought me to Constantinople, he took me here and told me to choose a team. I was wearing a white tunic that day, so when I saw the Whites I decided that they would be mine.'

'You must regret not wearing green.' Sigurd was merciless.

'Not at all. Because one day the Whites will win . . .'

'If a murrain strikes down the Greens and Blues and Reds first.'

'And I will have more joy from that single victory than you will from a lifetime of seeing the Greens roll past the finishing post.'

Sigurd shook his head sadly. 'You will die a bitter man if you wait for that day, Demetrios.'

Thankfully, a fanfare of trumpets rescued me. We fell silent as the Emperor rose from his throne.

It was the first race of the afternoon, and the hippodrome was as yet only three-quarters filled, but its spectacle remained undiminished. The arms of the arena stretched away from where we sat, alive with the colours of all the races and factions of men in their tens of thousands. In the distance, above the far gate, four bronze horses reared up as if pulling their golden quadriga into the air, while the great dome of Ayia Sophia crowned the horizon. Along the spine in the foreground were the statues and columns, the monuments of a thousand years of competition towering above us. There were Emperors and obelisks, set beside half a dozen effigies of Porphyrius and the other charioteers of legend, to whose company the church had added saints and prophets. I could see Moses, clutching two tablets of stone as he hurried towards the north gate; Saint George, brandishing his lance; and Joshua sounding his horn from atop a sandstone column.

Down in the Kathisma the acclamations were finished. The Emperor retook his seat, accompanied by a thundering roar from the crowd as the gates sprang open and the chariots emerged. They were quick on the damp sand of the arena, and had passed the northern marker in seconds. The factions rose as their champions galloped past, great squares of blue and green, many hundreds of men wide, all shouting in unison. None wore White or Red, for few were fool enough to support the junior teams who raced only in support of their seniors.

The teams slowed as they navigated the first turn around the southern post. They were directly below me, now, but some fool follower of the Greens chose the moment to raise a wide banner which completely obscured my view. By the time I could see again, they were past the Kathisma on my right and almost back at the far end.

'Is that the Whites in the lead?' I asked, squinting into the distance. 'And the Greens, straggling along there at the rear?'

'If the Whites could race seven circuits as well as they race the first two, then perhaps one of their drivers would be immortalised in stone on the spine.' Sigurd was sitting forward on the lip of the bench, craning to see what was happening. He looked as happy as a ten-year-old.

'Tactics,' I muttered through my teeth.

As ever, the Whites had started well; as they came back towards us they led the Reds by a length, and the Blues and Greens by several more. But it was illusory, for the senior teams were biding their time, letting their horses stretch their legs on the opening circuits while their junior partners raced for the stronger position.

'They're taking their time.' Sigurd bit his knuckle, looking anxiously at his team. 'They don't want to leave too much to do in the turns.'

'They won't have to. Not with that lame mule on the outside.'

But I was speaking from hope rather than reason. I could see the Green and Blue drivers using their whips more freely now, goading their teams into an ever faster rhythm. The leading pair were beginning to tire – the Whites faster than the Reds, I feared – and soon all four would meet. Every man in the hippodrome was tense; some could not keep to their seats in anticipation, but bounced up and down like puppets.

'There go the Reds. Your Whites have gone too close to the spine. They'll never take this turn cleanly.'

It seemed Sigurd was right, for the Whites had kept an impossibly straight line coming down the stretch towards us and would need to rein in the horses almost to a standstill if they were to make the turn without crashing. Seeing his chance, the Red driver was fading away to his right, intending to cut inside the White chariot and force him against the far wall so that his allies the Greens could go through.

'Never mind that your horses can't run. Now it seems you have a driver who can't drive either.' Sigurd did not disguise his glee.

But his crowing was too soon, for the Whites were not slowing their approach to the turn. If anything, they were accelerating. I saw the Red driver look over at his challenger in disbelief, then start frantically lashing his beasts in a belated effort at overhauling the Whites. He heaved on his reins, trying to edge across the Whites, but there was not enough space and his nerve failed him.

With immaculate timing, the White driver leaned back in his chariot and pulled in his team. They seemed to slow almost to a stop, inscribed a gentle arc around the post below us, and began to canter away down the far side while the Reds, held off from turning and forced almost against the wall, watched the Blues and the Greens gallop past them.

'That won't help the Greens,' I shouted in Sigurd's ear.

'I thought the Whites were to knock out the Greens, not the Reds. Can't they tell one team from another?'

The noise of the crowd was overpowering; all were on their feet now, willing their favourites to snatch the lead from the Whites, who were slowing quickly. By the next turning post, if not before, the teams behind would have caught them and their race would be effectively over. I had seen it happen too many times before. But, as Sigurd had said, they still had to trouble the Greens long enough for the Blues to edge in front. In a straight, wheel-to-wheel contest, not a man in that stadium would have gambled against the power of the Greens' four horses.

The White driver now adopted a defensive strategy, standing almost side-on in the quadriga as he looked back to see his opponent. With every second that passed, he sacrificed speed veering across the track, trying to stop the Greens from passing while not impeding his Blue colleague. It was an awesome display of skill. But when your horses are tiring, and your opponents are nosing at your wheels, skill can be insufficient. They were about three quarters of the way down the eastern stretch, on the fifth circuit, when the Green driver turned his chariot slightly left. The White driver reacted immediately but was too quick: the Green had deceived him, and had just enough time to snake back across the track before throwing his horses into a skidding turn which must have come close to snapping his spokes. The White driver screamed at his horses to run faster, raining his lash down on their backs, and for a moment he and the Greens were galloping in tandem, as if all eight horses pulled a single, two-man chariot. The shouts from the crowd – from the factions, the gamblers, the fruit-sellers, even the morose man whom Sigurd had dislodged – rose in a cauldron of noise; Sigurd and I were bellowing out cheers and abuse like madmen. If the Whites could hold off the Greens until the next turn, I thought, they might have a slender hope of pushing them wide and upsetting their rhythm.

They could not. The Green driver, with almost indifferent ease, snapped his reins and watched the Whites drop ever further behind. By the time he reached the turn they were gone from his sight, and from there the distance only grew. The Blues tried to match his speed, but they had rested their hopes with the Whites and left their own charge too late. The noise subsided, and all around the hippodrome men began to reclaim their seats. Only the Green faction stayed standing: somehow they managed to sustain their cheering unbroken while their team galloped out the two remaining circuits.

'Not a bad race,' said Sigurd. 'We could have done better. He waited too long to attack. But I never doubted he would do it. '

'That,' I told him, 'is why I'll never support the Greens.'

Some of the Green faction had vaulted over the wall and run onto the track to embrace their champion, to wrap him in the victor's cloak and carry him on their shoulders in triumph. Down on my right, the palace guards had opened the gate to the Kathisma stairs, where the charioteer would soon ascend to receive the Emperor's blessing. The Armenians beside me were cackling with glee and swapping piled coins among themselves, while other spectators argued over whether the Blues should find a better driver, or if they should send their horses to pasture and bring in a fresh team.

I was about to search out a fruit-seller when a movement down on the arena floor caught my eye. A spectator had crossed the barrier and was moving down the edge of the track; as I watched, he reached the foot of the stairs, darted past the hesitant guards and began running up towards the Kathisma. Straight towards the Emperor.

I leapt from my bench in a panic. What if this was the moment I had been commanded to prevent, an assassin who would murder the Emperor in full view of a hundred thousand Romans? Could it even be the monk? He was too far away to see, and obscured by the stair wall which also protected him. The lumbering guards were at last giving chase, but he was well ahead of them and climbing ever higher. If he pulled a bow from under his tunic now, I thought, he would have clear sight of the Emperor.

Not knowing what I could do, I ran. Not down, for that was too far and too crowded, but up, towards the long arcade which swept around the rim of the stadium. It was almost empty at this hour, save for a few children who had come to escape the noise and bustle, and I sprinted along it as if driven by Porphyrius himself, around the bend and down the straight to the place where steps fell away towards the Kathisma. So quickly did I take them that I almost tumbled headlong to my doom, but my desperately outflung arms managed to steady me on the shoulders of a passing wine-seller.

I reached a mezzanine, level with the second floor of the Kathisma, and paused. The interloper had stopped on the winner's dais, an exposed platform before the Kathisma where the garlands were bestowed, and was on his knees. Patzinaks had sprung down from the imperial box to surround him, but they kept a wary distance as he finished his obeisance and rose to his feet.

'Prince of Peace,' he declaimed, 'the least of your subjects begs an audience. Hear my petition, Lord, that you may know the mind of your people.'

He spoke loudly, in a voice well-drilled by some theatre or market. His words carried across the ranked benches, for all about him had fallen silent; further off, I could hear the murmurings as his oration was repeated around the hippodrome.

I could also see the Emperor from my vantage, ensconced on his throne like a statue of Solomon. He neither spoke nor moved, and his guards and courtiers followed his example.

I found the silence ominous, but the orator seemed to draw strength from it. 'Why, Lord, are your lands ravaged by heretic barbarians, occupying our homes and eating our bread? Why do you tolerate their invasion, and feed their appetites for ransom and plunder? Every man in your realm would rather die defending his home from such carrion, than invite them in as wolves to the flock. Lead forth your armies, Lord, and drive them from our shore as once you routed the Normans and the Turks. Will we be snared by their wiles and slaved to their power? No.'

He was not alone in answering his own question – from all directions, voices began to echo his defiance.

'Will we see the Kelts defiling our daughters, plundering our treasury and sleeping under our roofs? Will we be forced to declare, against all the teachings of the church and of God, that the Spirit proceeds from the Son? That our Patriarch should be the slave of a Norman Pontiff? That, in the manner of the heretics, we should choke on unleavened bread when we feast at Christ's table? No!'

Now I could hear the 'No's' resounding from the far side of the arena as well. Still, though, the Emperor did not move.

'These barbarians are an abomination before God and His church, and before all who truly believe.' The orator had worked himself into a frenzy; his arms swung wildly and his face burned red. 'We have them in the palm of our hand: we should not stretch it out in friendship, but squeeze them in our fist until their blood runs from our fingers. Prince of Peace, your people beseech you to lead your army into battle and win them a victory to rank with your triumphs at Larissa, at Lebunium. Or, if you will not do so, then let some other member of your family lead them, and rout the barbarians from our homes. Defend the honour of Christ and the empire. Kill the barbarians!'

His words were like a wind on embers: hardly had he spoken them than the cry was taken up by the crowds around him. Quickly, their neighbours joined them, and then their neighbours' neighbours, until all the stadium shook with the chant. It was louder than any cheer I ever heard for a charioteer, louder even than the acclamation when the Emperor was crowned. 'Kill the barbarians! Kill the barbarians! Kill the barbarians!'

In all this the speaker was forgotten. Looking back, I saw Patzinaks surrounding him, dragging him from the platform, but he had worked his mischief. Whichever party or faction had employed him – and no doubt that information would be worked out of him in the dungeons – they had made their point. Whether the Emperor was wise to put his faith in the barbarians, to entrust the recovery of Asia to them, I could not know and did not care, but it was clear now that he had spoken truthfully in his garden. If he died, there would be war. And though the chanting, hate-filled faces around me seemed confident enough, I feared that in that battle there would be no victors.

κ γ

It was a long season, the Great Lent that year, but more from fear than penitence. A black mood hung over the city, the anger of ten hundred thousand people against the barbarians who starved and mocked them. It seemed they had stolen even the sanctity of our fast, for what was praiseworthy in fasting when there was nothing to eat anyway? Every day Helena went to the markets, and every day she was gone longer, trying to find what scraps were to be had. Most stall-holders had little to do but gossip, and even at the far end of the Mesi the ivory-carvers and silversmiths sat by their doors and watched their hands grow smooth. Only the churches kept their custom – increased it, even, as their incensed domes resounded with the prayers of a city begging God for food, deliverance or vengeance.

And all this while the smoke of the barbarian camp rose from across the Golden Horn, from behind the walls of Galata. More of them arrived, of all their tribes and races, and it took great purpose from the Emperor and the unbending Patzinaks to keep them quartered in distant villages, prevented from joining with their compatriots in Galata. In the city, the scuffles between Romans and visiting Franks escalated: one day a watchman was almost blinded when he intervened to stop some young squire being stabbed by the mob. None of the barbarians passed our gates after that, and my duties receded even more into the confines of the palaces.

It was wearing, lonely work, for there was little for me to do save watch. Once, early in March, I actually went to Krysaphios and asked to be released, but he would not allow it: the Emperor, he said, was adamant that every risk should be countered. So I continued my uncomfortable vigil, well rewarded but ill satisfied.

In those grim days, as the bastions of winter held out against spring, the one consolation was the friendship of Anna. Though she would not forgive me my gamble with Thomas, she had accepted my invitation to dinner before Great Lent, and many more in the weeks which followed until the invitation was scarcely needed. She became a welcome guest in our home, sitting with us in the evenings and sharing our meals, and if her monks or my neighbours disapproved, they did not show it. Those who knew my family best, indeed, declared that it was a blessing for my daughters to have a woman in the house, instead of the faltering attentions of a father too much preoccupied with his own affairs. And they were probably right, for my daughters found the season a great burden, and I think Anna was some comfort to them. Helena was particularly morose in those weeks, and even lost interest in hectoring me to arrange a marriage. Which was useful, as there were few respectable families who would countenance a union in those uncertain times.

For it was as if we lived the eight weeks of Great Lent amid a pile of tinder and kindling, while sparks showered down over us. There were skirmishes against the newly-arrived barbarians in an effort to keep them hemmed in at Sosthenium on the Marble sea, and it was rumoured that the Emperor had assembled an army at Philea, a single day's march away. Then there was the gossip, which I had on my own account from several merchants, that the cargoes they supplied to the barbarians were now much reduced by order of the Eparch, that the Emperor was trying to starve the men and beasts of the barbarian army into submission. None of these sparks set the city aflame, but all knew that it would not smoulder forever. And still the stream of envoys who visited the barbarian captains returned unanswered.

It was on the Wednesday of the Great Week of Easter, the last week of the fast, that the web which the Emperor had spun around the barbarians began to unravel. Anna was at my house, drinking soup with us after attending the evening liturgy, and we were – as so often in those weeks – discussing the possibility of ridding ourselves of the barbarians.

'You work all your days in the palace, father,' Helena said, 'what do you hear there?' She was far more reasoned and thoughtful in her conversation when Anna was present.

'Little more than what I hear on the streets, and in the markets,' I told her. 'Either the grocers are particularly well-informed, or the secretaries in the palace are equally ignorant.' It was true – there was barely a single piece of news I had heard in the palace which was not common rumour in the forum. 'But I saw a grain merchant I know today, and he told me – in confidence, naturally – that this morning he was ordered to keep back all his supplies from the barbarians. Unless they have started growing their own wheat and cattle, they are going hungry. Nor have they had any fodder for their horses in two weeks, that I know of.'

Anna drained the last of her soup. 'Is that wise? I have a cousin in Pikridiou who says the Franks are growing bolder. Yesterday they left their camp to plunder her village. Only the strength of the Patzinaks checked them.'

'Why don't they just go away?' Zoe demanded. 'Our walls are too high for them, and our armies are too strong – why do they stay here making us miserable?'

I put my hand over her small clenched fist. 'Because they and the Emperor both desire the same thing, the lost lands of Asia, and neither will forfeit it. They cannot reach those lands without the Emperor's permission, and he will not give it unless they surrender their claim. He cannot dislodge them save by force, but if he uses force he will break the alliance and lose all chance of invading Asia. We are like two serpents, so tightly coiled together that neither can bite the other.'

'They're both barbarous.' Helena, as ever, saw the problem with the clarity of conviction. 'Why should great men squabble and sulk, like Achilles before the walls of Troy? The true purpose should be to liberate the Romans – the *Christians* – who live under the Turkish yoke. What does it matter which army frees them?'

'It matters greatly.' I looked at her firmly. 'Ask Sigurd what the Normans did to his country when they conquered it. Every man became a slave, and the kingdom was booty for their lords to plunder. They are murderous and cruel, these barbarians; their rule would be just as bad as the Turks'. Perhaps worse. That is why the Emperor resists them.'

'Then why . . .' Anna broke off as a furious thumping erupted from the bottom of the stairs. She eyed me inquisitively. 'Did you expect others to join us?'

'None that I invited.' The sudden noise had jolted me with shock, spilling my soup across the table, but now I steadied myself. 'I will see.'

I crossed to my bedroom and pulled out my knife from the chest where I kept it. Then I descended the stairs.

'Who's there?'

'Sigurd. The eunuch commands you to the palace.'

I groaned – it seemed there was no hour of day or night when Krysaphios could not summon me. 'Can he wait until dawn, at least, when I will return there anyway?'

He could not.

I ran back up the stairs to the three expectant faces. 'I am called to the palace,' I said briefly. 'I cannot say when I will be back. Will you stay with the girls, Anna? You can sleep in my bed. I . . . I will take the floor when I return.'

Helena seemed about to complain that she could watch herself and Zoe well enough, but stilled her protest at a glance from Anna.

'Of course,' Anna said. 'Though I must be back in the monastery in the morning.'

'I hope even the chamberlain cannot keep me that long.'

The night was cold outside, though during the day I had begun to think that winter was relenting its grasp and making way for spring. Sigurd was waiting for me in the arch under the house opposite; he crossed the street and joined me as I closed my door.

'What is this?' I asked quietly as we strode up the hill. 'Have the barbarians moved?'

Sigurd shrugged. 'I doubt it – I saw nothing from the walls. A messenger arrived at the gate two hours ago and demanded I take him to the palace. I'd barely introduced him to the guard when some flummeried noble appeared and took him away. I was ordered to wait. Then one of the eunuch's slaves appeared and told me to fetch you there. Which I'm doing.' He paused, letting the stamp of his boots fill the silence. 'Even standing sentry duty on the walls was more honourable than being a eunuch's go-between.'

'You were doing much the same thing on the first night we met,' I reminded him.

'That was different.'

The moon was waning, but with still more than half its face showing it lit our way adequately enough through the pale shadows. We passed by the severe statues of the great squares, through the looming triumphal arches, down empty streets, and so to the palace.

Sigurd conferred briefly with the guards at the gate, and then at greater length with a clerk who sat at a table just within, scribbling away by the light of an oil lamp.

The clerk looked up at me. 'He will take you to the throne room,' he said, indicating a slave who had appeared noiselessly from behind a pillar.

'And you, Sigurd?'

'I will wait here.'

Without a word, the slave turned and receded into one of the main corridors. I had walked it many times in the past months, and always it had been thriving with all the ranks of palace life, from distant relatives of the imperial family down to the slaves and errand boys. Now it was empty, and the gaps between the pools of light on the floor seemed unnaturally dark. Soon we turned off the thoroughfare, and down a succession of dimly lit passages where the smells of oil and roses were replaced by dust and damp. Some of these areas were familiar, and others seemed so, but without my silent guide I would have been as lost as Theseus in the maze.

He brought me to an open peristyle and vanished. The arcades around it glowed with the warm light of many lamps, suspended from the roof on thick, golden chains, while in its centre a floor polished like silver reflected back the shaved disc of the moon.

I drew a sharp breath. It was not a silver floor, I realised, but a lake, a pool spread over the entire square, yet impossibly smooth, unrippled. A marble causeway was built out across it to an island in its centre, where I could see the silhouette of some dark structure rising from the water.

'Demetrios.'

I turned back to the arcade and looked about. The voice had come from my left, and from some distance, but I could see nothing. The thick columns which obscured my view drew my eyes up, and I gaped again as I saw their vast height, four times higher than a man at least, and far wider. I had seen larger, of course, not least in the great hall of Ayia Sophia, but the stark beauty of these stone trunks towering above the pool held an awe all its own.

I walked around the arcade to my left, looking down at the speckled images passing under my feet. They seemed to be cameos of bucolic life, or what some urban artist had imagined bucolic life to be: children playing or riding on donkeys, goats grazing, huntsmen chasing a tiger. But amid these idylls were flashes of brutality: a dog being ripped open by a bear, an eagle with a serpent writhing about its body, a griffin feasting on slaughtered hind. Protean faces in blues and greens stared out of the borders, wrapped with fronds and leaves, and from the gentle swaying of the oil lamps high above, one could almost imagine their features twisting and contorting as I passed.

I turned a corner and saw the origin of the voice which had called me: Krysaphios. He was perhaps half-way along the passage, but I was an uncomfortably long time under his gaze before I reached him.

'The Sebastokrator Isaak has sent me news,' he said. 'He has spies in the barbarian camp. They have found the monk there.'

'The monk?' He had faded in my thoughts over the past weeks. Though there had been every chance that he had not left the city, that he still sought a moment to strike at the Emperor, every day which passed without news of him had lessened that likelihood. He had become a phantom, a ghost who could slip into my thoughts – and sometimes also my dreams – but never assume substance. 'Where in the barbarian camp?'

'Near the wharves of Galata, in a lodging house by the walls. It is behind the warehouses, apparently, now abandoned by merchants who fear to transact their business in a barbarian camp.'

'Why was I not told that the Sebastokrator had spies there?' I demanded. 'How can you ask me to perform my tasks when there are vital factors I am ignorant of?'

'There are many things of which you are ignorant. I would have thought you might have guessed that the Sebastokrator keeps his own spies, as does every member of the imperial household. Did he not once ask you to serve him so?'

'Perhaps. But how will we entice the monk out of Galata? We may be invincible within our walls, but Galata has become almost a Frankish kingdom. Ten thousand of their warriors make a commanding body-guard.'

'We cannot entice him out. It has taken us weeks to find him, and if he sensed a single whisper of a trap he would disappear again. We must enter Galata and capture him. Or rather, *you* must enter Galata and capture him.'

I stared at him. 'I must enter Galata? How? Will a loyal widow hoist me through her window in a basket?'

'You will go with two hundred Patzinaks – they will protect you. You will be welcomed, because you will be escorting a grain convoy on behalf of the Emperor. While the barbarians are distracted, burying their faces in the trough, you and the guards will slip away and seize the monk before they realise what has happened.'

I shook my head. 'If we invade their camp, and forcibly abduct one of their acolytes, there will be war. No-one desires more than I that the monk should be captured, but in Galata his danger is caged. Surely that cannot merit risking all the Emperor's diplomacy?'

Krysaphios folded his fingers together and stared at me with the full displeasure of an imperial eunuch. 'The Emperor desires what I command. The Sebastokrator has agreed that it should be thus, and you will be the instrument of their will. Already the monk has proven that he can penetrate and corrupt our inmost halls and trusted servants: if he were to do so again, as the quarrel with the Franks comes to its crisis, there would be devastation in the empire. And there is not much time – two weeks, at most. Bohemond of Sicily, whom the Emperor defeated at Larissa, is hurrying here with his Norman army to reinforce the Franks. If they join their forces we will be helpless before them.'

I swallowed. This was news I had not heard in the markets – nor even in the outer wards of the palace. I remembered Sigurd's tales of the ruin the Normans had wrought on his homeland, and – far nearer my home – the barbarity when the Normans captured Dyrrachium and Avlona ten years earlier.

'When do we go?'

'So that you reach the walls of Galata at dawn, when they are least prepared. You will leave by the Blacherna gate and take the road around the Golden Horn.'

'Boats would be faster – and would make our escape easier if we met resistance,' I objected.

'But you could not cross the Horn until daylight. Then they would see your approach and prepare for it. By road, you will be hidden from them until you arrive. And I have already ordered the grain carts to meet you by the Blacherna gate.'

'Then it's as well we have two hundred men and a cloak of darkness,' I told him. 'The mob will slaughter us if they see wagons of food being taken from the city granaries to the barbarians.'

Krysaphios ignored my words. 'You will sleep in the palace tonight; I have ordered the slaves to prepare you a bed in the guard quarters. There are few enough hours already before you must leave.'

'I will sleep at home tonight.' I bridled against his dictating my least movement. 'I would rather half a night's sleep in my own bed than a full night in another's. I can meet the Patzinaks by the gate.'

Krysaphios flashed a look of petulance, but waved his hand carelessly. 'As you will. I had thought you would abhor distractions now that the monk is so near your grasp.'

'There will be no distractions.' Nor would there be any satisfaction, not until the monk was in chains in the dungeon. Even with two hundred Patzinaks to guard me, entering the barbarian camp would be walking into the jaws of a lion. I could scarcely believe that after this long chase, these many months' hunting, I might finally trap the monk. But even if I did, would it justify bringing the two great armies of East and West into open war?

I left Krysaphios under the shadows of those great pillars, beside the moon pool, and hurried out of the palace. The slave who had led me there appeared as soundlessly as before, and took me quickly to the outer courtyard. The scribe was still there, writing in the lamplight, and Sigurd with him, dozing on a bench.

'Is your axe still sharp?' I asked quietly, nudging his shoulder.

His eyes opened slowly, and I repeated my question. 'Or have long days on the rainswept walls rusted it?'

He growled. 'The only thing which blunts my blade is bone, and it has felt none of that these last two months. Why?'

'I am going on a dangerous errand tomorrow, and I would welcome a stout axe beside me.'

'What errand?' Sigurd watched me suspiciously.

'A dangerous one. It would be more dangerous for you to know more, though you can probably guess where the greatest dangers are to be found at the moment. Will you come?'

'I should be on the walls.'

'As you told me once before, the walls have stood seven hundred years without you. They might survive one more morning.' I spoke light-heartedly, but with Krysaphios' warning of the Normans ringing in my mind, the jest no longer held so much of its wit.

Sigurd rubbed his shoulder, then stood up. 'Very well, Demetrios.

You make a habit of needing my help in dangerous places, and my conscience has too much to trouble it already. When do we go?'

I arranged to meet him at the Blacherna gate at the end of the midnight watch, then slipped out of the palace and hastened home. The night was already old, and I began to doubt my wisdom in refusing Krysaphios' offer of a bed. I could not afford a tired mistake in the barbarian camp in the morning, for I might pay for it with my life.

I was now well known to the Watch, after so many weeks walking home from the palace after dark, and I passed through the streets undisturbed. The thought of the Normans still worried me, and the darkness of the shadows preyed on my fears all the way to my own door, so much that I felt a flood of relief when I had locked it behind me, mounted the stairs, and gained the safety of my own bedroom.

My frugal daughters had not left a light burning, but I knew my home well enough to navigate it blind. I stood there in the dark and pulled off my tunic and cloak, letting them drop unheeded to the floor. The air was cold about me, and I felt my skin pinch at the chill. Thinking I would have to rely on my soldier's habit of waking when I was needed, I felt for the edge of the bed and pulled myself under the covers.

Where I was not alone. I almost yelped in terror, a second before remembering my careless folly. Of course – I had asked Anna to stay with my daughters, had offered her the use of my bed while I was gone. How could I have forgotten, even with a hundred images of Franks and Patzinaks and Normans and war consuming my thoughts? And – worse – she was as naked as I, to judge from the smooth warmth of her skin against me. For a moment I could hardly move, paralysed by shock, embarrassment and a desire I had not felt in years. And to my further mortification, I was responding to her presence, firming and stiffening, pressing towards the hollows of her body.

I tried to pull away, but she mumbled something in her sleep and threw out an arm, crooking it around my shoulders and drawing me closer. Christ forgive me.

And she was not asleep, for the words she spoke next, though tinged with drowsiness, were perfectly clear. 'Demetrios? Is this your tactic, to lure unsuspecting women to your bed and then leap in unannounced?'

'I forgot you were here,' I said, desperately aware how false I sounded. 'In the dark, and with many worries troubling my mind, I . . .'

She put a hand over my lips. 'Be quiet, Demetrios. A woman wants a man who desires her. Not one who stumbles on her in the dark by accident as though she were the corner of a table.'

'But this is . . .'

'Sinful?' She laughed. 'I have spent my life probing the secrets of the flesh: I've found blood, bile, bone and sinew, but never anything that looked like sin. You were in the army – did you never seek company when you were far from home?'

Her plain speaking shocked me, but the way her fingers played over the small of my back beat down my consternation. 'A young man may find himself a slave to his urges,' I admitted.

'So may a woman.'

'I confessed it and was absolved. That does not license me to make it a habit.'

'But you have fought men, sometimes killed them. Why do you submit to anger but resist pleasure?'

Her manner was bewitching, and her persistent arguments inescapable. Nor was the resolve of my spirit constant in my flesh, for I had begun stroking my hand between her breasts, running it up to her throat and down the curve of her neck. I thought of my wife, Maria, and faltered a second, but the memory of her touch redoubled my desire, and I pushed harder against Anna's yielding body. She wrapped her arms around my head and pulled me towards her chest, dragging my lips over her in a welter of tiny kisses.

In my body there was now no resistance; every part of me was tugging, kissing or squeezing her, but my mind held out. Was this blasphemy? Did I defile Maria's memory, our marriage before God? But the Lord had not condemned me to the celibate life of a widower forever. And Maria, who had matched her elder daughter's pragmatism with her younger daughter's playfulness, would not, I thought, want me living the life of a monk in her name.

Perhaps that was true, or perhaps circumstance made me wish it true, but I was in no place for reasoned moral argument. I surrendered and sank into Anna's embrace, clutching her against me in our silent coupling.

κ δ

The Blacherna gate was cold when I reached it, and colder still for the sleep I had lost. Leaving Anna's caressing warmth behind had been hard enough, but as I plodded through empty streets to the walls, doubt and guilt and shame overtook me. How could I have surrendered to such abandon, and in the most sacred week of the year? What would my confessor say? How would the Lord God treat with me? With a long march through darkness ahead of us, and nothing but ten thousand hostile barbarians at the end of it, I had chosen a poor time to offend His laws.

Sigurd was already there. He had his axe on his shoulder, his mace by his side, and a short sword in his belt, yet still had the strength to carry two shields and another sword in his arms.

'These are for you,' he muttered. There was something about the night which hushed all our talk. 'I dug them out of the armoury.'

I strapped the shield onto my arm, and buckled the sword around my waist. The distance ahead of us seemed immediately longer.

'They've made these heavier since I was in the legions,' I complained. 'How can any man fight with this?'

'They've made you heavier since you were in the legions, I think.'

'Who is this?' The Patzinak captain, the same who had led the expedition to the monk's brother's house, jabbed a finger at Sigurd. 'We've no need of Varangians.'

'Sigurd is my bodyguard,' I explained tersely. 'He must accompany me.'

The Patzinak looked unimpressed, but shrugged and moved away to the head of his men.

Sigurd glared at me. 'Two months ago I was bodyguard to the Emperor. Now it seems I protect only those whom no-one could possibly want to kill.'

'Maybe.' I hitched the shield further up my arm. 'Let's hope that you can still say that in the afternoon.'

A shout from the front of the line ordered us forward. Two columns of Patzinaks began marching, followed by the squealing rumble of the lumbering grain carts. The oxen pulling them lowed their displeasure; their coats were glossy with the moisture in the air, and breath steamed from their snub-ended noses. Sigurd and I joined the after-guard at the tail of the column. High above us tiny squares of yellow glowed in the windows of the new palace, where perhaps even now the Emperor dreamed of conquests, but they vanished as we passed through the arch and onto the plain ahead. The moon was gone, and clouds had covered the stars, so we travelled almost blind, with only the huffing and squeaking of the ox-carts to break our solitude.

Those carts might have been a wise idea as a disguise, but they were nothing but a hindrance on that dark journey. One got stuck in a rutted stretch of road, and had to be heaved out by Patzinaks; then their weight forced us to pass by all the bridges, and travel to the very tip of the Horn. The shield dragged on my arm, and when I tried lashing it to my back, as I had in the legions, the straps almost strangled me.

'To think it is Great Thursday,' I murmured, as much to myself as to Sigurd. 'We should be at prayer, not warring with our fellow Christians.'

'If they feel likewise, then you can be at your church by noon.' Sigurd's strides were, as ever, a foot longer than my own, and I hurried to stay with him. 'If not, then you might yet find time to talk with God today.'

We straggled on, and I grew glad of the oxen for they were the only ones of our group whose pace was slower than mine. Now we were heading back along the northern shore of the Horn, following where it curved in to form the harbour. I could see lights across the water here, small fires rising on the crests of the hills, though the greater part of the city still lay in darkness. We should be close to Galata now.

As if to confirm my thought I heard a call from ahead, and the sound of two Patzinaks conversing in their fractured language. We must have reached the picket line surrounding the camp, must be little more than a few hundred yards away. The night was falling away, receding into a grey half-light which opened our surroundings to my eyes, and in the distance I could see the dark shadows of the walls of Galata. We had timed our arrival well: their sentries would be rubbing their eyes and thinking of sleep, thanking their God for another night unharmed, while the rest of the camp would be in their beds. Including, I prayed, the monk, in the small house by the far wall, on the street behind the warehouses.

I threaded my way to the front of the column, with Sigurd close behind. 'Do you remember the plan?' I asked the Patzinak captain. 'As soon as the gates are open we leave the wagons and make straight through the camp along the main street.'

The captain gave an unpleasant smile. 'If the monk is in there, we will find him.'

'Alive,' I reminded him.

We were within twenty paces of the gate before the challenge came, a thin shout from a boy who sounded little older than Thomas.

'Food from the Emperor,' I called back. 'Five wagons of grain. Open the gates.'

'Why does the grain come before dawn?' There was doubt in the boy's voice, but whether from nerves or suspicion I could not tell. 'And why is it surrounded by men in arms?'

'So that you can enjoy your breakfast, and so that brigands on the road do not empty the wagons before they reach you. The Emperor does not wish you to be hungry.'

That drew derision, followed by a long wait, perhaps while the boy conferred with his superior. I began to doubt Krysaphios' plan, to wonder whether we would be left standing at the gate while the Franks took the carts. What would we do then? We could not invest Galata with two hundred men, and we could do nothing which might spark a war unless we were sure of getting the monk.

Without warning, the gates swung open.

Even the Patzinaks, barbarians who would charge the walls of Hell itself if ordered, seemed to shrink as we marched into the camp. As we had hoped, there were few Franks about at that hour, but all those we passed stood by the roadside and watched us in hungry silence. Their arms were folded across their chests, and hate was plain on their gaunt faces. Even the sight of the grain carts rolling in behind us did

219

not soften them, though a few of the children scurried away from their parents' sides into the alleys behind, doubtless spreading word of our arrival.

'You have to wonder why the Emperor allowed them to set their camp within a well-fortified colony,' I said to Sigurd, breaking the hostile silence which surrounded us. 'They might have been more co-operative with nothing stronger than canvas to protect them.'

'Perhaps he wanted to prove he trusted them. Or perhaps he wanted them trapped, easily surrounded and watched. Walls make prisons, as well as forts.'

'Whom do they imprison now?'

We reached a square, the main forum of Galata. There were more Franks here, many of them women and children with baskets for carrying home the grain. They surged forward as the ox-carts halted, but our column of Patzinaks never dropped a step. From somewhere behind us a man shouted that we should halt; we ignored him, and kept marching. I had to credit Krysaphios' cunning, for the grain served its purpose: with the choice between stopping a company of Patzinaks or eating for the first time in days, every one of the Franks chose to serve his stomach.

Unhindered, we crossed over the square and entered the twisting road which the Sebastokrator's spy had described. It followed the line of the coast a few dozen yards away, but so thick were the buildings against it we caught only the merest glimpses of water. It seemed almost deserted, perhaps because of the hour or perhaps because all its occupants were gorging themselves in the forum. Whichever: the fewer people who saw us capture the monk, the safer we would be.

As we progressed deeper into the town, the shops and taverns which had lined the road gave way to warehouses, taller and heavier build-ings which pressed against the sides of the street. They had few windows and fewer doors, and none of the wondrous smells that surrounded their counterparts on the far side of the Horn. I had heard that the business of trade had almost died since the barbarians arrived, and since the Emperor began his blockade. Certainly there was none of the industry of stevedores, factors and merchants I remembered from my last visit.

We had now come clear across the town of Galata; ahead of us I could see the bulwark of the western walls barricading the end of the street. And just before it, tucked into a crevice between two warehouses, in what must once have been an alley, a thin house.

I tapped the Patzinak captain on his armoured shoulder, and started at the speed with which he spun about. He was broad and squat, almost like a boar, and the links of his scale armour strained against each other, but there was a worry in his grizzled eyes which unsettled me.

'That is the house,' I told him, pointing to the thin building. 'We should get some men behind it, but there seems little point garrisoning the roofs of the warehouses.' They towered over it on either side, and it would have taken the leap of Herakles to escape that way.

The captain jerked his head, and I heard the rattle of armour as two dozen men turned down an alley behind us to guard any retreat the monk might attempt.

'Do we knock on the door?' he asked slyly.

'We knock it down.'

He shouted an order and six men ran forward. Instead of swords they carried axes – not great battle-axes, like Sigurd's, but woodsmen's tools for hewing trees. The core of our company assembled opposite, ready to charge the moment the door was broken, while the rest broke into two parties guarding either end of the street. It seemed a ridiculous force to apprehend a single man, but I knew him too well to think it extravagant.

'Now.'

Two axes swung against the door, their blades biting into the wood and gouging deep rifts out of it. I saw the Patzinaks heave to get them free, then sweep them round again into the timber. It splintered and trembled, but did not give. Its strength must have frustrated the assailants, for they pulled their axes clear again and struck a third, thundering blow.

One of the men swore and turned to his captain. He shouted something angrily in his own tongue, which I could not understand.

'What did he say?'

'He says . . .' The captain's words choked off inexplicably; he clutched his neck, and turned to look at me, as my eyes opened wide in horror. An arrow had transfixed his throat, and blood streamed out of it down over his hands. He sank to his knees in silence and I stared, uncomprehending, but even as I looked I heard more cries around me, and the buzz and rattle of arrows in flight.

'They're on the roof!' Sigurd shouted. 'Get into the building! And get your shield over your face,' he added. He charged across the street and slammed his shoulder against the scarred door of the house. It was a blow to topple an ox, let alone the ramshackle door of a makeshift tenement, but Sigurd recoiled from it as if he had struck stone.

'They've barricaded it,' he called. 'It's a trap. Raise your shield, curse you.'

Still reeling, I found the wit to lift my shield arm across my eyes as I crouched on the ground. It was not a second too soon, for even as I did so I felt the blow of an arrow thudding into the leather, inches from my head. The impact threw me off my balance, and I tumbled onto my side, before thick arms dragged me to my feet and pulled me into the shadow of the warehouse.

'Their archers are on the roofs,' said Sigurd grimly. 'They were expecting us.'

'But they cannot have had time since we arrived to assemble . . .'

Sigurd cut me short. 'Time enough. And for who knows what else besides. We must escape before they bring reinforcements.'

Keeping my shield over my head, I peered out. A dozen corpses already lay spilled out in the road, but the rest of the Patzinaks had managed to huddle themselves into four circles, holding their shields above them and warding off the worst of the onslaught of arrows.

'If they keep that formation, they can retreat to the docks,' I thought aloud. 'We can find a ship to evacuate us.'

I would have crossed to the nearest cluster of men and explained my plan, but Sigurd held me back. 'We won't find a craft that can hold two hundred of us and just sail away. We'll be trapped with our backs to the sea – we'll be driven into the water or massacred. We have to make for the square, for the gate.'

'That's half a mile away,' I protested 'We can't go that far scuttling like crabs.'

'We can if the alternative is death. And once we get away from these warehouses, the archers will be behind us. Unless they have more further along the route.'

Who knew where the barbarians would be? But I could not ponder it, for suddenly – as quickly as it had begun – the chattering of arrows on the walls behind me stopped. Nor was it just where we stood, for

I could see the Patzinaks in the street relaxing their locked shields a little, peering out from their makeshift shelters.

'Have they run out of arrows?' I wondered.

'All at once?' Sigurd glanced up grimly. 'I doubt it. This will be some new devilment. We should move now.'

Even as he spoke I heard a rumbling in the ground, as tremors before the earth shakes. Was even God against us now? The Patzinaks in their circles looked about nervously, shields half lowered. The rumbling grew louder, and Sigurd must have recognised it a second before the rest of us, for I heard him shouting for the men to form a line just as the barbarian cavalry galloped around the bend in the road. Some of the Patzinaks gaped, petrified with horror, but discipline and instinct triumphed in the majority and they began spreading across the street with their shields before them. We did not have spears, but it takes more than spurs to force a horse into a line of men, and if a single beast pulled up it would throw the others into disarray, opening a gap for us to charge into.

But we were undone. The archers above unleashed a fresh volley of arrows, striking down those Patzinaks whose attention was on the oncoming knights: they were caught between the two onslaughts, unsure where to face, and died helplessly. Sigurd strode among them, trying to marshal some form of order, but confusion frustrated his commands and there were too many spaces in the line to check the cavalry.

They broke over us in a wave of spears and blades, thrusting and chopping and hacking at any who withstood them. One galloped inches past my face, but the wall behind me broke his swing and forced his sword away from me. I lunged blindly with my own weapon, but he was already gone and I stabbed nothing but air. Then the space about us was clear again, and I stumbled forward into the street. The ground was littered with blood and shields and broken men, some of whom lifted themselves to their feet, but many more of whom did not. Sigurd still stood, a mountain above the carnage, pulling his axe from the chest of a Frank he had unhorsed and bellowing orders, but there were few who listened. An arrow struck the road by my foot and I ducked down again, but the archers must have had their fill of easy slaughter for their shots were sporadic now.

I waved my arm to the far end of the street, where the cavalry were regrouping. 'Their next charge will surely sweep us away,' I called. 'We cannot withstand them.'

'I will fight to the death,' Sigurd answered, his face crimson with blood and anger. 'There is no honour in surrender.'

'There is less honour in leaving my daughters orphaned. Die for the Emperor, if you must, but do not waste your last strength in some skirmish of no account. The barbarians will value us far more as hostages than as corpses.'

The keenest of the Frankish cavalry were already beginning to urge their mounts forward, kicking at their flanks and bellowing the war-cries of their race. Lances tilted down; they would be upon us in seconds.

'The Varangians never surrender,' Sigurd shouted wildly. 'We do not leave the battlefield before our enemy, except in shrouds. Stand and fight!'

But his was a lonely voice in a lonely place. Whether Varangians would indeed have fought to the last I do not know; the Patzinaks would not. All around me, those who could still stand cast down their swords and shields and lifted their arms to show they were finished. For a moment I thought the Franks would ride them down even then, but at the last they divided themselves and rode into a circle around us. Sigurd alone resisted the inevitable defeat, snarling and prowling and hurling challenges at our captors, but at length even his head dropped, and his axe fell to the ground.

The barbarians did not address us, but let their spears speak for them. Those ahead began to ride away, while those behind advanced, jabbing at our heels. They did not even allow us time to drag our wounded to their feet, and I saw at least one man, still alive, casually trampled under the cavalry's hooves. Shame and fury were evident on all our faces, none more than Sigurd's, but we were impotent: the Franks could have butchered us in seconds.

They herded us like swine back to the forum. The grain carts were gone, doubtless swept clean of all their load, but a crowd many faces deep had gathered. They were expecting us, I realised, taking in the gleeful expectation around me, just as the archers and cavalry had expected us. It sickened me to think of the ease with which we had been trapped.

Four tables had been dragged together on the far side of the square to form a crude platform, on which a dozen of the Frankish captains now stood. All were in armour, and many had their faces obscured by helmets, but the man standing at their centre was bareheaded – and familiar. He was the fair-haired duke, Godfrey, who had received Count Hugh's embassy in his tent: I remembered he had treated the count courteously, if warily, while his brother pissed on the floor. Though I was numb from the battle, from the forced march at spear-point and the peril of our predicament, the sight of him gave me reason for hope.

Hope which vanished as the leader of the cavalry cantered around the square, reined up his great bay stallion before the stage, and tugged his helmet from his head. His dark hair sprang out in unruly curls, as though he had just risen from his bed, while beneath it the skin was as cold and pale as ever. Baldwin, I remembered, the unlanded brother of Duke Godfrey.

He slipped from his horse and crossed to his brother, a triumphant smile on his face. He spoke brashly and quickly, waving his arms towards his captives and directing his words as much to the crowd as to his brother. He spoke in Frankish, but there was little misunderstanding the vicious exultation in his voice. He seemed to be pressing some sort of argument, for several times the duke interrupted him sharply, but the mind of the crowd was clearly with Baldwin. When he addressed them directly they cheered and applauded, while when he jabbed his finger at his brother they whistled and jeered.

They must have agreed on something, though, for at length Baldwin leaped down off the platform and advanced towards us.

'No doubt he comes to tell us how much our ransom will be,' I whispered to Sigurd. 'Did you understand any of what was said?'

Sigurd shook his head, the agony of surrender still plain on his face.

Without waiting for a translator, nor making any effort to discover which of us was the leader, the barbarian captain approached the nearest of the Patzinaks. The guard's arm was bleeding, gashed by a spear, but he lifted his chin and drew back his shoulders as Baldwin stopped and stared haughtily down on him. He let his head drift away, then snapped it back and spat full on the Patzinak's face. The Patzinak flinched, but otherwise kept still, while Baldwin grinned around at the approving crowd, accepting the murmur of agreement which greeted him. He was still facing them, still grinning, while his hand dropped to his sword-belt. And the grin never left his face as he spun about, pulled his sword from its scabbard and, in a single arc, sliced it across the Patzinak's throat. There was not even time for surprise to register on the murdered guardsman's face before he was dead on the ground. Blood began spreading across the stones around his body.

A roar of jubilation erupted from the crowd, and Baldwin gave a mock bow, wiping his blade on the dead man's sleeve. His brother looked on with silent disdain, but he could not defy the mob whose cheering only grew as Baldwin took two exaggerated steps towards the next Patzinak. His blade hovered before the man's face, darting left and right; then, as the guard tried to duck from its path he reversed the sword and stabbed it into the man's leg. The guard howled with pain and doubled over, presenting his neck to Baldwin's hungry blade. He probably did not even see the blow which killed him.

I closed my sickened eyes, then reopened them and looked to Sigurd. 'We cannot endure this,' I hissed. 'He will murder us all for sport, if the crowd do not tear us apart first. We must escape.'

'You said we would be worth more as hostages than corpses.' I had never heard such bitterness as was now in Sigurd's voice.

'I was wrong. But if we are to die, we should die on our feet. And if we can avoid it altogether . . .'

There must have been four score of us captive in that forum, and Baldwin's barbarity had kindled the same determination in every soul. Now one of the Patzinaks acted. Refusing to be a willing sacrifice, he charged towards the edge of the square where the crowd was thinnest. The knight there raised his sword to chop him down, but the Patzinak ducked away under the horse and escaped it. I saw his hands grasp the barbarian's leg and start to pull, while his shoulder must have collided with the beast's ribs for it reared up on its hind legs, unseating its rider. He fell to the ground with a cry of terror, and in an instant his sword was in the hands of the Patzinak, who lunged towards the crowd with a great shout of defiance.

Desperation filled my lungs. 'Now,' I shouted. I snatched Sigurd's arm and pointed to our right: as the Frankish cavalry and their rabble surged forward to stop the lone Patzinak, a gap had appeared in their cordon. I sprinted towards it with Sigurd close behind, crushed my fist into the single man who barred my way, and stuck my knee into his groin to be certain. He collapsed from my path. More cries and shouts sounded from behind me as Sigurd cracked and shattered the limbs of those who tried to stop him.

We were free, but I could hear the noise of many footsteps running after me. Whether they were barbarian pursuers or Patzinaks who had followed us out I could not tell and dared not look, but they pushed me on up a thin alley away from the forum, away from the confused commotion of the Frankish mob. I ran past the first two roads which turned off my path, swerved into the third and ducked immediately down another lane, hoping it would not prove a dead end, for the sounds of pursuit were everywhere about me. It was empty, but would not be so for long, and with so many barbarians we could not keep running around this maze for ever. I saw a crooked shed leaning against the wall of a house and made for its door, praying to my God that it would not be locked, while Sigurd pushed past me, scanning for any enemies approaching ahead.

The door resisted my first touch, but a frantic kick broke through the rust on its hinges and it swung open. I turned to call Sigurd back, for here we could wait until the barbarians passed, but the shout died in my throat.

A barbarian had found me. He stood behind me watching curiously, almost lazily, though there was nothing the least slack in his arms and shoulders. The blade he held at my neck did not tremble an inch.

He had both grown and withered in the last two months. His beard was now full, though still close to the chin, and hunger had chiselled away at his face to reveal the man beneath. But he was thin, far thinner than after weeks of the monks' hospitality, and if work had kept his arms and legs hard with sinew it had also stooped his back a little. What had it done to his spirit?

He seemed unsure what to say, but this was no time for long silences. 'Are you going to kill me, Thomas? Or turn me over to that demon Baldwin to be dismembered?'

'You are the enemy of my people,' he said harshly.

'I am your friend. I saved you from death, once, you remember.'

'You tied me up like a thief.'

'And then set you free.'

I saw the tip of his sword decline just a fraction before his arm stiffened again. 'You are the enemy of my people. You try to starve and kill us.'

'Will you orphan my daughters because we serve different masters?'

The mention of orphanhood must have bitten his conscience, for he went very still, and suddenly the eyes which stared at me seemed to be those of a child again. I thought to say more, to evoke his own parents, but I did not want to twist the knife of memory too far. He would not have forgotten them, I told myself: if their loss could sway him, then it would be so, and if not, then I would die.

'I do this for your daughter,' he whispered at last. 'And because you save my life.'

'Thank you.' I could hear more shouts, and the echo of horses' hooves drawing near. 'Can you help me get to the harbour? To find a boat?'

Thomas shook his head. 'No boats. The Greeks take them all. And my people look for you there. Go away. Go up to your friend on the hill.'

Panic and incomprehension stalled my mind for a moment, before I realised whom he meant. 'The merchant Domenico? You mean him? Is he still there?'

Thomas shrugged. 'I see him sometimes. He help you.'

That was something I would discover myself. I had not seen the merchant Domenico since before the Feast of the Nativity, and he was closer in kin to the barbarians than to the Romans. But Thomas spoke truthfully of the alternatives: the Emperor *had* ordered all boats away from Galata, to complete the barbarians' isolation, and it was in the lower reaches of the city, around the docks and gates, that the search for us would be thickest.

'Will you lead us?'

Thomas did not answer, but turned his back on me and began moving up the street at a half-run. I followed with Sigurd, who had watched my conversation with Thomas in silence.

'Do you trust him?' he whispered as we approached the corner.

'I would not choose to trust him. But it is not my choice to make.'

'It may still be the wrong choice. We should have knocked him down and left him in a corner. Then at least we would have had a sword.'

'It will take more than a sword to escape from this trap.' I spoke shortly, for ahead of me Thomas had not stopped at the corner, but had run straight out into the crossroads, and I heard frantic shouts erupt as he came into view. He turned to acknowledge them, and I watched in helpless despair as he shouted back, waving his arms confidently. Were we betrayed? I could scarcely stand to wait there, helpless, utterly ignorant of whether he summoned our doom or our salvation. Beside me I felt Sigurd tensing himself, as if to spring forward and strike Thomas down, and I touched his arm to stay him. If Thomas had revealed us to his countrymen, we would be powerless.

Thomas turned and began walking towards us, moving with an almost insouciant air. Only when he was out of sight of the main road did he drop the pretence and hurry to meet us.

'I tell them you are not here,' he said curtly. 'They go.'

'You sent the Franks – your people – away?' As I listened, I could hear the truth of it, for the noises which had been almost upon us were now fading to a few lingering shouts. We waited until they were almost silent, then followed Thomas away from that place, up into the streets which led inland from the harbour. Thomas was a sure guide, and as the shore and barbarians receded he grew ever quicker, darting around corners and seeking out crevices if danger threatened. Once he was so fast I thought he might intend to maroon us, but he always reappeared, beckoning us upwards.

And suddenly we were in the mouth of an alley which faced a lime-washed wall, and the gate I had passed through once on a December afternoon. Thomas pointed at it.

'Domenico.'

I took his arm to thank him, but he drew away abruptly.

'You can come with us,' I told him. 'After this you have earned your freedom. You can live in the city and make a new life.'

He did not answer, but disappeared back down the hill. Back to the barbarians.

We crossed to the gate, and endured a terrified wait while the suspicious doorkeeper approached, argued with us, took our names to his master and finally returned, grudgingly, to admit us. The courtyard was little improved from when I had last visited – worse, in some respects, for the orange trees had not taken to their soil, and had shed most of their leaves onto the unpaved ground. The façade remained incomplete and unpainted, but there was no sign of the workmen or their tools. I doubted Domenico would have wanted too much ornament with barbarians for neighbours. Somehow, though, through invasion, siege, famine and war, the little merchant had managed to keep as plump and well-groomed as ever. Only the rims of his eyes told the strain he was under as he welcomed us to his house.

'You stretch the laws of hospitality, Demetrios,' he admonished me as we sat in a cool, unwindowed room deep in his house. 'I do not usually entertain outlaws.'

'Nor do you now. The law of the empire still holds here.'

Domenico giggled nervously, and wiped his brow on the arm of his gown. 'Is it the law of the empire that imperial soldiers are executed in a public square by a Frankish lunatic? That a hysterical mob rules the streets of Galata with the justice of the sword?'

I leaned closer, urgency in my eyes. 'Were you there in the square? Did you see what befell us?'

'Me? No, indeed no. But I hear much.'

'There was an argument between two of the barbarian captains, the Duke Godfrey and his brother Baldwin. Do you know what they said?'

We were interrupted by the arrival of a servant bearing a flagon of wine and a plate of smoked partridge. I downed my glass as soon as it was offered, and gobbled the tender meat like a glutton.

'You no longer observe your fast,' Domenico observed.

'Not today,' I admitted between mouthfuls. I could serve my guilt later. 'But tell me of the barbarians.'

Domenico sucked some fat from his fingers. 'My report is that Baldwin, the younger of the pair, declared that the Emperor had shown his true intentions, that after penning them up, starving them of food, and heaping indignities upon their holy quest, he had declared war. To this, he averred, there was only one response. They must invade the city itself, and drag the impious usurper from his throne. Only thus would the honour of God be satisfied.'

'Let them try,' snarled Sigurd. 'I saw no siege engines in their camp. If they assault the walls and legions of Constantinople with their rabble, they will learn what happens when the Emperor goes to war.'

'So said Duke Godfrey. But his brother answered him that he had a spy within the walls who would open the city as the Lord opened Jericho to Joshua. He added a few slurs against the prowess of your race which I need not repeat, but the crowd adored it. Especially when he demonstrated the ease with which your soldiers died.'

I poured myself more wine, splashing it over the rim of the cup in my haste. 'Did he name the spy?'

Domenico looked at me severely. 'And perhaps reveal when he would strike, and by which ruses he would open the gates? No, he did not. But there were other things he said, which I guess would interest you greatly. A Norman army is coming . . .'

'I know.' I lifted my hand wearily. 'In two weeks it will be here, and then there will be twice as many barbarians to contend with. This is not news to me. Surely Baldwin will wait until then.'

Domenico sighed. 'You do not know how their minds work, Demetrios. Baldwin has not come to see the holy sights of Jerusalem, nor to help his Norman rivals gain a throne. He has come for himself, and he is terrified that if he delays others will snatch his prize. That is why, even as we speak, his army straps on its armour and prepares for battle.'

'You seem well acquainted with the barbarian's plans.' Sigurd curled his fingers into fists, and let them loose again. 'How does a merchant come to know the minds of our enemies so well?'

'In the same fashion as I come to have meat and drink on my table when all around me eat rats. I listen for what I want, and pay generously when I find it. Baldwin and his brother hold sway over this colony, so I learn everything I can of them, in the hope that one day the information may avail me something.'

There was a silence in that dim room, while each of us summoned our thoughts. At last I spoke. 'If the barbarians are marching on the city, in the hope that a traitor will undo us, then we cannot delay. We must get word of this to the palace, and warn the Emperor of their intentions.'

'You cannot leave this house,' said Domenico. 'Baldwin has unleashed the mob in this colony. It is a calculated act, to stir their blood to a frenzy and to affirm their loyalty, but if you venture from here you will be slaughtered. Far better to wait until the rage has subsided and the army has left. Then we can leave in the cover of night.' He saw the objection rising in me. 'They have no boats, and it is a long march around the Horn. They will not take the city by surprise.'

'And their spy?' In my heart I had already named him as the monk. 'What if he works his evil before the Emperor is alerted?'

Domenico shrugged his round shoulders. 'What of it? If you go tonight, he may have acted before you arrive. But if you go now you will certainly be too late, for you will never reach him.'

'And tonight you will help us escape?' pressed Sigurd.

'God willing. If the mob have not burned down my house and looted all I own. Though I hope they will not come this far – the hill should deter them, I think.'

'And in the meantime?'

'In the meantime you should stay in here. There is more food if you desire it. Or you could pray. It is, after all, the day for it.'

I did pray in the long hours which followed, repeating the pleas of the prophets again and again until a dark look from Sigurd silenced me. After that I kept my prayers in my heart, while Sigurd prowled around that small room like a bear in its cage. Sometimes we spoke, but neither of us could muster much effort, and our words inevitably fell away unheeded. Domenico's servant brought some bread and water, which we ate gratefully, and a little after that I managed to hold back the horrors from my thoughts long enough to fall asleep. Once I awoke thinking I heard shouting in the distance, but it came no nearer and soon I slipped back into dreams.

I woke again to a tugging on my arm, and opened my eyes to see Domenico peering down on me.

'It is dusk,' he said. 'In half an hour, when it is dark, we will go.'

I rubbed the grit from my eyes, and took a sip of the water he had brought. 'Have the barbarians gone?'

'Their army left many hours ago, but the rest of their camp are still in the streets seeking out what little plunder remains. It will still be dangerous to venture among them.'

'Not so dangerous as when we came here,' I said. 'You have saved our lives today, and I will not forget it.'

The merchant sat down opposite me, the chair creaking under his weight. 'In truth, my friend, I do not do this because of my love for your people, though I bear them no grudges.' He peered nervously behind him, where I could see the dim figure of Sigurd sleeping on a bench. 'The Emperor's blockade has all but ruined me, while every day from my window I see the ships of my rivals unloading across the bay.'

'If I reach the palace alive,' I told him, 'and if there is a single man in the palace who will listen to me, you will have the grandest mansion which stands in the shadow of the old acropolis.'

'I hope so, my friend. I hope so. My father in Pisa will be unhappy if I return a beggar.'

We sat there in silence and darkness a few moments, the only sound Sigurd snoring in his corner.

'Tell me what else you know of Baldwin,' I said. I was too alert to sleep again, and Domenico was not so well known to me that silences were comfortable.

He shrugged, sucking on a dried fig. 'Little things, pieces of gossip and hearsay. He has brought his wife and children – did you know that?'

'I did not,' I admitted. 'Does our climate agree with their health?'

Domenico chuckled. 'It will do, when they are queen and princes in his new kingdom.'

'He has no lands in the west? In Frankia?' It was half a question, half a statement, for I remembered the Count Hugh taunting him to such effect in his tent.

'None. His father was a count, and his mother heir to a duchy, but he was the third son and so got neither. According to rumour, they intended him for the church, but you have seen the temper of his soul. I do not think he was long in the great cathedral school at Rheims. After that . . .'

Domenico was never a man to diminish a tale which could be expanded, but he broke off in confusion at my shout of astonishment.

'Rheims? Baldwin was at Rheims? The barbarian town, where they keep the shrine of their Saint Remigius?'

'I believe so.' Domenico was looking up at me in alarm, while behind him Sigurd stirred from his sleep. 'I have never been there. Why?'

'Because the monk was at Rheims – that was where he joined his order, and was turned against the Romans. Where Baldwin must have found him.' I remembered the monk's brother describing his cruelty. 'I imagine they found much in common. So when Baldwin came east, and needed a man who could pass for a Roman yet had the barbarian faith in his heart, he chose the monk, Odo.'

Domenico watched me in puzzlement. 'You believe this monk – the man who once approached me to fund his scheming – is Baldwin's assassin.'

'I do. You said he had brought his wife and children, that he wanted to claim a kingdom in the east because he had none in the west. What richer prize than Byzantium itself?'

Much of this I had suspected, or believed, but finally to have a definite connection between Baldwin and the monk made me course with triumph. Though there was no triumph yet, I reminded myself, while the monk walked free and the barbarians were in arms.

'We must go and tell the Emperor,' I said.

Domenico edged open the door. It must have been as dark outside as within, for it admitted no light.

'We can go,' he announced.

'Then we had better move quickly.'

★   ★   ★

Armed with long knives which Domenico gave us, we hurried out of his courtyard and down the hill. His house was unscathed, but barely fifty yards away the devastation began. You could almost see where the crowd had stopped, the high-water mark of their destructive flood: one moment the houses we passed were intact and unharmed, the next they were roofless ruins, their doors beaten from their hinges and every window shattered. Smoke filled the air, the acrid fumes of human misery, and I had to hold my sleeve over my face to keep from choking. Domenico had spoken of a mob, but there must have been a method to their savagery for not a single building had been bypassed or forgotten. Even now, the dull wind brought more shouts of havoc and spoliation to my ears.

I shivered. 'The Lord God help us if they get inside the city. He Himself could not have visited greater destruction here.'

We descended lower, Domenico leading us uncertainly through smouldering streets and rubble-strewn alleys. We saw no-one, living or dying, and fear whetted our ears such that we were quick to hear if any approached. Several times we crouched in the ruins until we were sure that danger had passed, and our progress was fitful until at last the slope tailed away onto the flat ground by the shore. We came onto a broad street – the same, I realised, that we had trodden that morning. We had felt strong then, invulnerable, but how many from that column were alive now?

Domenico scuttled across the road, into the shadow of a warehouse, and beckoned us after him. It had probably been empty even before the looters reached it, and though it was scorched black, the new bricks of its walls had saved it from the worst effects of the flames. Its door had not been so fortunate, but that was to our advantage as we followed Domenico under the charred lintel.

He swept an arm about him in melancholy. 'Once, this was to be the cradle of my fortune; now it is its tomb. But in this week of all weeks, we should remember that salvation also can come from the grave. Help me raise the floor.'

We crouched on our knees, and pressed our fingers into a groove where he directed. When we tugged, a broad square of planking came up in our hands, opening a shallow pit to our view. On the packed earth within lay a small boat.

'The wise merchant guards against every risk,' said Domenico proudly. 'And thus never loses everything.'

'If you can get us across the Horn, you will gain a great deal more.'

We bent over the hole and lifted out the boat by its prow. I was glad of Sigurd's strength, for Domenico did little but fuss: together we managed to haul the craft across to the door by the wharf. The hull rasped and grated horribly as we dragged it over the floor, the noise redoubled by the towering walls, but the barbarians must have exhausted their appetite for plunder, or indulged it elsewhere, for none came to trouble us.

With a final push, Sigurd heaved the boat over the edge of the wharf and watched it splash into the black waters of the Horn. There was a ladder bolted to one of the pilings which even the Franks had not bothered to destroy: we slid down it, and soon we were splashing away from the dock, away from danger, away from the horror that had once been Galata. Though looking across to the far side of the Horn was no comfort, for by some unknown devilry there seemed to be flames there as well. I lay back against the thwart and stared at the sky, floating between the shores of a world on fire.

Κ ϛ

It was like some vision of the apocalypse, for around the entire sweep of the bay flames licked into the night. In Galata they were burning out, dying slowly, but along the coast the barbarian's progress could be measured by the heights to which the fires still rose in every village and settlement. To my horror, they did not stop at the bridge, but continued back along the southern shore even into the city itself. I stared out through the darkness, trying to judge if any were near my own home, but it was hidden in the hills. Where were the barbarians now? Had they entered the city, as Baldwin had promised they would, as the flames seemed to herald? Was the empire betrayed into slavery? I wanted to weep, but tears would not come. The last time there had been violence in the city I had spent three days and nights at my door, sword in hand, refusing to sleep lest the mob come for my family. There would be no consolation if I had failed them now.

Sigurd made a crude boatman, but he managed to bring us across the Horn, between the moored ships, and towards the walls. They were clear to see, for on that night even the waves burned: sea-fire had been spread over them, to deter all who might approach and illuminate any who did. I could smell the oily smoke, hear the spitting as the flames danced and swayed on the water.

'Where are you going?' I asked Sigurd. We seemed to be heading north-west, towards the headwaters. 'Take me to the gate of Saint Theodosia, so I can return to my house and find my children.'

Sigurd never looked back. 'We're going to the new palace. The Emperor will be there, unless he has changed his ways. We need to warn him of the danger he faces.'

I almost laughed. 'Look around you – he can guess at the danger, if he still lives. I must see to my family.'

'We all have families, Demetrios. But if the empire falls to the Franks, we will wish they had never been saved.'

I was too feeble to argue, and I said nothing more as Sigurd sculled the boat to the stone pier by the new palace. We were close to the barrage of sea-fire now, and I sat up in the terror that the current would carry us into it, but a small opening had been left and Sigurd deftly worked us through it. Guards came running, and I saw with relief that here at least Romans still held the walls. Their faces glowed orange in the firelight, as indeed did the stones, the water and even the air about us, but there was mercifully little panic in their faces.

'Who approaches?' they challenged. 'Declare yourselves, or we will burn you into the sea.'

'Sigurd, captain of Varangians, with news for the Emperor. Is he here?'

'He is. He directs the war on the barbarians from his throne.'

'War?' I echoed. 'Is there now a war between us. Have they entered the city?'

The guard laughed. 'They have sacked the outer villages, and paraded before the walls, but it will take more than a rabble of men and horses to force our defences. The city is safe enough – for the moment.'

'But what of the fires?'

'Our own mob. They came into the streets this afternoon, demanding that the Emperor unleash his full might on the barbarians and make the Lycus red with their blood. When he refused there was violence, and some set fire to the tax collector's office. But the Watch have the ringleaders now, and the streets are under strict curfew.'

'Thank Christ for that,' I breathed.

'Thank Him when it is finished,' reproved the guard. 'There are still barbarians beyond our walls, and great anger within. But for now, I will take you to the court.'

We scrambled out of the boat and came through the water-gate into the new palace. Everywhere was in turmoil: companies of soldiers hurried between the walls, and in the courtyards whetting wheels scraped plumes of sparks from steel blades. Spears and shields were stacked all about, while serving boys from the kitchen laboured under baskets of arrows. We climbed many stairs, often pausing to let files of guards push past, until at last we came to the great bronze doors. A dozen Patzinaks, armed and helmed and with spears in their hands, barred the way.

'The Emperor is in council,' their sergeant growled. 'He will not see petitioners. The secretary . . .'

I cut him short. 'Is the chamberlain within? Tell him that Demetrios Askiates and Sigurd the Varangian have returned from Galata. Tell him we have news which must be told.'

Whether from the surprise of being countermanded, or the flat certainty in my voice, the sergeant disappeared through the door, and emerged humbly ten minutes later to confirm that the chamberlain would see me immediately.

It was probably the most exalted gathering I would ever witness, I thought, as the bronze doors closed behind me. I had entered the room where I had once met the Sebastokrator, the broad chamber built atop the walls overlooking the plain. It was filled with the light of many candles, and with the glittering array of more generals, counsellors and their retinues than I could count. Apart from Isaak and Krysaphios, I recognised the Caesar Bryennios, the Emperor's first son-in-law; the great eunuch general Tatikios whom I remembered from his triumph against the Cumans; and myriad others in gilded armour and the regalia of their offices. All stood save the Emperor himself, who sat on his golden throne in the centre of the room and inclined his head to the arguments which flowed about him. On the marble floor, between the pointed shoes of his courtiers, I thought I saw blood.

I was too shabby to be noticed by that shimmering assembly, but Krysaphios noted my arrival and gradually slipped around the edge of the throng to greet me in a corner.

'You have returned,' he said calmly. 'When we saw the barbarians marching from their camp, we feared the worst. Particularly when we received reports that some of our soldiers had been executed.'

I stared into his shifting eyes. 'It was a trap. If the monk was ever there, he was not in the house when we arrived. Instead we found barbarians, hundreds of them, waiting for us. They cut down many of our force and took the rest captive. When they started murdering prisoners for the sport of their crowd, we escaped. They know that the Normans will come, and they are eager to seize the spoils for themselves before that day.' I leaned closer. 'When the barbarian captain Baldwin addressed his army, he told them he had an agent in the city who would see to it that the gates were open to them. I have discovered that he was taught at the same school where the monk learned to hate Byzantium. He and the monk must be in league.'

To my surprise and chagrin, Krysaphios laughed openly at this news. 'Your effort does you credit, Demetrios,' he told me, immaculate condescension in his voice. 'But you are tardy with it. The Emperor's enemies have already revealed themselves.'

I stared about the room. The Emperor Alexios still lived and breathed – so much was obvious. 'Was the blood on the floor . . . ?'

'The monk's doing? No. Those windows through which the Emperor surveyed the battle make an inviting target from without. Many Franks tried their aim with arrows, and one struck the man who stood beside the throne.'

'I winced to think how nearly we had been undone. What was this battle you speak of?'

Krysaphios glanced back to the middle of the room, where a stout general was making an impassioned oration against the barbarians, recapitulating their historic offences. 'I told you that the barbarians had revealed themselves as our enemies: so much was obvious, as soon as they had ambushed your expedition. After they left Galata, they pillaged their way around the Golden Horn until they arrived at the walls. The palace by the Silver Lake is entirely destroyed.'

'They left little untouched in Galata either.'

'Then they drew up their army over there' – Krysaphios pointed through the windows – 'and began an assault on the palace gate, trying to burn it open. All afternoon they launched themselves at our defences, while within our walls the mob rioted and demanded war.'

'But the Emperor did not succumb?' I said, remembering the words of the guard by the sea gate.

Krysaphios' eyes narrowed. 'Not yet. Invoking the sanctity of the day, he ordered the archers to keep to the walls and fire over the barbarians' heads, or at their horses if they pressed too close. Even now, when they hammer at our gates, he holds out hope that there can be peace and does not admit his folly. But fortune will desert them tomorrow. Even the Emperor cannot defy the howl of the mob forever, and when the barbarians attack again he will have no choice but to destroy them. As many have long demanded.'

'But what if he commits to battle and does not destroy them? What if they pierce our defences and break in?' I saw scorn rising on Krysaphios' lips, and hurried on. 'What of the monk? Surely tomorrow will be the day he strikes.'

Unexpectedly, Krysaphios chuckled. 'The Great Friday of Easter – a good day for martyrdom. But the Emperor will never be alone; his guards, family and commanders will attend him constantly. And it would need more than one man to open our gates, against the will of all who manned them. If even that concerns you, then stay and keep watch. Unless you again prefer the familiarity of your own bed.'

'There is enough of the soldier left in me that I can sleep where I am needed. But I fear for my daughters. If the mob riot again tomorrow and they are caught up in it, I will not forgive myself.'

Krysaphios' lip turned a fraction upward. 'Every man in this palace has a family, Demetrios, and all those wives and sons and daughters must wait in their own homes with the rest of our people. Do you really struggle between your obligations to two girls, and your duty to the millions in the empire?'

I had no patience for such contempt. 'If the empire cannot protect my family then I have no use for it; my duty is to my kin. You yourself might understand if you had more than a mule's seed.'

I regretted those words even as I spoke them, but the toil of the day had crushed my patience and loosed my wits. I saw anger sear Krysaphios' cheeks and did not bother to wait for its eruption.

'I will go and guard my family. If I were you, Krysaphios, I would not stand too near the windows tomorrow.'

I turned on my heels and walked stiffly from the room, invisible to the gilded company who still threw the same arguments between each other. Neither Krysaphios nor the guards tried to stop me, and once I was past the bronze doors there was too much confusion for any to notice. I descended the stairs in a daze of bitter misery, and had just gained the second courtyard when I heard running steps behind me, and felt a hand on my arm.

I turned, to see a handsome, apologetic-looking young man. His dalmatica was of the finest fabric, fastened with a brooch in the shape of a lion, while the ornament on his *tablion* betold a rank far above his years.

'My apologies, Master Askiates.' His voice was light, and his manner friendly. 'My lord Alexios the Emperor saw your departure and begs you to stay. He fears he may need you tomorrow.'

'The Emperor was wrapped in a council of war when I left – can he really have seen me?'

'My lord Alexios has both eyes and ears, and he does not always use them in unison. Will you stay, by his invitation?'

It was hard to resist the easy humour of this youth, but the single purpose in my mind overrode all else. 'I must return to my home. I worry for my daughters' safety, and I fear there will be more danger in the streets tomorrow.'

'And the Emperor shares those concerns. He will send his guards to bring them here.'

At a stroke, all my resistance ebbed away. Though the palace was far from safe, and though any battle in the city would rage fiercest here, I would rather see my daughters by my side in a stout fortress than at the mercy of the mob. I nodded my agreement. 'I will stay.'

The young man smiled, though there was a strain in his cheeks. 'Thank you – it will relieve the Emperor. God alone knows what else will on this accursed day.'

'Accursed indeed if my doings are his only comfort.'

'Today has been bad. His enemies have risen, and his friends circle the throne like dogs; his choices are few, and ever diminishing. Yet these are merely the first breaths of the storm.' He played absently with the clasp of his brooch, scanning the sky as if for a portent. 'Tomorrow, I fear, it will break.'

κ ζ

It was the Great Friday of Easter, the holy day when Our Lord was crucified, and I woke in fear. Not fear of the barbarian armies who massed to strike us, nor of the assassins who might haunt the palace halls, nor even of the mob who could tear the city in two at their Emperor's cowardice. It was fear of my daughters, fear that they would wake too soon in the small chamber where we had been lodged, and see their father curled shamelessly on a mattress with a woman who was not their mother.

Anna must have sensed that I stirred, for she twisted herself so she could see my face. 'I should go. There must be some in need of a doctor here, after yesterday's violence.' She shook her tangled hair. 'And though your daughters guess much, there are some things they should not see.'

'Some things their father may not wish them to see,' I added quietly. My spirits had leapt when Zoe and Helena arrived at the palace with Anna, she having still been at my home when the guards came. When at last I had finished roaming the passages near the Emperor's apartments, well after midnight, I had been grateful, if cautious, of her embrace.

All thoughts left me as a stern knock came from the door. I was on my feet in an instant, trying to kick the blanket free of my legs, while Anna rolled against the wall and affected sleep. I heard tentative sounds from the far corner, but by the time Zoe's head had peeked above the covers I was at the door and looking into the unblinking face of a guardsman.

'You are summoned.'

I had grown tired of this abrupt phrase, seemingly the only form of invitation familiar to the guards, but I was glad of an excuse to be out of that room, and followed willingly. The smudged light I saw beyond the windows suggested that the dawn had not yet come, yet still we had to force a way through the bleary-eyed functionaries bustling about, until at last we came to a door guarded by four Patzinaks. My escort spoke something unintelligible to them and they stepped apart, flanking the door.

'Go up,' said my escort. 'We wait here.'

Trying to affect calm under the Patzinaks' hostile stares, I pushed through and began climbing the stairs beyond.

After a time, I began to wonder if this was some joke on the part of the guards, for there seemed no end to the stairs, only a succession of turns and counter-turns leading inexorably up. Nor did it seem that any others attempted the ascent: I passed no-one, saw none descending, and heard nothing but the lonely sound of my own footsteps. Even the slitted windows were sunk too far through the walls to reveal anything but grey light beyond.

I turned another corner, identical to every other, and saw a slab of sky above. I ran up the last dozen steps, and emerged onto a broad, flat platform. It was a high place, as high as I had ever been in my life and perhaps as high as man could build without provoking the jealousy of the Lord. By day it must afford an extraordinary view of the city, and all the lands for miles about, but in the pre-dawn darkness I could see only a skein of embers spread across the landscape. A low wall lined the tower's edge, utterly out of proportion to the depth of the drop beyond. Certainly inadequate beside the magnitude of the imperial life it now had to protect.

I dropped to my knees, glad of the excuse to be hidden from the dizzying space around me, and prostrated myself.

'Get up. By tomorrow you may have to save your homage for another man.' He spoke gently, but there was a weariness in his face which gave his words an unintended bitterness.

'Is your confidence in me so low, Lord?' The altitude must have enfeebled my mind: how else could I presume to jest with an Emperor?

He stretched his lips a little under the thick beard. 'Confidence? Demetrios Askiates, you are one of the few men in whom I keep any confidence. Every one of my generals thinks me a coward, or worse, and my subjects denounce me in the streets. Many of my predecessors have found their eyes put out and their noses slit open for less.'

'They pray that you will live a thousand years,' I protested, but he rolled his eyes in impatience.

'I have ruled fifteen years already,' he said. 'Longer than any since the great Bulgar-slayer himself. Yet what will a later Theophanes or Prokopios write of my reign? "He spent his life fighting the barbarians when they attacked, yet willingly surrendered them the empire when they came as guests."' He turned to the east, where a smear of crimson heralded the sun's rising. 'I stood here when Chalcedon burned with the fires of the Turkish army, when a single mile of calm water kept us from their advance. Without the Franks, and the Normans and Kelts and Latins and whomever else the pontiff of the west sends us, the Turks will come again, and they will not pause at the shores of the Bosphorus.' He kicked the balustrade, and I tensed for fear that he might trip and topple over it. 'My counsellors and their mobs do not understand that we no longer have the might of our ancestors. We cannot march across the world, as a Justinian or a Basil could. We are a nation rich in gold but poor in arms, and if I am to protect my people I must let others fight in their place.'

'Then it is little wonder that your generals chafe, Lord.'

The Emperor laughed. 'Little wonder indeed, and far greater wonder that they have left me my throne this long. In fifteen years I have never sought war – why would I? If I win, my commanders grow stronger, and scheme to put themselves in my place; if I lose, then thousands more Romans are left to the depredations of our enemies. Only by turning those who would attack us against each other can I keep my people safe. Except now the barbarians will not be turned, and the precarious edifice which passed for my policy is revealed as a conjuror's trick.'

'Yet the walls remain strong,' I argued. 'As long as they are manned, the barbarians can do little more than ransack the suburbs.'

'The walls remain strong while their garrisons are loyal. How long will they support a coward who resists every provocation of the barbarians?'

The scarlet sun was rising now, filling the east with a cold red light, while above us great banks of clouds surged against each other, scarring the sky. The first bells were ringing in the churches below, and I could see their many domes gleaming crimson in the dawn. I shivered, and the Emperor must have noticed for he warmed his tone a little. 'Keep faith, Demetrios, and keep close beside me. Have you not guessed their plan?'

I started. In the night I had conceived a hundred plots which the barbarians might have devised, but none which seemed probable.

'They mean to kill me today.' He assessed the prospect calmly. 'When I am dead, I will change from coward to martyr. The mob and my generals will throw open the gates to avenge my memory, and the barbarians will rout them. That is what I would do. While we keep to our walls they cannot harm us, so they must tempt us out. As long as I rule, we will keep inside, so they must remove me.'

'You could stay here, Lord,' I suggested, 'on this tower. Then none could approach, and you would be safe until the barbarians were gone.'

Alexios shook his head sadly. 'If I stayed up here, isolated and alone, I might as well be dead. My generals would issue orders which I could not countermand, and there would be a battle. No, I must stay in their midst, exerting what power I can, and you must see to it that the barbarian agents – this monk, perhaps – do not overcome me. While we hold to our walls, we will be safe.'

I looked over to the west. The light had touched it, now, and I could see the fringes of a vast army gathering itself for war. They must have spent the night in the fields, cold and damp, but I guessed they would have kept the rust from their swords. And somewhere among them would be Baldwin, buckling on his armour and dreaming of making our empire his by nightfall.

The Emperor had nothing more to say. I followed him back down the long stair as the sounds of our own army rose from the court-yards below.

It was two hours or more before the barbarians showed any semblance of order, two hours while I lingered in the throne-room trying to keep my eyes on the space around the Emperor rather than the events beyond his windows. It amazed me how the pugnacious, lively man I knew from the rooftop and the garden could still himself into the statued poise demanded by ritual. He sat on his golden throne, turned so that he could look out at his enemies, and kept motionless while a stream of courtiers and soldiers paraded past. Most of their petitions he did not even acknowledge, leaving Krysaphios to answer; a few, if the question was particularly confused, or the supplicant well-liked, he answered with brief changes of his aspect, stern or gracious as was demanded. I wondered that the weighty debates of empire could be settled thus, but never did I sense that he left any doubt as to his meanings.

And all the while, the low chants of the priests rose and fell in the background. As the Emperor could not attend the ceremonies in Ayia Sophia, an altar screen had been erected behind him, and three priests sang the melancholy songs of the Great Friday liturgy in private. Perhaps if my faith had been deeper I would have found solace in them, in the promise that even the worst suffering and death would be redeemed into eternal life, but in truth it only unsettled me to hear the brutal narrative of the passion. How it played on the Emperor I do not know, but he gave the appearance of ignoring it, save when the priests scurried out for him to perform some role allotted to him by custom. Then his audience would pause, while he recited his part or did as was required, before resuming his business. Incense rose with the music from behind the screen, and the scent, coupled with the ceremonial familiarity, slowed my senses and left me uncomfortably lethargic.

As the morning drew on, the room slowly filled with courtiers. They clustered around the fringes and conversed in hushed tones, so adept at hiding their voices that even I, standing almost beside them, could hardly discern a word. Their presence piqued my unease and restored my vigilance; perhaps overmuch, for now there were too many faces to scan, too many hands to watch for hidden daggers or sudden movements. Though the air from the open windows was cool, I began to sweat, and I wondered again how the Emperor could seem so frozen under the radiant weight of his grand robes.

At about the fourth hour, the bronze doors opened to admit a familiar figure, the barbarian Count Hugh, with a quartet of guards before him and as many pages behind. I stiffened, and nodded to the Patzinak captain to keep close to the throne. I had been assured of Count Hugh's loyalty to the Emperor, or at least to his treasure, but having a barbarian so close, on this day of all days, seemed unspeakably reckless. The Emperor, as ever, gave no sign of discomfort.

'Count Hugh.' Krysaphios spoke from beside the Emperor. 'Your kinsmen are again marching in arms against us. We are a peace-loving people, but in their hearts there is only war. Will you go to them, and press upon them our fervent desire for their brotherhood? Those who befriend us are rich in the blessings of life; our enemies enjoy only the pains of death.'

Count Hugh swallowed, and touched his throat to straighten the glittering pendant he wore. 'You know I am always at my lord the Emperor's command. But there is a madness in my kinsmen which I can neither cure nor explain. They have forgotten all that is good, and are seized by a thirst for blood and war. Loyal as I am to my lord, I do not think they will hear me.' He lowered his voice a little. 'They may not even respect the honour of my station.'

Krysaphios seemed about to speak angrily, but the Emperor forestalled him. It was the subtlest of movements, a drop of the chin and a slight widening of the eyes, but it must have been a deafening shout in Krysaphios' ears for he recomposed himself and continued: 'The Emperor reminds you that on this holy day, all Christians should unite in friendship. As our Lord Jesus Christ preached: "Blessed are the peacemakers, for great will be their reward in heaven."'

It was not the gospel as I remembered it, but it seemed to pacify Count Hugh. He shifted the weight of his enormous lorum, so heavy with jewels that I feared it might crush him, made his obeisance and departed in haste. From beyond the door, I heard the sergeant calling for horses.

Left to his own desires, I suspect Count Hugh would even then have delayed his embassy as long as possible, but the Emperor must have made his will known throughout the palace, for within a quarter of an hour I saw their small procession trotting out of the gate below and across the plain towards the barbarians. I moved my way around the room, so as to have both the Emperor and the Franks in my sight.

Count Hugh and his entourage had just dropped into a dip in the landscape, and out of our view, when the doors were thrown open with a crash. I spun around, my hand on my sword, to see the Emperor's brother Isaak marching in heedless of manners and convention, and entirely without the customary retinue.

'What is this?' he demanded of Krysaphios. 'The barbarians are massing to attack again, and the legions sit in their barracks polishing their shields. They should be behind the walls, ready to be unleashed as soon as we have our enemies trapped under them.'

248

Krysaphios stared at him dispassionately. 'The Emperor believes that the sight of our army in the streets would incite the mob to demand action, and raise the risk of a precipitate attack by an intemperate commander.'

'Does the fear of the mob now guide the Emperor's policy? Has he lost all faith in his captains, that they cannot be trusted to keep their men in order?'

'If captains could be trusted with strategy, they would be generals.' Krysaphios was less patient now. 'And we have companies of archers who will hold the walls.'

'And will they aim at clouds, as they did yesterday?' Isaak was red with anger. 'Every time we do not crush these barbarians, they grow bolder. Defeat is the only lesson they will learn – defeat by the force of our arms.'

The grains of the argument threatened to grow swiftly, but in a second the Emperor had stilled his chamberlain and his brother both. It seemed that he did no more than stretch out the fingers on his right hand, as if admiring his rings, yet Krysaphios and Isaak and all the assembled courtiers fell silent, and turned their gaze on the plain outside. Count Hugh was returning, galloping back as if the furies themselves chased him; he was comfortably in advance of his escort, and had entered the gates, climbed the stairs and been admitted to the Emperor's presence before the last of his group had even reached the walls. All that time no-one spoke, save the priests who continued their ceaseless chanting behind the screen.

Count Hugh's splendour was much diminished by his errand, though his pride was unbowed. There were gaps on his lorum where gems must have been shaken loose by the violence of his ride, and mud was splashed halfway up the skirts of his dalmatica. The jewelled cap he wore so constantly had slipped over one ear, which glowed as if it had been slapped.

Krysaphios still waited before he had performed the full homage before letting him speak.

'My Lord,' he said indignantly. 'It is as I warned you: they are completely deaf to reason and charity. They called me a slave – *me*, a lord of the Franks and brother of a king. Their king, no less. How can I treat with such men?'

'How did you?' Krysaphios was unsympathetic, but Count Hugh's answer was delayed, for the three priests suddenly processed from behind their screen and walked solemnly before the Emperor. One held a tall cross on a wooden staff, the second a censer, and the third a golden cup. He tipped it to the Emperor's lips, while the others flanked him and sang their acclamations. When he had drunk, all three retreated, never once acknowledging the watching multitude.

Count Hugh glared at them, and continued. 'I did as my lord the Emperor wished. I told them that all should offer their allegiance to the greatest power in Christendom. I reminded them that they were far from home and allies, and that rather than seek to overthrow the noble Romans they should be grateful of their aid. I appealed to their love of all good things in earth and heaven, and they laughed at me. *Me*, the brother of . . .' A stare from Krysaphios ended his aside. 'They said: "Why beg for a treasure we can seize ourselves, and from a king whose crown will have fallen before we are even within his walls?" I would have argued, but they grew tired of the interview and I feared they would kill me if I delayed longer. "Run to the Greeks," they said as I left, "but you will find no safety there. For we are coming, and none can resist us."'

'And they are coming indeed.' The Sebastokrator Isaak spoke from beside the windows, through which the lines of the Frankish cavalry could now be seen advancing towards us arrayed for battle. 'Now will you hear me, brother?'

Krysaphios looked to the Emperor, still as a rock, and back to Isaak. 'Your brother reminds you that unless they have built an army of siege engines in the night, the walls are secure. We can withstand a thousand such attacks.'

'And every time our men will die.' Isaak was speaking to the entire room now, as much as to those about the throne. 'Are we to widow our women and orphan our children because we do not dare oppose the barbarians? I say it is better that a few should die in the glory of battle, than that the barbarians should pluck us from the walls one by one.'

'Your pardon, Lord,' Count Hugh broke in. 'I beg the Emperor's indulgence, and leave to retire to my apartments. The effort of my embassy has exhausted me.'

Krysaphios waved him away, though I saw that the Patzinaks followed when he left. Hugh would not be resting, I thought: he would be stuffing his trunks with all he could salvage, lest the barbarians make good their threats.

'My Lord.' Now Krysaphios addressed the Emperor. 'It is plain the barbarians distrust Count Hugh. They fear he has betrayed his race, and so they do not respect his overtures. But Christians should not fight while there remains a hope of peace. Send another envoy, one who would awe the barbarians with his resolve and stature. Send one of your generals with a light escort, for the words will carry more weight from a soldier.'

'And a legion of cataphracts will carry more weight still.' Isaak stood in silhouette under the window arch, while behind him the barbarians drew ever closer. 'You yourself could ride out, brother, and still they would not heed you. Do you hear that?' He paused, allowing a distant roar to penetrate the room, as of a waterfall or high wind. 'That is the mob. They know the barbarians approach, and they demand action.' He crossed to the throne, and I too moved nearer, for I had not relaxed my suspicion of him. 'You cannot deter the Franks with words. In this course you will not weaken them by a single man, while your enemies in the city will pull us down in riot and murder. If we attack, in a single stroke we will restore the loyalty of our people and destroy the barbarian threat.'

'And leave ourselves open to the Turks.' For the first time since entering the room, Alexios spoke. 'If we hold firm we will see off the mob, the barbarians and the Turks, but if we waver, any one of them can destroy us.'

'Forget the Turks!' Isaak was shouting now, heedless of protocol and decorum. 'Do you see Turks hammering on our gates demanding our blood? We have survived these fifteen years because we focused always on the greatest danger, not on those which might come later. This is not some game where you can plot your tactics many moves in advance, and sacrifice the lesser pieces for a greater end. Here every move risks destruction, and all you will sacrifice is yourself. Ourselves. Please, brother, forget this madness before it overwhelms us.'

It was astonishing watching these two brothers, so alike in form and so disparate in temper. The greater Isaak's frenzy, the greater Alexios' composure, and when at last he gave his answer it was still Krysaphios who spoke for him.

'We will send the captain of the Immortals, with ten of his men, to warn the barbarians of their folly.'

Isaak seemed about to tear himself apart with rage, but Krysaphios continued: 'Meanwhile, order all the legions of guards to assemble behind the gates.'

'I will summon them myself. And send your words to the captain of the Immortals.' Isaak hissed between his teeth, made the slightest of bows, and strode from the room. The noise of the mob grew loud as the doors opened, then subsided when they snapped fast. Again the chants of the priests were the only sound we heard. The courtiers looked at the floor and did not speak, uncertain perhaps how to respond to the Emperor's public confrontation, or worrying whether they were bound to a doomed allegiance. I watched them each in turn, flicking my eyes from one to the next for any hint of rebellion. All were sullen, but none seemed fired with murder.

'There.' Krysaphios saw it first – or perhaps the Emperor signalled it to him – the first horses of the Immortals' expedition. They rode on massive beasts bred for the purpose, capable of bearing a man cased entirely in armour into the heart of battle. I had seen them charge several times during my time in the army, and on each occasion I had marvelled how seldom they needed lance or mace, how quickly their weight alone tore through enemy lines and scattered men before them. Isaak was right: nothing could convince the barbarians of the might of our arms if they did not.

I counted them as they came into view from under the walls. Their captain rode in front, with four cataphracts flanking him and another four after them. That should be force enough, I thought. But there were more, trotting forward row after row: twenty, then sixty, then a hundred.

'I ordered ten men.' Every man in the room looked to the Emperor, who had half-risen from his throne to stare at the sight before him. There was nothing of the statue about him now: his face was alive with horrified anger, and every limb shook with rage. 'Call them back now, before the barbarians take them for an assault.'

Orders were shouted out of the doors, and I heard trumpets sound from the ramparts, but the cataphracts had little ground to cover and already the head of their column neared the barbarian vanguard. They were too far away to hear, and too close to the barbarians to turn: we could only stare, as if watching a mime-show. Neither army slowed;

the cataphracts kept to their unforced pace, and the Franks to their relentless advance. They were barely fifty feet apart now, and still closing; I watched for an opening in the Frankish ranks, wondering if they would admit the embassy, but they stayed locked together.

'Turn back,' a voice whispered.

Then a cloud of darts and javelins fell from the sky, and the battle began.

Even before the first arrows struck our cavalry had responded: they broke from their column, and cantered to form a double line facing the oncoming Franks. The missiles would have done our men little damage, for their armour was more than its equal, but I saw several horses already felled, their riders struggling to be free of their harnesses before the barbarians were over them. With a shout which reached even our ears, the Franks lowered their spears and charged. Our cataphracts spurred to meet them, and for a second I saw only two waves of brown and black and silver rushing against each other, closing over the ground between them. Then they struck, and the shapes of single men were lost in a sea of battle.

'We must reinforce them, your Majesty.' Krysaphios spoke urgently, but without the confusion which had gripped the rest of the room. 'A hundred against ten thousand – they will be slaughtered to no gain.'

'If I send out more men, there will merely be more slaughter. And why were there even a hundred to begin with? I gave orders for ten.'

'Lord, the mob . . .'

'Forget the mob. My office exists to restrain them, not pander to their craven dreams. We have the hippodrome for that. Where is my brother?'

'At the Regia gate with the Varangians, Lord,' a young courtier volunteered. 'He awaits only your command to march to the aid of the cavalry.'

'He will have a long wait then. Go and order him, in my name, that he is on no account to leave the city.'

The courtier made to leave, but a word of command from Krysaphios paused him. The eunuch's eyes moved across the room and fixed on me. 'Demetrios, you know the Varangian captain. These instructions would be better heeded if they came from you.'

I was hardly used to refusing direct orders before the Emperor, but my sense of duty rebelled. 'The Emperor needs me . . .'

'He needs you where you are sent. Go.'

Though I had many misgivings, I could not disobey: I ran for the door, slipping on the marble floors in my haste. As I steadied myself on a column I looked back at the Emperor, hoping perhaps for a word to countermand my errand, to keep me where I felt most needed. He did not see me, but stood before his throne gazing out of the arched windows in silence, while the nobles around him argued loudly and openly. Only the priests seemed unaffected, continuing their liturgy even while the fate of the empire was decided on the plain before them. I could see them coming around the edge of the screen even now, bearing an icon for the Emperor to kiss. I had to admire them their devotion, their pious indifference to the mundane, even if it seemed almost sacrilege to ignore such extraordinary events. Perhaps I envied them.

The Emperor caught sight of them and sank back into his throne, ready to enact the ritual. Doubtless he should have resumed the utter impassivity which was his appointed role, but the cares of the moment had stripped away all talent for pretence and he watched with open interest. Nor could he even keep from frowning a little, as if some thought or sight had jarred in him. His face was towards me, and – fearing that he frowned at my delay – I was about to depart, when I realised that his eyes were fixed not on me, but on the approaching priests. I followed his gaze. Two of them I recognised, having been there since the morning, but the third was new: he must have come in to allow the other a rest. His knuckles were tight about the tall cross he held, and he stared on it with almost feverish devotion, tipping his head back as if he basked in the sun of heaven. The pose accentuated the angles of his sharp face, particularly the crooked line of his nose, and I saw that he must be recently come from a monastery, for the skin of his scalp was still pink where the tonsure had been shaved.

Too slowly, I recognised what I saw. Perhaps the Emperor had seen something unholy about him, or perhaps he had just been surprised by an unfamiliar face, but he could not have known who it was: that, after all, had been my task. I hurled myself across the room, staving aside any who blocked my path and screaming warnings as I went.

And the monk struck.

κ η
___

There was nowhere for the Emperor to hide, for the monk had him trapped on his throne. Most men would have been stilled by terror, or thought only to squirm feebly aside, but the Emperor had the instincts of a soldier and in that instant threw himself forward. It was still too late. As the two priests looked on, speechless at this murderous apparition, the monk brought his cross down like a mace on the Emperor's head. The pearled diadem shattered; blood spouted from the thick hair and poured off the Emperor's neck and shoulders as he fell face-first to the floor. I expected the monk to lift his weapon for a second blow, but instead he put one hand on the golden cross and pulled it from its shaft. As it came free and clattered to the floor, I saw that it was no ordinary staff he held, but a naked spear, whose point had been hidden in the crucifix. Still no-one in the room moved, petrified by the sudden onslaught. The Emperor groaned, and tried to raise himself on his arm, but the monk kicked him in the face and lifted the spear over his head. He screamed something in an unknown tongue, untrammelled triumph wild in his eyes, as he drove the spearhead down onto the Emperor's neck.

All this time I had been moving towards him, too quickly to think, and my frantic oblivion carried me just far enough. I charged into the monk, too late to stop his blow but soon enough to knock his aim awry. The spear sank into the Emperor's back and he howled with anguish, while the monk tumbled to the ground under my impact. Thin fingers clawed at my face, scratching my eyes, and as I tried to fend them off the monk rolled me onto my back and sprang away. His spear stood upright in the Emperor's back, swaying like a sapling in a storm; he pulled it free and swung it in a half-circle around him, keeping any who would approach at bay.

But there were none save me, it seemed, who would approach.

Though dozens of guards and nobles crowded that room, not one of them moved. Perhaps it was from cowardice, or shock; more likely they feared to intervene on one side or another while the empire hung in the balance, but they held back, pressed together in a circle of watching faces which surrounded us like the walls of the arena. It was as if the monk and I were the two anointed champions, Hector and Ajax, and the world ceased its wars while we fought our mortal duel.

But I had no Apollo to guide my hand, nor even a sword. The monk was approaching, lifting his spear with evil purpose. Perhaps he recognised me as his pursuer that day in the icy cistern, or perhaps he had reconciled himself to death in the cause of death, but there was a calm about him as the bloodied tip of his spear followed my futile evasions. I backed away, keeping my eyes fixed always on his. 'The thrust of a spear begins in a man's face,' a sergeant had once told me, and as long as I held his gaze he would struggle to beat me.

But my concentration was undone. I took another step back, and felt something jostle my arm; instinct drew my eyes around to the man I had collided with, one of the priests, and in that moment the monk lunged.

It was the priest who saved me. Not by any act or intercession, though perhaps he offered a prayer, but through the sheer depths of his fear. He saw the monk move before I did, and in his haste to duck away he brought me to the floor in a tangle of limbs. The spear rushed over my head, too fast to change its course, and as I threw out my hand to break my fall I felt an iron chain underneath me. It was the censer, dropped by the priest in his fright; I lifted it, and as the monk's momentum carried him over me I swung it through the air with all the force I could summon. It cracked against his face in an eruption of hot oil and screams, though whether they were the priest's, the monk's or even my own I did not know.

I found myself on my knees, my skin burning where the liquid had splashed it. The priest was beneath me, wailing piteously, but the monk still stood and still held his spear. One half of his face was seared with a crimson welt where the censer had struck him, and his eyes were clenched with pain, but it seemed he might yet find the strength for a single, final blow.

Then his mouth opened wide and the spear fell from his hand; blood dribbled down his chin and his eyes bulged open. His thin body convulsed as his soul broke free, and his empty corpse sank to the ground.

Behind him, Sigurd looked distastefully at the short sword he held, its blade bloodied almost to the hilt. He dropped it silently onto the monk's body, then pulled me to my feet as we ran to the Emperor. The monk's spell was broken and there was uproar in the room, shouting and recrimination, but it seemed Alexios was almost forgotten. Was he dead? Would all he had worked for, all I had sworn to protect, be undone? Krysaphios was kneeling at his side, one hand on his blood-smeared neck, and he looked up urgently as we approached.

'He lives,' he said. 'But barely. I will have the guards carry him to his physician.'

'We will go with him.' Sigurd made to follow the guards who had answered Krysaphios' command, but the eunuch stopped him abruptly.

'Not you,' he said. 'You are needed for greater matters. Look.' He pointed to the window, where I could see the cataphract remnants being pressed back by the barbarian host. 'Soon they will be at the walls, and if we do not have a force to hold the gates then our cavalry will be massacred in full view of the mob. You know what would happen then.'

The blood and battle and noise and confusion had left my mind dangerously brittle, scarce able to register the words he spoke, but his mention of gates sparked a vital memory which I dragged into my thoughts. 'The gates,' I mumbled.

Krysaphios regarded me like a fool. 'The gates, yes. We must protect them.'

'But that was their plan. The Emperor guessed it. When the monk killed him, the mob would open the gates in fury and the barbarians would pour in. Now that the monk has failed, they too have failed.'

Sigurd glanced outside. 'It seems they do not know they have failed.'

'Then we should prove it to them.' The demands of the moment overpowered my daze, and pulled together my thoughts. 'We must show the barbarian leaders, Baldwin and Godfrey and their captains, that their effort is futile, that the gates will never open except to unleash the full power of our armies.'

'There is a simpler way,' said Sigurd. 'Unleash the full power of our armies now. Then they will not doubt their defeat.'

'No! That is what the Emperor almost died to prevent. He will not thank us if we now squander that hope without a final effort at peace.'

Krysaphios and Sigurd looked at each other, and then at me, and for a moment we were a single trio of silence in the tumult of the room.

'Very well,' said Krysaphios. 'But how do you propose to reach the barbarians?'

There was no question of our leaving by the palace gates with the enemy so near, and we lost precious minutes riding along the walls to the Adrianople gate. This quarter of the city had become an armed camp, and the waiting legions were arrayed in long, unblinking rows behind us – as much to keep the mob from the gatehouses as to strike at the enemy, I think, but they kept a path free for us to pass. We were seven in all: Sigurd and I, three Varangians, an interpreter we had seized from the chancellery, and the dead monk tied over my horse's back. He slowed me considerably, for these were steeds of the imperial post whose strength was all in their speed, not cataphracts' beasts, and I had to shout after the others not to leave me behind.

The crowds were thicker by the Adrianople gate, for there were fewer guards to restrain them, and I feared lest our exit give them the opportunity to push through. Their faces were contorted with hate and fury, while the rocks and clay vessels they threw upset our beasts and impeded our progress. If they had known what the man I carried had attempted, I did not doubt they would have torn his dead limbs apart and danced on the bones. I probably would have fared little better.

Thankfully, the gatekeeper was a man equal to his task. He left his gate closed until we were almost upon it – so close that I could barely have pulled up my horse in time – then heaved it open just wide enough to admit a single rider. Sigurd, in the lead, never hesitated, and my horse followed his true course through the gap with mere inches between my legs and the wood. There was a thud as the monk's head caught the edge of the gate, but the rope held him in place and we were out of the city, galloping down the Adrianople road towards the right flank of the barbarian army. Though they had seemed so many from the throne-room, they were some distance from us now, in the hollow between our ridge and the shore of the Horn. They appeared to have concentrated all their might on the gates by the palace, where the walls were nearest and where, I supposed, the news of the Emperor's death might be expected to reach them first. Their foot soldiers were at the base of the outer walls, some wielding siege rams against the gates, others trying to shore burning pieces of timber against the masonry, perhaps trying to collapse it. Their mounted knights were drawn up further back out of bowshot, waiting for a breach to be made, while archers tried to keep our defenders pinned behind the ramparts. On the slope which rose behind them, a sheaf of banners were planted amid a cluster of men on horseback.

Sigurd slowed his horse so that I came up beside him. 'I should be sallying out of those gates at the head of my company,' he muttered. 'Not skulking around the enemy's flanks.'

'A glorious battle is what we hope to prevent,' I reminded him. 'And in any case, the flanks are where the enemy are always weakest.'

'Not so weak that six men and a corpse can turn them. Look.' Sigurd pointed his axe to our right, and a wave of apprehension coursed through me as I saw a score of the barbarian cavalry galloping towards us. Sparks flew where their horses' hooves struck rocks, and their spears were couched low.

'We can outpace them,' I said, glancing towards the hill where the barbarian captains stood. 'These beasts were bred for speed.'

'We can outpace them,' Sigurd agreed, 'but we would only spur ourselves into the end of the sack. There is a company of spearmen on that hill, and it will take more than half a dozen post-horses to break their line.'

I looked back to the approaching horsemen, who were now fanning out to envelop us. Battle would be futile, for they outnumbered us four to a man: even the Varangians would succumb against those odds. Reaching under the ill-fitting mail hauberk I had hurriedly pulled on at the palace, I felt for the hem of my tunic and tore at it. A thin strip came away; I knotted it about the end of my sword and waved it desperately over my head, shouting the one Frankish word I had learned. 'Parley! Parley!'

Thankfully they did not carry bows, or they might have brought us down before ever coming into earshot. But the brevity of their weapons, and the unlikely threat that our gaggle of Varangians posed, drew them close enough to hear our vital pleas. I saw their leader slow his steed, and cock an ear to what we said, while his men spread into a loose cordon about us.

I looked to the interpreter, who seemed struck dumb by our situation. I doubted he had ever expected to be plying his trade in the midst of a battlefield.

'Tell them that we ask for a parley,' I shouted to him. 'Tell him that we come from the Emperor, that we must see Baldwin or Duke Godfrey.'

Somehow the interpreter found voice to stammer a few words in the Frankish tongue. The barbarian listened impassively, his face masked by the thick cheeks of his helmet, then answered brusquely.

'He says he will not take us to his captain,' the interpreter told me. 'He fears we are assassins.'

I reversed my sword, and let it fall from my hand. It stuck upright in the soft ground, the white ribbon on its blade flapping weakly in the breeze.

'We are not assassins.' Though it would have been of little use against their spears, I felt exposed without my sword, but I forced calm into my voice. 'Tell him to take this to Baldwin.'

I withdrew the monk's garnet ring from my pocket, where I had carried it so many months, and threw it to the Frank. His hands were clumsy in their mail gauntlets, and he almost dropped it in the mud before trapping it against his saddle.

'Tell him that I have news of Odo the monk.'

I could see nothing of the barbarian's thoughts, but I guessed he did not like this errand at all. For long, painful seconds he was silent, doubtless wondering whether he should slaughter our little band and be rid of us. Beside me, I heard the interpreter mumbling a plaintive *Kyrie Eleison* to himself, heedless of those around him.

Christ have mercy. Christ have mercy. Christ have mercy.

Without realising it, I had shut my eyes as I echoed the words of the prayer in my head. I jerked them back open, to see the Frankish leader passing the ring to the man beside him and barking a few short commands. The subordinate nodded, pulled his horse about and kicked her away along the ridge towards the captains' standards. None of the other Franks moved, and their spear-tips never lowered so much as a finger's breadth.

I could not count the time we waited there, for every second seemed an eternity. On the plain before us the barbarian army had withdrawn a little distance, and my hopes rose that perhaps they had learned the futility of their assault, but it was only to regroup. Again they attacked, charging forward under a hail of arrows, their shields flat above their heads. I hoped we had stout men on the walls, for though our archers held back many of the horde, many more managed to raise ladders to the battlements and scale their heights. I imagined the legions drawn up in the city, swords unsheathed and bowstrings tight, waiting on a single command to throw open the gates and join battle. There would be a slaughter indeed if that happened, for even against our unyielding walls the barbarians were fighting like wild dogs.

The clanking of harnesses on my left drew my attention away from the battle: four horsemen were approaching along the ridge, their leader riding a great bay stallion which I recognised from the ambush in Galata the day before. The Franks who encircled us moved apart as he cantered towards us, spear in hand, and it seemed for a moment he would charge us alone until he reined his beast in just before me, staring at the corpse I carried. Though his helmet covered much of his aspect, the death-pale skin it framed was unmistakable.

I cut the monk free and let him drop on the ground. 'This is the man you hoped would murder the Emperor and break open the city,' I said, ignoring the echo of a hurried translation. 'He has failed. You have failed.'

A second man spurred forward. A few locks of fair hair crept from under his mail hood, while his face was grim. He spoke angrily to his companion, making no attempt to disguise his words from the interpreter.

'Is this true, brother? Is this the man you claimed would . . .' He broke off, aware that his words were heard and understood, and whispered urgently in Baldwin's ear.

'Duke Godfrey,' I began. 'Since you came, the Emperor has desired only peace and alliance, for all Christians to unite against our common enemies. Many voices in the city condemned him for his generosity, but he withstood them against every provocation. Even as your army assaults his walls, he does not retaliate with the full force of his might.'

'Because he is a coward,' Baldwin spluttered. 'Because he knows too

261

well the strength of Frankish arms against his rabble of eunuchs and catamites.'

'Silence!' barked Godfrey. The wind snapped at the great white banner with its blood-red cross which the herald carried behind him. 'I never sought this battle, even when the king sent his mercenaries to attack us in our camp. For two days I have submitted to your demands, Baldwin, and the gates have not opened as you promised they would.'

'Nor will they open,' I pressed. 'The Emperor has survived your plots, and will destroy you from the comfort of his walls if you do not abandon the battle now.'

Baldwin's eyes were black with hate, deeper than the depths of Sheol, but his brother was unmoved.

'I will call back my army,' said Godfrey, 'if the Emperor will allow me to pass on to the Holy Land, where I have ever sought to go. There have been enough . . . delays.'

'He will not let you pass without the oath,' I reminded him. 'But I am not the man to argue that with you. He will send an embassy to your camp tonight. You would be wise to let them approach unharmed.'

Godfrey nodded, and without a word of farewell turned his horse back towards his captains on the hill. The company who had surrounded us fell in behind him, and I saw several galloping down the slope to take the news to their army.

Baldwin, though, did not move away. 'I do not know your name, Greekling,' he hissed, 'but I know there is no proof to a word you have said.'

'Your brother's response gives me proof enough.' I sensed Sigurd raise his axe a little beside me, and hoped he would be quick enough if Baldwin succumbed to the desire so plain on his face. For the moment, though, the Frank saved his violence for his words.

'My brother is a coward to match your king. Retreat and delay are his only strategies.'

'Then he is a wiser man than you.'

Baldwin's spear twitched. 'As wise as a Greek?' He sneered. 'Even if I *had* found this cruel little monk, and turned his murderous thoughts against his king, do you think that he alone could have opened your city? Do you think that *I* told him when the Emperor might walk within bowshot, or admitted him to the secret doors of the palace? Would *he* have assumed the throne when the Emperor was dead? Would I have even imagined turning my army against the city unless there were men inside – men of power and stature – who invited me?' He gave a savage laugh at my stunned confusion, but before I could speak he had stabbed his spear into the monk's broken corpse, so deep that it stuck in the mud beneath, and kicked his horse away.

'Assume the throne?' I repeated numbly. A terrible panic broke over me, choking my trembling limbs. 'So there is an enemy . . .'

Sigurd's words echoed my own. '. . . in the palace.'

The wind roared against us as we galloped across the plain, ducking our heads close against the horses' manes and crouching in our stirrups to smooth our path. The barbarian army was in full retreat now, straggling back towards what remained of their camp. The weariness of failure was all about them, and none troubled us as we skirted their flank, racing towards the palace gate. I scarcely noticed them. One name alone was fixed in my mind, a looming horror of what he might purpose and the chaos which would ensue if he did. Several times my thoughts grew too terrible, and in frustration I kicked my unfortunate mount all the harder.

'Look.' They were Sigurd's words, brought back to me on the wind, and I snatched my eyes from the ground before me to look further ahead. We were nearing the walls – I could see the black scorches where the barbarians had tried to burn the gate, the spent arrows and bodies littering the field. Some I recognised as cataphracts, great rents hacked into their armour, but most were Franks.

'At the gates,' Sigurd called, indicating with his fist. I looked, and for a second thought I would be pitched from my saddle, so slack did I slump. The gates had opened, and a great column of soldiers was marching forth: not stretcher bearers or gravediggers come for the fallen, but a full legion of Immortals arrayed for battle. Some of their out-riders broke ranks to spur towards us, but Sigurd waved his Varangian axe in the air and they slowed, hailing us with urgent shouts.

'What are you doing?' I demanded. 'The Emperor gave orders that you should hold at the walls. The barbarians are broken, and you will only antagonise them by appearing in such force.'

'We mean to do more than antagonise them,' barked one, an officer. 'The Emperor is dying, and we are commanded to rout the barbarians in their retreat. Against our cavalry, they will be like wheat in the harvest.'

'Does the Sebastokrator command that?' A great emptiness swelled within me: I had failed. The Emperor would die, and with him all hopes of peace with Franks, Turks, even among the Romans themselves.

But the officer shook his head. 'The Sebastokrator remains at the Regia gate, I think, waiting with the Varangians. He has given no orders that I have heard.'

'Then who has . . . ?'

'The chamberlain, or regent as he soon will be. The eunuch Krysaphios.'

It was as well Sigurd could speak, for I was struck dumb. He pulled off his helmet and stared hard at the Immortal officer. 'Do you recognise me, Diogenes Sgouros?'

Though there was not an inch of his body not cased in steel armour, the Immortal still seemed to cringe. 'You are Sigurd, captain of the Varangians.'

'Do you doubt my loyalty to the Emperor?'

'Never.' Sgouros' voice was fainter now. 'But the Emperor is dying and . . .'

'Dying is not dead.' Sigurd rested his axe on the pommel of his saddle. 'Do you remember the legend of the Emperor who feigned death to test the loyalty of his men?'

'Yes.'

'Do you remember what he did to those who failed him?'

'Yes.'

'Then unless you wish a similar fate, Diogenes, draw up your company here and do not move one pace nearer the barbarians until I or the Emperor himself bring word that it pleases him you do so. Do you understand?'

Sgouros' helmet seemed fastened too tight under his chin: he struggled to breathe. 'But . . .'

'If you fail, even witlessly, there will be a terrible vengeance,' Sigurd warned. 'And not the vengeance of the Komneni, too quick to forgive their enemies, but the vengeance of Sigurd, who has never yet forgotten a wrong. Will you risk that to prick at the heels of a few broken barbarians?'

The throne in the great hall of the new palace was empty, the only clear space in the room. Every general and courtier must have had word of the Emperor's wounds and rushed to stake their place in the succession – or to pray for his healing, as they doubtless later protested – for Sigurd and I could barely pry them far enough apart to push ourselves through. I searched desperately for Krysaphios, trying to pick out one sumptuous head among the golden throng, but it was Sigurd, with his height, who saw him first. He was standing near the throne in a circle of nobles, speaking pointedly and forcefully, though his words were lost in the din. His eyes darted over the surrounding faces, seeking out disagreement or disloyalty, and he did not see our approach until Sigurd pulled away a whimpering acolyte and loomed over him.

'What did you do with the Immortals?' Sigurd demanded. 'Why, after the barbarians had surrendered did you order our cavalry to destroy them, when it was the Emperor's dearest wish that they should be spared?'

I saw Krysaphios glance to his side and tilt his head a little, as if beckoning someone. Guards, I guessed. 'The Emperor is dying, and whoever succeeds him will rely greatly on his chamberlain as he accustoms himself to rule. If you disagree with my policy out of sentiment for a weak-willed fool, whose nerve failed in our darkest hour, you would do well to reconsider. I will have need of strong warriors when I serve the new Emperor, but only those who obey.'

The circle surrounding him had eased a little, for many were clearly uncomfortable with our talk and uncertain where to display their loyalties. I tried to discomfort them further. 'Did you ally yourselves with the barbarians from the beginning, Krysaphios? Did you really mean to give our empire over to their tyranny, until you saw just now that they were defeated?'

Krysaphios' cheeks swelled out like a serpent's. 'That is treason, Demetrios Askiates, and you will not escape its penalty this time. Nor will you have even the consolation of righteousness when your daughters are screaming in my dungeon, for none have worked against the barbarians more diligently than I. Would I give over the triumph of our civilisation to a snivelling race of animals, scarce fit to tup in the gutters of this city? I will be remembered as he who saved the empire, while the Emperor Alexios will be anathemised as a godless traitor, a lover of barbarians.'

I heard a commotion in the crowd behind me: the eunuch's guards, I presumed, coming to drag me away. Sigurd was lifting his axe, though he could hardly have wielded it in that room, but I was still. The jibe about my daughters had shattered my will, for they were still in the palace, and if I resisted the eunuch he would surely visit unthinkable horrors on them.

'Tell me,' I said brokenly. 'Did the Emperor die of his wounds?'

'He will.' Krysaphios raised his eyes to the heavens. 'We searched, but his physician could not be found to heal him.'

The last words of his sentence seemed unnaturally loud, but it was only as he stopped that I realised it was because the rest of the room had fallen silent.

'And who sent my physician away this morning?' Though slowed with exhaustion, and more strained than before, the voice was undeniable. I forgot Krysaphios, and turned in wonder to the bronze doors. They were flung open, and between their mighty posts, leaning on a stick and with a bandage for a crown, there stood the Emperor Alexios.

All in the room fell to their knees, then scrambled from his path as he advanced on the throne. He walked stiffly, and his eyes were clenched with pain, but his words rang clear as ever. 'Who ordered the hipparch to send a hundred men when my brother ordered ten? Who ordered the Immortals to massacre the barbarians when they had surrendered the field? Who now stands beside my throne and schemes to fill it with his puppets?' He reached us, and I saw a phalanx of Varangians drawn up beyond the doors behind.

'You are recovered, Lord.' Krysaphios alone had not bowed to the Emperor, and he did not do so now. 'Thanks be to God. But your mind is clouded. The daze left by the assassin's blow cannot be bound up with linen.'

'Nor can his spear-thrust, if there is no physician to call on. If the chamberlain has ordered him to count herbs in the Bucoleon while the Emperor lies bleeding. Thank God indeed that I found another in my palace.'

At last I understood how the Emperor had outlasted the innumerable reverses of his reign, why his armies' loyalty had never wavered in defeats which would have ruined his predecessors. Even now, limping and gasping, there was a power in his face which was more than mere authority: perfect certainty, the unanswerable knowledge that he would prevail.

Even so, Krysaphios resisted it, flicking his eyes over the room in a search for allies. None showed themselves. 'Lord,' he pleaded, 'let us not quarrel in victory. If I have erred, it was in the service of the empire. Surely such sins can be forgiven.'

'You conspired with the barbarians to murder me,' said Alexios. 'You of all my counsellors. What did they promise you? That when they had sacked our city, and ravaged our women, and carried off our treasure, you would be left as their regent? Or did you think you could . . .'

'No!' Krysaphios almost screeched the denial. 'How can you call me a traitor, when you yourself would have given half the empire to those demons?' He crouched down, as if to perform homage or kiss the hem of the Emperor's robe, but instead he lifted his own garments high over his waist. There was a gasp of disgust from the crowd, and many hid their eyes, but many more stared in ghoulish fascination at the eunuch's exposed loins. His organs were entirely absent, as a carzimasian, but the horror of his unnatural flesh was magnified still further by the brutal mesh of scars which covered it.

'Do you see this?' he screamed, pointing crudely. 'This disfigurement? This is what the barbarians do to their enemies – for *sport*! Give them a captive and their evil minds turn only to cruelty and torture.' Mercifully, he let his robes drop back to the floor. 'I would give my last breath of life to save the empire from their violence – and yours also, if you would not heed my warnings.'

'You tried to kill me.' Alexios' voice faltered with pain. 'You would have unleashed civil war, and opened the empire to the worst depredations of all our enemies.'

'If I conspired with the barbarians, it was only to lure them into revealing the black truth of their hearts, so you could witness their evil. But you would not see it. Your love of conquest blinded you, for you would rather rule a despoiled empire than protect your people. And now, because I guarded the people you would have forgotten, I will be sacrificed.'

'As you never tired of telling me, I am merciful – too merciful – to my defeated enemies.'

'You lie.' All this time Krysaphios had been edging back through the crowd, retreating from the Emperor's gaze; now he found himself at the brink of the room under the windows. 'You will cast me into the dungeon for your torturers to unleash their craft upon.' He snapped his head up and met the Emperor's eyes. 'But I have been a prisoner before, and I will not submit to that *mercy* again. Let the barbarians come, and let them tear the flesh from your empire: I will not see it.'

With a final, sobbing sneer, he bowed his head and stepped off the parapet. Alexios started forward, one arm half raised, but Krysaphios would have hit the ground before he had covered half the distance and he went no further. A great sadness shrouded his face.

I ran to the window and looked down. The walls were high here, and sheer, dropping unbroken to the rocks below. The ground was blurred in the fading light, its details indistinct, but amid the muted stones I could still see the eunuch's body. It lay stretched out like a fallen angel, a fragment of gold against the darkness.

κ θ

A web of incense hung under the great dome of Ayia Sophia, its curling tendrils caught in the sunlight which fell through the windows. One shaft struck just behind the Emperor's head, shining off the back of his throne and illuminating the hazy air like a nimbus. On his right sat the patriarch Nikolas, on his left his brother Isaak, a triumvirate of unyielding glory. Elsewhere in the city they would be ringing bells and singing songs for the great feast of Easter, but here the vast crowd was silent, watching the ceremony unfold.

At the front of the hall, the barbarian captains sat in a line on chairs inlaid with silver. Duke Godfrey was there with his brother Baldwin, and the three ambassadors I recognised from the day of Aelric's treachery; others whom I had not seen before were there also, and, at the far end of the row, Count Hugh. He was apparently reconciled now with the kinsmen who had mocked and despised him, though he seemed uncomfortable in their company. His companions looked no happier, every one of them sour-faced with suspicion.

Trumpets sounded, and as the heralds recited Duke Godfrey's name and titles, he rose and approached the throne. From my position in the western aisle I could not see his face, but the silence of the congregation left his words perfectly audible in that cavernous hall. Prompted by the interpreter, he spoke the words of the oath that had been agreed the night before: he swore to respect the ancient boundaries of the Romans, to serve the Emperor faithfully in battle and to restore to him all lands which his ancestors rightfully held. Seven scribes sat at a table recording every word, and when the oath was taken the Emperor's son-in-law, Bryennios, stepped forward to present a golden garland. There would be much more gold to follow, I knew, for the Emperor was ever generous to his defeated enemies.

Duke Godfrey retook his seat gracelessly, wearing the garland like a crown of thorns. Then the heralds called his brother and I tensed, while across the hall seven pens sat poised in the air to see what he would say. For a second I thought he had stepped too close to the throne, that he would bring the Varangians rushing down on him, but now he was on one knee mumbling indistinct allegiance. He did not wait for Bryennios when he was done, but marched back to his seat stiff with shame. A rash of pink scarred his cheeks like plague-spots.

The oaths took almost an hour, followed by anthems of acclamation and the liturgy of Easter. When the patriarch put the cup of Christ to Baldwin's lips I feared he would spit it back, but he managed to choke it down under the stern eyes of his brother. Then there were more hymns of praise and unity – the message doubtless lost on the barbarians – and at last the long procession into the cheering crowds of the Augusteion. A double line of Varangians had parted the mob, forming a human corridor between church and palace, and as I emerged into the sunlight I saw the last of the Emperor's retinue disappearing within. The Emperor might be generous to his enemies, I reflected, but not kind: three hours in church followed by the rigours of an imperial banquet would reduce the Franks to the utmost misery. Doubtless they would find compensations.

'Weren't you summoned to feast at the Emperor's table?'

I looked up. Sigurd was standing by a pillar beside me, surveying his men with quiet pride. 'I've spoken enough with barbarians,' I told him. 'And not nearly enough with my daughters.'

Sigurd nodded. 'There'll be more barbarians soon enough. The logothete reports that the Normans will be here in a week.'

'They won't cause trouble.' Weariness spurred my hope, but reason agreed. 'Word of the Franks' humiliation will spread to them; they will think again before defying the Emperor openly.'

'And this time there'll be no mad eunuch urging them on. Though if there is,' Sigurd added, 'he'll know better than to draw Demetrios Askiates into his schemes.'

I smiled at the compliment, though I did not deserve it. 'I served Krysaphios' purposes all too well – he could have no complaint of me. He wished me to discover that the monk was in league with the barbarians, that they plotted to usurp the Emperor, so that he might have a pretext for insisting on their destruction. He judged me perfectly – it was the Emperor's stubbornness he underestimated.'

Sigurd bridled with mock temper. 'It was the Varangians he under-estimated,' he told me, waving an arm at the burnished cohorts before him. 'If not for my sword in that throne-room, Demetrios, your head would now be raised on a Frankish spear. And the Emperor's beside it.'

I laughed. 'You are restored to favour now. And the eunuch is gone.' In my heart I could still find pity for Krysaphios, for the terrible wounds he had suffered and the treachery they had driven him to, but I could not forgive him for balancing the empire on a sword edge.

'Krysaphios had not learned the lesson of the past,' I mused aloud. 'He was of a generation who believed that the imperial office was their tool, to be filled, used or discarded as they saw fit. A generation who turned all-conquering glory to invasion and rebellion in fifty meagre years. They never saw that the throne is too much like a serpent's egg – most dangerous when it is empty.'

To my chagrin, the Varangian laughed at my melancholy reflections. 'Will you use the Emperor's reward to retire and write epigrams? And can this be the same Demetrios Askiates who four months ago was so reluctant to tie his fortunes to those of the Emperor?'

'Now I have no choice. I am marked as the Emperor's man, with all the advantage and prejudice that brings.' When you save a man's life, I thought, you buy it with a small piece of your own.

In the sky above, a breeze pushed away the scrap of cloud which had covered the sun and I smiled. 'And you, Sigurd? Are you invited to the Emperor's banquet, or will you join me for the Easter meal?'

Sigurd swelled. 'Do you believe that the Emperor would allow him-self into a roomful of his enemies without due precaution? I will be in the Hall of Nineteen Couches, watching for any Frank who waves so much as a quail-bone at him.'

I left Sigurd shouting orders at his company, and pushed my way grad-ually out of the Augusteion towards the Mesi. It felt strange to be watching the Emperor from a distance again, the untouchable statue I had always known; those few days when I had fought and argued and battled with the greatest men in the empire already seemed far removed. Now the crisis was past and his orbit would draw apart from mine, into the rarefied circles where even the most magnificent moved with caution. He would be locked behind a hundred doors, every one watched jealously by an army of functionaries, and his words would come from the mouths of others. Through every tribulation he would maintain a perfect stillness, for he was the keystone of the empire, locking in the vaulting ambition of his nobles and keeping it off the shoulders of the people below. Though a single gem from his robes would have supplied a year of my needs, I did not envy him it.

I turned off the Mesi and followed the road towards my house. The streets were filled with families and children and roasting lambs fresh from the market. The smell made me hungry after long hours standing in the church, and I was glad to see my own family already had the coals dutifully glowing under the meat.

'Did the barbarians behave?' Anna stepped away from the spit, leaving Zoe to turn it. 'Or am I called to the palace to bandage the Emperor again?'

'Sigurd should see to it that you aren't needed. Except perhaps to sew up some barbarian skulls. I fear your career at the palace may be finished.'

Anna lifted her eyebrows. 'For a man who claims to be a master of unveiling mysteries, you can be unduly ignorant, Demetrios. My career at the palace is barely begun, for the empress herself has sent word that she requires a physician to attend her. I think the Emperor will be keen to keep me near, now that he has found me.'

'I thought *you* found *him*.' The smoke of lemon and rosemary played in my nose, stirring new hunger in my stomach. 'Bleeding and dying in the corridors of the palace, while his attendants fluttered helplessly.'

Anna poked a knife into the lamb, and watched the oily juices dribble down its side. They spat and popped in the fire. 'I think this is cooked. Helena is just fetching some bread from the house.'

I rasped my knife over a stone, and began slicing meat off the bones. It was troublesome work, for heat rose off the coals and fat splashed my hands, so I did not hear the footsteps behind me, nor even look when the shadow fell over me.

The sound of a plate crashing against my doorstep drew my attention though. Helena was standing there amid shards of pottery, staring at something past my shoulder like Mary in the garden. I turned, and almost dropped my knife in the fire in astonishment. It was Thomas, seeming taller and broader than ever as he stood over me, yet with a nervous hesitancy in his face.

'I come back to you,' he said simply.

I could see he did not speak to me, and I was about to launch a hail of questions when I felt Anna's hand against my arm.

'You'll need another plate,' she said, nodding to Helena's feet. 'At least.'

'I will bring two.'

Thomas had suffered the murder of his parents, the abuse of the monk and now, I guessed from the scabbed blood on his cheek, the betrayal of his race. He had also saved my life. Sharing my table was the least he was due. How much else he desired I could guess from the silent, awkward looks which he and Helena exchanged, but I would address that later. Now I served him the thickest cut of the meat, filled his cup to overflowing and did not say a word when I saw his hand entwined with Helena's, nor even when they mumbled an excuse and walked down the street to where the cypress tree grew. It was not a day for argument.

Much later, after the sun had set, I climbed to the roof with a flagon of wine. The streets below were dark, save a few patches of glimmering embers, but the sky was laden with stars. I squinted at them, picking out the ancient constellations which governed our lives. There was Lyra, and Krios the ram and Argo, and a hundred others I had forgotten or could not piece together. When I had named all I could I gave up, relaxed my eyes, and watched the fragmented lights swirl together in patterns of my own imagining. Sometimes beasts and heroes would emerge, sometimes the shapes of leaves or fruits, but most often they were simply the formless weavings of fancy.

Drawing my eyes down, I looked out over the roofs and domes which surrounded me, and let my thoughts descend from the stars to the lands beyond the empire. From the west, I knew, the Normans were coming, and behind them the Kelts, while to the east and south lay a wilderness of Turks, Fatimids, Ishmaelites and Saracens. No wonder the Emperor had more than once nearly died holding their dangers in balance. Doubtless while his empire provoked the lust and envy of the world he would do so again. But tonight his power endured, and under the heavens the queen of cities slept.

Τελος

273

Acknowledgements

Two noble historians, a princess and a knight, were indispensable companions in this project. Anna Comnena's *Alexiad* and Sir Steven Runciman's *History of the Crusades* (both published by Penguin) provided the historical core of the story, and there were few days when I did not refer to one or both of them. Both works were as enjoyable as they were rigorous, and in the general chronology of events, particularly the battles in Holy Week, I have followed their leads as closely as possible.

As with Alexios Komnenos and his empire, a wise marriage and supportive family were invaluable in realising my ambitions. My Greek parents-in-law offered hospitality and valuable feedback on the draft manuscript, while my mother was always on call for scriptural or religious references. My sister Iona accompanied me on my intercontinental research trip, and was frequently summoned out of libraries to provide a classical anecdote or Greek translation. As for my wife Marianna, from the moment she provided the original idea she has had an immeasurable influence as fan, critic, proof-reader and muse.

Out of the family fold, Jane Conway-Gordon encouraged this at an early stage, and proved that the Byzantines have nothing to teach her about the shadowy arts of agenting. Oliver Johnson at Century was a generous and convivial editor, as well as doing duty as a relocation consultant. The vast resources of the Bodleian library in Oxford unfailingly turned up the most obscure works which my meandering researches demanded; I could not have written the book without them. Many friends in Oxford and London provided much-needed relief from the work, and in the process probably learned far more about eunuchs than they ever wanted.